WIRELESS...
IN THE FABRIC OF TIME

E. I. Johnson

INKWATER PRESS

PORTLAND • OREGON
INKWATERPRESS.COM

For LJ, Bugoy and Angel

For this book, I'd especially like to thank Lloyd, my best friend and confidant for his sharp, meticulous, blunt (but amusing) comments. Not only did he show amazing patience while I was writing the novel, I wake up every morning knowing that I'm lucky to have him catering to my obsessive details and giving me confidence and support 24/7.

ACKNOWLEDGMENTS

My book would not have come out without the help of many wonderful people I've encountered. I'd especially like to thank the following:

To my long-suffering and ever helpful friend and writing mentor "Charlise Brown Whiteside," who, soon after we first met, encouraged me to pick up a pen and journal and re-explore the world of writing.

To Bruce... who thinks I am a super hero. Thanks for believing in me and giving me confidence, support and love. I couldn't have written this book without him. He was my inspiration.

To Ellie Parnes for her determination to edit this book even when I wanted to give up. Thank you so much Ellie, for hurling my book into the literary world and giving it life-support. I'm fortunate to know & work with you.

To Linda Weinerman - Editor/Publicist who handled the final editing and salvaged this novel. She also deserves my heartfelt gratitude. She's fabulous and gifted. If I got anything right, it's because of her; all I can say is I'm grateful that she was around.

For all the people who have a role in my book. I would like to thank each and every one. Without all of you, this book would have not made it.

Melinda Mondrala - Universal Music Publishing Group, Los Angeles Ca. - Who guided me through the UK music licensing process.

Kester Harding - Universal Music Publishing Ltd., UK / Film & T.V. Department

Elton John's Team, UK

Ted Goldthorpe - Sony Music Co. - Who guided me to contact Matt Goss artist management with regards to licensing.

Matt Goss - Website Team, UK

Mr. Ray Light - Matt Goss, Team in UK

Ellen Burke - EB Music Services / Representing Matt Goss - Who was there for me when I needed her and rescued me from stepping into the fray to get things possible for my music license to be released.

Susan Markheim - Azoff Music Management / Representing Matt Goss

Carol King - Chrysalis Music, Los Angeles, CA. / Representing Kevin Savigar: For her integrity; she took the initiative and rescued me from the corporate maze.

Jonathan Belott - Hal Leonard Corporation Music Publishing

Coretta Frank - Creative Design Firm - Web Site Designer: It's been an honor and privilege to work with you. You're a genius! Please thank your staff for me.

Lorraine Thompson Castle - Country Diner Media / Innovation - Cover design: She's fabulous, gifted and hard working. I could have not found a better person to work with.

Thressa Smith of Inkwater Press: Who saved the novel from an untimely release. I'm truly grateful for what you have done for my book and your intervention to make things possible.

Virginia Martin - Director of Inkwater Press: I'm fortunate and grateful that she was around to save me from my publishing dilemma, and taking the lead on this process.

Masha Shubin & Her Assistant Tricia of Inkwater Press: For using their magic wand and making me believe that nothing is impossible.......

Michael Davis - Author Services of Inkwater Press: He always knows what to say when the going gets tough. You have an extra ability to make sure everything is just as it should be with my book. I'm so fortunate to work with you.

Valerie Szenberg - Who guided me on my French translations.

Giovanni Migliorini - My Italian instructor who guided me on my translations.

Mr. David Applegate - In reference to my British dialogues.

To My sister-in-law Brenda who once told me get an eyeglass you'll read better!

To Ate Vicky, who once said she loves my fictitious tales.........!

TABLE OF CONTENTS

CHAPTER ONE

CIRCUITOUS ROUTE

Stephenson University, 2008

I T IS A BEASTLY HOT, HUMID FRIDAY NIGHT IN MAISEN BEACH, FLORIDA. The hottest June in sixty years has brought the coastal college town crowds to the beach in search of relief. But they've been disappointed. Even the breeze off the ocean feels like it is blown from the exhaust of Crystal River's nuclear silo. Most of the students agree that the nights are four times better at the beach. The ice cream stands and bars around the campus are handing out free cold drinks during the final week of college exams. This is the highlight of the year for the social wasteland of central Florida with its ungodly heat.

The date is June 12, 2008. It is the wee hours of the morning. Dark hair, brown eyes, athletic build: twenty-two-year-old Von Muir Carmichael, a self-proclaimed computer and cartoon geek who loves *anime*, has just returned from a late-night fraternity party.

He steps out of his metallic green sports car, with an assured physical presence. He wears his favorite Abercrombie & Fitch classic Bull-Point Oxford shirt proudly like a uniform.

1

He slides his car keys inside his sharply creased denim jeans while whistling and listening to an old Elton John song on his iPod.

It seems to me a crime that we should age / These fragile times should never slip us by / A time you never can erase / As friends together watch their childhood fly / Making friends for the world to see / Let the people know you got what you need / With a friend at hand you will see the light / If your friends are there then everything's all right.......

Von controls the touch screen of his 10th generation iPod video-camera-phone by speech command. He whispers a word to the voice-activated menu navigation; the volume turns up and rewinds the previously played song automatically, without the need for a traditional navigation interface. Then, he slides the little gadget back into his shirt pocket and puts his earpiece back on.

For Von, he has only two things on his mind: graduation in twelve hours and his late thesis.

As he walks to his dorm, he feels a last-minute anxiety attack. Through the fog of his mind, reality sears like a hot knife, reminding him of the results of his final exam, the several job interviews he has lined up, a possible job offer that is brewing with a large New York research firm, the task of picking up his grandmother's ring (that has been stored for years in the bank safe deposit box), and the ordeal of planning a surprise wedding proposal to his girlfriend, Bessie. Oh, yeah, Bessie, the ever-unpredictable, typical young gal who captured his heart from day one.

Due to a sudden onset of intense apprehension and fear of the real world, he decides to take a silent walk around the campus. This may be the coolest time of the day to clear his head with an early morning stroll. He feels the intense humidity still lingering in the June night air as he pauses for a moment – just a reminder of the intense heat that wafts from the pavement during the day. He stops in the narrow service alley behind his dorm to gaze up at the night sky. The early morning darkness and thick atmosphere saturate his clothes as he tunes in to the peacefulness. It is a safe place he has grown to love over the past four years.

The campus walkways are empty at this hour. The street lights overhead are bleary by the fog and conjure shadows over the buildings that appear to seize every sleeping dorm. Von has always liked when the campus is empty, and the throng of clamoring students are still asleep, in their rooms. He likes walking the school grounds alone at night. It appears a welcome reprieve from the constant drone of adolescent college students who flood the campus by day, who feel compelled to greet one another constantly in some reassuring ritual which he welcomed as a freshman but has grown tired of over the years.

Von remembers when he first started. The student ambassador assigned to mentor him had said that former students through the years told stories of seeing two friendly ghosts walking around the campus at night holding hands. Perhaps it is the thought of that ghost, or just the empty campus feeling, that Von likes because he feels that it spurs everyone to share the feeling of what it must be like to be a detective at night.

Von reaches a corner not too far from his apartment dorm. He is fearful of the changes he knows are coming right after graduation and the fact that he will be out in the real world. Everyone realized it's a safari out there. He has a gut feeling that his time with his buddies and two pets will be limited. He is sad just thinking about it.

What am I going to do? I wonder if Mom and Dad will ever put up with them. I don't have any other choice.

Von tries to picture his nuisance of a thirty-five-pound, *fat* cat of no known origin they all call *No Neck*. This was one cat that could not find the off switch. You know, how most cats, when presented with a bowl of food, eat as necessary over time. *No Neck*, however, never saw a bowl of food she could not eat in one sitting.

Then there is also Von's favorite pet and close confidant: an ornery, grungy, blind old dog with brindled, short, matted hair that led to the name *Swamp Dog*. An accident a few years ago left the dog with a slight limp. This dog has vacant, blue eyes that appear to be cold and intimidating. But who could not like this dog that defends his turf by jumping backwards as he barks with his nose pointing off in the wrong direction all the time? Or perhaps it is the ever-present different colored scarf around his neck everyday that says to strangers he has a home despite appearances. *Swamp Dog* has been with Von since he was a pup, and the dog is Von and Mick's oldest friend since childhood.

Von stops walking, and realizes how much he loves living in a beat-up, apartment-style dorm just across the street from a fraternity house. From the parking lot, he can usually see into the small patio, which is mostly filled with college seniors who wanted to be on their own.

His room, like all the other senior students, opens on a patio. He is always proud to tell everyone that he shares his apartment with his friend Mick and that they share a big room, almost double the size of a regular master bedroom, with a makeshift three-panel divider in the middle for privacy.

As he turns into the back alley to the street, he pulls a tiny box in his pocket. He pauses for a few minutes and looks at it using the light from a street lamp.

Thanks, Grandma, Bessie will love this ring, he says to himself and puts it back in his pants pocket.

He walks towards his place and notices that the light inside his place is still on, still flickering like a bug zapper. Earlier, in the evening, Von planned to attend a study group but he was confident that his last exam would be easy and decided to go to the frat party with Mick, despite his impending exam. This was his last chance to cut loose as a student.

He wonders how tired Mick must have been to have forgotten to shut off their light before going to bed. He walks around the courtyard to open the sliding door. As he approaches, he feels a strong static charge of electricity in the air. It appears to be coming through the sliding doors. It's an eerie feeling, so Von decides to use his keys to get in the front door instead.

When he reaches his room, he finds that the door is unlocked. The first thing he does is look around, empty the front pocket of his denim jeans and change into his cargo shorts. His pockets are still stuffed with nickels and dimes from doing his laundry earlier that evening. He jumps into his bed, pulls his covers over his head, and closes his eyes to take a short nap, hoping to get over the spins – the only reminder that he was a bit over-the-top at the party.

Damn it, I still need to send the darn thesis to Professor Richmond…as soon as I get my head straight…and I need to speak with Bessie, he says to himself as he scratches his head.

Von is startled by a mysterious noise coming from inside their dorm room apartment. He looks around and finds no one except Mick, who is sound asleep in his bed. He finally decides to goes back to bed, and this time he hears another sound.

Knock, knock, knock.

Knock, Knock, Knock...

Von slaps his face, hoping to sober his senses. He feels a throbbing in his head, and thinks he's having a migraine attack.

Who could it be at this hour? he thinks to himself. He squints to focus through the dark haze, appearing to scowl. His heartbeat begins to race. It is so fast that it doesn't feel or sound like a regular heartbeat. Von feels like his heart is coming out of his chest.

Am I having a panic attack, or am I so out of practice that a late frat party, a mix of drinks, and weird junk food have me on the floor?

Darn it. Do I have to get up? Mick, it's your turn, dude! he thinks as he scans his darkened room. Emptiness confines their room. A quick look at the darkness outside proves it is the dead of night. He rolls from side to side on his bed, tangling his legs in his soft cotton, 400-thread-count woven comforter. It's hard for him to tell if the room is spinning because of that last shooter or his nerves about leaving the security of college for the unknown. Moments later, he relaxes and starts to drift off to sleep.

A muffled sound coming from the sliding door to his bedroom makes him roll out of bed from sound sleep. He finally peeks through the sliding door but can't see anyone from the low lighting outside. He moves onto the other side and sees that a man is squeezing sideways through the porch door, one foot already inside their patio. Von's heart starts to race once more and feels as though it is crawling up into his throat.

"So...this is how a panic attack feels, hmmm. Mick... Mick...there's a dude outside trying to break in. Can you hear me, dude? Wake up!" Von whispers. He hears no comment whatsoever from Mick, and Von can see Mick is out cold. Von hears Mick's heavy breathing of deep sleep with his mouth wide open, ready for the flies to dive in.

From under the Ralph Lauren designer sheets that Bessie gave him for his birthday, he moves the bed back and forth against the wall to make noise, hoping Mick will wake up.

Ouch! Damn static from the carpet is annoying, he says to himself. In the darkness, he stubs his toe on the side of his Pottery Barn night stand that he bought from one of his fraternity buddies who moved out last semester. It hurts like only the hurt of a surprise injury when half asleep and unprepared to deal with pain. Von bites his lip to keep from sounding out. Angry and scared, he just wishes Mick would speak to him or wake up. He needs back-up to give him the courage to take this guy down, whoever he is. Von squeezes between the makeshift panel divider. He crawls over the boxes and luggage by the door. They are heavy and filled with electronic devices. He reaches stealthfully for the wooden practice sword that he uses in his martial arts class. With one hand, he opens his backpack, shuffling through his notebooks and devices while clutching the sword in the other.

PINNGGG, PINNGGG! The intruder is knocking hard on the bedroom glass door with what seems like a coin, making enough noise to rattle even Mick, who Von sees is beginning to stir.

Who knocks at this hour?" I wonder who this nut case is? Burglars don't knock, do they? As fear fades, the anger surfaces. Still clutching the sword, he comes upon the Military Strobe light he and Mick bought at the Army Navy Store. He jerks it out of his black backpack, dumping the rest of his *electronic* gadgets everywhere. With the wooden sword in one hand and a Military Strobe light under his armpit, he angles himself, ready to pounce on whoever the intruder is, friend or foe, outside the entryway.

While Von braces for the intruder's attack, he hears the turn of the door knob. The door abruptly flings wide open. Instinctively, he attacks, slashing his wooden sword in a fluid reflex motion toward off the perpetrator. He strikes a solid blow to the old wooden bird feeder standing just outside the sliding door. The feeder flies off its base, hitting whoever is out there, making a loud noise as it crashes to the ground and shatters. Von sees Mick, who is still sound asleep, mouth agape, oblivious to the clamor. He thinks that if only *Swamp Dog* were around tonight instead of over at his parents' house this week due to graduation, he would scare the robber by barking continuously.

Von sees the surprised assailant lose his balance and fall and bang his head into the dead ficus plant that Von got for Mick. Emboldened by his success, Von assumes the defensive position he has practiced countless times. With the perpetrator concealed in the darkness, Von repeats his fluid slashing motion first to one side, then the other. His wooden sword resonates with a whooshing sound as it cuts through the thick night air. The intruder-turned-victim gets up swinging.

"Von? Dude, hey, stop it, man. It's me, Dex. What's wrong with you?"

"Dex? Oh, I'm so sorry, I didn't know it was you, man," Von answers in disbelief, still clutching his sword as the adrenaline pumps through his veins. He is too in the moment and too stunned to say much else. Von and Mick haven't heard anything from Dex since he started his training with the FBI in D.C. So much time has passed, and Dex didn't even send an e-mail. Von had begun to accept that he and Mick might never hear from Dex again. They fantasized that Dex had been inducted into a covert training program, which would have perfectly fit Dex's childhood dreams.

"Sorry, dude, did I hit you hard? I thought you were a burglar, man."

"It's cool. I'm okay. Next time, I'll remember to knock!"

"Dex! Was it you knocking earlier inside my room?"

"No! I just got here, man!"

"Anyway, what are you doing here, man? Where've you been all this time? Do you have any idea what time it is? Thank goodness I didn't have a stun gun. I could have hurt you, dude."

They both laugh until tears stream down their cheeks and their stomachs ache.

"Von, I need a hand, dude," Dex says, regaining composure.

"What's wrong, Dex? Aren't you graduating? Are your grades in trouble, dude? Why didn't you e-mail me or something this week? I thought you'd gone to a classified training program for the government you always talked about. Why did you leave us hanging for so long?"

"I'm fine, Von. I was wondering if you'd mind helping me load up my SUV early in the morning before the traffic gets heavy. I'm leaving for D.C. first thing tomorrow, and I really need to get a jump on it," Dex wipes his eyes with his dirty sleeves.

"SUV? That's not big enough for all of your stuff."

"It's okay; I got a hitch and I rented a trailer to load the rest of my things."

"You're moving out of your apartment tomorrow? Jeez, man. That's fine, I can help you out," Von replies, feeling sad knowing that everyone will go separate ways after commencement ceremonies.

"Great, dude," Dex says, backing away from the window onto the back patio. He accidentally knocks over the dead ficus, which had long since overgrown its pot. "Oops! I'm sorry. Hey, I'll see you in a little while, okay? Can you meet me at Adam's place at about seven? Please?"

"Adam's? Seven o'clock? Argh. That's way too early after this night. I guess it's okay – what the heck!" Von says looking at his watch. "It's graduation!"

"Bye, dude!" Dex shouts as he heads off into the darkness.

"Of course, no problem. Just wake me up if I'm late whenever you're ready to go, okay, man? I will leave my cell phone on just in case I oversleep," Von says with a smile, knowing this might be the last time he was together with his buddies. Before Dex leaves, Von asks, "Wait, do you have a minute? Where have you *been*, dude? I thought you left early to train with the FBI in Washington." Von tries to stretch his arms, thinking it might clear his stupor.

"I was in D.C. for several weeks. You know it was all about the interviews...all that bull," Dex responds. "I start my training next week, but hey, got to go. I still need to finish packing, so we'll talk later, dude. In few hours, okay? And hey, Von, it's your graduation tomorrow, and you're still in your dorm? What're you still doing here, man? Are you going to be here all summer?"

"Well, you know…a lot of last-minute things to do. We made arrangements for a late move-out. I'm excited about graduating but not about the awards, my parents' big party, and that long ceremony. They should just mail us our diplomas or at least cut down on all the formal crap," Von notes wishfully.

"Man, everyone knows formality is part of the tradition, dude. I can understand why it would be quite tedious, especially since tomorrow is also your birthday! Thought I forgot? Oh, by the way, Von, advance happy birthday,"

"Thanks, Dex!"

"Hey, do you know that the night before college graduation is an important milestone in life, my dad always tells me and my brother Clyde. He harped on it for sixteen years, if you take kindergarten into account. For you, dude, not only is it your graduation, it's also your twentieth birthday. So, welcome to the real world, I guess. Anyway, I really got to go. I'd like to get at least an hour or two of sleep before heading out to D.C." There is a little sadness in Dex's voice.

After their conversation, Von is wide awake. He sits down on his bed and turns on his laptop. He notices a familiar message on the screen: "Low Battery: You should change your battery or switch to outlet power immediately to keep from losing your work." He plugs his laptop into the electrical outlet and notices that the surge protector, which is jammed with wires connecting to all of his electronic gadgets, is completely tangled in a snarl of twisted wires.

"Damn, now what? This is an accident waiting to happen. How the hell did this get so bad? Why'd I let this become such a mess?"

He gets down on his knees and reaches for the clump of wires under his bed. Methodically, he untangles them one at a time. He thinks to himself, This is an unfair test. Finally, he sorts out the wires and is confident there is no danger of a short circuit. He tries to resend a copy of his final thesis to Professor Richmond, thinking that this is his last act as Von the student.

Suddenly, a disturbance occurs among the devices. The scanner is acting strange. It's flashing and doing something he has never seen. While Von focuses on his scanner, he feels another huge surge of static electricity tingling right in his core and through his body, making his hair stand straight up. He thinks maybe his life should be flashing before his eyes. He recalls the odd news story about how many Floridians die each year from being electrocuted in their bathtubs or by their phones. Unexpectedly, a loud crack of what sounds like thunder and a blinding flash strikes the room. The room seems to be hit by lightning, which illuminates the previously gloomy dorm. In the glare of the bright light, Von feels something strange on his arm. Then, the light flickers and comes back on once again. A few seconds later, he feels it again. Is he hallucinating? No, it's real.

But how and where is it coming from? he wonders. Von senses another electronic crackling radiating toward him from the machine. He sees that part of his hand and left arm are pulled inside the scanner by this unknown source. The electronic field pulls his hand through the metal as though it did not exist. In an instant, Von's arms are sucked into the interior space of the flashing machine.

Von instinctively resists the force by pulling his arm back towards his body. But it still pulls at him harder with each numbing second. He tries to fight off the force, but this is impossible. Desperate and stunned, he reaches for the power cord and yanks it off the machine, but the inexplicable force intensifies with each second.

"Holy *crap*, what the hell?!" Von yelps and pulls his hand free, expecting to see a bloody end piece. Instead, his hands are intact – still tingling, but intact.

"Bizarre...freakin' *weird*," Von blurts with excitement, as he always does at the end of his favorite ride, the Scorpion at Universal Park. "Let's do that again. Okay, I'll tap the scanner *slowwwwwly* one more time...like this," Von says to himself. Then, he hears a loud sound.

WHOOOOMP! WHOOOOMP! WHOOOOMP!

"Gee whiz, there it goes! Oh, shit...my hand...make that my entire arm," he says, thinking he is still in control.

Schhhluup! Schhhluup!

Whoosh! Whoosh!

He hears the sound of his hand going through into the scanner like it is going into liquid plasma...Maybe more like that fake pancake syrup at the *Maizen Beach Diner* near his school.

*Wait a minute...*Von thinks, *How bizarre is this? I'm standing here in my room, near my bed, drooling, with my arm inside my scanner and my pants down? What's wrong with this picture? I don't get it?! Man, this is a trip.* He tries to twist his body in a sinuous writhing motion. His arm wriggles around in the sappy digitizing device.

Shoot! Am I going to change into a pattern of dots and turn into text? Is this why I'm in this sappy, digitized, pixilated mess? Von feels an object that seems like it is freezing below zero. The object is squeezing his fingers.

Am I majorly stoned? I think I just lost my mind. Something just pulled my arms. Damn it...what the heck was that? I'm going to smack Mick for giving me that pot. I hate this feeling of losing control. Von wonders if he really is losing it. He whispers, "Whoa! Whoa! Look at me, pen and all; I think I just went through my scanner. This can't be happening. I have to laugh, thinking that if Mick could see me laying flat on my face, laughing and swearing, trying to get the taste of the ink from my pen out of my mouth…which tastes a whole lot better than that wacky weed he gave me. I can really see how gross the carpet is from this angle. That huge old stain from Mick's unfortunate mix of an open can of Pepsi and beer he was drinking while eating his midnight ice cream snack is still here, a blended palate of disgusting colors…It never bothered me before, but now that I'm so close, it's filthy!"

In my mentally screwed up state of mind, I will push to my knees and wipe the tears from my eyes. Oh shit…What the hell?! Oh man…I'm never smoking that weed again!

"HEEG!" he yells. Did someone just grab me by the throat and pull me, or am I really hallucinating? Von begins to laugh uncontrollably. Damn it, I knew I shouldn't have smoked that weed!

Laughing at his hallucination, he kicks his own leg, holding onto this thing around his neck and picturing his tears running down his face as he kicks and squirms like any intelligent weed smoker. *Damn, this doesn't help much*, he thinks, trying to regain control of his thoughts.

He begins to cough as whatever it is tightens around his neck, like a hand, squeezing him with a firm grip. *All right, dude! Let me go!*

"GAAACK!!" Von gasps for air. Yeah! That's it…*it's gotta be the brownies. They must have put some funky weed in those brownies.* Von consoles himself, trying not to scream. He looks at his hand inside the scanner, and his eyes bug out of his head.

Seriously, I probably look like one of those cartoon dudes who've just seen that ditsy redhead in a thong bikini. I'm probably going to have brain damage or something. This is bad, and this feels real. My vision's getting all funny, and I can't breathe, Von says to himself. When I come out of this, I swear I'll never go near weed or booze ever again.

He pulls himself from the scanner and runs as fast as he can. Something feels strange, though. He is running faster than his dreams could imagine. There's no resistance. He throws his head back, howling in both fear and delight, sensing that ride-at-the-park rush again.

"Let me out of here!" He screams, trips, and falls. But instead of stopping on the ground, he feels that he goes right through it. Von realizes that this isn't just a bad trip. This is the real thing.

"Holy *crap*!" Von's jaw drops open. He rolls over, gets out of bed, and stands in the center of his dorm room shaking uncontrollably. "I'm getting a CAT scan first thing in the morning." He tries to regain control of his functions.

Still dazed, he peeks around the divider and see Mick in his bed, halfway in a daze. Von hasn't a clue what just happened. He looks at the clock, which reads 3:30 a.m. He looks at Mick again and sees that his mouth is wide open as he sleeps soundly with no notion of what Von has just been through.

He glances through the doorway to the empty hallway and finds no one. He shuts the door quickly but quietly with speed attributed to apprehension that the slightest noise could bring about uncontrollable events.

Von flashes back to the present, realizing that graduation is less than twelve hours away and that he still needs to scan and e-mail his late thesis. To keep his promise, his thesis needs to be the first thing his professor sees in the morning. However, Von is hesitant and still mystified by what has just happened. For now, he knows he can only get on with it if he is in denial. His emotions have to be pushed aside so that he can move forward. Denial soon steps in, and he tries to ignore what just happened as his curiosity mixes with the thought of much-needed sleep that entices him to overlook the strange event.

Von hopes it has just been one of those weird nights, when there have been far too many cups of coffee and a year-end party warping his perception of reality. He tells himself that maybe if he gets some sleep, everything will be fine in the morning.

He is too exhausted to struggle with his fragile grasp on reality any more for one night. Von sticks his DocuPen handheld scanner in his back pocket and crashes onto his bed with his shoes and clothes still on. Lying on the bed, he sees Professor Richmond's e-mail address on his Black-Berry next to him.

He feels a strange movement beneath him as though his whirls are coming back. The bed seems to be turning, spinning like a magic carpet ride. He wonders if it is still the flashback from the earlier drug experience he was coaxed into and wonders how long this effect will last. It's like sky-diving without a parachute. He feels like a stone dropping into a dark state of limbo, right out of the air, high above the sky. He can hear himself screaming loudly as he plummets to the ground as though he has jumped from a skyscraper. The sight of what looks like lit windows speeding by nause-ates him; he waits for the splat of his body parts.

Rationalizing this to be an out-of-body experience at best or a psychotic breakdown at worst, he wonders what could possibly happen next.

Crap! What the hell's happening now? Now I know how friggin' *Curious George* feels! Von says to himself. Dan-gling from his bed pole, holding on for his dear life with both hands, he rolls his eyes in shock and disbelief. What...

the…heck?! Wait…if this is a trip, then…hmm…shouldn't I be able to get out of this? I mean, after all…this is just a dream, right? This is another one of those moments that has reinforced the stereotype that all potheads are morons.

Holding his backpack like a child's security blanket, Von closes his eyes and then moves aimlessly on the wings of the unfamiliar wind. "Shoooot! Here I goooooo!" Von yells. As he was being lifted off by energy as strong as the category four hurricane that hit the Florida coast in the summer of 2004. Soon, he has no sense of his own existence and realizes he has given himself up to the heart-stirring sensation that surges throughout his being. He feels as if he is exploding into fragments of himself, like something out of a strange Disney animation, and it seems his soul is dissipating everywhere.

In an instant, he is split into molecules, is zapped inside his DocuPen handheld scanner, and instantly vanishes into thin air. A sudden, loud noise and a feminine voice is heard in the hallway of his dorm. A clap of thunder rattles the dorm with its uncontrolled wrath, followed by a flash of lightning simultaneously illuminating every corner of the dorm.

"Quiet, dude!!!!" He hears Mick yell.

CHAPTER TWO

MIND'S EYE

V on wakes up on the following day and hears loud voices outside the room. His face is flat on the floor. He wonders why on earth he is waking up on the floor of his room. *Where is the carpet?* he thinks. The awful *beige* filthy carpet with pizza stains, red wine, soda, you name it…is not there. Gone?? Instead, the ground is an old hardwood floor. Von is completely confused and wonders if this is his room.

Ouch! Damn, I feel awful…My head…What the hell did I drink last night, paint thinner? he wonders.

Without his contact lenses he can't see a thing. The glowing lava lamp in the corner of the room that he gave Mick is gone. Von is overwhelmed by a cold nightmarish feeling rushing over him. Not only is his mind bewildered, but his senses are obscured, too. The room smells different; it is more pungent, like old soccer socks, only perfumed to disguise the source.

"Mick must have put one of those damn smelly deodorizers under the bed. I hate that fake smelly stuff," he says to himself. Then, he tries to locate his iPod station receiver, which is always on top of his dresser. The colorful iPod screen that normally stays on all night is missing. Nothing is as it should be. Normal is no longer normal, though Von searches for something, anything, familiar. He gets up and promptly falls right back on the floor. His legs are still tingling, asleep and wobbly.

"Ouch! I got a freakin' cramp. Damn it," he says in a low voice so no one can hear him. He wants to turn on the lamp, but he can't find it. This seems a bit like Murphy's Law.

He moves quietly while limping to avoid making any noise that might wake up his roommate, but it is strange that he doesn't hear Mick's snoring or groggy voice telling him, "Quiet, dude." Von wonders where the partition in their room has gone.

"Damn it, did someone rearrange the room while I was totally stoned or sleeping?" he says, still talking quietly to himself. Von stumbles into what he thinks are his videogame controllers but he realized it's someone's shoes. "Crap! Whose shoes are these?" He feels very strange in this room. He can only guess by the way his body aches that he has been lying on the floor quite a while

The last thing he can remember clearly from the night before is stepping out of his car after the fraternity party with Mick. There is a dull ache in his head and a pain in his calf muscle that he guesses has something to do with how much he had to drink or inhale.

Then, he wonders if he has been carried somewhere outside of his room while he was asleep. He can only speculate that he is the victim of a practical joke perhaps orchestrated by a fraternity. All of a sudden, something slides from his head. He picks it up to see what it is.

"What the–? What *is* this? I'm wearing an elf night cap... a damn bonnet? Who am I, *Scrooge?*" Von has decided that some buffoon has played a mischievous prank on him, and he throws the nightcap on the floor. "Damn it, my picture is probably all over the Internet by now! Some joke. Mick?" Those mentally defective loonies. I'll smack the heck out of them! Von says with great trepidation in his voice.

"Hey, dude, are you awake? Where the heck are you, man?"

He wipes his eyes with his sleeve while limping. Still, no one answers him. He reaches for his eye glasses next to his bed and neither they nor the bedside table itself was there. Even without his contact lenses, Von realizes the room is very small and has no furniture. "Damn it, the dorm RA must have taken all of our stuff since we're leaving so late," he guesses. "But when could this have happened?" Von knows the RA explanation really makes no sense at all.

Where the heck am I? Ouch! I hope I won't be limping tonight for graduation. Mick and his fraternity friends must have added some special ingredients to the brownies. I'll kill them!

He tries to convince himself that there's some sort of rational explanation. Okay, this is what happens when you party with the frat guys, he lectures himself firmly. I must be hallucinating. Hoping to shake off the effects of the unknown toxins, he paces the room in a semi-conscious state. He tells himself over and over again that it has just been a dream. But doubts creep in as he does a reality check that says his walking feels real, and he feels awake, so how can it be a dream?

From the corner of his eye, he sees that there is a smaller unfamiliar desk behind him with no phone, no computer, and no entertainment system that he and Mick assembled last semester in that spot. He looks around quietly from the dark and can't see his new generation PlayStation 4 or Xbox either, which he and Mick purchased together at *Circuit City*. Von looks to the left side of the room and wonders where Mick's bed is.

"Did he move out of the dorm without telling me? That moron…moves while I'm sleeping. He couldn't wait to get out of here," Von imagines. He grabs for his cell phone in his front pocket and takes it out. He presses #2, Mick's speed-dial number.

Von wants to wake up Mick, wherever he is, and he knows Mick will hear it since he always keeps his cell phone hidden under his pillow practically attached to his ears. But Von hears a mechanical operator voice from his cell phone: "Sorry your long distance carrier is out of roaming area. You are calling out of your network." Von is frustrated and stomps his foot on the dusty wooden floor.

"What the heck is that message about? What do you mean 'out of roaming area'? Damn, my service isn't working again. Wait a second…Have I mailed my cell phone bill this month? I think I did…and I'm pretty sure it has a stamp, not like Mick, he never put a stamp on any of his mail. And sure enough, it always comes back…*return to sender.* Okay, Von, okay…focus and get serious here for a second. Damn it! They should have more cell towers in this friggin' college town," he sputters angrily to himself and puts his cell phone back into his pocket.

He decides not to worry about what he just heard from his cell phone. Still undeniably baffled as to what is going on, he struggles to sort out the situation. Von looks for the light switch, usually on the left side of the room, and it is now gone. Instead, there is an old nightstand, with what seems to be a kerosene lamp on top of it. He thinks it is one of those kerosene lamps from past centuries.

"How do you use this darn thing? Mick must've bought this junk at the flea market and left it for me," he tells himself and tries to figure out how it works. Von shakes his head, wondering whatever happened to their regular lamp.

Von sees lights coming from outside in the hallway through a crack in the door. Someone opens the bedroom door. A person comes inside, and Von is startled. He assumes it's Mick's friend, one of the guys that was at the party the previous night. He is annoyed that this person would just open their bedroom door without knocking, but he doesn't bother to say anything, knowing some of Mick's friends are real characters.

"Hey, guys…what's up, man?" Von says with a smirk and before he realizes what's happening, as he is wiping his eyes to adjust to the lightless, shadowy room, a very tall, largely built man jumps on him and grabs his neck. Von reels when he feels the hot sting of a fist on his jaw, and his mouth opens his surprise. The punch knocks Von out cold. The man lights the lantern and ties Von up with some kind of leather strap, continuing to strangle him.

"*Vis is tewwibuw. Well, Oi suppose d' sensible t'ing ta do is turn 'im ova'. Aawight, William,*" a man with a thick British accent speaks.

"*Well, go on, 'is barely alive.*" Another man gives orders.

When they finally revive him, Von feels too ill to try to figure out what's going on. His head hurts too much to think. Then, he remembers what his dad said before: "Drinking water before bed helps. When people drink alc…blah, blah, blah…." Damn, why's Dad's lecture suddenly on my mind? I really think I am hallucinating…alcohol poisoning, maybe?

Watching the motion of people around him, Von feels an unhealthy sensation of dizziness that turns his stomach. Sweat breaks out across his forehead at the realization that he is going to get sick…and soon. He tries to keep still, slowly, tentatively. Perhaps his feelings are reflected in his face, because a man next to him takes a big step back.

"Hmm, Oi mean, look aht dem clothes, just look aht 'im. Front buttonfly closure…cut trouser? It go'fringe hem? Look at dem stitching. Well, fancy that, eh? 'E looks like a thief. Oi 'ave no doubt dat's exactly wot 'e is. Dem clothes from Bond Street. He pro'ally steal em' inside em' store. Fa' sure e's a me'derir and a thief," a man with a British accent says.

"Good 'eavens!" a man yells and looks at Von.

Von tries to open his eyes to be as wide awake as possible. He pushes himself out of the chair and slams the heel of his hand under the man's jaw. The man's head snaps backward, and he falls unconscious. Another man hears the rumble, jumps behind Von, swings around while grabbing some kind of a metal pipe, and gives Von an uppercut.

"Hey, why'd you beat the crap out of me? What the hell are you doing, man? You're hurting my neck, damn it. Mick, Mick, your friggin' frat friend is going crazy! Get them out of here! This is *not* funny, dude." Von keeps yelling and trying to push the man away from him.

"'E isn't from 'round 'ere, dat's fa' sure."

"Gawd knows w'ere 'e came from. It's a bit odd!" The man looks at Von's face.

"What do you want?" Von finally asks, but the man doesn't say anything, just stares at him. Von tries to remain calm under this stranger's angry gaze. Then, the man abruptly turns and exits the room. Von breathes a sigh of relief, but it catches in his throat as the men returns ten seconds later...with an old *cricket bat*. Grim as death, he stalks toward Von...

"Don't ya fink yer be'aving ratta' oddly? Where de devil did ya' spring from?"

"*Oh, blooming 'eck!*" Another man speaks.

"No, *wait!* Shit!" Von yells. The man hauls back and swings. A loud *SMASH* is heard all over the room. The bat misses Von's head by a fraction of an inch but hits his left arm, making a sharp snapping sound as it hits his shoulder. Suddenly, no one else is in the room.

"*Just as well...*" a man whispers to another fellow next to him.

"Shoot! That's it, I'm filing a report for fraternity hazing. Damn it! I think they broke my freakin' shoulder. Oww!" Von screams in pain from his injury.

"*Ghastly little lad, aint 'e?*" another British man yells.

"*It's ol me own fault. Can't keep me bleeding trap shut. Me temper ge' t'e better of me self,*" a heavy-set dormitory worker yells.

"Wha...what the hell just happened?!" The room's suffocating silence is the only answer Von gets. Then, a man comes back and gives Von a sharp blow in his face.

Von feels something loose inside his mouth. He thinks he has just lost a couple of his back teeth.

"Phttt!" Von spits on the side of the chair.

"Good lord, t'at wos ratta' rude."

"Ya caun 'ang on ta yer tooth fa' a bit, lad."

The man won't let go of Von, and five other men surround him this time. Another man ties his hands tighter behind his back with a rope on top of the leather. A very largely framed man slugs him in his stomach, and the other one gags his mouth with cloth. Dizzy and lacking clarity and strength, Von cannot move and faints for a moment.

When he regains consciousness, he looks around with one eye half open. Von sees a small group of men staring at him in the corner of the room that he doesn't recognize. They're all wearing some kind of costume, and they are all staring at him. One of them tries to poke his chest.

"*Ows t'e lad?*" a man asks.

"*E's pretty bashed 'bout a bit, actually, John.*" Two men speak in front of Von.

"Hmmmmmmm? Grhmmmmnn!" He tries to yell but can't. *What have I done? Why are they doing this to me?* Von is angry and irritated. He tries to think as fast as he can to figure out how the hell he can get out of this and if this is some kind of a fraternity hazing…or was he kidnapped, but by whom? And why?

Damn it, I didn't join any fraternity. I'm a senior for God's sake! They must've mistaken me for someone else, shit, Von thinks as the cloth is still inside his mouth.

Damn it, who are these people and why am I here? He hears a voice next to him yelling.

"*Good 'eavens, we 'ave t'e me'derir, we 'ave t'e me'derir!*" an older British man interrupts.

Von looks at the man with a dazed look on his face and wonders what is going on. He is stunned to hear what this man has said. He can't say or do anything because he is tied up and gagged at the same time. Another British man angrily walks over to Von and grabs him by the throat.

"If ya starts ta foam aht de flamin' mouf', it means ye'r goin' berserk. Stay w'ere ye'r lad, or Oi'll club yer louse-bitten 'ead."

Von takes a minute to orient himself after that big hit to his stomach. He tries to recall the previous evening in his dorm room apartment, but he cannot ignore the people around him. He needs to do something to fight back.

Unexpectedly, a man comes forward and takes the gag out of his mouth.

"Goddamit let me *go*! Ouch! You broke my freakin' ribs and my shoulder, man!" Von yells as soon as the man takes the cloth out of his mouth. "What are you guys *doing*? I don't remember seeing you on campus. What have I done to you people? Is this some kind of frat hazing? I didn't sign up to join this semester. You've mistaken me for someone else. Untie me, let me go, and I'll just think of this incident as a practical joke. Let me go! Let me go!" Von shouts.

"Whatever this is, you got the wrong guy. This is some sort of case of mistaken identity," Von tries to reason.

"Me dear chap, ya don't really expect us ta answer that one, d' ya? We caun't let ya go. Not til de constables ge' 'ere. Ya killed a young fella' next door. Ya cut 'im into bloody pieces," the man says.

"T'e body wos mutilated in t'e most g'astly manna'. 'e wos found lyin' on 'is bed, 'is entrails placed around 'is neck...really awful mutilation."

"Oi'll ge' on wiv t'e arrangement, if I may?" another man chimes in.

"Please my dear fellow, please do," a man behind Von with an upper-class accent instructs a bearded man next to him.

Von looks around. He sees a body stuffed in the closet, strangled and suffocated where it may have sat for three days before it was discovered, now waiting for someone from the morgue to come.

No wonder it smells in here... Von says to himself. "Wai...Wait a minute here, buster. Murder? Who murdered who? Are you telling me that I killed *him*? I didn't kill anyone. This is not funny anymore. Is he really dead, or is that one of those fake microfiber dudes that sorority girls have in their dorm?"

"Wot's 'e talkin' 'bout?"

"Never mind. We'll soon catch on. It's a pity 'is just an odd chap."

"Hey, I was sleeping here in my bed. You guys are sick. This is not very funny. This is an over-the-top frat joke."

"Bed? T'is ain't yer bed, lad. Sorry, son, ye'are in mi' bed." a man yells back.

"Don't ya fink t'at wos ratta' rude ta tell us its 'is bed?"

"Not at ol. 'e should kno' tis ain't 'is bed."

"Mick! Mick! Mick!"

"'Oo ar' ya callin', lad?, 'Oo is Mick? Would sum'un fetch t'e constable – 'e's going berserk," the angry man says.

"Carry on, wot's takin' 'em bloody ages ta ge' 'ere?"

"Sum'un' 'ad betta fetch de constable ta pick up tis' loofy," another man answers.

"T'at's a brilliant idea."

Von still assumes that they might be friends of Mick, who loves serious practical jokes, so he guesses they are waiting for him to end these games. But what's with the dead body? Is he hallucinating? It certainly smells real. Now, how can he solve this crime when all the evidence points to him into a different era? The clock is ticking for Von.

"'ave ya got an accomplice in t'is crime? 'Oo is 'e?" a man in his late twenties seethes.

He thinks he'll try to play the game with these guys... get it over with and wait for Mick to arrive and get him away from these loonies. Losing his composure, he goes along with the game.

"Mick is my accomplice. Okay, okay, we killed the bastard next door. He didn't return my damn Xbox games, so Mick and I decided to kill him, satisfied?" Von says with a smirk.

"Is anyt'in' t'e matta'?"

"Blimey! 'e said Mick's 'is accomplice. W'er is 'e?" the man asks as he punches him in the chest. Von tries to wriggle away to avoid the sharp blow of the man's fist. A very tall, curly-haired man with sideburns is wearing what looks like Shakespearean attire. He scowls down at Von, and Von wonders if he is really hallucinating. He blinks and tries to keep the image before him from blurring and distorting. And just the thought gave him a case of heebie-jeebies for some reason.

"Mick? He went to Circuit City to pick up some games to shove up your you-know-what," Von laughs. "Oh, stop it! Would you guys just stop it already, I'm just playing with you guys. You morons! We didn't kill anyone! I was just playing your game. Now can we stop this? I have a headache, and I just sprained my ankle. Okay, if this is part of a frat hazing, you guys got the wrong man. Besides, isn't it a little late to do this? It's the end of the semester! I'm really not up to these jokes right now. It's not funny. I really have a lot of things to do for tonight's events," Von begs.

"Don't b' daft." The men stare at Von very closely. Then, Von notices that his clothes are drenched with blood. His shirt and his cargo shorts are dirty, and there are blood stains on his fingers. Did he really kill this man?

What the heck? How did I get into this? Von asks himself silently and notices everything from his fingers to his legs is covered with blood. He thinks that he must have really injured himself bad, but why are his clothes covered with blood? Did he really kill someone? He glances down and touches his cargo shorts. The blood is still damp.

This doesn't make sense, he thinks, weary with confusion and a bit queasy. *What the hell happened?* A bizarre sensation quivers inside his stomach...must be some kind of a gut reaction similar to a panic attack. Something feels wrong, very wrong. Everyone stares and whispers around him while waiting for the constable. He can't figure out what is going on. His right ankle starts to throb. He wants to rub it to make it feel better, but he can't because both of his hands are tied. He feels a pain behind his head as well. He tries to stand up, but he's a little woozy and both of his feet are tied as well.

"*Stay w'ere ya ar', until t'e constable ge' 'ere, ya 'ear me?*" The man pushes Von back to the chair.

"What's with the British accent, guys? That is too much, dude," Von snaps back at the guy next to him. The man just stares back at Von and ignores his remarks. *Damn, did I pass out in some foreign dude's dorm last night? Never seen any of these British guys before. What the hell happened?* he wonders while looking at his blood-stained shorts.

Heck, I think I may still be dreaming. I must still be dreaming, he thinks to himself firmly while trying to shrug off the hangover that he speculates was from the previous night's activities. He blinks his dry eyes and notices a couple of blurry figures emerging from the shadows towards him.

"*William, make sure 'e's tied properly. Watch 'im till t'e constable gets 'ere, I'll shoot off now t'en*," a man instructs.

"*Aawight, 'ere ya ar' an' off ya' go*," William responds and hands the man some evidence they found near Von's belongings.

Von squints his eyes twice and realizes that this bad dream is not in his imagination after all.

I feel like I've left the lunar mission without my space suit...Everything looks and feels different.

Half in apprehension, half with disgust, Von opens his eyes, dizzy and confused. The men with British accents are still standing in front of him. All of the men appear to be dressed in costumes. It seems that each person is outfitted with authentic period dress from the early 1900s. Everyone is wearing a hat.

Frustrated, Von begins talking to himself: I've never seen guys wear hats like this, and what's with the hair? And those clothes? What the heck are they wearing? These guys are lunatics. I'm definitely filing a complaint after this. I don't care if I lose Mick's friendship. Right now, I'll play their freakin' games so I don't get hurt too badly.

While eyeing Von, one of the men opens the curtain window next to where Von sits. He looks around and sees a strange environment outside.

Since when does Florida get so foggy and dark? And it looks freezing outside...during the month of June? he wonders to himself.

"It's a bit of a fog out t'ere," a man says as he looks outside.

"Hey, is that tree real? Damn, that's freaking huge, man. What did you guys do to Mick's dead ficus plant?" Von squints his eyes for a few seconds; he tries to focus on looking outside and notices that the small, dried, dead ficus potted plant Mick left on their patio last week seems to have transfigured into a huge, dark tree. He is certain this tree he is looking at wasn't there before.

"Hey, that doesn't look like Florida out there. What happened?" he whispers in shock. A man next to Von hears him talking to himself. Von shrugs his shoulders, very confused. "I really don't want to be in this game, you know. I'm too busy, man. I still have a lot of things I need to do before graduation tonight. Beside, you guys are playing this practical joke a little too seriously, man."

"Is it yer 'abit, sir, ta' enta' a conversa'shun wif'out introduc'shun?"

"What's your problem? What are you talking about, dude?"

"Oi said, is it yer 'abit ta simply enta' a conversa'shun wif 'out introduc'shun? Don't ya speak till yer spoken to. And me name is not Dude. It's William," the man repeats with growing irritation.

"I'm truly sorry, William, if I've offended you, I just don't want to be in this game. Anyway, are all of you Mick's friends? Where is he? I still feel nauseous from last night's party, man. Give me some slack."

"Wot's t'e big fuss, t'en? Hmm?" the man responds with a cold shoulder.

"Whoa, whoa, you are getting too serious here, man, Hey, it's cool. Okay, I get it; Mick must have signed me up for this, right?" Von asks. But no one in the room knows what Von is talking about. They all look at each other, wondering if Von is going insane.

"Chuck it, will ya? Blimey!"

"Damn! You guys are something…You don't even break a smile for a second, do you? It's unbelievable," Everyone just stares at him, knowing that they have never seen him before. They have no idea who he is. They all think that he is the murderer everyone has been looking for. Von tries to convince himself that the guy in front of him is so deep in his character that there is no point in telling him to relax.

Does he think he's an actor? Von sighs heavily and realized that this strange group of men doesn't seem like they are from *Stephenson College.*

Am I having a nightmare? "*Ouch!*" he cries. He feels the tip of his nose and sees that he is bleeding. The blood is dripping onto his shirt. *Damn it, another nose bleed. That makes twice this week. Is it possible to have a nose bleed in a dream?* he wonders. Von wipes his nose with his sleeves and looks around at one of the men with a British accent, who stares back at him with narrowed eyes.

"*'Ave ya something ta say? Wot's yer name, lad, 'oo ar' yeh? Go on. Look aht t'e state 'f ya.*"

"I-, I-" Von stammers. He feels that he might not be dreaming after all, but he's not where he should be. He asks the men next to him, "Who are you? Where the heck am I?" A glance around the room doesn't offer any new information. At least nothing recognizable is there. Now that the window curtains are wide open and all of the lights are lit, he notices that the room is very small and consists of unfamiliar beds, a small dresser that doesn't belong to him or Mick, and a couple of nondescript foxhunt paintings on the wall.

"Blimey, can't speak, eh?"

"Who are you, man? Where is Mick?" Von asks again, growing more and more frightened.

"Mick? We 'aven't found 'im yet, and why wod'ja' want t' kno' w'ere Mick is?" a man responds, as Von looks around the room with a wider eye.

"I want to speak to Mick, that bastard. I'm in this freakin' shit because of him,"

"Rubbish! I'm fa' mor' interested in yer concern, young fella.'"

"Oh, would you just *shut up*? Just shut up! You know Mick is my roommate. Enough of this...," Von says, still feeling a little off-balance.

"*Bloody atrocious! Aawight, the constables'll be 'ere ta question ya 'bout the murda',*" a man illustrates.

"Constables? You mean the cops? Hey, I didn't murder anyone. I was just playing with you guys earlier to shut you up. *This* is why I never signed up with any fraternity. I don't believe in hazing. This is unconstitutional, you know?" Von responds shakily.

"Caun ya explain w'y ya 'ave blood ol ova' yer clothes?"

"I had a nose bleed. It probably dripped all over me, you shithead. The body has been dead for days; tell me how the hell I would have wet blood on my clothes from a dried-up corpse?" Von announces with a frightened look on his face. "Excuse me, why are you calling me Lad? My name is Von! Let me tell you, morons, it isn't funny anymore, and it wasn't funny to begin with."

"*Eh?*" One of the British men sighs. "*It's such a pity. I must warn ye' that playin' us like vis is unacceptable.*" The man was growing quite angry.

While Von listens, he becomes queasy and faints. One of the men fetches strong smelling salts, and Von soon recovers enough to sit up. He examines his nose again and then looks up, questioning what just happened. Everyone is silent around him.

"*Aawight, Oi'll ask ye' again, 'oo ar' ye?*" the man asks. "*W'ere ar' ya' from?*"

"Carson Hall, you idiot!" Von responds, still lightheaded but also angry and frustrated.

"I beg yer pardon?" the man questions.

"C'mon guys, you know, Stephenson College…in Florida," Von whines, exasperated and still feeling nauseous, now with a headache. He wonders why he even bothers to mention Florida.

The man pulls Von's face from both sides.

"Fla'rida? 'ow terribly clever ye ar'?"

"Yes, and if you guys don't freakin' let go of me, I will never be on time for graduation."

"*Gra-dua'shun?*" the man repeats what Von has said, emphasizing the wrong syllables and making the words sound odd and foreign.

"Yes, it's June 12, 2008; it's graduation day. What's wrong with you people?"

"Eh?"

Von explains, "Yes, *Florida*! Don't act like you've never heard of it. S-T-A-T-E, State of Florida!" Von speaks with irritated exaggeration.

"Tat's a bit obvious, idn't it? Oi 'ave neva' 'eard of it," the man replies. *"'ave any'un 'eard 'f it?"* The man asks around the room.

"Lad, it is 1908...not 2008, Oi' fink 'is goin' bonkers on us, 'is a nutter?" one of the men says, and everyone but Von laughs heartily. The men shake their heads and don't say a word. Von takes a deep breath. "Prove to me it's 1908, then. C'mon, prove it. I'm getting tired of this ridiculous joke, so come on, I dare you!" Von shakes his head and tries to stand up from his chair.

"Ey, 'ere's an Exeter tabloid, wight 'ere: June 12, 1908. Ya look a bit shell-shocked. Wot else wod'ja' wunt ta see?" one of the men says.

"That's obviously a fake. You probably had that printed at the Maizen Beach mall."

"Use yer loaf, lad! Wot's t'e 'Maizen Beach mall? C'mon tell us," a man responds, and Von feels dizzy, nervous and doesn't know what to say.

"What do you mean loaf?" Von asks.

"Loaf..." the man points to his head, looking at Von and trying to figure out where he came from.

"Ah! You mean use my head? I'm using my head, and this still doesn't make sense." *Forget about Florida*, Von thinks for a minute or two, suspecting it would prove hopeless to try to make them listen. *I suppose if I really have time-traveled, Juan Ponce de Leon hasn't discovered Florida yet, and that's why these strange men haven't heard of it. Wait a minute, did he say 1908?*

Ponce de Leon discovered Florida in 1513. Why don't they know Florida? I thought I was bad in history.

"H's daft as a brush! Oi can't go on vif is," a man comments.

Von starts to feel lousier by the minute. He refuses to faint again, though blacking out seems like a comforting alternative to trying to sort out what really is going on. He thinks about what fainting did to him a few minutes ago. *Not again,* he thinks. *No way am I fainting, no way.* Von feels pale as he sits down on an old chair.

"May I please have a glass of water?" Von asks

"Ya need sum'tin t' drink?" a man asks.

Why does everyone around speak with different British accents? Lower class and upper class ...Ohhh, I get it – different accents, for different regions. That's what it is, right? Von says to himself.

"'E's an odd chap!"

"What did you just say?" Von asks the man, who ignores him. "Can you just please give me a glass of water."

"T'at's rubbish, askin' fa' a drink," a man replies

"Yes, indeed," another man responds.

"Bit frightening. 'Oo can he be?" The man stares at Von from head to toe.

Von feels the blood rushing from his face. He sits down quietly; attempting to get up again only causes a severe pain at the base of his skull and makes him nauseous.

In his daze, he has an eerie sense that he knows one of his abductors. Even though it doesn't look familiar, the twin bed, with a small, blue, wool blanket beside him, is the only spot he needs to be at that moment. Von tries to slowly move his right hand to the back of his head, expecting to feel a bump or cut, but cannot reach for it because his hand is still tied up.

Hangovers never feel like this. I've had enough drunken nights with Mick when I've woken up with injuries, but none like this.

He reaches back for his head and finds it a little damp. *There are absolutely signs of injury that could be causing this strange hallucination. Well, aside from an injury, could it be that Von Muir Carmichael is mentally deranged? he asks himself. I know this is all Mick's fault. I need to get some coffee, find him, and beat the shit out of him for doing this,* Von thinks while he scratches his head.

CHAPTER THREE

MURDER OF THE CENTURY

"*E*y, lad! 'ey, wake up!*"

"*Wot's t'e lad doin'?*" a man enters the room and asks someone.

"'E's kipping on t'e bloody floor."

"'Ey, wake up!

Von opens his eyes when he hears one of the British men yelling in his ear. As he reawakens, he finds himself on the floor and more confused than ever.

"It's been a dream...just a bad dream," Von whispers with hope. The British man is still standing in front of him. He hears a voice above him. Someone is holding him. Von is wrapped in something warm, and someone has propped him against the wall like in *Weekend at Bernie's*. Trying to ignore the throbbing in his head, he thinks to himself, *How can this be happening? Mick gives me one cocktail, and the next thing I know, I'm a candidate for the funny farm and One Flew Over the Cuckoo's Nest gang. What the hell happened to me?*

He squeezes his eyes tighter, concentrating on waking up. He peeks from under the covers and he sees that the men are still there and staring at him.

"Absolutely rubbish, ye' 'ad us worried there fa' a bit, lad. Blimey, wot am oi going ta do wiv' ya, lad?" a man asks while looking at Von. *"Good 'eavens chap, ye 'avin us on 'bout blimey Flar'da, eh?"* The man runs his fingers through his hair. Von pulls the covers over his head and turns towards one of the other British men.

"Tell me *sumfing,* I mean something. Shooot! This British dialogue is freakin' contagious." Von whispers, stiffly holding himself. "Where are we?"

"Oxford, lad. Aawight, don't tell me ya don't kno' w'er ya ar'?"

Von has not paid attention to what the man said and asks another man a favor. "Can you please take me to Carson Hall? I'm feeling sick, and I can't take this game any longer." Von swallows hard.

Finally, the man responds, "Lad, ya 'ave ta stay 'ere until t'e constable ge' 'ere."

"Excuse me, where did you say we are, and what's the date? I think this bad hangover from the party last night is confusing me. I can't seem to understand any word you just said. And do me a favor: speak *softly* and *slowwwwly.*"

"Oxford, England, son."

"Wai…wait a minute here, buster! I'm sorry? *What* did you just say?"

"Oxford, England."

"What do you mean *Oxford?*" This time, Von is furious.

"Oxford, England, an' 'tis 1908. T'ats t'e bloody truth."

"But…that's not possible!"

"Go a'ead… wot year do ya bloody fink it is? D ya 'ave a propa' explana'shun, ey? C'mon, out wiv it."

"It can't possibly be. How the hell did I get here? Does this mean I time-traveled?"

Another man points out to Von that he is indeed in England and it *is* 1908. Then the man exclaims, *"So! Ya'ar tryin' ta tell us ya'ar from the bloody future! W'ot the bloody 'ell did'ja' drink at the pub? Ya' really fink y'ave come from 2008?*

"E's bloody daft, ain't 'e?" a big bearded dormitory worker comments as everyone laughs, looking at Von.

"Don't call me daft. Hey, don't get personal here, okay? I'm not stupid, you know. I don't know where I am. I don't know what's happening," Von replies with despair and confusion.

"E finks 'e's from the bloody twen'y-first century, William. 'e finks 'e's the fella from time yet ta come," Von overhears a man say.

"The constable is 'ere. We 'ave ta 'and ya ova' ta' 'em" a man tells Von.

"Go a'ead, lad. Ya tell the constable yer a time-traveler. Fa' sure ye'll end up in asylum ."

A man in a dark British police uniform and a plain-clothes man enter the room, and one says, *"'Ello evryone, Oim Chief Inspecta' George John Littlefield, an vis is Detective Constable Andrew Walta'."*

"*Is vis de' suspect?*" Chief Inspector Littlefield, wearing an old-fashioned, khaki-colored suit, says.

"E's de me'derir, Chief Inspecta'. We saw 'im 'is clothing full of blood. We found 'im 'iding in that room. 'e said e's a man from de bleedin' future," one man reports.

"Aye, if you'd prefer ta tell de magistrate before we 'ang ya. It must be grand to 'ave a talent like dat." The Constable laughs with this nasty remark.

Crap! I really did time-travel, and I'm going to a prison in 1908? Damn it, I don't belong here. Is this for real? Von asks himself. He tries to stand, but the constable pushes him back in the chair where the man tied him up earlier. The

Inspector unties Von's feet and drags him in the corner of the room to interrogate him.

"Sir, I'm not your man. I really belong to another time… in the future…please, you have got to believe me, sir," Von says with tremors in his voice.

"*T'at's nonsense! Bloody rubbish! Ya' a bit wicked, yeah. Prove ta us t'at ya not of vis time!*" Detective Constable Andrew Walter, a man with a large mole on his nose, says.

"We 'ave ta tike 'im ta Scotland yard. We need ta ge' 'is fingerprint."

"*Fingerprint?*" Wait a minute! They can do fingerprinting in this era? Shoot! That's not possible! Is it? I guess they can…I remember Dex did a research paper once for his forensics class. He mentioned the *Fingerprint Bureau* was formed in 1901 in England, and Sir Edward Henry was in charge of it. They used the process in 1902 when a guy named Henry Jackson was jailed for burglary. The fingerprint identification classification system was made in Scotland Yard. I remember Dex has said that it was called *Bertillion's anthropometric system or something*. Yeah, that's it. Shoot! Does this mean they will have a file of my fingerprints in this era? Whoa, that's kinda cool, actually. Hey, wait a minute, it's not really cool if I end up getting hanged in this time warp…Von thinks to himself.

"Sir, I really don't belong here…Excuse me…Sir…Hello? Please, you have got to believe me, sir?" Von begs with tremors in his voice.

"*I fink t'at is propfa' wicked an' we should a be talkin' it, yeah?*" A man made a comment to a fellow next to him.

"*Aside from yer trouser an' bloody shoes, wot else caun ya show yer not from 'ere?*" another man chimes. "*We 'ave showed ya Exeter tabloids dated 1908 an' ya did not believe us, lad. Ye' fink ye'r from t'e bleedin' future? Make us believe t'at ya're a time-travela'?* a man asks.

"I'm *not* a murderer. I have nothing to do with any of this."

"Ya don't com' from 'round 'ere, da ya?"

"Oh, no, sir. I'm from Florida."

"T'is is bloody daft lad, 'ow dija ge' 'ere t'en? Ya should be talkin', yeah?" Detective Constable Andrew Walter asks.

"Look, all I know is that I came through my scanner and landed here. I don't know how it happened or what's going on." Von shakes his head, desperately trying to clear it, and explains. "I was in my dorm, trying to send my thesis in an e-mail to Professor Richmond. My scanner started acting up, and I felt and saw static electricity. I rubbed my eyes because I was tired, and the next thing I knew, I woke up and I was here." Several of the men watching Von were staring at him and silent for a moment.

"Wot's a bloody scanna'? An' wot's an 'e-mail,' lad?" Chief Inspector George John Littlefield asks wide-eyed.

"A scanner is a device that converts visual information into digital data. And e-mail is electronic mail."

"Wot'd ya mean 'digital data'?" a curious man asks.

"Hey, everyone knows what digital data is."

"Go on, out wiv it, and tell us wot bloody 'digital data' is?"

"It's data that…consists at its most basic level of just 0s and 1s," Von expresses while everyone looks at each other, laughing and wondering what the heck he's talking about.

"'Ow do ya' send t'is 'electronic mail? Tru 'orse-drawn mail carriage?" a man cracks.

"Oi kno'…Oi kno' 'ow 'e sends it," another man chimes. *"'e sends it tru 'Aerial Post,' courtesy of King Edward."* The man breaks into laughter.

"Awfully astonishing lad, ya' most proa'lly 'it yer 'ead somew'ere, eh?"

"Look...I don't know what the heck is going on. All I know is that I fell through my scanner, nearly got killed by some kind of electronic tornado, and then I fell out of the sky or something and ended up here. I *wish* I'd hit my head. That would explain some things..." Everyone laughs heartily listening to Von's befuddled response.

"Believe me, I didn't kill anybody. Please believe me! I'm not the murderer you are looking for." Von begs for his life.

"Awfully sorry, lad, ya said ya came in t'rough yer scanna'? T'at's splendid, 'ow'd ya d' t'at?" William asks Von.

"No freaking clue, Blue Boy. At first I thought it was because I was high."

"It's a bit of a stretch, lad. Wot'd ya mean 'I'?"

"High, as in from the weed I smoked at the party...id-iot," Von responds sarcastically. "I'm from the U.S., I mean, America, although that doesn't matter, considering that I just *fell through my scanner.* So I guess where I come from doesn't make a difference. You guys are ancient history...make believe. Fictional. As in *not real*, Blue Boy. But this kind of shoots that theory straight to hell, doesn't it?" Von retorts.

"If ya fink ya' came 'ere from 'ere-afta', 'ow' bout ye' tryin' ta tike me wif ya? If ya disappear in front 'f me eyes, den ye'ar a time-travela'. If ya' don't, we take ya ta Scotland Yard fa' murda'," the Chief Inspector says to Von.

"Are you guys serious? You really want me to disappear in front of everyone, now? How?"

"Wot'eva ya were doin' befa' – maybe ya'll ge' back ta yer own world," the man next to Von says.

"Go on, give't a w'irl," a man tells Von. All of the men continue to laugh.

"In t'at case, Oi'll wear a rope around me waist...if ya ge' back in time, ya' could tike me back wiv ya," a man chokes back his laughter.

"Splendid! Quite astonishing! I supposed," a short, burly, middle-aged British man yells sarcastically.

"Well, that saves us an introduction," Von says dryly. "And you would be...?"

"Oi told ya, lad. Me name is William."

"Are you sure it will work, dude? Okay, I'll try..." Von blinks in surprise at the men's suggestion. I don't think it's that easy...but I'll try, he thinks. Von shuts his eyes and says goodbye to everyone. "I wish it works, I wish I just disappear. Thank you for helping me and suggesting this idea. What's your name, dude? Von asks the man standing closest to him.

"Mi' name is Sir Oliver Robert, but don't worry, lad. Ya' just shut yer eyes an' give it a go ... go on, lad!"

Von feels a warm sensation all over his body. Where has he heard that name before? And his face...the man's face looks familiar as well. Could it be possibly that he has actually seen this man before?

"Ye' really tellin' us ye' came 'ere from some otha' place one 'undred year in t'e future?" a man asks again, unable to believe Von's claim.

"Yes!" Von answers. The man breaks out into laughter, a laugh so full of delight that Sir Oliver joins in. Von shuts his eyes. *Get me out of here*, he thinks. He tries to imagine his dorm. What did it look like? It was so clear, right there at the edge of his mind.

"Outa' me way, ye swine. Oi've ge' a job ta do!" the man laughs hysterically.

"Well...I guess this is *goodbye*. I'm getting the hell out of here!" He saluted the men sarcastically, using his index and middle fingers to touch his right eyebrow briefly.

"*Toodles!*" someone shouts.

"*Farewell* to you, too. I'm hoping to leave the way I came." Maybe if I really shut my eyes, reality will creep back to where I had left off before. All I need to do is find the right moment, and I will go back to my own world in 2008, Von whispers to himself.

He is desperate to get back to the only world he knows, back where all of his friends and family are waiting, back where Bessie is. *My own world*, he repeats to himself. He opens his eyes...and his new friends are still there, staring at him.

"Damn it, I can't transport myself. Argh! I know I can do it!" he says, squinting his eyes with intense concentration.

"*Good show, lad. Well, Oi'm not surprised,*" one of the men says.

Von cannot accept that he stepped into a portal of time when his handheld scanner, only the size of a pen, took the decisive action while it sat securely in the back pocket of his pants as Von laid on his bed.

In reality, Von now realizes he truly is no longer in hot, humid Florida. He has to accept that, for some unknown reason, he has traveled back in time into the upper-crust, well-bred, aristocratic society of one of the oldest British universities. He has stepped into the old-fashioned world of gas-lit streets in Oxford, England, 1908. But he still cannot figure out who Sir Oliver could be, although he is sure he recognizes him from somewhere. Suddenly, the inexplicable images become vivid and real. Von feels faint when he realizes how he knows the name. Yes, he knows one of the men in the room.

Oh NO! It can't possibly be, or can it? Sir Oliver Robert? Sir Oliver Robert? Von repeats to himself. *It can't possibly be real. That is Mom's dad. How can this be?* Von moans in distress. *This man is my grandfather? I really* did *time travel. How can this be?* Von turns his head to look at the group of young, refined, well-dressed British men standing beside several dormitory workers. He turns and shakes his head again to see if he's dreaming, and there he is, with his grandfather a hundred years in the past. He remembers a black-and-white picture that his mother showed him many years ago when he was a child. Now, he is seeing his grandfather in living color. While all of this is running through his mind, Von realizes he has not eaten and is fiercely hungry. But it feels as though all that is left is fear.

"'E's lookin' white as a ghost," Constable Andrew Walter notes.

"Go on, put yer 'ead between yer knees, lad. Per'aps ya betta' sit down a sec," Sir Oliver adds.

Von feels queasy as he looks at his young grandfather in flesh. The group of men is still there in front of him. He grapples the fact that it is 1908, and he is in his grandfather's dorm. Von feels the need to get away from this group of men for a while to come to terms with what has happened, so he asks, "Will I find the John down the hallway?"

After a short silence, the man with the pipe answers him. *"An' 'oo's Jo'n, might I ask?"*

"Is anything t'e matta?" Inspector Littlefield asks.

"May I please use your John? Could you just tell me where it is?"

"We don't kno' 'f ani Jo'n t'at lives in tis' dormitory. Is t'at another accomplice 'f yers?" the detective asks.

Everyone looks at each other, bewildered.

The man frowns. Obviously, he does not understand. To convey the seriousness of his demand, Von dances up and down like a monkey and points to his private parts.

"Good Lord! 'is ge' ta urinate," the Constable grins, and everyone in the room laughs. *"'e needs t'e wat'r closet."*

"T'e lavatory? Oi will tike 'im ta t'e wat'r closet," Constable Walter ties both of Von's hands and heads down the corridor with Von into a dark room. Von realizes the man is taking him to an actual water closet. Von whips his head around and asks, "Wait, please, mister, untie me, please. How do you expect me to use the toilet? And please don't trap me in the *water closet*! I don't want to go in there! What's a *water closet*, anyway? Please, please, I just need to use a bathroom!" He begs as the Constable pushes him inside the dark cubbyhole. He screams, loudly protesting.

"Yes, vis' is t'e wat'r closet," the Constable responds, and then he steps through the doorway.

"Will sum'n watch 'im outside t'e wat'r closet?" the Chief Inspector says. *"Constable Walta', don't let 'im out 'f yer sight!"*

"Okay, okay, stay calm," Von tells himself, cautiously moving in this unfamiliar space, which is just a bit bigger than an old telephone booth. It is pitch-black and very narrow. Von tries to look for a light switch, and finds two kerosene lamps attached to the wall near the toilet tank way above his head. He thinks again how bizarre this whole thing is and how strange it is that he and a young version of his grandfather were in the same room.

"Damn it!" This dude's bathroom stinks! *Ah, dorm life. What's new? At least these people have something in common with my roommates,* Von thinks and shakes his head about most college men's lack of social graces.

While the Constable waits outside the water closet, Sir Oliver snoops around the room where they found Von. He eyes what seems to be a small box. He flips it over this way and that way. He notices the small colored screen in front of him and can't even guess what its function might be. While Sir Oliver examines the item, he accidentally touches a button. Tiny words appear: "E-MAIL & WEB." At the same time, he hears a voice. "Touch-Sensitive icon wimax mobile…Welcome," On the side a tiny label reads: 20 megapixel high resolution camera.

"You have four new messages," the voice says. Sir Oliver wonders where it came from. He puts the device closer to his ears and hears it again. "Please enter your password and then press pound," a voice says from inside the contraption. Unable to think of another option, Sir Oliver responds to the mysterious voice.

"Is any'un t'ere?" He understands the meaning of "mail" but can't grasp what "e-mail" or "web" could possibly mean. Then he notices a word sketched onto the device: VERI-ZON. It means nothing to him, even though Sir Oliver is known for having an incredible lexicon.

"Shite, " Sir Oliver exclaims. *"Good lord wot's ol t'ese' mysterious words? Wot kind of apparatus is vis?"*

He struggles to figure out what these strange items are and where they are from. The message reads: Note to self: URL (Universal Resource Locator) is an address to a computer website. When you type a URL into your browser, your computer finds the website and loads it. All URLs begin with "http://" which stands for "hypertext transfer protocol." URLs usually end with a "something." Next to it is a little metal device. He picks it up and it reads: Flash drive contains 50 PETABYTES of data. "Wot language would that possibly be?"

Then, Sir Oliver discovers a *pamphlet* next to the strange device that fascinates him. He tries to examine it more closely; a small word on top of the cover reads: *MANUAL*.

And before he can scan through it, he hears Von emerge from the water closet and angrily ask, "Who was the last one to use the water closet?"

Nobody answers Von. A man walks toward Von and says to him, *"No more 'f 'yer rubbish. Tell us befa' the Constable tikes ya ta Scothland Yard."*

"*Scotland Yard?* The metropolitan police force of London? Please, I'm not a thief. I'm not a beggar. Please…don't take me to jail. I really came from the future. I know it's hard to believe, but it's the truth. I really don't know how I got here. Please don't send me to jail," Von pleads.

Good 'eavens, from t'e look of yer rubber-soled shoes, those the kind of footwear thieves' wears. Ta enta' a premises so no'un'll notice them, frightenin' eh?" a burly man accuses, pointing to Von's feet.

"Why won't you believe me? I am not a thief or whatever you call them. You've got to believe me, Sir. I wish I could be David Copperfield, the great illusionist, so I could get out of this mess. I don't even like magic! I mean, I don't even know anything about it! Excuse me; please let me have this seat. I'm feeling sick."

"David Copperfield? 'e's just a bloke in t'at Dickens story. Wot ar' ya on 'bout? Wot ar' ya creepin' 'bout, lad?" the man asks again.

"I don't know what you just said but…I'm so tired and upset that I cannot take another one of your questions," he blurts out.

"Oi'll ge' sum'un ta 'elp me transport 'im in the wagon so Oi caun tike 'im ta the station," the Chief Inspector says.

"Untie 'im, an' 'ave 'im ready fa' transport." The Chief Inspector motions to the Constable. As soon as Von hears that he will be transferred and taken to the jail, he panics and takes the chance to escape.

This is my last chance. If this is a freakin' hazing, I will prove to them I can fight back. If I'm really a time-traveler, I really need to fight back or I'll die in this era and will never be born in my own time.

He looks at the Constable standing beside him, grabs what looks like a nightstick hanging behind the Constable's trousers, and warns everyone to stay back.

The Constable backs off. Another British man who works in the dormitory tries to corral Von, but Von is in motion. He makes a single turn, spinning, catching the man completely off guard by the heel of his hand, driving up into the guy's throat.

"Back off, and let me go!" Von yells, when another man behind him tries to grab him. Von is putting all of his weight into a single fluid attack, a sweeping kick, and the Constable and a couple of British dormitory workers fall, catching the bench to try to fight back. Von is unbelievably fast, giving them three jackhammer punches until all of the men are down.

"Grab 'im! Grab t'e lad," the Inspector commands to everyone ahead of him.

"Oi can't, Oi can't! T'e bloody bloke micked me light!" the stocky man's head slams into the bench, blood spraying from his nose, and he's out cold. The third British man is writhing on the ground, gasping for air and struggling to fight.

"Shoot 'im t'en..." the Inspector declares as Von puts his foot down like a vise onto the second man's arm, shattering

the bone as the man starts to scream before being silenced by Von grabbing the Constable's pistol and putting it right up against the Chief Inspector's forehead. He's right on the edge of pulling the trigger and tells everyone to back off or he'll shoot.

"*E's go' a bit of a berk, inspecta'*," a man yells.

"*Go on, shoot 'im,*" the Inspector hollers.

"You're going shoot me? You're going to shoot me? Okay, c'mon. I'll shoot the freakin' sh-t out of you, before you shoot me! I'm not going die in this era..." Von yells, and he is, ready to shoot anyone. He is losing his temper as well as all of the kindness and patience he showed them earlier. Now he is ready to shoot anyone who would stop him from being born in his own time.

Von slams the gun against the Inspector's temple, and the fight is over. He stands there in silence with an unconscious British dormitory worker at his feet. Blood is on his pants. The Inspector and the Constable are holding their heads, trying to get up.

"*Wot just 'appened 'ere? 'ow'd 'e do vis?*" the Inspector looks at Von in disbelief, seeing his gun in Von's hand, thinking the young man is so quick to take them all down by himself, and seeing the way he holds his gun and aims it at everyone.

"Thank goodness for martial arts," Von whispers to himself, as he's done this motion a million times before when he used to practice with his martial arts buddies. Then he stops, throwing down the gun, running off into the darkness.

Into the darkness Von doesn't know where to go. Feeling the tenderness in his ribcage and an acute pain coming from his shoulder blade, he sits for a few seconds on the ground. He gets up and realizes he doesn't know the town, so he hides behind the dormitory alley when out of nowhere a man strikes him in the head and knocks him cold. When they revive him Von screams while the Constable and Chief Inspector tie him to the four-wheeled trap-carts used for transporting inmates. His wrists are tied with a cord, and another cord is tied around his body and arms. Von hopes that staying calm will help him get out of this horrible situation.

He rests his head on the side of the wagon and lets his mind wander. He is oblivious to the crisp snap of the Constable's whip, urging the horses on the rough road. It is going to be a long ride to the police station. The Chief Inspector is silent for a while, until he says, in a strained voice, *"I don't believe tis' lad is a time-travela', Constable, I 'fink 'e is a t'ief an' a murdera an' 'e needs ta b' 'ung."*

Von overhears the Inspector talking about him as though it were a dream but realizes it is not. His senses are suddenly in overdrive again, with the thoughts replacing his daydreams. He hopes for another chance to escape, but the horses have picked up the pace, making any attempt to jump with his hands bound impossible.

Racing downhill, they hit a rut that catches the Chief Inspector and the Constable by surprise, almost throwing both of them off the right side of the wagon. Von does a one-hundred-eighty-degree turn from his seat and hits his face on the side of the wagon. At the base of the hill, the Constable regains control and slows the team down just before a sharp turn.

Now at a walk, the horses seem reluctant to pull the heavy wagon through a low spot in the road that recent rains have turned into a mud hole. The horses refuse to go on, but the Constable cracks his whip, forcing the horses to struggle through the deep mud. As the horses are about to reach the dry bank, the wagon wheels stop as the axles disappear into the muck.

Von hopes this will bring one last chance for escape and watches intently as the Inspector and the Constable descend into the mud on foot with wooden seats they have removed from the wagon to use as levers. Their uniforms are covered with filthy manure and mud, and the darkness gets deeper.

It is hours before other officers are sent to find them, but Von is watched constantly, leaving no chance for escape.

"Oi'm sorry Inspecta', wos Oi dreadful?"

"*Not at ol. Carry on… T'e night clouds 'ill soon b' drawin' in,*" the Constable whispers.

"*I caun't understand w'y it 'as grown so dark,*" says the Inspector in a low voice. "*Gawd lor', I fink a storms comin'. Frightening we'aven't git a lig't on vis' cart.*"

"*We 'ave,*" says the Constable. From the floor of the cart, he reaches for a heavy, carved iron lantern.

"*W'ere on eart' did ya ge' that?*" asks the Inspector.

"*I ge' it unda' the cart, Inspecta'.*" the Constable responds, while staring at Von.

"Oi fink we'll ge' there momentarily."

"*We're almost there, Inspecta'.*"

"*Awfully brilliant,*" the Inspector hollers.

The conversation is cut short by a loud bang and a blaze of light, which awakens Von from his well-needed nap. A shot shrieks past Von's ear.

"My God! Someone has shot at us! I almost got hit here, you know," Von yells. "I don't want to die by a gun shot while I'm *time-traveling.*"

"That's beyon' b'lief, Inspecta'."

"What's the matter with you people? Aren't you worried we almost got shot?"

"*Vis is extraordinary,*" the Inspector says, "Most extraordinary."

"What's extraordinary? We have to get out of here. We're being shot!" Von shouts with fear and anger.

"Ge' out? We 'ave ta move on till we ge' ta the *sta-shun,*" the Constable replies as he slows the cart down upon reaching the steep, narrow entrance of the police station.

"Frightenin' so at times, ain't it?

"*Right, ho!*" the Constable screams.

Von feels more and more anxious as he gets a glimpse of the police station. The two men help him get out of the cart, as both of his hands are still tied behind his back.

"*Ya seem ta b' a fine fella'. Too bad yer a criminal. Oi caun't believe yer a murdera',*" the Constable tells Von with a cigarette in his hand.

"*Aawight, befa' ya get inside vis' cell, ya need ta sign tis' pap'rs,*" the Constable hands Von a piece of paper to sign. Von examines it and sees that he needs to write his residence on the form. If he writes his real address, they will think he is officially insane. After his prior beating, he is sore and afraid of what would happen.

The Constable goes inside the cell Von is assigned. When he finishes checking the cell for Von, he walks back to his desk.

What address do I tell them if I don't know of any address around here? Von asks himself.

The Constable snatches the paper from Von.

"*Give me t'at en' let me finish it fa' ya,*" the Constable says to Von. He then asks Von several questions regarding the murder weapons, until he notices that Von didn't declare his address. "*Tell me, in wot part o' town d' ya' live? C'mon, lad.*"

Von tries to avoid the Constable's question, but when he realizes he must answer, says, "Sorry, Constable, I do not remember where I live."

"Don't ge's'irty wiv me, lad," the Constable says to Von.

Von hears several police discussing events for the following morning. Another constable then arrives. The constables discuss that the execution early the following morning. An inspector interjects that there will be two separate executions: the first is a thirty-five-year-old man with a history of crime who killed a young constable. The constable next to Von remarks that the man fired shot into each of the policeman's eyes, leaving him dead on the road, still holding his baton. The Inspector says that everyone in town thinks this man deserves to be hanged.

"Awfully sorry ta ask...Will there be anot'er execution afta' that, Inspecta'?" The Constable asks.

"Indeed! Yes, indeed. Anotha' execution will tike place in few 'ours afta' t'at. Gawd lor', an eighteen-year-old lad will be 'ang fa' the murda' of a sixty-six-year-old dame whom 'e battered ta death in 'er 'otel room whilst tryin' ta rob 'er," the Inspector replies. He mentions that everyone feels sorry for the young man because several juries have made a recommendation for mercy. The juries were not convinced the young man had intended to kill but felt he panicked when the woman woke up and screamed. But, the Inspector mentions, the lad will be hanged anyway because of tainted evidence The Inspector describes the young man as calm and kind.

Von can no longer stand to listen. He has the gut feeling that they will find him guilty even with no evidence, and then he will never be born in his own time.

Von quietly takes out his camera-phone from his front pocket. He has the idea that he may as well try, so he punches one of his speed-dial buttons and then feels afraid to put the phone to his ear. If it works, if his call goes through, he'll know that this is just one heck of a nightmare – yes, just a dream, and that he really has become the random target of a frat's practical joke, caught up with a troupe of school theater performers who take their roles too seriously.

Warily, and hopefully, not daring to glance at the display, Von brings the cell phone to his ear. He is sure it will do something to help carry him back to reality… But, Von didn't hear anything. Only silence…that's it. So it's real; he really has gone back through time. Von traveled out of his cell phone service area…by thousands of miles away, a hundred years into the past! Then, the cruel reality of his situation begins to sink in. The Constable harasses Von regarding the information he "forgot" to indicate in the documents.

All of a sudden, black clouds appear, and earth-shattering thunder sounds. A massive bolt of lightning rockets out of the menacing sky, striking through a window where the Constable has been standing. A fire begins to flame near the Constable's desk, and a high-pitched sound comes from somewhere in the precinct. The noise is so loud that it hurts Von's eardrum and is heard all over the precinct. The Constable hides under his desk when, all of a sudden, he sees Von disappear right in front of his eyes. The Constable tries to grab him, but Von is gone.

The Inspector runs into the room and asks the Constable what the commotion is all about. He is cut short by a loud bang and a blaze of light which causes them both to lunge under the desk.

"*Wot's ol vis turbulence?*" the Inspector asks.

The Constable clarifies that Von has vanished into thin air, right in front of his eyes, after a sudden bolt of lightning and clap of thunder.

"W'ere's e' gone?"

"Oi 'fink the lad is a time-travela', Inspecta', 'e's gone," the Constable says.

"Do ya bloody believe that?" the Inspector asks incredulously. *"Wot do ya mean 'e's gone? Did 'e escape?"*

"Well 'e just disappear'd right in front of me eyes! Oi tried ta grab 'im, but it wos bloody frightening Inspecta'. 'e wos gone in front of me eyes. The space where 'e wos standing wos full 'f dark air. Oi couldn't 'ang on ta me desk."

"Oi can't bloody believe...that's nonsense," the Inspector responds with a puzzled look in his face. He then says abruptly, *"Ar' ya sure?"*

"Oi don't kno' wot ta say, Inspecta'. Oi'm puzzled me'self," the Constable responds.

"Don't be daft, Constable. Ar'ya tellin' me t'e lad is a 'arry 'oudini?"

"'arry 'oudini? Wot d' ya mean, Inspecta'? The fella wo' performed t'e legendary Mirror Cuff escape, an impossible-to-pick set of locks act ot the London Hippodrome in 1904?"

"'Cmon, t'is lad is not an illusionist..."

"If he is not a time-traveler or illusionist, then w'ere d'ya fink' e's gone?

"Oi 'ope back w'ere 'e bloody belongs," the Inspector responds, shaking his head. *"Well, O'im dashed. Not a word of vis, naturally, ta ani'un' or the whole town will fink we've gone loofy ourselves. Ya 'ear me, Constable? We 'ave ta be discreet,"* asks the Inspector.

The Inspector leaves the precinct with a peculiar feeling, wondering if the young man really is a time-traveler.

"Yes, of course Inspecta', not a word ta ani'un' in our force. The Constable responds to the empty room as he sits down.

CHAPTER FOUR

ALTERED LIFE

I magine falling asleep in Florida the night before commencement ceremonies for your college graduation in
2008, then waking up the next morning to find yourself in a dorm room at Exeter College at Oxford University
in England, being accused of murder, bloody and beaten,
and the year is 1908! How surreal it would be to meet your
grandfather at a time when he is a college student, just a bit
older than yourself?

There is no lifeline to connect you with all things familiar to prove you traveled back in time. No Wi-Fi or any kind
to link your laptop to the web or cell towers, so you can't
call your buddies – or your parents – to bail you out like you
have done without a second thought so many times before.

You are the lone tree falling in the woods making the
sound no one would hear. What would you do, if your entire
life changed in a blink of an eye?

Von is distraught when he awakens and realizes he has
returned to the Exeter dormitory, not his own dorm, from
the sudden electrical blast…the strange-looking people are
wearing unfamiliar clothes, parading in front of him as they

were the first time he encountered them. These men wear dark, heavy suits and black derby hats. Looking from the inside window, Von can see the old-fashioned carriage cars and horses plodding on cobblestone roads. Primitive-looking signs along the streets read: "Carriage rides for 5 pence."

Is that a British pound sign? Did I really travel back in time? How did this all happen? What just happened to me?

Von realizes he has no choice but to adapt to his new reality. He must adjust to a world one hundred years in the past and make a new life for himself as long as he is here.

Inside the British dormitory he finds the bloody clothes of the dead body hanging off of a dorm closet. He is repulsed, and to make it worse, he's not completely certain he isn't responsible. But the next thing he knows, he stumbles across another body in the water closet. This time it is so bloody that it looks like the parting of the Red Sea from where he is standing. He's not sure if he should report it to anyone in the dorm. If he does, he knows they would implicate him.

Am I being stalked by a killer? he wonders. To top it all off, Von knows that when the police find him, he will be arrested again for another murder. As he enters the water closet to use the John, just when it seems things can't get any worse, a man who Von thinks is the real killer appears in front of him. This man tells Von that he believes that Von is a time-traveler and wants to return to the future with Von in order to escape the murder he committed.

The mysterious man asks, *"Oi needs ta speak wif' ya, lad, tonight aht de pub. Com' early."*

"Who are you? What do you want from me?"

"Listen ta me, chap, ya got ta show up, an' I'll tell ya 'ow ya got 'ere."

"Did you just say you know how I got here?"

"Had me on a toast, didn't ya? I saw ya covered wif dark clouds. It's a daft blooming 'ell. Ge' out of 'ere. Oi'm famished. I ain't eatin' anything. Oi'v go' ta ge' me stomach sum meal. T'morrow ya see me back 'ere."

"But I don't know my way around here. I don't know where the pub is. Why should I listen to you? Why should I see you later?"

"Wot ya goin' ta do? Sit around like golliwogs, I suppose? Dat's yer lookout. If ya don't, I'll find ye an' cut yer bloody t'roat like de rest of 'em, took me fa' a mug, a stupe, eh?"

When Von hears that, he is assured that he is in fact talking to the killer. "What do you want from me?" he asks. He is not sure if he should follow the man's orders and meet him later or stay away from him. If he stays away from him, the man may find him as he said he would.

"Ya don't 'ave a choice, sonny. Tike me wif ya, or de bleedin' copper tikes me ta jail. At de pub Oi'll strangle ya like de rest."

"I will do my best."

"Not anotha' pack of bleedin' lies. Git yer arse o't 'ere! Might ya try and scamper off. Crumbs!" the mysterious man responds as he leaves the dark, shadowy room by which he was standing.

I don't like this world, I don't live here, and tomorrow I'll wake up in my own world, Von tells himself.

A loud voice breaks into his thoughts.

"T'e bloke is back! Fetch the Constable! Blimey, ow'd 'e escape t'e station?" a man yells with a shocked grin on his face. He then turns to Von and says, *"ow'd ya ge' back 'ere? 'ow'd ya do t'at t'en?"*

Another man responds, "Oit doz not matta'. Aawight, get on wiv it an' telephone t'e Constable, quick!"

Von doesn't know how he got back to the British dormitory. All he can remember is that he punched a speed dial number into his cell phone while he was at the precinct. Next thing he knew, he was back in the old dormitory in the same corner where everyone found him earlier.

"I don't know how I got back here. I don't know," Von tells the man and surveys his surroundings.

"Will sum'un' alert t'e Scotland Yard Constable? T'e murdera' is back 'ere," a group of men yells to someone Von cannot see.

"Please, sir, let me explain…I don't *know* how I get here, and I don't *know* how I transported myself back here tonight. Please listen to me. I think I transported myself here with my wireless gadget from the future. I don't understand how it happened, but I think it did," Von persists.

"Aawight t'en, d'ya 'ave anything ta show yer from t'e bleedin' future? Go a'ead, show us sumfing," the man tells Von, staring at him.

Von tries to get something from his pocket. He goes to the corner of the room to locate something that he can show to these people to prove that he is from the future. He hopes that if he does so, they might at least give him the benefit of the doubt that he is not the murderer. But a sound coming from somewhere interrupts him. It sounds like his cell phone's ringtone.

Rrringgg! Rrringgg! Von hears over and over. It's a familiar sound to him but not to these other men.

"Wot is t'at sound? Di'ja 'ear t'at? W'ere is it comin' from? Caun ya 'ear it, too? It keeps followin' me!" one man says.

That sounds like a cell phone ring, Von thinks. *Oh my god, it's my phone! Holy crap! That's my phone! That's my freaking phone! My phone rings in this era? This is so Cool!*

Von screams in excitement, and everyone turns to look at him as he picks up what looks like a small metal box with a little piece of thick wire sticking out of it.

"It's my phone! My cell phone!"

"*Yer off yer trolley, lad. Wot's a 'cell'fon'?*" a man asks, smoking his pipe.

"*Wot's 'e go' in 'is 'and?*"

"I wonder who it is!" Von looks at his phone and realizes he has no signal or caller ID. "Damn it! This sucks! My *picture caller ID* doesn't work here. I can't see who's calling." He answers his phone hurriedly, hoping he'll have even a slight signal, so he decides to move around.

He then hears, "Hello?! Hello?! Von, can you hear me? It's Mick, dude. Where the hell are you, man?" *It's Mick!* Von thinks.

"Mick, I hear you, man! You won't *believe* what's happened to me!"

"Try me," Mick responds. "Where the heck are you? You missed graduation, dude. Your mom and dad were *pissed*... and worried. Are you in New York? Did you get the job offer at that investment firm?" Mick peppers Von with a continuous line of questions.

"Dude, easy with all this questions! You're cutting off, man I can't hear you! I, uh, don't have good reception where I am," Von says. "No cell towers here, dude."

"*E's talkin' to 'Dude' in t'at tin can metal apparatus. W'os 'Dude'? Does any'un' kno' 'Dude'? Good Gawd. 'Is 'e goin' loofy on us?*" a man with thin wire-rimmed eye-glasses asks.

Von hears what the man has said but ignores him while talking to Mick with excitement.

"What are you talking about? Where are you?"

Von manages to sneak into the corner of the room while the men argue about what they've just heard and seen. "Mick, you won't believe it man. I've gone back in time! I've gone back hundred years, and it sucks, dude. I wish you could be here...or get me back to reality," Von admits.

"Righteous, dude! Can you change my final grades in Business Calc.? Shoot, I didn't freakin' study the night before coz' I went to a party instead. I think there is still time to do it before Professor Hinkley submits the grades at the registrar this week," Mick exclaims, laughing.

"Listen, I've really gone back in time, Mick! I'm not joking, man. I'm serious."

"What do you mean you're *in the past*?"

"Don't you get it? I time-traveled, dude!"

"What the heck? Are you messing with me?"

"No, man, I'm telling the truth. I wouldn't lie to you about this. Damn, I don't think I could make this up!" Von refrains tirelessly.

"Sweet, man! So...can you go into the future, too?" Mick asks, half teasing, half curious, and laughing.

"I don't know, dude, I don't even know how I got here."

"Dude, why would you want to go into the *past*, anyway? That's where all the trouble starts. Didn't you once say to me that it makes you nauseous when you change zip code? Dude, not only did you change zip code, you're way out of your calling range," Mick laughs at Von. "We don't want to see all those girls that we've been avoiding in the past!"

"I didn't *try* to go back in time," Von responds, exasperated, wishing he had a better explanation.

"I thought you needed like a magic machine or something to do that," Mick scoffs. "I'm hanging up, man, cause you're nuts."

"No! Don't. Do not hang up on me, I beg of you. Something big is happening, something that validates my entire life, I feel it."

"What could *that* be, dude?" Mick asks impatiently, half teasing Von.

"Are you sitting down?" Von asks to see if Mick is really paying attention to him.

"Yes!" Mick replies, laughing, ready to hang up.

"No, you're not. I'm serious!"

"I am now. Okay, What's up?" Mick complies, feigning interest.

"That night, after the frat party, I was zapped into my scanner and ended up here, on June 12, 1908. All I can remember was trying to send my late thesis to Professor Richmond, and then *BOING*! I woke up and I thought I was back in our dorm room. I thought it was just one of those bad dreams I get when I smoke and drink too much."

"Then...?" Mick asks.

"'I'm home,' I said to myself. I'm alive. As I looked at myself and rolled over in what I thought was my bed, I realized what happened...Well, after lots of confusion, I figured it out. It's real, man. I swear!"

Mick is baffled by what Von is saying. He doesn't know if he should believe him or laugh about it. He pauses for a moment and thinks what questions he needs to ask Von. "Are you sure you're not hallucinating, dude?" Mick asks seriously.

"C'mon. I'm not hallucinating. I'm with my grandpa in England. He went to college here, you know? He's *our age* now! Believe me, man."

"Oh, I do. Of course I do!" Mick answers jokingly and sarcastically. His reaction is definitely being influenced by the little bit of wine he had in the afternoon.

"Dude, here's the kicker..." Von says, exasperated. He hopes Mick will believe him, after all these years of friendship... They've been best friends since the fifth grade.

"What's the kicker, man?"

"I can't get back home. I can't get home, dude!"

"Why? Are you hiding from that chick from last night's party?"

"No, moron! You know me better than anyone. I am *not* making this up, Mick!"

"Okay, dude, easy man. I'm still a little hung over from last night. Okay, start over again, would you? Your grandpa from your mother's side or your father's side of the family?" Mick laughs uncontrollably.

"Mom's side of the family. Seriously," Von answers, desperate for a more serious reaction from Mick.

"Ohh, the one who studied in England? Didn't he bite the dust before you were even born?"

"Yes. This is what I'm telling you..." Von is irritated with Mick's sarcastic remarks.

"Then how can you be with him, dude? Are you hallucinating or something? I thought you didn't experiment with the, uh, recreational chemicals? You really have a vivid imagination, man," "Can't you just fast-forward a hundred years if you're really where you say you are?" Mick asks earnestly but still not knowing whether Von is just joking with him.

"Well, it's not like that. It's not like I can hit a button. I wish."

"That is so cool, man, By the way dude, before we get any further in this conversation can you do me a favor to change all my grades in business class while you're back in time? Seriously, I think Professor Mansfield gave me a freaking D on my final exam. Maybe I'll get accepted into my master's program after all!"

"Mick, stop it! Believe me, it's true!"

"Okay, Von, this is not funny, dude! What have you been smoking without me? The mind can play games with you on that stuff, you know."

"Man, what do I have to do to get you to believe me?!" Von pleads. "Wait, Mick, your connection is cutting out. Mick, I'm losing you, man. Mick! Can you hear me? Can you hear me?"

"Yep! I'm here, dude. Get back here from wherever you are! Too many video games for you. Your imagination can't handle all those games," Mick stammers between bellows. "So, did you chicken out proposing to Bessie?"

"Mick, that's my other problem. Remember you asked me at the frat party why I looked a little odd?"

"Yes, dude, I remember. Then, out of the blue, you whispered to me that you are going to propose to Bessie. That knocks the socks off of me, man. Damn, I thought we were still going to be in a master's program right after college? Why would you want to marry her right away? Is there a bun in the oven, dude?"

"No, you moron. All you think about is wild parties and all. There is no *bun* or whatever you're thinking. Nothing like that. And yes, I still want to get my master's degree, don't worry," Von insists.

"Didn't you say that you're going to tell me something else, aside from proposing to Bessie? Sorry dude, I was blasted last night, and I just can't comprehend anything after 2 a.m., you know? My brain doesn't seem to function at that hour," Mick responds patiently.

"Dude, dude, it's okay, man. What I wanted to tell you is about Bessie. She was with a dude in her sorority dorm.

They were kissing when I got there. I was going to surprise her to propose. So when I saw them, I left. I was furious, man. But then I thought I'd try to talk to her the following day and try to propose again, but things didn't work out because I was zapped into another era. I can't understand what happened?" Von sadly expresses.

"What are you talking about, man? C'mon, Von. Not Bessie. Are you sure it's Bessie you saw? You know that other sorority sister looks just like her...what's her name?"

"No. Mick, I know it's Bessie. And I've seen that dude before. He's from Georgetown U. Bessie has mentioned him to me. She said that he was trying to pick her up, but she told him she's involved. But then he continued to pursue her."

"Oh! *That* dude, yeah, I remember that dude. How can I forget him? He is the one who thinks he belongs to a membership of the *logo* club. I do remember him because he laughed at my cheap necktie I got from *Target*, remember? He knew right by looking at it that it's a *knockoff*."

"Yap...He said is there anything better than a whale, crocodile or pony on your shirt to tell the people his shirt cost more? So I guess he thinks it's a brilliant idea to get a polo pony tattooed on his chest. His brother got a crocodile tattooed on his neck. The crocodile tattoo represents Lacoste. The polo pony represents Ralph Lauren, you know?

"Wasn't he the same one that was so proud of telling everyone about his expensive black tie suit?"

"What about it?

"He said it belongs to his grandfather and was buried in it.

"Yeah, yeah, that's the one. Now we're on the same track, Mick. Yeah, he is the same one who said you need a certain 'look' or 'style'...what did you call him, then?"

"The *logo junkie* and *trust-fund baby*. Seriously, if he is not a freaking trust-fund baby, how the hell can he afford all those designer suits and outfits, man? Unless he's a fashion model and gets all those things for free. College students are supposed to be poor, you know? I thought he was with that *perfume-marinated chick* from Yale," Mick responds. "Yeah, Dex told us that during the college recruit week the chick was in the same booth with him. He heard a recruiter ask her if she has any skills. She proudly told the recruiter she can type 20 IMs per minute. The recruiter laughed so loud that she had to leave the interviewing booth to get a glass of water."

"Dude, you're so funny...ha! ha! ha! Everyone knows that *chick*. Her perfume is so strong it enters a room before she does! Anyway, sorry to open the topic about your fashion statement. I know you're still angry at the dude for insulting your style, but that's the same guy that *snatched* my Bessie away from me.

"Dude, dude, enough of this silliness. If this is really true about Bessie, get back here. You both need to talk. And take her for a magic carpet ride after you settle your differences," Mick laughs again.

"Mick, why won't you believe me? I thought you started to believe me here for a minute, but I guess you didn't."

"Okay, Von, tell me this...did you have your contact lenses in that night? You know you're nearsighted. You can't see clearly!" Mick cracks up, laughing uncontrollably.

"That wasn't nice of you to say that, dude. That's not funny, you know? Well, I thought it was her...and I just didn't want to get closer 'cause I don't think I could've handled it right there and then."

"Okay, Von, don't worry. Seriously, I'll find out if there's a new dude in her life. Do you want me to tell her you time-traveled?

"No, moron! Don't be silly, Mick. Please be serious for once."

Okay, I am now. So could we change the topic for a second? By the way, tell me, did you get the job at the New York Mercantile Exchange?"

"Yeah, I did. I am supposed to report there next week. Shoot! I need to call them. But how can I? And what do I say?" Von is worried.

"Hey, that's good, dude, congratulations. Also, are you coming to my party later or not? I don't have time for this! Cut the crap, and pick up an extra keg on your time-travel back for the party tonight." Mick ignores Von's pleas to listen to him. "Tell me, seriously, did you run away with that blonde chick from last night's party? She didn't show up at the ceremony, either. Everyone thinks you ran away to Vegas or something!"

"Who?"

"The blonde chick you were with last night? Damn, she's prrrrrretty, dude! So…who's cheating on who? Ha! Ha! Ha!" Mick cracks up.

"Mick, you got it all wrong. Yeah, I was upset with Bessie, and I was out of control without even hearing her side, so when I bumped into that blonde chick I kinda used the time to forget my problem at the moment, you know?"

"Aha! You're guilty now, dude! It seems like you didn't wait to mourn. You moved on right away! What I don't get is why are you using this time-travel shit excuse? It's the most ridiculous excuse you could have ever come up with. If you are upset about life or don't want to come home for a while, just say so. Don't make up excuses like this. No one is going to believe you, dude. I thought you were smarter than this."

"Mick, let's rewind this conversation here for a second... why are you saying this speech and asking me all these questions?"

"Well...the blonde gal didn't show up at the graduation. So everyone thinks you run away with her. Did you? On top of that, Bessie did show up at the graduation." Mick irritates Von.

"Oh yeah?" Von asks.

"Yeah, dude. Bessie was sitting next to your parents, waiting for you to show up."

"What? She was sitting next to my parents with that *dude*?" Von screams.

"No. No. You got it all wrong, Von. She was by herself, and I don't know where that dude was. You know what, this is really getting weird, dude. I don't know how much longer I can play this with you. Your disappearance the night before graduation, then Bessie being with that *Georgetown* dude, then you are nowhere to be found. It's all too bizarre."

"Mick, that's the problem! I know this is really strange. I know it's crazy, but I woke up in a dorm I've never seen before...here in England. What's really creepy is that I woke up with blood all over me, and they said I murdered some dude next door. I haven't seen any of these people before. At first, I thought these dudes were your frat brothers playing a joke on me. I thought you set them up to haze me or something," Von illustrates. "Then I realized it wasn't hazing after all. I really *did* time travel. They now accused me of murder, I've been badly beaten, and two of my back teeth have been knocked off, man. They took me to Scotland Yard police station – arrested me for murder I didn't commit! It's terrible here, dude."

"You're toothless? Man, you are gonna be in trouble with your parents. It costs a ton to get your teeth capped, man. This is crazy..." Mick says, starting to realize Von really is serious.

"Yes, it happened, and while I was at the police station, I heard that there will be an execution in the morning. A young guy will be hanged for murdering an old lady for food. And guess what? They know the dude was innocent, but they're gonna hang him anyway.

"I was freaked out, so I tried to call you, since I have my cell phone on me. For some reason, when I dialed your number, I was transported back to the British dorm. I don't have the faintest idea how I did all these things. Help me, Mick, I need to get out of here."

"Would you stop being ridiculous? I think you're delirious from whatever you had at the party last night," Mick snaps.

"Dude, are you hiding in the girls' dorm? Seriously, where the heck are you?" Mick asks.

"Mick, please listen to me. Seriously, I really traveled back in time. I know it's strange, but it's the truth, man." One of the men finds Von and tries to interrupt him. Von says, "Excuse me, would you please? I'm on the phone here, do you mind?!"

The man stares and listen to Von's conversation.

"Who was that?" Mick asks, trying to listen if Von was really talking to anyone or if he was hallucinating.

"I don't know his name. Some British guy. He's eavesdropping." Von eyes the man suspiciously.

"They're real? The people are *real*? Ahhh! Holy crap! You're not alone?" Mick teases.

"Stop it! I'm serious, I'm not hallucinating, I'm not hung over, and I'm not crazy!"

"Okay, Von, I want you to repeat after me, dude, are you listening?"

"Yes!"

"Okay, repeat after me. 'I am Von, and I'm going to walk out of this mess and not let anyone know I'm hallucinating-"

"Mick, dude, I'm not! Look, I'm going to take a picture with my phone and send it to you. Tell me if you get it." Von takes a picture of the dorm room, managing to fit a couple of the men into the photo without them noticing. He waits a minute and asks Mick, "I'm waiting, dude, did you get it?"

"Yeah...What the heck was that?" Mick asks, now completely confused. "Who are those dudes?"

"I know what you mean. I thought I was in the Performing Arts Department. I thought these people were planning for a summer drama program about the early 1900s. Don't they look like they are wearing costumes?"

Mick finally begins to believe Von and hurriedly responds, "This is bad news, dude. That means these guys have been dead for a hundred years if you're in 1908, right? Dude, touch the friggin' rewind button...or fast forward, whatever it is...just press it now!"

"Hey, what about using aluminum foil? Do you remember, Dex uses it when his cell phone antenna breaks? For some darn reason it works, man," Mick teases.

"Dude, seriously, I need your help getting out of here. I'm stuck," Von says sadly.

"How do you expect me to believe you that you're really in the 1900s?" Mick is very serious this time.

"The picture isn't good enough?"

"Well, it *is* kind of eerie," Mick responds. "How do I explain this, man? What do I say? Hey guys, guess what? Do you know that Von time-traveled? I can't say that, dude!

Someone might think I'm on drugs or something. I'm serious, I don't know. I want to help, but I don't know how. Seriously, I don't know what to say to you, dude. Okay, cut the crap already, and pick up an extra keg on your time-travel back for the party tonight." Mick still joking, ignores Von's pleas to listen to him.

"Mick, you're fading, man. Hello? Hello? Mick?" Von yells.

"I said, pick up an extra keg for tonight's party, okay?" Mick yells.

"Mick, are you there?" The line goes dead.

"Mick! Mick! Noooo!" The connection was lost, and Von is petrified. He sits down on an old chair that is close by, looking dazed and shocked, still holding the phone close to his ear. After a moment, he slowly puts the phone down in his lap. He buries his head in his hands, trying to pull himself together. What now?

I don't get why this happened to me. I'm just an ordinary guy who was supposed to graduate from college today. I have a mother and father, a girlfriend, a life. And I want all that back! Von thinks. *I wasn't trying to escape from anything…I just wanted to attend my graduation today and hopefully get that job from that investment firm…and propose to Bessie so that I can snatch her back from that Georgetown dude. Damn, I didn't hurt anyone. I was a good person. I was just trying to send an e-mail to my professor, and now I'm here. How did I get here? How did I get here?*

I've got to get back home. All I want is to be able to go home. I don't belong here. I don't like it here. I don't like it here…

CHAPTER FIVE

RIPPER VS. SERGEANT PEPPER

I t would be nice to be able to plug in his computer and try to get an Internet connection, but he can't right now.

"There's no way they have cell towers in this era," Von says aloud to himself. After the big bloody chaos in the British dormitory earlier, the rest of the occupants try to keep their distance from Von until the Constable gets back to fetch him.

One man overhears, and after having watched Von during his entire conversation with Mick, the man concludes, *"Oi fink 'e's one of the finest theatre actors Oi 'ave eva' seen."*

"E strikes me as genuine, sum of them things 'e wos sayin'... 'e is completely gormy of our surroundin" Sir Oliver Robert states.

"An' 'oo speaks like t'at?" the man with the pipe asks.

"Sum'un' 'oo's a theatrical actor, 'e appears ta speak English, t'oug' not very well." another man replies.

"Terribly sorry, lad, may Oi 'ave a word wiv' ye 'bout yer situation?" Sir Oliver asks.

"My situation is that I want to go home. Today is my college graduation. I just want to go home..."

"As fa' as we're all concerned, ye' might be Jack t'e Rippah!" Sir Oliver replies with astonishment.

"If you can say that about me, I can say you must be Sergeant Pepper!"

"'Oo is Sergeant Peppa'?" asks Sir Oliver.

"Oh, forget it!" Von says.

"Oi beg yer pardon?" Sir Oliver asks.

Von refrains from saying anything about Florida and Stephenson College again. The man wasn't very impressed when he mentioned it earlier. And although Florida has been a state since 1845, these guys do not seem to be aware of it. Von decides to just be quiet and listen to Sir Oliver.

"Oh, an' ye made us believe t'at ye 'ave found a 'gap in time?" Sir Oliver asks.

"Yes, yes, you got it! Why won't you believe me? You of all people should understand..." Von realizes that Sir Oliver won't grasp what this means, and hesitates to explain. "Would someone please give me an *Aspirin?* Does anyone even know what Aspirin is? I also need a triple antibiotic for my cuts."

"Wot is it, lad?"

"Aspirin...It's for pain. I need something for pain. I'm having a lot of it recently. And do you have any kind of antibiotics?"

"Wot is it fa?"

"Antibiotics are medicine to fight infection," Von responds.

"Well, we 'ave acetylsalicylic acid fa' pain and antiseptic to clean yer wound. I picked me personal supplies aht t'e chemist yesterday," Sir Oliver offers Von. *"An' let me look aht yer shoulder, lad."* He puts an old wooden sling on Von.

"It's broken," Von says with indignance.

"*Yer arm'll be fine. It's sprained, not broken,*" Sir Oliver says as he inspects Von's arm.

"*Time-travel caun't possibly 'appen, lad. It doesn't exist, fifteen minutes or a 'undred years, we 'ave ta slog along in t'e time we 'ave,*" Sir Oliver tells him.

Von pulls out his PDA and other gadgets. "Sir Oliver, may I show you my wireless devices from the future? If you still believe I am not a time–traveler, please explain to me where I got these." Von tries to show the wireless gadgets to Sir Oliver and the other men when suddenly a man grabs his backpack.

"Give it back!" Von yells and lunges for the bag. Cradling Von's backpack in one arm, the man attempts to open it with his free hand but with no success.

"*Wot else d' ya 'ave in yer possession,*" one of the other men asks.

"*Wot's ol tis t'en!*" another man yells

"Those are my electronic gadgets. They are essential parts of my everyday life."

"*Go'dget? Wot's a go'dget?*"

"PDAs, cell phones, and laptops are some of the gadgets. Okay, tell me, Sir Oliver, do you have PDAs in this era? *Do you?*" Von questions angrily.

"*Ow'd ya rememba' ol t'em long names? Wot is t'at? W'ere'd ye ge' it, lad?*" another man asks.

"I told you, I brought it with me from the future. If you don't believe me, explain to me why I speak and dress differently from all of you. And tell me how I have a picture of you in my PDA. A picture of you with my great-grandpa, which is your father. A picture that has not yet been taken but will be years from now," Von contradicts angrily.

"*Aawight, wot t'e bloody 'ell may Oi ask is a 'PDA'?*" the man asks furiously, staring at Von.

"Look, this is you and your father, is that right?" Von shows the photo to Sir Oliver.

"*Yes, t'at is mi father,*" Sir Oliver answers, confused, "*but Oi don't rememba' t'at pho'ograph bein' taken recently. An'...Oi look a bit older in t'at photograph.*"

"Of course you don't remember it...because it hasn't happened yet. It will happen in the future," Von replies.

"*Ow'd ya' do t'at? Oi mean, were'd ye' ge' mi pho'tograph? Oi don't kno' wot ta say...*" Sir Oliver stammers.

"It was given to me by my mother, and I downloaded it to my PDA."

"*Wot d' ya mean downloaded?*" a man asks.

"It means that it was transferred into a computer and my PDA."

"*Ar' ya my descendant? My offspring?*" asks Sir Oliver.

"Yes!" Von replies. "Unless you can give me an answer that will make sense...or maybe I am dead..."

"*Ya'r not dead. Sit down...look 'ere...Oi'd like ye ta look aht viz Tabloid. Does ani 'f viz look familiar ta ye?*" Sir Oliver asks.

"Nope! I've never seen that newspaper in my life."

"Awwight, as reluctant as Oi am, Oi feel that Oi must now personally intervene," Sir Oliver whispers to Von.

"*Listen, lad. Oi've a business matta' ta attend ta. Oi'll be back momentar'ly an' discuss vis furt'er wiv' ye. In t'e meantime, Oi want ye ta sit an' waif fa' me,*" Sir Oliver instructs Von.

"*Now, ta come straight ta t'e point, Oi considered t'e matta' very carefully. Oi do not 'ave a 'eart of stone, and it is not me intention ta drive ya ta t'e wall,*" Sir Oliver reveals.

"Thank you, thank you very much, Sir." Von is hoping for the best.

"Now, while yer attitude 'as 'ardly been conciliatory, I've no desire to injure an innocent man fa' what matta' or to cause any unnecessary distress to ya."

"Oh, please, Sir. You don't understand how happy I am knowing that someone in this era understands me. Again, thank you," Von gratefully says.

"Now, if yer prepared, Oi might be able ta meet you 'alfway. Ya may 'ave overstressed certain facts 'bout ye being a time-traveler, so ya and Oi need to discuss certain matta wen Oi ge' back from me engagement." Sir Oliver winks at Von to make him feel more comfortable.

"Sir Oliver, may we suggest t'at we fetch t'e Constable an' 'ave 'im tike care 'f tis matta'?" the man with the pipe suggests.

"Yes, let's not worry 'bout tis an' go on wiv' t'e task fa' t'e day. Let me 'ave t'e bloomin' Constable 'ere an' 'ave t'e boy taken ta t'e station. Let 'im explain t'at 'e 'as come from t'e future. Ha ha ha," a man with wide spectacles laughs.

"No! Let me 'andle viz, an' Oi'll b' t'e one ta call t'e Constable if it com's ta t'at. Oi'll tike viz lad ta t'e Constable me'self," Sir Oliver tells the other men.

"Be careful, Sir Oliver, 'e could b' a very dangerous lad. We'll leave ya wiv' 'im, t'en," another man complies. *"G'day, Sir Oliver, an' a pleasant ride ta ya."*

The men leave, shaking their heads as they stare at Von. Von's face is white as a ghost, and he is clearly sad and dejected. Sir Oliver comes closer to him and pats his shoulder to console him.

"Listen! Don't go anyw'ere. Stay right 'ere, an' Oi'll return momentar'ly ta 'elp ya 'ide until we can figure ouf wot ta d' wiv ya," Sir Oliver assures Von.

"Please don't call the police. I'm not a thief. I really came from the future, and I really don't know how I got here.

Please, you have to believe me. Don't let them take me back to jail," Von pleads.

"*Settle down, lad. Alrig't t'en, we need ta discuss tis matta' furt'er. Oi shall com' back momentarily an' 'ave a word wif ya afta' me engagement. Rememba', I forbid ya ta promenade. Stay right 'ere until I come back,*" he reminds Von.

"I will, I will..." Von replies. "Sir Oliver? Am I here forever?"

"*Oi don't know, lad. Viz is strange ta me as it is ta ye.*" He looks at Von, wondering if he is really a time-traveler who will be his grandson in the future.

"*Oi'll b' back momentarily, I've ge' business to attend to.*" He leaves the room quietly and shuts the door on his way out. Sir Oliver can see that Von is an honest, frightened, young man who could never have committed the crimes he is charged with, so he decides that they will join forces to bring down the actual killer when he returns from his appointment.

CHAPTER SIX

RIFT IN TIME 911 OPERATOR

Von walks towards the window and observes the people from outside the dormitory. He sees a man pulling something from his suit pocket. He opens the object, glances at it, and frowns. He wears what seems to be a silk hat, a dark suit with a tiny lapel. Then Von looks around and sees that everyone outside is dressed in early twentieth century clothing. He knows that he has never seen so many mustaches and hats in his life.

A woman in early twentieth-century clothing steps into a fancy carriage. She wears a vintage-looking long-sleeved dress. Behind her, out on the tracks, Von catches a glimpse of carriages with very delicate designs around them. Then he sees a chauffeur pick up a newspaper, the name of which he recognizes: *The British World*. It is a newspaper that he saw in a museum on a field trip with his high school history class with Mrs. Norphy.

Shit! Did I really travel back a hundred years? I must have… he thinks. He sits down on the chair next to the window, utterly confused about what's going on with him.

He tries to sneak outside Sir Oliver's room, hoping that nobody sees him. He goes inside the dark water closet. Von unzips his pants, and then his phone rings again. He immediately grabs it from his back pocket and answers quietly.

"He-hello?! *Hello*?! Hello? This is Von, who's calling? Is anyone there? Hello, can you hear me?" Von vaguely hears a voice on the other end of the line but can't recognize the voice. Then the line is disconnected again.

He decides to go back to the room, hoping to be able to use his cell phone. He tries to dial one of his speed-dial numbers, but it doesn't work. He tries many times and gets frustrated. He decides to go back to the water closet quietly to see if his phone works there, and for some reason, it does have a signal.

Then he thinks of a crazy idea. He doesn't know what the heck he is doing anyway, so he might as well try. He dials "9-1-1" to tell them he's gone through some 'rift' in time.

"Hello, 911, hello? Can you hear me?" Von says, feeling like he is losing his mind.

"Yes, sir, you have reached a 911 operator. I can hear you. May I ask the urgency you wish to report? What is your name and location?"

"Hello! My name is Von, Von Muir Carmichael."

"Sir, could you please repeat your message. I cannot hear you. Hello? Hello, sir? I think I lost him," the operator says to someone on the other end of the line.

"I said my name is Von Carmichael. Can you hear me?"

"Yes, sir, I can hear you now," the operator responds to Von but is unsure of whether Von can hear her.

"Wow! This is great! You can hear me, great!"

"Von Carmichael, where are you? What is your emergency?"

"Ma'am, can you please try to triangulate my location? I was wondering...Well, you see, I have GPS microchips in my cell phone, and I need your help. Do you think you can track me down? I've traveled back...Well, I've somehow gone back in time...Please help me. I will be executed here for a murder I didn't commit if you don't help me get back to real time."

"I don't think I caught what you just said. Mr. Carmichael, we have too much static on this line. Please repeat. We are trying to trace your call, but we can't seem to track you down. Where are you calling from? Can you hear me? Tell me where you are, and we will send someone to help you."

"Operator...I said I need someone to track me down. I'm in Oxford, England. I need help to get out of here."

"What did you just say? You are where? Back in where? Please speak up, sir, I can barely hear you. We can't seem to understand what you just said. Please speak louder. The connection is not clear. Did you say you're calling from an Orchard?"

"Operator, no, I said Oxford, Oxford, England. I've gone back in time..."

"Sir, did you just say Oxford, England? Did I hear you correctly? Please repeat, you are cutting off."

"Yes, I said Oxford, England, and I'm back in time. The year is 1908," Von is nearly yelling with frustration.

"You said you are...back in time? Is that correct?"

"Yes! That's what I just said, is there something wrong with the connection?" a frustrated Von replies.

"Mr. Carmichael, calling 911 is a serious matter. It is only for emergency, not for any kind of jokes or prank calls."

"This is a very serious matter operator. Do you understand? I swear, I promise this isn't a prank. I'm back in time, about a hundred years. Please, *please* don't hang up. What could be more serious than this? I don't know what to do. I will be executed here for a crime I didn't commit, and I can't get home. They hang people in this century. Please help me. Hello, can you hear me?" Von hears no response. "There's not much time! I need you to report this to the police. My name is Von Muir Carmichael. I've time-traveled and been abducted by British men!"

"All I can remember is: I was in my dorm sleeping, and when I woke up, I was here in Oxford, England and it's 1908. I am being accused of murder, and I'm bloody from being beaten earlier by this British man for the crime I didn't commit."

"Have you had some alcohol or any kind of mind-altering substance recently, Mr. Carmichael?"

"No! Well…I was at a frat party the night before…but, wait a minute, here…what does that have to do with anything? I'm not on any kind of drugs. I was really abducted. Operator, believe me…my ribs are tender, my shoulder blade is dislocated. Two of my back teeth got knocked out. I don't even know these people. What else do you want to know? Please, please, I'm telling you the truth, I've been abducted.

"Oh, really? Abducted?" the operator mocks, near ready to hang up the line.

"Please. I know what you're thinking, but it's real! I'm in a British dormitory. They are waiting for the Constable. They're going to kill me! You need to-"

"Awfully polite abductors to give you a phone to use," the operator remarks.

"It's a cell phone, not a regular phone, operator."

"A cell phone? I'm not aware of cell phones in 1908? That answers it…That is clever!" the operator responds.

"No! You don't understand!" Von yells. His voice trembles uncontrollably, desperate and frustrated. His cell phone begins to make a *"BLIP"* sound continuously. He pulls it away from his ear. He looks at the LCD display and starts to worry...

"If you were really in trouble, you would have called the cops wherever you are...wherever you 'time-traveled.' We're in Florida, and now I've got to take a *real* call on the other line," the operator retorts. The next sound Von hears is a *Click!* and the connection is gone.

Von is confused and angry that the operator hung up on him. Then, he remembers he can dial *215 on his cell phone, and a service provider representative will come on the line, so he does that.

"He- Hello? Hello?"

"Yes, may I help you?" the cell phone representative answers.

"Ah, yes, my cell number is 888-555-1234. My service is equipped with a GPS chip, so would you please tell me if you can track me down or send me a message to my phone and tell me where I am?" Von asks.

"Can you please verify your account information, sir?"

"Oh, for heaven's sake...I'm in a crisis here, you know. Can you just do it...quick? I can't speak too loud right now, and I need help."

"Please verify your account, sir, for security purposes," the representative insists.

"Okay, okay. My name is Von Muir Carmichael. The last four digits of my social security number are 0216. The billing account address of this account is care of my school, and that is *Stephenson College*, 222 College Town, Box 778, Maizen Beach, Florida 34455," Von gives the information with a sarcastic attitude.

"Thank you, please hold, and one of our customer service representatives will be right with you."

"Hey, hey, don't put me on hold. I don't want to repeat the information I just gave. I don't want to waste time here, you know."

"Please hold..." the representative puts Von on hold, without listening to the rest of what Von has just explained.

"He- hello? Damn it! Please don't make me listen to the damn elevator music!" Von screams.

After a few seconds, a male service provider representative comes on the line.

"May I help you?"

"Oh, please, stop asking me if you can help me or not...I need for you to find out if you can track me down. I have a GPS tracking device. I want to know if I can receive signals from *global-positioning-system* satellite. Do you think you can see where I am?"

"Sir, I am looking at your tracking device right now in our system, but for some reason, we can't seem to track down your location. Is it possible that you're in dense building or maybe you are around tall buildings?"

"No. No. I don't think so. I don't know where I am. Well, I know where I am, but...it's kinda difficult to explain. I just want to know if someone out there can find me."

"Mr. Carmichael, you see, this device is best in open locations, outdoors where your cell phone receives signals from the satellite. The accuracy can degrade if your cell phone, for example, is buried in your backpack, which obviously in this case it is not. But we have a backup system that may be able to locate you by specific city by identifying nearby cell phone towers. By the way, for just a five more dollars, you can upgrade your GPS, sir."

WIRELESS IN THE FABRIC OF TIME • 85

"Please don't give me a sales pitch right now. I really don't need it."

"Okay, sir, would you tell me what city and state you are in?" the man starts to slow down a bit, hearing that Von is uptight on the other line.

"Okay, all I know is I'm in Oxford."

"Sir, did you say Oxford?"

"Yes, you heard me right."

"Would that be Oxford, Mississippi?"

"I repeat, I'm in Oxford, England."

"Mr. Carmichael, I don't think I heard you quite right there for a second. You said Oxford Heyland? There is no town and state listed under that name. Would you kindly repeat? Besides, you are getting too much static, and I am losing your connection," the man asserts.

"No! No! You've got it all wrong. I am in Oxford, England, and let me tell you why I want you to track me down…I have time-traveled to a British dorm in 1908, and I am being wanted by the cops here for a murder I didn't commit, please help me."

"How funny! Okay, sir, good joke." The man hears Von sighing. "Is this some kind of a joke? I can see your account is accurate and all the information you give us is correct, but this does not make sense. What do you mean time-traveled? How could you call us if you have time-traveled?"

"I don't know, I can't answer that. All I know is whenever I am inside one of these *water closets*, I do get a cell phone signal. It's weird, but it works, man. I don't freakin' understand."

"Sir, I would love to help you, but what is a *water closet*?"

"A water closet is an old-fashioned toilet that has a water tank way above your head with a chain on the side. I really don't get why my cell phone would work whenever I am inside on one of these. It must be their specs that bring the signal to my phone, don't you think?" Von proudly explains to the man.

"Hey, guys … I've got a live one here." Von hears the man joking around." Okay, sir…Call us when you get back in town, and thank you for calling. Have a great day." *Click!* The man hangs up.

"Damn it, damn it…why can't he believe me?" Von whispers, and, hearing footsteps outside the door, he hides, trying not to move or make any sounds. Then he hears loud voices outside the door, and people trying to open it.

"Is any'un' in t'ere?" a voice asks irritatedly. *"Is any'un' usin' t'e wata' closet?"*

"I'll be out in a minute," Von replies, but he hesitates to come out, scared that they might turn him in to the Constable before he gets the chance to meet with Sir Oliver, who seems to be on his side.

"'Oo is t'at?" a voice asks another person and tries to open the door.

"Don't kno'," the other voice says. Von hears the two walking away.

Von waits a while before he comes out of the water closet. He sneaks quietly back to Sir Oliver's room. He is exhausted and falls asleep on the couch. Before he goes to sleep, he looks at his watch, and it says 9:00. He's not sure if that is the time where he is right now or the time back home. The second-hand dial seems to be working; he hears it ticking.

He gets up and sees a tin of biscuits. He opens it and takes a few. He is hungry and thirsty and wants a glass of cold water. He realizes there isn't a refrigerator in this room. He finally appreciates the conveniences they have back in the dorm. Everyone has refrigerators. He sees a pitcher with water in it, so he smells it to see if it's okay. He closed his eyes and sips a bit to quench his thirst. The water tastes awful and is not drinkable even for his cat.

How can they drink this water? It tastes moldy or something, Von thinks.

He is bored, angry, and confused, so he decides to wander around the town of Oxford and see what their everyday life is all about.

Frustrated, and disappointed, he plugs his earpiece into his iPod and walks over to the newsboy, while listening to his music, and glances at the stack of papers at the boy's feet. It is definitely the same paper that he saw earlier, *The British World*, which hasn't been published for years. The lead story today is about King Edward VII.

I've seen that front page before, in the Public Library files; it was printed June 11, 1908. It was part of the research paper I did for Ms. Norphy, Von muses.

He takes out his camera phone and snaps shots of the surrounding area to send to Mick. He notices people looking at him with his earplug iPod in his front pocket, and they are undoubtedly filled with curiosity on who he is. He decides to go inside a nearby restaurant to eat. *Here,* he thinks, *I'm existing in both times, the past and the future. Heck, I don't know. I may just make the transition.*

Then he knows for sure, he really has traveled back in time! He realizes that Von Carmichael does not exist. He won't be born for nearly a hundred years. And in just about one hundred years, he'll be missing, having disappeared from the sizzling Florida weather and from his university and having traveled through time.

He is sad just thinking about it. As his mind wanders he keeps an eye alert to his unfamiliar surroundings. He suddenly realizes that he doesn't have any money. Several people in the restaurant are staring at him from head to toe. He feels very uncomfortable sitting at a table by himself, so he decides to leave. He gets up and goes to check out the bathroom, to see if they all have the same water closet. The bathroom is small and dark. There are no windows. He goes inside, closes the door, and turns on his cell phone.

He tries to call Mick, but he sees that someone beside him is staring at him suspiciously. He hides the phone inside his pocket and decides to wait until the man gets out of the bathroom. The man fiddles around, pretending to need more time. A few minutes later, he becomes impatient and finally leaves. Von leaves as well and tries to retrace his steps to the dorm. On his way back, he remembers what the mysterious man said earlier. He wanted to see him in some kind of a pub. He looks around, trying to see if he can spot the pub the man mentioned. He walks through a dark alley, and then sees what seems to be an old, rugged-looking place. Outside, a sign hangs: 'COWICK BARTON PUB.'

I think this is the one. He said it's near a canal and on the Topsham Road, Von thinks. He goes inside the gloomy pub. Everyone stares. He tries not to look at them, but he knows that even though Clint Eastwood could be ready for a showdown, he is not ready for anything that could happen here. As he walks around the pub, a man grabs his elbow and pushes him in the corner of the room.

"Blow me down. I kno' ye'r not from around 'ere, boy. Tike me wif ya, I've seen ta many Bobbies. I kno' wot they caun do wif me in jail 'round 'ere. It's the bloody black 'ole of Calcutta," the mysterious man says to Von with an angry and hurried tone.

"Take you with me? Where?" Von asks, surprised.

"Fa' away from 'ere. If ya chuck me ouf now, I go ta prison. If ya don't tike me wif ya, ya will neva' see t'morrow, ya 'ear me?" the man warns as he grabs Von's left arm and twists it.

"Owww!!" Von squirms a bit.

"Ya shan't forget. I ain't done wif ya, sonny. Belt up! Dat's not ol dat'll 'appen if ya don't bloody tike me wif' ya. I kno' 'oo y'are. I 'eard t'ose men in de dormitory…Dey fink y'are de killa'. I kno' betta'…I saw ya 'ow de dark cloud ge' ya 'ere from somew'ere. I kno' ya'are a time-trav'la," the man reveals. *"Go on, meet me 'ere t'morrow at de same time. We'll leave t'en."*

"You saw me come from the future? How did I get here? Do you remember what you saw?" Von asks eagerly.

"I saw t'unda an' lig'tnin' from above, an' ya com' from de sky. Oi may appear ta be daft but still go' some in t'is loaf," the man insists as he points his head.

"The sky? Where? What do you mean, the sky?" Von asks again.

"Don't kno'…don't exactly rememba'…It's a bit of a mystery me-self. I 'eard a big blastin' sound, rig't afta' I killed de bastard…in de room next ta w'ere dey found ya. Bleedin' 'ell…Tike me wiv ya, an' ya'll be safe wiv me. Ot'erwise, I'll kill ya like de othas, ya 'ear? Wot do I've ge' ta lose ta kill anatha' one like ya? Oi've a spot of trouble wiv de law…" the man warns.

"But I don't even know how to get back. Was I riding on something? Believe me, I'd like to get back to where I came from, but I don't know how I got here or how I can go back. I am working on going back, but I don't know how. If you tell me how to do it, I'll gladly take you with me, man – I mean, sir," Von promises.

"I shan't jolly well 'fink so. I don't care 'ow ya d' it. Jus' d' it! Smarten yourself up a bit. T'is is yer funeral, sonny," the man yells, as he takes his knife from inside his jacket and shoves it dangerously close to Von's neck.

Von feels the cold knife beneath his neck, so he abrupt-ly shuts up. He can't even open his mouth to say another word.

"Push off, out of 'ere! Rememba', t'morrow, in t'is pub, ya shan't forget! Go on, push off...Yer acting unpaid dogsbody." He slams Von against the wall, yanks his head back, and holds the knife against Von's throat to threaten him. Then, he takes his hand away from Von's throat and leaves the pub. Von follows him but can't see where the man has gone. He has just disappeared like a gust of wind. Von walks away, out of the dark alley near the pub and is able to trace his steps from Sir Oliver's dorm.

He hurriedly dials Mick's number but then decides to go to the bathroom again to call him. He opens the door quietly, hoping nobody is in the hallway. He sneaks out qui-etly and quickly runs inside. He takes out his cell phone and presses Mick's speed-dial number. He hears that it is ring-ing. He counts eight rings.

"Hello?"

"Hello? Mick?" Von whispers. "Mick, it's Von. Can you hear me?"

"Yeah! I can hear you, man. What's up, dude? Hey, still time-traveling, eh? I'm pissed off at you, man, for not showing up and bringing the keg. Thank goodness Stewart brought some wine from his father's wine cellar. Dude, I had an awesome time. It was a blast."

"Oh yeah? What'd you guys do?" Von asks.

"Damn, I don't remember, dude! So, where did your magic carpet take you this time, huh?" Mick chuckles. He hears a sound from his phone...*Clinggg! Clinggg!*

"Mick, seriously, I'm still in England, dude, and I don't have a magic carpet. I have told you a million times that I was zapped here from my handheld scanner."

"*Okay*, chill out. Whatever…it's cool, man. Hey, hey, wait a minute…what's this? Von, I just got more pictures you sent from your phone. Where the heck are you? It looks like you're in a theater with some actors in weird, old-fashioned clothes! What's going on? Seriously, where are you, man?"

"Mick, I told you I was zapped back in time. I took that picture from my grandfather's friend's dorm window. He was visiting a friend here in Oxford when I zapped myself in here through time travel. I'm here in England, in 1908, dude!"

"C'mon, if you really traveled back in time, how could you call me? There's no such thing. Where are you calling from, seriously? You're getting kind of creepy, man," Mick remarks annoyingly.

Von keeps his mouth shut, biting back the bitter sarcasm he hears from Mick. "From the bathroom, dude, I swear. I am in the water closet, as they call it. Besides, I've got my Instant Cell Phone charger Energizer Energy To Go."

"Ahh. Yeah, that needs double A batteries to power up your cell so you can talk anywhere, anytime, right? But what's a freaking water closet, dude?"

"Mick, you're not listening, are you? I told you they call their bathroom *water closet*!"

"Never heard of it, dude."

"Listen, man, I met the killer that these people were looking for. He asked me to meet with him in a pub near an alley. He threatened me that if I don't bring him back home, he'll kill me. I talked to him, Mick. I talked to the killer."

Mick feels his heart stop. He's sure his best friend has slipped over the edge. "Okay, dude, easy…this must be a panic attack you are experiencing because we're all going out on our own after graduation, and I understand. It's a safari out there, dude."

"*No!* Stop. Damn it. I'm serious, man," Von is frustrated with Mick for not believing his dilemmas.

"Okay, dude, are you telling me they call their freakin' bathroom water closet? Are you really serious? You can get a cell phone signal in one of those closets? Dude, wait a second, they really have cell phone towers or antennae in their bathroom? How weird is that?" Mick says again, with a big sigh in his voice.

"No! They don't have cell phone towers or antennae in their freakin' bathrooms. Would you just shut up, and listen to me for a change?" Von takes a picture of the water closet and sends it to Mick.

"Dude, what do you mean closet? Does it look like a regular clothes closet, Von?"

"I've been telling you, Mick, it's what they call the crapper here, man." Von simplifies. "By the way, earlier when I was on the crapper, my phone rang. Someone tried to call me twice, but we got cut off. I think something with their darn toilet here messes up the signal. It's probably their diagnostic or procedural diagram of the old pipes, or maybe it's some kind of mechanical system connected with their toilet. I don't know, dude. Look, I took another picture, and I'm sending it to you. Mick, let me know when you get it," Von instructs Mick as he sends another picture from his cell phone.

Mick waits patiently, not knowing what to believe or expect. Is his buddy losing it, or was he really captured by old British dudes from another time?

"Okay, did you get it?"

"Yep! What the heck was that?" asks Mick. "Why is the crapper tank so high?"

"I don't know. I guess it's how they make their crapper here in this era, I need your help. I need to get out of here

– I'm stuck. I don't want to be executed for a murder I didn't commit!" Von pleads.

"How do you expect me to believe you? Why would some old British dude do this?" Mick asks, abruptly losing his sense of humor.

"Mick, would you stop it!? I am really seriously in danger here, dude."

"Well...I am seriously trying to comprehend this on top of my hangover, Von. I don't know if you are having a nervous breakdown because you missed your graduation and saw your girl with another dude...Heck, I don't know. Besides, are these British abductors real? Do things like this really happen?"

"Mick, Mick, they are not abductors...They didn't kidnap me. They just happened to be here when I got zapped from my scanner. They are real people. Shit, I don't know how to explain this anymore. Is the picture from my cell phone not good enough?"

"Well, it *is* kind of eerie, dude," Mick admits. "How do I explain that to someone? What do I say? People will think I'm doped up or something." Mick tries to figure out if this all makes any sense.

"This is serious, man. I don't know. I'd like to help, but I don't know...Seriously, I don't know what to say. By the way, have you called your parents yet?" asks Mick.

"Nope! I don't know what to say to them!"

"Tell them the same thing you're telling me. Tell them you have traveled back in time. At least it won't just be me who thinks you're going loony, I can just hear what your dad would say now, dude. He'd think you've lost it, man! Seriously, Von, you really have to call your parents, they are *sick* worrying about you. Your mom's been calling my mom, and she's so upset. Please, dude, you've got to call them. Even if they don't believe what you're going through, tell them. At least it would be nice for them to hear from you, okay, dude?"

"Speaking of calling…have you seen or spoken with Bessie?" Von asks.

"Yep, I don't know what to tell you. Do you want to hear the good news first or the bad news? You have a choice."

"Shit! You're so annoying, dude!" Von yells.

"Annoying? Well, for the sake of our friendship, I'll give you the good news. Okay, the good news is your optometrist will be proud of you that you can see better at night. Got that, dude?"

"Yeah, yeah. C'mon, just tell me, man."

"Okay, the bad news is…one of the sorority girls confirmed that Bessie was seen with another dude. I'm sorry, Von!" Mick blurts.

"Shit! I need to speak with Bessie. I want to speak with her right away. If I don't, I'll never be with her again. Please help me get out of here, man," he pleads.

"Get out where? Where, dude?"

"Here in England, dingbat!"

"*Sorry*…tell me, how do I get you out of there? Do you want me to zap myself inside your handheld scanner and pick you up on the other end of it, huh?"

"Ahhhh! You're hopeless, Mick."

"Von, I don't know what to tell you, dude, this is really between you and Bessie, man. I'll do anything you want me to do, but it's in her court now if she wants to be with you or that dude. Look at it this way, while you're time-traveling, she can be with that Georgetown dude. Then, maybe she'll realize that it's you she cares about and throw Mr. Georgetown out of the picture when you return from your magic carpet ride," Mick jokes again.

"Mick, seriously, I don't know what to do. I'm scared, Mick. I can feel now that we will never be together…if I really get stuck in this era, for sure I'll never be with her again, man."

"Okay, dude, in spite of you being creepy, I will try to give you the benefit of the doubt that you are time-traveling…" Mick says but is brushed off by Von.

"Call you later, dude. Be sure your cell phone is fully charged so I don't reach your voice mail instead. Got it? Gotta go, man. Someone's at the door," Von puts his cell phone back in his cargo pants. He opens the door and gets out of the water closet. A man looks at him strangely, but he walks past him and goes back to the dormitory. He walks quietly, enters Sir Oliver's room, and hides behind the thick curtains. As soon as he closes the door, he hears someone trying to open it. He hears voices and someone knocking at the door.

"Sir Oliver, ar' ye t'ere? It's William, Sir Oliver. May I 'ave a word wiv' ye, sir?" the voice outside the door yells. Von hears more voices and footsteps but can't figure out what's going on. He wants to peek outside the door but doesn't, scared he might be seen. Besides, Sir Oliver instructed him to stay put inside the room, so Von hides behind the curtains.

A few minutes later, it seems to be quieter outside the door, but Von stays still. Then, he decides that it is taking too long for Sir Oliver to come back. He is bored waiting for him, so he ventures out for another walk hoping around each turn to find something familiar.

All at once, his cell phone rings again. He thinks Mick has called back. Von tries to answer it as fast as he can to avoid attention.

"Hello?" He- Hello?"

"Von, where the heck are you, man? You promised to help me move out of the dorm, but you didn't show up."

"Dex, Dex, is that you, man? Thank God you called…"

"Yes, it's me. Who do you think it is?"

"Sorry, dude, I was really planning to help you move out, but, well, I just told Mick…I time-traveled, dude."

"What the heck are you talking about? Man, are you stoned or something? And who are you talking about?"

"Mick!"

"Mick?" Dex asks curiously.

"Yes, I told Mick earlier."

"Argh! Whatever, Von! Just you know, I was really disappointed, but I'm cool. I'll keep in touch with you later, man."

"Hey, Dex, sorry, dude. I'm serious man, I wasn't making excuses. Something really strange happened to me. Would you do me a favor and track me on my GPS system? Send a message to my cell and see if I get it or not. Then when I answer, you'll know where I am at or something."

"Dude, I'm kinda late, so I can't play stupid jokes right now…maybe later toward the end of the week when I get to D.C., okay, bud?"

"No. No. Really, I need your help, man," Von pleads.

"Okay, dude, whatever you say, man. Take care, and we'll talk later, okay? Gotta go," and Dex hangs up as Von feels guilty about Dex not believing what he's just explained.

He tries to call his dad's cell phone, but it doesn't work properly. He dials it several times, and finally, his dad answers.

"Hey, Dad! Dad, it's Von. Can you hear me? Can you hear me, Dad? Hey, before you say anything, I want to explain…"

"Who is this? Can you speak louder? I can't hear a word you said. I just got a new hearing aid, and I'm still not used to it."

"Dad, it's Von. What I'm about to tell you will knock your socks off. Dad, I've time-traveled. I'm in Oxford, England. I don't know how it happened, but it did. And I need for you to track me down through my GPS. Please, Dad. Do that for me, would you?"

"Young man, I still didn't understand what you just said. I think you must have a wrong number," and his dad hangs up. Von tries to call back his father right away, but his phone keeps giving him the same message: "All circuits are busy now. Please try again later," the automatic message repeats.

Von walks around the town frustrated, trying to keep himself sane. While looking around his new surroundings, he remembers what he learned from Ms. Norphy's class. He remembers that Ms. Norphy had told the class that Edward VII was first the Prince of Wales and later King. Edward VII was a broad-minded, fun-loving man, and he mixed with men and women of all classes. A privileged few gained access to his personal circle of friends known as the 'Marlborough Set.' Wealth rather than birth was a passport to the society he dominated. He favored ripe bodies and ripe minds and lovely women with curves that emphasized their womanhood. He liked to be surrounded by handsome women of mature years with generous natures. Damn-it! *That's it*, Von thinks. *That's all I remember from the whole freakin' class!*

CHAPTER SEVEN

UNMASKING THE WIRELESS

Sir Oliver returns to his room looking for Von. He is furious that Von has left despite his strict instructions. While waiting for Von, Sir Oliver decides to snoop in some of Von's belongings that he has left in the corner of the room. He sees what seems to be a gray metal folder. He lifts the top, and it opens. Inside it is a label: "This laptop belongs to Von Muir Carmichael. If found, please call 555-1234." Sir Oliver wonders what this metal-looking thing can do? He opens it and hears: "You can now use Windows Vienna."

"Wot is a laptop?" he asks himself aloud. He searches and sees the DocuPen portable scanner. *"Wot an odd-looking pen t'is is."* He wonders about that, too. But what he is most curious to look at is the colorful book with a bold note written: 3D pictures. Then Sir Oliver hears a voice: "You may now check your e-mail through your external display. It's not necessary to open your notebook. Please remember your device is *breath* activated."

"3D? Wot could t'is possibly be? T'is is amazing." He says to himself. The picture is so true-to-life that he pulls out

his chair behind the window, sits down, and scans through it. *"Breath activa-shun? Wot' could possibly be a breath activa-shun?"* Sir Oliver starts blowing, huffing and puffing. *"'ello? Any'un 'tere?"* He waits for someone to say something. When he doesn't hear anyone, he shakes his head and starts looking at the book next to it.

The book title reads: *BLACKBERRY.* A small written description describes what this edition was referring to: *YOU CAN BE POWERFUL.* A line catches Sir Oliver's attention, then draws him to a tiny line, which reads: *The Most Powerful Handheld Anyone Can Have.* He gets more curious by the minute.

He turns the pages, revealing the quality of the pamphlet. He pulls his spectacles to his eyes. *"T'is absolutely is rubbish!"* he yells, not able to make sense of the words.

As he continues to inspect, he scans through the pages and finds a startling discovery: the inside of the manual shows more vivid pictures of a small metal box with letters and numbers except this one is almost similar to a miniature typewriter. The book describes the BlackBerry PDA. He runs his fingers over two of the pages and is confused.

"T'is isn't possible." Then he sees Von standing few feet away from him.

"Hello…Sir Oliver!? You are back, how was your meeting?"

"It wos fine, were've ye been, Lad? I gave ye' specific instructions not ta go anyw'ere."

"I was bored, so I went for a walk."

"Ye went off fa' a walk? W'ere?"

"What is wrong, Sir Oliver? Is everything okay?"

"Did ye look around town? Ye 'ave ta tell me wot is going on? Or wod'ja rat'er talk ta t'e constable?"

"Of course not!" Von tries to calm down.

"T'en, wod'ja bloody tell me 'bout t'is metal appar'tus? 'ow do ye' explain t'is?"

"I am from the future, that device is from the future. Why can't you believe me?!" He shouts, trying to persuade Sir Oliver.

"No! Unless ye tell me 'oo ye really ar'?" Sir Oliver threatens. *"Wot is t'is, a hoax, lad?"*

"It's not a hoax! The metal device you are holding is my laptop, and the manual is for my PDA; don't worry about it, Sir Oliver," Von replies with a little hesitation.

"I do beg yer pardon? Wot is a 'and'eld, laptop, or BlackBerry? Wot language ar' ya speakin'?" Sir Oliver responds, confused.

"Listen, I'll turn on my laptop in a second. I think I have enough battery power to work on it. But I can't promise you internet connection, since you people don't have wi-fi, WIMAX, or broadband here."

"Y MAX, Y PIE or Bro-Band? I nearly died of shock, if I may say so?"

"I'm not a bad person, Sir Robert," Von insists.

"Ye ar' an illusionist."

"No! No! I am not!"

"Oh, may I remind ye, lad, t'e year is 1908, an' tis metal apparatus is made in 2008?"

"I…I know. I don't know what to say," Von says, searching for the words to explain.

"C'mon, lad. It's a bit ridiculous. No such thing of this matta'. Tell me…or I will fetch t'e constable," Sir Oliver sighs.

"It is the truth; that's the manual book for my Black-Berry handheld…and the metal device is my laptop from the future."

"I don't have any control over the fact that my electronic device was built in 2007. It's a year old, you know. Actually, I really need a new laptop. There are better ones out there now…better than this one. Do you know, that they now have quad core, detachable mini display with 100 terabyte drives, and it includes the new version of *Windows Vienna?* Not only is it breath activated it is also sweat activated. How cool is that, huh?" Von asks his future grandfather, without even thinking he's way too ahead with his new technology .

"Go on. Will ye' bloody tell me 'oo ye really ar'?"

"I told you and I will say it again, I am your grandson from the future," Von relates matter-of-factly.

"'Ow can ye' be me grandson from the future? I don't 'ave a wife."

"I don't know how to explain it, but I am your grandson, All these things that you see in my backpack – my wireless gadgets – I accidentally brought with me, when my scanner zapped me here," Von defends himself and sits down.

"Sir Oliver, have you read about Dr. Lee De Forest, the famous radio inventor, and Guglielmo Marconi, an Italian inventor?" Von asks. "Well, Marconi discovers the impact of wireless and development of modern communications which successfully send and receive telegraphic signals over a short distance without wires."

"Well, lad, I'm familiar wiv Guglielmo Marconi's work," he replies, curious to see where Von is going with this.

"Dr. Lee De Forest did the first public wireless exhibit in 1904. In the future, Sir Oliver, we have figured out how to use wireless everywhere." He breathes. Would you please believe me, Sir?" Von asks. "I'm telling you the truth. I'm your grandson. I don't know how I transport myself or even explain how I got here, but I'm here for a reason. Everything you see in that bag is from the future. Everything I said to you is the truth."

"I caun't possibly believe t'is an' yet, looking at yer electronic devices..." He says, as he looks over the gadget in Von's backpack brought from the future.

"The PDA?"

"No, no. T'e telefon. T'e un' ye 'ave in yer 'and." He stares at Von and waits for his future grandson to continue the lesson.

"Oh, that one?" Von's eyes wander to his cell phone.

"Well, lad, t'e only conviction I caun find is t'at t'is book an' ol 'f yer electronic devices ar' really from w'ere ye com' from..., w'ich means t'at ye' ar' a time-travela' from t'e future. 'Ow is t'at possible, lad?"

"I've been telling you that, but you don't seem to believe me," Von says. He sighs, a world-weary sigh that seems out of place in a man so young.

"Ar' ye 'ere ta tike me ta t'e future'? Is t'at w'y ye'ar 'ere? I'm not longin' ta live in a different time. I like it 'ere."

"I don't know why I'm here!" Von exclaims. "I'm afraid, and I don't know what's going on or why I'm here. My family has told me that you died. I really don't know exactly when you really died. We never talk about it at home. I'm not sure if I'm here to stop it. I don't know if I *can even* stop it. Maybe no one can. I don't think that's how time-travel works. I think there are restrictions. I don't think you can change history." Von says this with sadness.

"I 'ope ye' won't betray me confidence." Sir Oliver warns. "T'en tell me 'ow time-travel works, an' per'aps I caun figure a way ta get 'round t'e restricshun."

"I don't know. I didn't plan this at all. I didn't time-travel on purpose, so I can't answer your questions," Von replies, feeling helpless.

Von walks toward the bed, and a look of sadness spreads across his face. Sir Oliver notices this and asks, *"Wot is it? Wot's wrong?"*

"I'm afraid I can't tell you the answer."

"Per'aps I caun't understand t'e science be'ind ol t'is time travel, I don't understand ani 'f t'is," Sir Oliver replies encouragingly.

"These devices you see me with are the everyday tools of life in my time. The technology has taken us to the moon and back. Where do I begin? The telephone evolved into the cell phone, and with the discovery of digital technology came wireless, streaming everything. Within a few years time, our daily lives became intertwined and interconnected with technology. Handheld computers, capable of launching rockets, were as common as eyeglasses." Von explains.

"Wot's digital?" asks Sir Oliver. *"Oh, forget it, lad! I don't understand wot ye'r talkin' anyway, so w'y should I bot'er t' ask'? I'm sorry, lad."*

"I understand, Sir. don't worry. I seem to recall that your era has just started a new technology in the field of-"

"Yes, indeed. I'm not properly informed of technology, but I'm very much interested in medical research on dipt'eria, tuberculosis an' polio," Sir Oliver interrupts. *"Medical research is t'morra's miracle. Now t'at we bot' concur ye 'ave time-traveled t' t'is era, I supposed ye 'ave ta learn ta survive in t'is era fa' awhile."*

"Okay. Is this the Edwardian Era? I'm familiar with it through what I know from my history class. It is true that wealth, birthright, and manners are the prime qualifications for commanding respect and obedience from others. Is that true?" Von asks.

Sir Oliver replies with a bit of a laughter in his voice, *"Is that wot they fink of us?"*

"From what I learned, people from this era have luxurious banquets and extravagant clothes." Von goes on to say.

"Yes, ye'r partly correct, lad. T'e trut' is only few elite ar' concerned 'bout such' mattas'. Most ar' just tryin' ta survive through t'e winta'!" 'ow'd ye kno' ol t'at?" Sir Oliver wonders, surprised at this young boy's depth of knowledge.

"From school," Von replies.

"Quite astonishing fa' a young man."

"Jeez, Mick and Dex would love the Edwardian Era. It's always time to party!"

"Ave ye said somet'in'?" asks Sir Oliver.

"Nope!" Von replies, smiling. "I also know that the Edwardian Era is all about life-changing social reform, technology, and the arts. I think we could have some fun together in your time!"

"I guess I 'ave ta observe an' learn wot ye' caun teach me." Sir Oliver.

"It's an amazing world out there. It's not my kind of world, but I guess it's the old-fashioned world that has come full circle and is now modern in my time," Von, thinks aloud.

"I didn't understand wot ye' just said, but I suppose I 'ave ta trust ye," Sir Oliver replies.

"Well, what do we do now? Where do we go from here?" asks Von.

"Put some of me clothes…'ere…." He hands Von an armful of clothing. He changes out of his and is ready to go out with Sir Oliver.

The pants are a little loose and a bit too long for Von, and the sleeves are uncomfortable, but he makes do knowing that it will feel better to fit into his surroundings and he looks much more appropriate for the time. On their way out,

Sir Oliver stops in front of the door and asks Von to try on a hat hanging on a stand by the entryway.

"Ahh! It's rather smashing!"

"Hat? I don't wear hats. They make my hair flat, and they're uncomfortable!" Von retorts.

"*Everyone wears a 'at. If ye notice outside, almost everyone wears 'em,*" he insists.

"This sucks! I hate hats. I don't even like to wear my favorite baseball cap." Von mutters to himself. "Do I really have to wear this?" He tries not to whine, gesturing to the hat, grimacing.

"*I'm sorry, lad, but ye' most definitely do,*" Sir Oliver says unsympathetically, without apology. "*D' ye realize t'e commotion yer modern clothes would cause? Do ye' require anyt'in' else?*"

"Nothing!" Von blurts, hoping to cut off any further wardrobe discussion. "Sir Oliver, the hat looks great! How about if I wear it off to the side like this?" Von says sarcastically, yet still hoping Sir Oliver will see how foolish he looks and let him leave it behind. He realizes that he is acting just like he did when as a freshman his mother took him to Brooks Brothers to be fitted for his first "grown-up" clothes. All of his pranks and back-talk then didn't help him either!

Von frowns as he looks at himself to see what he is wearing. He wonders if he should be glad that there isn't a mirror nearby. His outfit consists of dark leather shoes, a long-sleeved white shirt that goes almost to his knees with one of those lacing things at the neck. It all reminds him of a Shakespearean actor in a play. An expensive leather belt goes around his waist, but by far the worst part is the hat: uncomfortable and ill-fitting. He reassures himself that this is just a temporary costume. He knows he would never hear the end of it if any of his friends could see him wearing it!

He remembers what he learned from Mrs. Norphy's class about British men's dress at the time. The suits were always dark and heavy. In the summer, out in the country, men might wear white flannel, and there was no such thing as a summer-weight suit. The shirts had high collars and detachable cuffs for easier washing. Almost every man wore a hat. Farmers wore straw hats, the wealthy wore silk hats, and middle-class men wore derbies...always a damn hat! This is going to be a long hard slog no matter what role he ends up playing.

Von emerges from the dressing room, and he is visibly disdainful in his very uncomfortable new clothes. He already misses his comfortable jeans, shorts, and loose t-shirts. He can see the Sir Oliver has something more to say:

"Ye can't possibly wear yer rubba' footwear. Wod'ja kindly tike off yer plimsolls? Terribly sorry, lad, no rucksack, either. We don't carry 'em around 'ere. I suggest ye leave 'em in t'e dormitory," Sir Oliver tells Von.

"Are you being funny?"

"No, no, I'm delighted! Truly delighted of yer company."

"Okay, give me a second to take out my stuff." Von puts his backpack on the side of the bed and tucks his Black-Berry and cell phone into his pocket like a security blanket. He discovers that his grandfather's trouser pockets are way too deep, and he feels his PDA and cell phone slide all the way down to his knees.

"I say it's a bit big on ya. Needs a bita' sewin'. Ya look smashin, lad."

What the heck? Von thinks. He reaches deep into his pocket, removes the gadgets, and places them in the inside pocket of his black four-button suit. Von stares once again at Sir Oliver in disbelief, amazed that his fate has landed him in a time warp, back in 1908, and that his new friend, as it turns out, is his grandfather as a young man! He pauses to take another deep breath, more like a sign to regain his perspective.

"In a way, it's neat to go back and learn about the family you thought you knew, but how?" Von says to himself quietly.

"Did ye say today's yer commencement? Wot d' ya read at yer university, young fella?" Wot standard 'f educa'shun 'ave ya reached?" Sir Oliver asks.

"What do you mean? What book do I read? I read a lot of books at my university," Von responds.

"Not books... Wot's yer career?" Sir Oliver asks.

"Oh! What is my major? Well, I have a degree in Business Technology, and yup, today is my college graduation." Von replies, trying to impress his future grandfather.

"Fine vocation fa' a young fella. It's quite an undertakin'," Sir Oliver remarks, admiring Von's wits and smart new appearance.

"Sir Oliver, I can't believe I'm here...in 1908. Do you know that that World War I is still six years away, and World War II is over thirty years in the future?" Von says, bewildered, losing his poise once again.

Sir Oliver struggles to keep calm; his heart races and his breathing quickens at the thought of Von's words. Collecting his composure he asks Von, *"War? Wot war? T'ere's goin' t' be a war?"*

"Yes, there will be a war in 1914. I mean, there was a war in 1914," Von says, confusing himself. "By the way, Sir Oliver, do you know anything about the Olympics? Aren't the Olympics being held here this year? You do know what I am talking about, don't you, Sir Oliver?"

"Why of course, Oi caun tike ye' t'ere t'morrow afta' our business wiv a scientist wo could 'elp ye wiv yer dilemma," Sir Oliver

says. *"Very interesting subject. Tell me, wot do ye kno' 'bout these Olympic events? It's a bit of mystery…"*

"Well, from what I remember, the host city is here in Great Britain. The official opening of the games will be by His Majesty King Edward VII. In fact, they will be held here in London from April 28 through the month of October of this year," Von says.

"That is splendid, lad, very interestin' ta kno'. Wot else 'appened during t'e Olympics?" Sir Oliver asks.

"Well, according to the research paper I did for school, the 1908 Olympics were first awarded to Rome but were reassigned to London," Von says with a smile on his face, proud to speak with such authority that he can share with his grandfather.

"Wot 'bout the athletes? Do ye' kno' anything 'bout 'em?"

"From what I read, at the opening ceremony, the athletes marched into the stadium by nation, and most countries sent their selected national teams. Archers like William and Charlotte Dod became the first brother-and-sister medalists. A man named Oscar Swahn, sixty years old, was the oldest competitor to earn an Olympic gold medal. Surprisingly, he won the running deer shooting event in a single shot," Von details. He can't believe that the paper he did for Ms. Norphy's boring class is proving to be useful.

"Wot 'bout other sports an' events. Ar' there ani significant events that Oi should be lookin' forward ta watchin'?" asks Sir Oliver curiously. *"If Oi appear particularly interested, it's because Oi've been asked ta provide support services at several 'f the events. Oi am still debating if Oi should accept. The absolute straight truth is…I know. It's ol so beastly. It would b' splendid ta kno' wot supplies Oi s'ould carry in advance!"*

"Sir Oliver, are you a medical doctor?"

"Oi'm most certainly not. I will be providing support to the field officials."

"Well, 1908 was the first time diving and field hockey were sanctioned. And the final match for middle-weight, Greco-Roman wrestling between Frithiof Martensson and Mauritz Andersson, was postponed a day to allow Mr. Martensson to recover from an injury. Well, Mr. Martensson came back to win the match. Then there was Ray Ewry who won the standing high jump. He became the standing long-jump record holder for the third time and the only person ever to win eight gold medals in individual events."

"T'is is fascinating…my colleagues will b' in attendance at the events. Oi def'nately fink tat Oi should 'ave ya accompany me there."

"Just to let you know, the event that made the news around the world was the dramatic ending of the marathon. After a 26-mile run, the first man to enter the stadium was Mr. Dorando Pietri of Italy, who proceeded to collapse on the track five times before reaching the finish. He was finally disqualified when officials carried him across the finish line. I don't suppose you would be able to show up with an oxygen tank and a bottle of electrolyte solution at the finish line?" Von jokes.

"Wot is that ol 'bout, lad?" Sir Oliver says with some annoyance, realizing that Von is having a laugh at this expense.

"I suppose I could buy ya a ticket. Would you really like ta go? There's a private view t'morrow. If you'd care ta have an invitation ta watch t'e first Olympics eva' held in London. Oi want ye ta experience 'istory bein' made right in front 'f yer eyes," Sir Oliver says.

"Oh, yes, please. I'd like to see it."

On their way to a tea party, a Scotland Yard Inspector stops Sir Oliver, and Von quickly walks ahead of him, hoping the constable won't notice him.

"Sir Oliver, may I 'ave a word wiv ya, sir?" the constable asks.

"*Yes, 'f course,*" Sir Oliver replies as he gestures to Von to keep walking as it is evident that the Inspector has stopped him for questioning.

"*Good day, Sir Oliver. We were told t'at ya were wiv' t'e lad wo' murdah' t'e youn' fella' in t'e dormitory. Wod'ja kno' w'ere we caun find 'im?*" the constable asks.

"*'e escaped mi' carriage on our way t' bring 'im ta ye. Oi d' not kno' where 'e could be,*" Sir Oliver replies.

The Inspector interviews Sir Oliver and informs him that the police were alerted by his friends in the dormitory. Sir Oliver holds to his claim that Von escaped while tied in the carriage on the way to Scotland Yard.

"*Well t'en, let us kno' 'f ya see 'im,*" the constable responds politely.

"Inspector, may Oi ask wot 'e is charged wif?"

"Well, Sir, we are trying ta ge' the truth of a delicate matta'."

"*Ow did 'e escape unda' yer watch at t'e station?*" Sir Oliver asks the constable.

"*Oi don't kno' wot ta tell ya, Sir Oliver. 'H just disappeared. Well, wot I'm trying ta say is... 'e escaped,*" the Inspector admits. "*The Constable on duty is being reprimanded fa' the incident.*" The Inspector is hesitant and embarrassed to tell Sir Oliver that Von had disappeared right in front of him, but the stutter in his voice gave him away. He is even ready to let the case drop. He remembers warning his Constable earlier not to tell anyone that Von evaporated, as they knew that they could both lose their service pensions.

"Oi will telephone the station if we 'ear anything, Inspector. I take this matter very seriously, indeed." Sir Oliver says as he begins to walk away.

"Good day ta ya, Sir." The Inspector replies, as he climbs into his carriage and leaves.

Sir Oliver sees Von up ahead sitting on a bench waiting for him. He implies that the Inspector was looking for him and that he was vague about how he escaped custody. They both have a good laugh about how the Constable and the Inspector can't accept what they saw right in front their eyes.

Von and Sir Oliver go to a late-afternoon tea where Sir Oliver introduces Von as a relative who is visiting from another part of Europe. He hopes this will explain Von's strange accent and manner. Young women clamor to engage Von in conversation, fascinated by his unusual dialect and grasp of things not in their usual tea conversation. Some of Sir Oliver's business associates are also in awe of Von. Everyone thinks he is very mature and knowledgeable for his age.

A young woman and her family who are especially impressed at Von's interest in commerce and trade offer him the use of their chauffeur and carriage for the duration of his visit. Von politely thanks them and expresses gratitude for their generous offer, but hoping to avoid undue attention, he declines.

"Lad, ya've impressed a lot 'f young ladies today. Oi 'ave neva' been wiv someone 'oo's attracted so many women. Oi'm overwhelmed by the gracious gifts ya've been offered, an' it wos wise 'f ye ta decline," Sir Oliver says with a smile on his face.

"Thanks. I learned some parlor tricks from Mick and Dex," Von says, grinning.

"Tricks? I'm awfully sorry but wot does it mean? Ar' t'ey Casanovas 'f t'eir time?" he asks, with a confused look on his face.

"Casanovas? Dex? Mick? They aren't Casanovas. They're gamers; they like video games, although Dex loves the occasional foot massages," Von can't help laughing at the thought of how absurd it is to think of his awkward friends as Casanovas.

"Lady Stephanie wos most impressed, if ya rememba'? T'e brief impres'shun Oi gained on 'er wos t'at she wos an intelligent, an ratha' ambitious young lady. Smashin' ain't it, lad?

"Any runners in her department?" Von asks.

"Do ya mean has she go' any suitor? Followers, if Oi may say so?"

"Yes, yes, suitors."

"Oi fink she go' 'er eyes on ya, lad."

"Really? Me? Why me?"

"Come now, lad. Surely ya 'aven't lost yer eye fa' a pretty girl? She's ratha' pretty, isn't she?"

"Yes, she's gorgeous, but I'm sorry I can't possibly reciprocate. Not in this era. I'm not comfortable. I'm sorry to disappoint you, Sir Oliver."

"Well then, she'll 'ave ta look elsewhere, Oi'm afraid."

Von and Sir Oliver are ushered into another room where there is a sumptuous buffet. In the other parts of the tea room, a variety of food is served buffet style. Von is offered a small plate of food by one of the servants. Though normally a picky eater, Von accepts the plate, not knowing what to expect. Small portions of truffles, caviar, oysters, ham, beef, quail, imported jams, crumpets, and fresh butter are laid out on the table presented with fresh flowers and fruit. Von's plate has a bit of cheese and crumpets, which he manages to eat without dropping on the floor before heading back to the table for more delicacies.

"They don't have cream and butter like this in Florida. It's so good! Here goes the low fat!" Von jokes as he is served a slice of the salted ham.

This is unbelievable. How can I be eating with these people? They've been dead for centuries. This is so weird. I can actually feel the sensation of the food in my body. My stomach is really full. The drinks quench my thirst. This is all real! Unbelievable, Von thinks.

One of the young women's attendants approaches Von with a note. On it a young woman with whom he has been talking asks him if he can accompany her to one of the events that she will be attending in a few days. Von can't recall exactly which of several girls she might be and declines respectfully, excusing himself to use the water closet.

Damn, I'm twenty-two years old, and even though I was born in 1988, here I am in the early twentieth century talking to several girls born long before even my parents. This is so not real, Von keeps thinking.

CHAPTER EIGHT

ARISTOCRATIC GRAMPA

S ir Oliver and Von leave the gathering and decide to stay at a house nearby owned by Sir Oliver's family. Inside the carriage driven by the family chauffeur, Von quickly glances at his new-found friend, his grandfather.

Von realizes that a man like Sir Oliver Robert, an MFH, Master of Fox Hounds, is the epitome of an Edwardian aristocrat. To get to know each other during the ride, Sir Oliver tells Von that he is an ex-soldier and also an all-around sportsman, landowner, and *courtier*. In Von's mind, anyone who meets his young grandfather surely sees him as a man with an assured physical presence – one of those men who always dresses immaculately. Sir Oliver always wears a Chesterfield overcoat and his conservative clothes proudly like a uniform. His top hat is always tilted rakishly to one side. His resonant voice, which is strong and deep, shows command of the language and unwavering self-confidence, giving the first impression of a truculent man, but his demeanor is decidedly warm and gracious.

"I don't think I got any of his style, manners, and mannerisms. He's definitely not a cool guy, kinda uptight..." Von thinks.

Von also realizes that his grandfather exudes an air of superiority, a façade shared by the ruling classes in this early twentieth century when social status is a birthright. Von knows just by looking at Sir Oliver that he really is a gentleman of considerable taste. He mentioned that he is a collector of fine furniture, which he uses to complement the family heirlooms in his large London townhouse. He is a patron of English artists who paint romantic landscape, like JMW Turner, and George Romney, the noted portrait painter.

A sudden stop of the carriage makes Von jumpy, and he realizes they have reached his grandfather's house. The house looks old-fashioned from the outside. He steps out of the carriage and stands at the entrance of Sir Oliver's family estate. Von's jaw drops when he sees the spectacular landscape of the gardens.

"It would be betta' if we stayed 'ere fa' t'e night," Sir Oliver says to Von as he steps out of the carriage himself.

"Sir, I'm really very honored to be asked."

"I 'ope t'ere's no truth ta t'e allegations. Oi shall stand behind ya."

"I'm more than delighted that you trust me in spite of the fact that your other friends think I murdered those men."

"In view of t'e circumstances wif yer modern apparatus an' in t'e light of yer honesty, Oi fink t'e best thing would be fa' us ta forget t'e whole entire business. Oi'm quite prepared ta forget ol about it, on one condition. On condition t'at ya will reveal all your time-travel electrical apparatus fa' me to inspect."

"I'm cool with that. I have no problem showing it to you," Von replies as they enter the house. A footman opens the door for them.

"Come on in, lad. Oi'll just go an' take me hat off. Oi can't fat'om taking ye back at the dormitory. Oi 'ave informed everyone ye escaped on the way ta Scotland Yard. Yer electronic apparatus convinced me yer from anotha' time…Oi've neva' seen anyt'in' of the kin'" Sir Oliver tells Von as he enters the his family house. *"Tis 'ouse belongs ta me family. They're on 'oliday, the servants ar' 'ere. If ye need anything, ask t'em. They will take care of yer needs. May Oi remind ye ta address t'em as mista' or miss followed by t'eir first names. Tat is 'ow we address our servants. Oi'll wake up early t'morrow ta ge' t'e rest of yer belongin's.* And the servants took Sir Oliver's luggage inside.

"Yes, Sir Oliver. I will do that."

"Very well. Ye should address t'e chef as Monsieur Paul. 'e's not a cook. 'E's our chef de cuisine. Me father inherited 'im from 'is family."

"I will try to remember that, Sir Oliver," Von insists.

"Very well. Befa' Oi retire fa' t'e night, mi' Oi ask if ye enjoy'd yerself wiv t'ose young ladies ye met at t'e event? Ye seem'd ta impress t'em wiv yer wit an' intelligence, lad," Sir Oliver says to Von in a gentle yet proud manner.

"Of course, and thank you for introducing me as your relative. I really can't believe that I eat, breathe, and smell the past. I could never have imagined that I would experience this in my wildest dreams," Von replies.

"Should I fetch t'e scullery maid ta ge' ya food? Will ya be requiring me fa anything?" the servant asks Sir Oliver.

"No, not fah t'e moment, Oi'm off ta bed." Sir Oliver sees Von looking at a photo tintype of him in uniform. Before Von has a chance to ask, Sir Oliver, volunteers that in 1902 he served in the second Boer War, in South Africa, one of the most significant events in the history. He relates that malaria forced him to return home to recuperate before

completing his commission, a circumstance which he deeply regrets as a question of honor.

Sir Oliver states with pride to his future grandson that the British Empire's power and prestige was never greater than during the Boer War, but that the High Commissioner of Cape Colony in South Africa, Alfred Milner, wanted more. He wanted the economic power of the gold mines in the Dutch Boer republics for the Crown. He also wanted to create a Cape-to-Cairo confederation of British colonies to dominate the African continent. As reward for his achievements, Milner expected to be appointed Magistrate of the newly expanded territories.

Von sees that Sir Oliver's face quickly grows sullen and a distant gaze appears in his eyes as the memories of war flooded back. After a brief pause he looks up at Von, showing an uncharacteristic glimpse of self-doubt, but then he goes on to say that the war was a true test of British imperialism. He explains that the enemy was using nontraditional guerrilla tactics and superior German rifles to leverage their inferior resources. Victory came at too high a price, and the legacy of high death rates among captured women and children in the detention camps is deplorable. It is clear that Sir Oliver could not conceal his shame for the Empire's failure to manage the war.

"Well, it's rather late, an' Oi 'ave got a lot 'f t'ings ta attend in t'e morning. Ye're welcome ta use som' 'f t'e clean clothes in t'e closets." Sir Oliver walks Von to their guest bedroom and retires for the night.

When Sir Oliver opens the guest bedroom, Von sees a great four-post bed with richly carved posts standing in the middle of the room, a heavy, tasseled coverlet, and ancient fox-hunt art hanging on the wall. By the bedside stand a small oak chest and a two hundred-year-old chair. The seats are upholstered in contemporary needlework. Von notices that the front legs are standing on ball-and-claw feet, a decorative treatment dating from around 1700. A writing desk near a window is supported on brass quadrant brackets.

"Oi'll send t'e maid in ta light t'e fire an' turn down yer bed."

"You don't need to do that, Sir Oliver. I can manage to turn down my bed. Really, it's not necessary," Von insists, but Sir Oliver doesn't seem to hear a word.

A chambermaid knocks on the door and fills the pails with hot water. Von helps carry them to a small vanity table to wash his face and get cleaned up.

"Oi'll put some coal on the fire, sir. T'ere, dat should soon burn up, now, sir. Den, ya'll be a bit moe' cozy." As the chambermaid finishes putting in the coal, she turns his sheets for him.

"Will dat be satisfactory, sir?" the maid asks Von.

"Ah, yes, of course. Thank you." Von takes some money in his pocket that was given to him by Sir Oliver earlier and tries to give some to the maid as a tip.

"Oh, no, sir. T'ere's no need." The maid leaves the room.

Von feels strange just thinking of sleeping on the same floor as his grandfather, who has been dead for more than sixty years. The idea makes his head whirl. But then the events of the past day come back, and he feels sick...and miserable. He has a dry mouth and a headache. He feels like he has another hangover, but this time he knows it's just nerves. His stomach grumbles, and he knows he is starving. He would kill for a few Tylenols, some of Mick's elaborate midnight snacks, and a crispy, buttered bagel.

I guess I can wait till morning to have another one of these amazing meals. Shit! I've got time. Just a hundred years' worth, he teases himself.

A chambermaid returns with a flat covered copper pan filled with warm ash from the fireplace. She slips it under Von's bed sheets and gives Von a polite nod as she leaves the room. She returns with another pot in hand.

"Here's your chamberpot, sir. I will ge' it in da morning to clean."

"Hey, what's this for?" Von asks.

"Fa' urination or defecation in yer own bedroom, sir," the maid replies and leaves.

"Say, what?" Von looks at it and scratches his head. *No way I'm going to pee or release my bowels in there. Yikes! I would rather go outside and pee in the bushes if I can, or I'll use the bathroom all the way at the other end of the house. I don't like this gas-lit room, with its ridiculously massive ornamental tables. An open-flame light is burning steadily behind a frosted shade. On the small marble-topped table beside me is a copy of the* Oxford World Review *newspaper. I'm lying here, snugly tucked in under a thick quilt with my nightgown and nightcap. I tried to refuse to wear this nightcap, but Sir Oliver said it would get too cold when the coals in the fireplace across the room burn out. If Mick and Dex could see me now with this stupid nightgown and nightcap, I'm sure they would take my picture with their digital camera and post it on the online college Face-book,"* Von thinks, as he starts to sleep.

In the middle of the night, a loud noise is heard in front of the Roberts' property. Two British officers in dark blue uniforms knock, pounding at the door vigorously. It takes a couple of minutes for the Mr. Barrington, the butler, to get up, put on his robe, and open the door.

"Oi should like to speak with Sir Oliver Robert."

"Well, ya can't. He's in bed. Do ya kno' what time it is?" the butler asks.

"Oi apologize for that. Oi am aware of it, of course, but this is a serious matta' that Oi'm engaged with, and Oi require to see 'im at once," the Constable insists.

"Oi'll see what 'e says," the butler says. He heads to Sir Oliver's room and knocks.

"Sir Oliver, wake up."

"Wot? Wot is it?"

"An officer from the metropolitan police is 'ere, Sir."

"What does 'e want?"

"Oi fink they come fa' the young lad. 'E didn't say, Sir. Just that it's serious."

"Yeah, it betta' be." Sir Oliver puts on his clothes and goes to the living room where the constables are waiting.

"Sir Oliver Robert?" the uniformed officer asks.

"Wot's that to ya?" Sir Oliver answers sarcastically.

"Inspector Jason Lithgow, Sir. Oi 'ave been issued a warrant fa' the arrest of a Von Muir Carmichael. I 'ave reason ta b'lieve 'e may be staying in yer 'ouse."

"Wot reason could ya 'ave to suppose it?"

"Acting on information received, Sir, that ya ar' knowingly harboring 'im 'ere."

"Is t'is yer usual behavior, Constable? Ya walk into a respectable 'ouse at t'is time an' intimidate me servants?"

"We're suspecting a murder, Sir."

"*Suspecting?* If Mr. Barrington said 'e is not 'ere then, ya may believe 'im. Yer information is wrong. Oi understand the lad wos employed 'ere briefly. Fortunately, Oi wos wise enough ta send 'im packing when Oi learned 'e's in trouble. We 'aven't seen 'im since then. And if ya wish ta dispute the honesty of miself and me staff, Oi suggest we discuss t'is in front of yer superior, eh?"

"Very well, Sir. Oi'll take yer word fa' it. Fa' the time being," the Inspector answers.

"Oi beg yer pardon?" Sir Oliver demands.

"Oi needn't warn ya about obstruction, Sir Oliver. Per'aps if ya'd allow us ta see yer premises?"

"At tis time of t'e night?"

"It won't take very long, Sir."

"Ya fink t'is is a dosshouse for strays?"

"Oi beg yer pardon, Sir. It's a normal practice."

"Well, it may be where ya come from. Not 'ere in me 'ouse. Tis a private residence an' me guests can come an' go as they please. As fa' as yer concerned, ya don't please me at ol'. Ya come 'ere in t'e middle of t'e night getting decent people out of their beds and an' asking t'is and t'at, an' ya call t'is reasonable?Oi call it interference," Sir Oliver reiterates.

"Ya refuse, Sir?"

"Oi shall do no such thing. Certainly Oi refuse. The idea of it."

"Then Oi regret to tell ya Oi shall 'ave ta apply fa' a search warrant."

"Ya 'ave no right ta do it, no such thing so don't pretend ya has."

"Under the provision of criminal justice act, 1887…I may obtain a search warrant ta any premises wo' is 'arboring a criminal. He lodge wif ya' few days ago."

"I said to ya, Oi understand the lad wos employed 'ere briefly."

"I supposed ya'd be prepared ta accompany me ta the station an' make a statement ta tis effect?"

"Station? Yes. Yes, of course. Glad to, Inspector. Oi just need ta fetch me hat. Inspecta', would ya by any chance know Sir Jeremy Robinson, the assistant commissioner?" Sir Oliver Robert asks.

"Ah, yes, Sir Oliver."

"Commissioner Robinson is a very good, old friend of mine. Always delighted to do anything to 'elp the police."

"Ah, well…now Sir Robert, if ya were to assure me…Ya don't need to come ta t'e station wif me."

"Oh, no, no, no. Wot was yer name, Inspector? Oi will be seeing Commissioner Robinson t'morrow night an' just wonder if…" Sir Oliver tries to continue to make the Inspector uneasy and nervous, and it works.

"Jason, Sir. Inspector Jason Lithgow."

"Ah, well, Inspector Jason, we must do things properly, mustn't we? Can't make any exceptions now. Commissioner Robinson would be absolutely furious if 'e got word of anything like that, so it's down to the station and get everything signed, sealed, and witnessed like ya said, right, Inspector? Off we go then…"

"Very well, Sir. Robert, if ya insist."

"Oh, much, much better. 'Twould be splendid," Sir Oliver says to the inspector, and they stand to leave.

"If ya excuse me, Inspector, Oi'll just go and ge' me things on." Sir Robert excuses himself and hurriedly goes to the room where Von is sleeping.

"Lad, wake up. The police…they kno' yer 'ere. They 'ave a warrant fa' yer arrest. C'mon, ge' dressed. The butler will show ya the back stairs."

"What exactly did the police say?" Von asks, half asleep.

"That they 'ave information ya are 'ere."

"There's a bobby in the yard, Sir," the butler warns.

"Who's Bobby?" Von asks.

"A policeman, lad." Mr. Barrington replies.

"If I may suggest, Sir, we've go' to find somewhere for him to 'ide," the butler offers.

"Indeed, Mr. Barrington."

"The housemaid's pantry down the landings, Sir."

"Right. Lad...'ave ya go' ol' of yer belongings?"

"Yep. Oh no. My cell phone. I left it in the bed." Von hurriedly runs back to his room, but on his way, he sees Inspector Lithgow's shadow and several other police officers waiting outside the premises. Von slowly tiptoes and carefully ducks his head.

CHAPTER NINE

CULTURE SHOCK

V on wakes up very early. He opens his eyes, goes to the window, and looks outside. He stands on the terrace, looking toward the lake. He sees old stables to his right at the bottom of the hill, arranged as an attractive courtyard. He goes downstairs quietly and finally sees the whole house in the daylight.

He notices the interior is filled with fine furniture, paintings, and sculpture. The bookcases are divided by Corinthian columns and contain what seems like thousands of books, plus a remarkable eighteenth-century "cabinet of curiosities" which includes fossils, natural history specimens, and an extensive collection of scientific instruments. Von sees that all the brass rods are clean and lacquered, together with all the picture rails throughout the house.

"Damn, am I in a museum?" Von whispers to himself. He walks around the house and can't believe what he is seeing, that he is inside his great-grandparents' London house. When he reaches the other part of the property, he sees paintings that seem to be family portraits and a large collection of watercolors by famous eighteenth-century artists.

Throughout the house are examples of arts and crafts and fascinating items collected from different trips or vacations that his great-grandparents have taken.

Von decides to look for the kitchen and get something to eat or ask one of the servants for food. As he goes towards the kitchen, he gets lost and finds himself in the dining room, which is on the ground floor of the house. He notices the fine mahogany, long table that most likely could seat twenty-four people. The chairs are tall and very intricate looking. He sits down and tries to get comfortable.

"Gee whiz, I need a booster seat to sit in one of these chairs. How do they reach the darn table? It seems way too high." He gets up and tries to locate the kitchen, but he opens the wrong door into the main room where there is a small, Victorian, coal fireplace and a Sir Oliver portrait. A servant is walking around and sees Von.

"*Would ya care ta 'ave breakfast, sir?*" the maid asks.

"Ahh, yes, please. I'm kinda starving right now."

"Would ya care ta 'ave it by de window or by de fire?"

"Uh…anywhere really is fine," Von responds.

"It feels a bit chilly, sir."

"By the fire then…"

"Very good, sir. Oi will return momentarily with yer meal.

"Cool!" Von answers back.

"May Oi beg yer pardon, sir?"

"Ahh…sorry, I mean that would be great to sit near the fire since it's a little chilly this morning."

"*Very well, then.*" She leaves the room to get Von's breakfast. A man in a dark suit enters the room where Von is waiting for the servants.

"'Ello. 'Morning, sir. Oi don't believe Oi had the pleasure meeting ya last night. Oi'm Sir Oliver's valet. Oi've laid out your clothes, sir."

"Ohh, gee, thank you very much. You really didn't need to do that for me. I can manage to choose my clothes. Besides, I didn't bring any of my own."

"Very well, sir, understood. Would ya prefer yer bath t'is morning, sir?"

"That's cool, but really I can bathe myself. I really don't want you giving me a bath. It will give me the heebie jeebies, man," Von tells the valet.

"Oi beg yer pardon, sir?"

"Ahh, everything is okay. I will let you know if I need your service, dude."

"Me name is Hargroves, sir." The valet leaves with a confused, nasty expression. The servant comes back to serve Von breakfast.

"Excuse me, would you know where Sir Oliver is?" Von asks.

"In de drawing room, sir."

"Should I be having breakfast with him?" Von asks.

"Quite awwight, sir. Sir Oliver wos up early fa' riding an' didn't care fa' too much breakfast t'is morning."

"Okay, I will look for him right after I have my breakfast. Thank you."

"Will dat be satisfactory, sir?" the servant asks.

"Yes, of course." Von takes the white linen table napkin and puts it in his lap. Then he whispers to himself, "How is is possible that when I eat, my stomach really is full? Is this some kind of hypnosis?"

Right after breakfast, Von goes back to his room and sees that the clothes that have been given to him temporarily are laid out on his bed.

No way am I wearing these early nineteenth-century suits! It's way too uncomfortable, he says to himself, but he changes and starts to go towards the library when the servants tell him where Sir Oliver is waiting. When he reaches the library, Sir Oliver is nowhere to be found. Von sits down at the far end of the family library and begins to reminisce.

How is it possible that I have to live in this time? It's not about acceptance. I can already see that I can blend in enough to avoid suspicion. At least it's not France; my French would get me hung! I remember how I once locked horns with Dad debating what life in Edwardian Britain was like. I guess I was right; it's more of another world. The truth is that history distorts the reality and hardship of life in the past. The Edwardian age was dysfunctional; history paints life in 1908 as a continuous string of parties, mostly banquets attended by gentlemen and ladies adorned in extravagant clothes. That's fine if you were born with a silver spoon in your mouth.

Just the thought that this image of extravagance and excess is said to be the lost golden age makes me sick. In reality, the lost golden age belongs only to the very few in Edwardian high society. For them wealth, birth, and manners are all that you need in life to succeed. Valuing anything else in life is beneath them. It's unbelievable that in this era, high society is a club; you either belong, or you don't. To be a member is everything. To be on the outside means to be doomed to a grim life with no hope of having the good life. If you ask me, it's a stupid era, and I can't imagine ever getting used to it. I don't care that my family has always been a member of the club. The sanctimonious code of conduct required for membership is not worth the price.

From of what I've read for Ms. Norphy's high school history class I recall that Edward VII is, or was, a man not only larger than life but also a man with a raunchy appetite for earthly indulgence, mostly in wine and women. Ms. Norphy said he favored ripe bodies and ripe minds. I didn't know what that meant at the time, but I'm beginning to get the picture; he liked big women with active fantasies. I don't get it! What's up with this dude?

I don't really know if I can buy into this tradition. The good Sir Oliver has been helping me understand the rules of the game. Unmarried girls of the Edwardian period are never considered "fair game" if they violate the code; they too can be struck off the guest lists, which means their chances of a good marriage and life are ruined. Talk about dressing for success!

The chief business of the upper-class girl of this time is to dine and dance until she is married, aspiring to become a frivolous society hostess. Once engaged to be married, she is not allowed to drive alone in a carriage with her fiancé, and she is expected to remain innocent and virginal. That would explain the invitation by the messenger and other strange dances I have been doing with these over-primped princesses. Once married, of course, the bride can be eyed thoughtfully by both single and married men. The good Sir Oliver explained that this depraved rule is how the King keeps his options open to philander beyond reproach. It's the pathetic reality of the day. Can you imagine this swinger set the standard for a whole society?

I'm boggled…How could I start a conversation with an Edwardian girl? What questions do I ask safely? I managed to play the game at the tea party, but that was all a short act. I doubt I would ever be able to be straight with a girl, in a normal conversation. I could show her how to play video games, but that approach hasn't even worked well for me in the twenty-first century. Here, I would have my dance card revoked!

How do I forget everything that I am? I have to be careful when I see girls beyond the age of 18 years old with loose, uncut hair. Truth is those are the girls I find most attractive. Sir Oliver explained that this hairstyle is a symbol of promiscuity. Girls who put their hair up signal that they are still virgins, and that they have reached maturity, and that they are available for marriage. Whoa! I've got to be careful, and pay close attention to the road signs. Dating here is serious business!

"Von!"

Sir Oliver's yelling interrupts Von's thoughts. He shuts the leather journal that he still carries from the future. Across the room, Sir Oliver is reading a book, but he drops his glasses on the floor and frowns at Von.

"Ya must learn ta b' quiet wen ot'er people ar' readin','" Sir Oliver says firmly.

Von frowns defensively at Sir Oliver's criticism. He does not appreciate being reprimanded, when he is trying so hard to absorb so much new information. Under Sir Oliver's disapproving gaze, he transforms a scowl into a polite smile.

"Sorry, Sir Oliver, I didn't know you were there. I was looking for you earlier, and I didn't see you," Von says as he quietly closes his journal, placing it on the side table as he gets up to his feet.

"Von, Oi've 'eard ye address t'e c'ambermaids by t'eir first names. Oi want ta remind ye ol family memba' should maintain appropriate relations'ips wiv t'e staff. As upper servants will work directly fa' t'e family, trusting an' respectful relations'ips should b' establis'ed." Although Sir Oliver is firm, he is also

quite gentle in his request, enabling Von to catch his breath and change the tone.

"I'm sorry to have made such a stupid mistake. I was so tired last night that I forgot my manners with the chambermaids. I'll always try to remember your explanation that footmen are a proclamation of wealth and prestige. I understand that they're representatives of the household and reflect the family. I grasp that it's to my advantage to develop an appropriate relationship with them."

"Totally necessary ta rememba' t'ese rules, lad," Sir Oliver reiterates.

"I promise to also remember what you had said last night that, as lower servants, they do not expect to be addressed other than to receive instructions, right?" asks Von, a little embarrassed about his social stumble.

"Ye'r correct, lad. Just as ye always rememba' t'e 'ousemaids 'ill clean t'e 'ouse during t'e day an' t'ey should make every care an' attention neva' ta b' observed doing t'eir duties. If ya d' meet, ya should expect t'em ta give way ta ye by standin' still an' lookin' away while ye walk past. By not acknowledgin' t'e chambermaids, ye will spare t'em t'e embarrassment 'f explainin' wot t'ey're doin' in yer presence," Sir Oliver responds.

"Sir Oliver, is it customary for the butler to be addressed by his surname, Charles, and the housekeeper by Missus or Miss?" asks Von. "And what about the chefs? How do I address them? Do I call them Mister?"

"No, lad, ye address the chef as Monsieur Paul. Ye caun neva' call ani 'f the male servants 'dude,' Rememba!" Sir Oliver replies, patiently teaching Von the house etiquette, while expressing his shock. *"It is 'ow'eva acceptable fa' the mistress ta address 'er by 'er Christian name."*

"I apologize for not knowing my manners with all this," Von says, embarrassed, although somewhat amused by Sir Oliver's angst.

"Don't b' embarrassed, lad, Oi'm very proud ye're adjusting," Sir Oliver replies. *"Von, Oi'll be taking ya ta a country 'ouse t'is weekend ta meet a colleague 'f mine from Wood Farm Estate in Staffordshire.*

"Oi want ta educate ye' on som' English manna' as a guest in a propa' English 'ouse."

"Do I need to meet these people? Do I need to come with you?" Von asks anxiously.

"Indeed. T'is fella' will give us informa'shun on where we caun meet Marconi, the fatha' 'f wireless tec'nology, as ye said," Sir Oliver appeals.

"Where exactly are we going?" Von asks.

"Well, lad, Oi am takin' ya ta a shooting party in a country 'ouse own'd by Sir Edward an' Lady Beatrice at Staffordshire. We leave Friday. We set off in the carriage in the morning, an' a dinna' at night. We ar' invited ta stay fa' the week.

"Sir Edward an' Lady Beatrice were just accepted into t'e ranks 'f high society, an' it wos crucial fa' a nouveau riche family like 'em ta 'old an' improve their position aht the top. Sir Edward an' Lady Beatrice ar' using their new assets, including their country 'ouse, their male servants, an' their French chef, ta maximize the effect 'f the most powerful so-cial weapon – the dinner party."

"Sir Oliver, would you tell me how I should act and treat the staff in an English country house?" asks Von.

"Well, son, t'e' junior staff must rise early an' work long 'ours. T'eir tasks ar' physically demandin', an' t'ey're told ta expect no time off. T'eir schedule's awfully formal an' rigid. T'eir meals ar' eaten in silence. T'ey sit in order 'f rank, an' t'ey speak only when spoken ta by a superior. Oim sorry ta say t'at t'ese servants 'ave

little access ta t'eir families, an' followers ar' not allowed," Sir Oliver instructs .

"What kind of a dinner party will it be?" Von asks, hoping he won't hear elaborate instructions in response.

"It will'b a stunnin' seven-course banquet 'f soups an' soufflés," Sir Oliver says. *"Afta' dinna', t'ey invited a major poet ta entertain t'eir 'ouseguests wiv a readin' 'f 'is poetry."*

"I'll do my best to behave well at these events, and I promise you to remember all the etiquette lessons you have given me," Von assures Sir Oliver. "Will there be young ladies my age at these events? I just want to be prepared."

"Oi understand, lad, an' 'f course t'ere 'ill be som' lovely young ladies," Sir Oliver responds.

"Tell me, Sir Oliver, do the girls in this era really receive little education other than learning to play the piano, to dance, and to have good working knowledge of French and German? Is it true that training in table manners is all that is considered necessary for a young lady, who can overnight become a society debutante?" Von asks curiously.

"Yes, but ye 'ave ta understand t'at 'coming out' an' 'being presented' ar' critical events in a young lady's life, an official recognition 'f adult'ood by parents an' all 'f society. Debutantes ar' expected ta look an' be'ave wiv t'e dignity 'f t'e 'ostesses t'ey will soon become."

"Isn't it true that throughout the season, all they do is just dance the nights away and spend their days shopping for their clothes, attending garden parties, and calling on acquaintances? Do they really enjoy themselves…their lives are those of leisure rather than freedom," Von wonders.

"Yes, an' wiv' in mont's, many ar' married an' find t'emselves playin' t'e role 'f a society 'ostess. 'Alf-educated girls wiv som' political power, t'ey're entertained by society an' entertain in return," Sir Oliver elaborates. "But don't worry 'bout ol t'ose t'ings, lad, ye will b' in a perfect setting when we ge' t'ere."

"Well, lad, ready fa' our expedition? Oi'll tike ye shoppin' aht Debenham an' Freebody. We're off ta me tailor. Fancied ta ge' yerself new evening clothes?"

"Shopping? But I don't have any money, Sir Oliver."

"Not ta worry, lad. We've go' ta ge' yer measurements, and I thought we'd see wot me old tailor could do fa ya? Off we go, lad. Ye 'ave ta meet mi tailor fa' tis special event. Shoppin' is intended ta b' a recreation. T'e shoppers flock ta t'e stores fa' t'eir exclusive items." Sir Oliver insists that Von change into his clothes in order to go out with him.

The two of them shop all afternoon. Sir Oliver generously buys Von's clothes and sets the tailors to work.

It's a lovely color on ya, lad. Me father 'as a suit not dissimilar ta t'is 'un."

"This is way too heavy, Sir Oliver," Von replies.

"No, lad. I don't fink it's 'eavy aht ol fa' t'e summer. Tweed allows t'e wearer ta breathe b'cause 'f t'e openness 'f t'e weave."

"Are you sure? Does it look good on me?"

"Oh, ya d' look smart. A stiff collar looks awfully smart, lad."

"How much does this cost?" Von asks.

"It's two pounds an' fifteen shillings, Sir Oliver," the tailor responds.

"Oh, good lord! Not cheap, is it?" Sir Oliver responds and pays with cash from a large purse-like wallet.

Von is surprised to see that the building where they shop is a huge store on Wigmore Street. Music greets the shoppers.

Right, there are no credit cards in this era, Von thinks. After a few hours, the family chauffeur picks up Sir Oliver and Von in the carriage and takes them back home. They both have an early night, exhausted from the day's shopping.

The following morning, Sir Oliver wakes up very early and sneaks into his dormitory room to get the rest of Von's things.

When Sir Oliver returns, Von is waiting at the family library. The maid brings tea, and they sit down to strategize their trip, hoping they will find a way to be introduced to the famous Italian inventor, Marconi.

CHAPTER TEN

LET THE GAMES BEGIN

O n a wet and dreary day in Oxford, Von and Sir Oliver are traveling by carriage to London to attend the 1908 Olympic Games. Von can hardly sit still with excitement. They enjoy the view, as Sir Oliver has been given VIP seating in exchange for his medical supervision at several events taking place over the many months of competition.

Under continually rainy skies, the Roberts' chauffeur reaches the 68,000-seat stadium in the Shepherd's Bush section of London. As soon as Von and Sir Oliver step out of the carriage, Von notices a man distributing pamphlets to a large crowd gathered in the streets. Von springs out of the carriage and runs towards the man to ask for some pamphlets.

"This is really sweet! What are the chances of this day? Some of these names are familiar. I never could have imagined that I'd experience this excitement first-hand," Von whispers to himself while looking at the pamphlets.

The minute Sir Oliver emerges from the carriage, he is whisked away by an official organizer sporting an armband to the officials' tent. The plan is to have a small table set up for him right on the field in some of the events. Sir Oliver quickly re-emerges, clad in a heavy blazer and perfectly fitted trousers. As he walks out to the event, which is flanked by hundreds of damp spectators under the constant drizzle, Von can think of only one thing to say:

"Whoa, I'm at the 1908 London Olympic games. How cool is this?" Von watches as the crowd cheers for their favorite athletes. The guards are pushing back against the crush of spectators, who are trying to get nearer to the competitors. Von tries to reach for his cell phone, which is tucked inside his oilskin coat, so he can call Mick. The crowd is so energized that he can feel his ears ring from the noise. Unable to hear over the crowd, he decides to put his cell phone back in his coat.

Von quickly works his way back towards where Sir Oliver is standing. Before Sir Oliver can be seated in a designated chair for the officials, he says a few words of encouragement to one of the athletes who is stretching out right in front of him. The athlete is the famous Italian marathon runner, Dorando Pietri. Speaking little English, he politely shrugs and goes back to his routine, which by then has drawn the crowd's attention. Sir Oliver notices that Pietri's color is a little off. He walks closer to Pietri, but he is too late as Pietri is moving closer to the enthusiastic crowd, psyching himself up for his main event set for the next day.

Von walks all over the Olympic ground, taking pictures of the events with his camera cell phone to send to Mick. People are staring at Von trying to figure out what he is doing. A beautiful young British lady notices Von and walks towards him. She smiles at him, and without thinking, Von smiles back. Uncomfortable with the situation, Von tries to put his camera phone in his side pocket without being noticed.

In the meantime, the young British woman is approached by what seems to be her chaperone and walks away, tossing a curious glance back at Von, who pretends not to react when he sees her beautiful hair flowing down below her shoulders. Before Von can process the social significance, he realizes the day is half over. He is awed by the level of competition. Von is left wondering how athletes in 1908 can be so good before the advent of modern day technologies and sports medicine.

Sir Oliver looks into the crowd and sees Von standing by himself in somewhat of a daze. He approaches him and tells him that he should go to the archery events:

"Lad, ye must see the archery events in the other part 'f the stadium. The rest 'f mi colleagues 'ill be watching 'em."

"In which part of the stadium is it being held?" Von asks.

"Follow the crowd that is 'eading to that field. Go on, Oi'll see ye momentarily," Sir Oliver says. Von follows Sir Oliver's directions.

The archery doesn't begin until half past two, which is an hour and a half later than the British crowd expected, and it goes into the end of the day. Von is surprised that women are allowed to compete with the men in archery.

"How can they function in that costume?" Von notices that Ms. Queenie Newall of Great Britain is wearing a white long-sleeved blouse and a long skirt that goes all the way to the ground. The natural way she moves makes it seem like she could actually be comfortable. Von wonders how well the men would do if they had to wear the same clothes and then laughs out loud at the vision of these conservative men wearing long dresses as they shoot their arrows. Fascinated, Von stores photos of the events in his cell phone file.

Lost in his own world, Von is surprised by Sir Oliver's tap on his shoulder.

"Bit of a fog in 'ere, aint it? Well, we ar' 'ere fa' two days, 'ave a lovely time. Oh, Oi betta' b' off, t'en," he whispers to Von, but Von tries to ignore Sir Robert and watches the archers. Remembering Sir Oliver's words, he leaves before the award ceremony and walks quickly to the other part of the stadium.

While walking around the grounds, Von overhears a rumor that the British royal family requested that the marathon start at Windsor Castle. Apparently, King Edward VII and Queen Alexandria want the marathon race to begin at the Castle outside the city so that the royal family can view the start.

Von hears an official comment that the distance from the Windsor Castle to the Olympic Stadium is about 42 kilometers, 195 meters, and that distance would allow the runners to finish in front of the King and Queen's royal box. That means 42 kilometers would be 26 miles, and 195 meters is 214 yards. The official seems unimpressed that Princess Mary insists that the start be moved to beneath the windows of the royal nursery on the Castle grounds, adding additional distance to the run, so that the royal children could watch.

Unbelievable! Von thinks to himself. *How can they do that?* Then, Von realizes that this is an era long before course certification is required.

Von wants to see a swimming event. The 200-meter breast stroke has always been his favorite, but he checks the time and sees the end of the day is near. He is not sure if they can stay until the end, so he goes to the middle of the main arena, Shepherd's Bush stadium, and waits. What a sight to see the swimmers in their full-length suits. They look like they do in the twenty-first century, when technology determines that sharkskin suits are faster than human skin. Von can't believe it has come full circle: the striking difference being that women are not allowed to compete. Von walks over to a pile of suits on the side of the pool and reaches to feel the material. He is shocked to find how thick and absorbent they are.

God, this must be like wearing a sea anchor! He thinks. As Von looks for the U.S. team, he sees Sir Oliver standing near the crowd and walks up next to him.

"Mingling amongst t'e British upper class, ar' we?" Sir Oliver remarks, smiling at Von.

"Well, I guess so, but would you kindly move over to this side, Sir Oliver, and tell me where is the U.S. representative?" Von asks.

"Lead on, lad. Wot's a U.S. representative?" Sir Oliver asks and tries to follow Von as he walks around.

"Ahh! I mean athletes from America?" Von responds.

"T'ere 'e is. T'e one wiv a long bathing costume…"

"You have to be kidding me, Sir Oliver; how can they swim with that outfit on? It is way too heavy!" Von says in a loud whisper.

"It's rather dark, ain't it? Ye 'ave ta b' quiet, lad," Sir Oliver insists and starts whispering.

With all the food around the events, Von doesn't eat much that day; he is just too overwhelmed. They have a big table for the volunteers. Sir Oliver walks Von over to the buffet table. There are *Scotch Eggs*, hard-boiled eggs and sausage meat, *Scone*, an American soda biscuit eaten with butter and often jam and cream, *Shepherd's Pie*, a dish made from minced beef and potatoes, *Toad-In-A-Hole*, a dish of sausage "bangers" in batter, *Bubble and squeak*, a cabbage-and-potato dish, *Fish Fingers*, which are fish sticks, and *Flap Jacks*, which are thin cakes made in a pan from oats and eaten at tea, but none of this appeals to Von's appetite at the moment.

He spends most of his time with Sir Oliver in the crowd studying the athletes. He finds a place close enough to the arena to pick up on the track and field competitors complaining about their running shorts. The Americans are complaining about having to wear knee-length running shorts. In defiance they have folded theirs to the mid-thigh, setting off quite a furor in the officials' tent.

The British have a lot of complaints to deal with, but they largely have brought it on themselves. It doesn't help that they use only English officials. Their only compromise is to adopt the metric system over the imperial system of measure. Von overhears the officials arguing with the English coaches, who fear that using the metric system will disadvantage English athletes, since 100 meters is almost 110 yards. English athletes have trained to compete in yards. The debate lasts for hours.

The following day, Von accompanies Sir Oliver to an early breakfast near the Olympic stadium. Sitting at the breakfast table eating his scone with butter and cream, Von reviews the Olympic catalogue while staring at Sir Oliver's plate full of a traditional English breakfast that consists of fried bread, kedgeree, eggs, and black pudding, which is a sausage made by cooking down the blood of an animal with meat, fat or filler until it is thick enough to congeal when cooled.

"Okay, I think I'll just have their oatmeal, or porridge… whatever they call it here." He shakes his head in desbelief, for all the food on Sir Oliver's plate is full of cholesterol and saturated fats.

"Sir Oliver, would you mind if I separate from you later?

"Where ar' ya off ta?"

"I really would like to see Dorando Pietri's marathon today."

"Aawight, lad, do not let ani'un see yer cellphone. It'll cause a lot 'f commotion," Sir Oliver insists. *"Don't miss the 400-meter race an 'our from now. Ye betta' 'urry or ye won't see anyt'ing through the crowd."*

"What time did you say this event starts? Von asks.

"Oi don't kno'. Oi guess at half past one. But it's bloody good fun, lad," Sir Oliver insists.

Von walks towards the other side of the stadium, where the men's 400-meter flat race between the United States' athletes J.C. Carpenter, W. C. Robbins, and J.B. Taylor, and Great Britain's W. Hallswelle is being held.

When Von reaches the stadium, he finds that the games are under way, and he has missed the race. Two men alongside the track are talking about a dispute. The announcer through a loud speaker says that the English officials are claiming that the American John Carpenter blocked Britain's athlete Wyndham Halswelle from passing him in the final stretch, so the British officials remove the finishing tape just as the John Carpenter is about to win the race. The race is declared void, and runners are ordered to run again. But the two remaining finalists, both Americans, Robbins and Taylor, refuse to appear. Mr. Halswelle is given a solo run over, completing the distance in fifty seconds.

Von cannot believe he is seeing this historical event unfold before his eyes. He remembers reading something about it, recalling that it is the biggest controversy of the London Games. In the end, John Carpenter is disqualified because of a maneuver that is legal under the American rules but prohibited by the British rules.

As soon as the 400-meter event is over, Von runs as fast as he can to the finish line of marathon. He is determined to catch Italy's Dorando Pietri finish.

Von melts into a crowd of 250,000, cheering on the marathoners lead by Pietri. He is so excited that he hardly notices a strange-looking man stepping on his foot.

"Ouch! Would you please move, Mister..." Von says to him, keeping a tight grasp onto his cell phone. The man looks at Von while shaking his head, not knowing what Von is doing. He is pushed up against Von again by the crush of the crowd.

"Wot ya got t'ere, lad?" the man asks, peering at Von's phone.

"Oh! Nothing," Von replies and tries to move away from the overly curious man. The man lunges at Von's hand, trying to grab the camera. Von is able to push his way through the crowd to safety and can see the man still searching the crowd for him. He hides behind two tall men, who also obscure his view of the race.

"Damn, I'm missing the best part of the freakin' marathon," he whispers to himself. Then, he sees Dorando Pietri of Italy stagger into the packed stadium. The runner is clearly affected by the hot, humid conditions and seems to take a wrong turn before collapsing. Just as the history books said, he is helped to his feet by doctors and then wobbles and falls three more times before being half-carried across the finish line by race officials. Von is caught up in the drama of

Pietri's agonizing finish, along with the cheering crowd. In the mayhem, no one notices the second-place runner, Johnny Hayes of the U.S., as he enters the stadium and crosses the finish.

Pietri spends hours near death after the race, but survives his ordeal only to lose the race. Judges disqualify him because he was basically carried across the finish line. British and U.S. officials argue for an hour, and fights break out in the stands.

Von remembers when Paul Hamm of United States won the gold medal and was pressured to give it back.

I remember how the international gymnastics officials asked Hamm to give up his gold medal as the ultimate show of sportsmanship, but the U.S. Olympic Committee told them to take responsibility for their own mistakes and refused even to deliver the request, Von thinks and smiles as he is reminded again that human error is the one constant that transcends time.

"Aside from experiencing ol t'is commotion, lad, did ye enjoy the events?"

"Thank you very kindly, Sir Oliver, I did. I really had a great time – maybe the greatest of my life. This is one experience I'll never forget, and I owe this to you, sir," Von replies, back showing his coach he has learned something about social skills.

Yes, Von has had the time of his life experiencing the 1908 Olympics up close and personal. Sir Oliver informs Von that they will be leaving the next day. Von is so disappointed to leave the games in progress. Sir Oliver reminds him that from London they will be going home to prepare for their shooting trip the following day.

Early the next morning, Von and Sir Oliver have breakfast together and discuss the plan for the day. Von is quiet as he finishes his porridge and thinks about his experiences. He knows that part of his joy came from the timelessness of the Olympics. Somehow he felt closer to home by losing himself in the competition. Noticing Von's distraction, Sir Oliver gets up to talk to the driver and review instructions for the ride home.

Von and Sir Oliver both return from the Olympics trip safe and sound. Both are exhausted from the excitement of the last three days and the long trip, so they go to bed early to prepare for the following day. Sir Oliver stays in his study, finishing official paperwork for the Olympic committee. In the meantime, Von rests in his room and tries in vain to reach Mick on his cell phone to share his adventure. A chambermaid brings a tray with tea, Bath Oliver biscuits, and water biscuits. Von is too tired to even look at what's on the tray and goes to bed to take a nap.

The family chef makes the most delicious meal for dinner. Von can not believe that his appetite is so strong. He loves the food and he now realizes that whenever he eats it, he really feels a difference. It's been weeks without junk food! For dessert, there is blancmange, a gelatin-like pudding dessert almost like a custard, with hot milk. Sir Oliver informs Von that he can eat his after it has cooled off because when it's cool, it solidifies, producing a jello-like dessert.

Von tries to taste his but doesn't care much for the flavor, but he is polite and eats half of it. He thanks Sir Oliver and the family chef for the wonderful meal.

After dinner, Sir Oliver heads to the drawing room to read a book. Von sits with him and writes in his journal.

"Wot a pity we don't 'ave a gramophone fa' ya ta listen, eh?"

"Ohhh, I know what a gramophone is. It's an antique record player, isn't it? I've never seen one, but I saw a picture of it. Doesn't it have a turntable for a disc record with a sound box is mounted on a pivot to allow the record groove guide that little stylus and a conical sounding horn? Does it really sound the vibrating needle amplified acoustically?"

"Yes, indeed, yer quite right, lad. It would b' nice fa' ya to listen to it."

"It's okay. I have my iPod with me."

"Wot's an iPod, lad?"

"Well, Sir Oliver, let me show you." Von takes out his iPod and shows Sir Oliver how it looks and works. "Okay, in the age of the digital device, iPods are portable digital audio players. See this middle part of it? It is designed around a central scroll wheel. Most iPod models store media on a built-in hard drive, while there are also lower-end models of iPods called Shuffles, which rely on flash memory."

"Good God, t'at's beyond belief. Oi'm sure it's a delightful device. Frightfully sorry, Oi fink t'ats enough excitement fa' today, lad. Oi'll soon catch on."

"Alright, Sir Oliver I'm sorry for all the confusion."

He is now assured that the time spent with his grandfather has been the best time of his life, in any era. Von goes off to bed with his new thoughts of belonging, and Sir Oliver goes to his room.

He and Sir Oliver share an early-morning breakfast before heading off to Staffordshire. After bumping along country roads for what seems like hours, their carriage drives through the formal gates of the estate, where screaming peacocks sound their arrival.

Stepping down from their carriage, they are greeted by the maids and escorted to their rooms. Von's room overlooks a lake. He is tired from the long drive, so he sits on the bed and takes out his leather-bound journal. He starts writing about his escapades of the last few days and falls asleep after writing just a few pages. He wakes up to a gentle knock in his door and gets up as fast as he can to open the door. It is Sir Oliver, and he advises Von to get ready for tea, which will be served in the living room with the rest of the company. Von hurriedly changes his clothes and goes down the stairs to meet the rest of the honored guests.

Von introduces himself as Sir Oliver's relative from another part of Europe. One young lady moves closer to Von, and Sir Oliver introduces her to him.

"May Oi introduce Lady Stephanie 'f Worcestershire?" Sir Oliver says grandly. Von acknowledges the introduction. After a few minutes, Sir Oliver excuses himself from the conversation and leaves Von with Lady Stephanie. Once alone Von says, "I'm glad we were formally introduced. After we met in London, I realized that we would not be allowed to be together again until after a formal introduction was arranged."

Von discovers that Lady Stephanie is a cultured daughter of Lord Fleming, head of one of the oldest families in the country. She and her brother George, who is an Ambassador to India, are prominent among the cultured and adventurous circle of Edwardian aristocrats.

"Warm tonight, my lady?" Von says and can't believe himself trying to speak like one of the Edwardians.

"Thunder in the air, rain later, Oi shouldn't wonder," Lady Stephanie responds.

"I'm not boring you, am I?" Von asks.

"Not at ol. T'is is an absolutely amazing evening."

"May I claim my dance, my lady?" he whispers to her. If Mick and Dex could hear me now, I would be the laughing stock of our group because they'd think I lost my marbles!

"I beg yer pardon?" She asks.

"May I claim my dance, my lady?" he asks again.

"Certainly." She smiles. After the dance, Lady Stephanie excuses herself and speaks with Lady Beatrice.

"We ar' serving unhulled strawberries afta' dinna'."

"With individual bowls of cream and sugar, isn't t'at so?" Lady Stephanie asks.

"Lady Stephanie, wot a wag you ar'!" Lady Beatrice comments.

"Very droll," Lady Stephanie smiles.

"One tries, Lady Stephanie," Beatrice responds, and she leaves as she sees Von eyeing Lady Stephanie.

"Charming fella', may Oi say," Beatrice whispers, and they both smile.

"Could ya spare me a few moments?" Lady Stephanie asks Von, speaking quite boldly for her era.

"By all means, Lady Stephanie," Von answers.

"Would yer room be convenient?" she asks.

"Well, of course, my lady," Von answers slowly, a little surprised at the question.

During the course of the night, Lady Stephanie becomes more and more interested in Von. Toward the end of the night, she invites him to her place, but Von politely declines. He still thinks of Bessie as his soon-to-be fiancée and cannot have anybody else in his life right now...especially not in this era.

"Ya 'ave paid me t'e greatest compliment possible," she whispers to Von and leaves. Lady Stephanie is very disappointed but is still hopeful that they can get together another time. When she retires to her room for the night, Von does the

same: he wishes a good night to Sir Oliver and the others and goes to his room by himself.

Bright and early, Von gets up to get ready for what everyone is excited about: the shooting party. Lady Stephanie and her family are there as well. Sir Oliver and Von sit at the same table, sipping tea and getting ready for their turns. Sir Oliver tells Von that these events are amongst the most extravagant of this time. Held in total privacy from the outside world, guests compete at shooting, perform their party tricks, and indulge in passionate and occasionally extramarital affairs.

"*Ow do ya fink Lady Ashby managed that 'at? In t'is wind? Oi quite thought Oi was going to lose mine,*" Lady Stephanie says.

"*Oi scarcely noticed against 'ers. Personally Oi found it ratha' vulgar, don't you fink so?*" Lady Beatrice responds.

"*Oh, did ya? Well, Oi fink those feathers were tremendous fun.*" Another snooty lady joins the conversation.

"*Well, Oi must say Oi did, too, but look at those colors, hmmm,*" another matronly lady interrupts.

"*At least t'e weather was lovely, apart from t'e wind, and there were some amazing hats. Absolutely amazing,*" Lady Stephanie says, trying to calm some of the jealous ladies.

"*Jolly good!*" Lady Beatrice ends the whole discussion, and all the ladies return to their own tables, waiting for their escorts, companions, or husbands.

The shooting parties tallied over two thousand kills for the day. Von is surprised to hear these details. He excuses himself with a headache toward the end of the day. He retreats to his room, locks the door, and sleeps all night.

When he awakens, he once again thinks about the mysterious man at the pub, the murderer, who must still be expecting to meet with him. Von decides to find Sir Oliver. He knocks on Sir Oliver's door and finds him dressed for the day.

"Sir Oliver, may I have a word with you?" Von asks.

"Yes, 'f course. Come in. Wot seems ta be t'e trouble, lad?" Sir Oliver opens the door to let Von inside. *"Frightfully sorry, ta 'ear t'at, lad."*

Von explains about the mysterious man. He tells Sir Oliver how they met and everything he knows about him. He also informs him about the man's proposition. Sir Oliver is upset to find out that Von is in a very dangerous situation.

"Wot'eva ye tell me goes no furtha'. Listen, we can't possibly talk 'bout t'is ta ani'un. We can't possibly tell the constables 'bout it, or they'll tike ye away. We kno' 'ow dangerous t'is man is, lad. Ye 'ave ta stay away from 'im. At the moment 'e doesn't kno' where y'are, an 'e's most certainly looking fa' ye in me dormitory. T'morrow, we leave fa' Italy ta meet wiv Marconi, an' we will b' gone fa' few days. Nobody will kno' where ye ar'. In t'e meantime, ye're safe wiv me."

"Thank you for your kindness. I will always be grateful for this," Von says.

"Oi appreciate yer candor. Oi'll try me best ta accommodate yer needs. T'at gave ya a bit of a fright, didn't it lad?" Sir Oliver asks. Von returns to his room to get cleaned up. He rests all day, thinking about his situation.

Towards the end of the week, Von and Sir Oliver get ready to leave the country house. As they are leaving, Lady Stephanie gives Von a piece of paper with her name and address written on it, hoping he will write to her.

"Send me a correspondence sometime," Lady Stephanie says to Von. She looks back to him as she goes inside the villa, hoping he will change his mind and stay. But Sir Oliver and

Von climb into the carriage and are taken by the chauffeur to the train station to see Marconi in Italy.

"Oi've been wonting a word wiv ya, lad. Wot in blazes hav' ya done wiv t'e young ladies, eh?" he asks.

"I didn't do anything, Sir Oliver. What have I done?" Von asks curiously.

"*Yer a nice-looking young man. Now, Oi don't mind a cuddle in the corner, but since t'en, Lady Stephanie an' other young ladies been mooning around like lovesick cows!*" Sir Oliver says, and they both start to laugh.

"Sir Oliver, I've done nothing as far as Lady Stephanie is concerned. I'm not going for that sort of thing right now. For the moment, no lady is coming into my life. In other words, I'm not interested getting involved with anyone in this era. I've got quite enough on my plate right now. All I want to do is go back home, back to where I belong, in my own time," Von says.

"Very well, then."

"Sir Oliver, if for some reason I couldn't go back to my own time right away, do you think I could extend my stay in your home? Could you use an odd body who would be absolutely worthless?" Vons asks, half laughing.

"*Yer not a duffer. Oi'll say, ya look upon me family's 'ouse as yer own…fa' always. Unless ye ge' tired of me temper. It's t'e very least Oi can do fa' ya,*" Sir Oliver says as he looks at Von's sad face.

"After all you've done for me, I could never repay you. I have to learn the lessons you've tried to teach me, learn to walk on my own two feet…and I am confident enough to rely on you completely," Von says earnestly.

CHAPTER ELEVEN

FATHER OF WIRELESS TECHNOLOGY

J ust several weeks ago, Von barely escaped the Scotland Yard police station. He has convinced Sir Oliver that he is his grandson from the future, and now the last thing Von wants is to get mixed up in any other kind of investigation. Yet here he is, letting his grandfather talk him into finding Guglielmo Marconi, the father of wireless technology.

The long trip, including the train, the ferry, and then the train on the Continent, makes Von fall asleep. Sir Oliver lets him nap, knowing that it is a good idea for Von to be able to relax.

"Oh jeez, what the heck was that?" asks Von as he jumps, half asleep.

"Oi wouldn't worry, lad, the train is a wee bit wobbly," Sir Oliver says as something comes to life with a low rumble. Von can feel the vibrations through the floor. Sir Oliver grabs hold of a bar near the boiler. Von takes a couple of steps back and sits down, gripping the wooden armrest. The

train shudders once and then feels like it is slowly lifted into the air. Von leans forward and cranes his neck towards the windows, trying to see outside. He sees some billows of steam and not much else. The train accelerates and then moves forward, turning in a wide arch until it faces wonderful scenery. It picks up speed slowly, faster and faster, and then with a flash of bright light, the ride is suddenly smooth.

"How far are we from Marconi's lab, I mean laboratory? Is he expecting us to arrive today or tomorrow?" Von asks.

"Not that fa'. Oi sent 'im a t'legram an' Oi wos 'opefull 'e go' it befa' we ge' there. Ot'erwise, we 'ave ta wait a few days until 'e ge' back from 'is 'oliday," Sir Oliver says. *"Ar' ya sure 'e invented t'e wireless tec'nology, lad? 'E did not, 'f course, invent t'e radio itself. Nobody eva' does invent anythin' from scratch, as each invention is t'e consequence 'f many previous discoveries an' research…especially t'ose done by Faraday, Maxwell, Hertz, Lodge, an' others."*

"Sir Oliver, in my point of view, Marconi can only be regarded as having invented the wireless telegraph in 1896. And radio only became possible with the invention of the amplifying valve in 1906 and the possibility of modulating a signal over a carrier wave, which happens later in your time," Von indicates. "One of my friends did a research paper on wireless technology. He said Nathan Stubblefield, a Kentucky farmer, was really the first inventor of wireless technology in 1892."

"'Oo would that b' lad?" Sir Oliver asks.

"His name is Nathan Stubblefield. My friend said he should be recognized as the inventor of radio. Have you ever heard anything about this man?" Von asks curiously.

"Does ani'un really recognize the poor man's inventions? Wos 'e ever mentioned in ani 'f the books from yer time?" Sir Oliver wonders.

"I'm not quite sure if Stubblefield developed and implemented the well-known tin-cans-and-string models that kids make, which were outmoded when the Bell telephone company moved into his town of Kentucky. A theory has said that Stubblefield tried a wireless phone because he figured stringing wires and poles all over rural Kentucky was expensive. Sadly, his invention and ideas were stolen.

"I remember there was another research paper that my friend and I found in the library. It was called 'The First Practical Test of Wireless Telegraphy Heard over Half a Mile: the Invention of Kentucky Farmer, Wireless Telephony Demonstrated beyond Question in 1902.' It's so strange that Stubblefield never marketed his invention. After his stunning success in Washington, he just packed up and went back to Kentucky. Then they found him dead at his home in the spring of 1929. His equipment was gone, and all of his records were scattered all over his basement.

"I think Nathan Stubblefield was one of the people who really worked tirelessly to contribute their new ideas in society. I'd like to meet this man if I can during my time travel. But time will tell if my wireless gadgets will take me to him by fate. He could probably help me get back to where I came from," Von says.

"'Ow'eva, 'e must be considered as the most important person 'oo contributed ta tike the invention out 'f the laboratories an' put it in everyday life. In t'is sense, 'e really is t'e inventa' 'f communication."

"Do you really think so, Sir Oliver?"

"As fa' as Oi'm concerned, nothing's any different, not in the least."

"Well, I don't know about your theory. I'm not quite sure."

"Ye' kno', radio wos dramatically different in t'is century an' yer century, as was the way we ol fink an' relate. Do ye agree wiv me, lad?" asks Sir Oliver, watching his future grandson sitting next to him.

"I agree with you, Sir Oliver. If I had to choose who got the award, I think that they should be both recognized for their own individual research," Von says, proudly presenting his knowledge to Sir Oliver.

"Lad, may Oi ask 'ow y'are familiar wiv 'is research? Oi 'ave 'eard from me colleague that Marconi 'ad a vision an' managed ta realize it against ol odds. 'E is, per'aps, one 'f the last inventors wo battled against nature's difficulties."

Von responds, "Marconi's success is a true epic adventure, believe me. His popularity, notwithstanding his fascist or radical role, is assured in history by his conforming to what people expect from a hero and an inventor.

"While Marconi's wireless technology played a central role in many extraordinary historical events, long after Marconi experimented with radio waves, the first real mobile phone was developed."

"Wot is a mobile phone?" asks Sir Oliver with his eyes wide open.

"Oh, a mobile phone is the same as cell phone. See this one?" Von takes out his cell phone and shows it to Sir Oliver.

"Ahh, t'at. Next time ye' speak ta yer friend, wod'ja let me 'ear 'im speak?" Sir Oliver suggests.

"Yes, of course," Von says. "My father told me that when cell phones first came out, they were so big. He said it felt like you were carrying a brick in your pocket rather than a phone. But it soon became an essential companion. Now, mobile phones are an integral part of our lives, and we've found many uses for them."

"As a matter of fact, cell phones and Starbucks coffee are the two twenty-first century essentials in my friends' lives."

"Starbucks? Wot is a 'Starbuck,' lad? Does everyone carry t'em, as well?" Sir Oliver inquires.

"No. You don't get it. Starbucks is the best coffee place. You can get the best lattes there. Let's put it this way: cell phones and Starbucks are absolute necessities in my time. Young people like me are the big users of cell phone technology. A teenager shows us where the future lies; they find ways to fit technology into their lives. You know, having been raised with the technology, we see it as the main way to study, communicate, or shop," Von mentions.

"That is amazing ta kno', lad, an' Oi'm impressed wiv wot 'appens ta technology in the future," Sir Oliver says.

"A friend of mine told me that at an airport in Finland, their soda machine has a mobile number instead of a coin slot. You dial the number, the Coke comes out, and the charge goes to your phone bill."

"Wot is a soda machine an' 'Coke'?" Sir Oliver asks, surprised.

"Oh, Coke is a drink, a carbonated beverage. Soda machines are where the beverages come out when people purchase them in a convenience store or at another public place."

"Very impressive 'ow technology evolves," Sir Oliver replies.

"Sir Oliver, it's in our nature to keep pushing the boundaries. Do you know that in less than one hundred years, our ability to communicate with each other has progressed beyond all of today's recognition? People in one century will see not one but many wireless revolutions, all likely to have at least as profound an effect on our society as did Marconi less than a century ago from my generation."

"Lad, 'ave ya 'eard 'f Professor Oliver Lodge? 'e is a British physicist, 'e perfected the device called 'coherer.' In 1900, 'e became prominent in psychic research, believing strongly in t'e possibility 'f communicating wiv t'e dead."

"Is it true that the growing fame of Marconi as the inventor of wireless was deeply hurtful for Professor Lodge, particularly when Marconi was granted his first British patent in March of 1897? According to research we found, Marconi publicly described the products of Lodge's brain as not his own. I think they missed the point. I really believe that Professor Lodge lacked the vision to see the potential application of wireless; Marconi, however, quickly understood and sought to exploit it," Von says, proud that he still remembers this information from his research group with Dex.

"Well, the poor fella' tried 'is best ta do the same as Marconi but wos' not as successful," Sir Oliver replies.

"Sir Oliver, do you know why Professor Lodge is not the rightful inventor of wireless? Is it true that he was too busy teaching to take advantage of what has turned out to be his extraordinary importance later on?" asks Von with serious curiosity.

"Oi caun't give ye the right answer ta that," Sir Oliver responds.

"Momentarily, we'll reach our stopping point. 'Ere is sum' money fa' ya in case ya need ta purchase somet'in'. Oi'm givin' ye two different kinds 'f currency, Italian an' British, fa' ye t' keep. Keep t'is piece 'f pa'pa wiv ye as well. Oi wrote an address 'f a place next t' a village. Oi would like ya t' 'ave it. Oi used t' love t' walk in t'e square," Sir Oliver says.

"Sir Oliver, I can't thank you enough for doing this for me. I will treasure these moments with you," Von says with sudden emotion.

"Lad, ye neva' kno' wot the futu'h brings ta us. Well, Oi'm sure sumfin' worthwhile 'ill com' along."

Von takes the note and the rolled-up money and puts them in his pocket.

When the train stops, Von looks around and realizes how beautiful this old Italian village is. At the train station, they are met by a middle-aged Italian man who speaks perfect English. A carriage waits for them. The chauffeur opens the side door, and the two men get inside.

As the chauffeur drives off, Von notices that the coastline is dotted with small picturesque villages, and the town stacked unsafely on steep, pale, rocky cliffs plunging into the sea. The streets are so narrow that two carriages can hardly pass and have to back up to yield to each other. He also sees that the coast is surrounded by dramatic limestone cliffs that reach as high as two thousand feet above sea level and plunge straight into the sea.

The island has olive groves, fragrant lemon trees, garden terraces filled with flowers, and spectacular views – a very beautiful, natural setting.

"Well, Oi fink it's goin' ta be an amazing 'oliday, do ya, lad?"

Sir Oliver introduces Von to Aldo, the man who picked them up. Von finds out that the man was educated in America and grew up in New York City. They stop at a small restaurant which serves coffee and light meals. Outside, the sign hangs: Caffè del Ristorante. A young Italian girl, maybe twenty years old, comes to their table and asks them what they need.

"Alimento o bevanda?" the girl asks. Von can't say anything in Italian, and he isn't entirely sure what she has just said.

"Food or drink? Ahhh…coffee, please," Von says.

"Caffè?" she asks.

"Oui, I mean, sì, senorina, and biscotti por favore," Von says, attempting to speak some Italian. The young lady smiles, and Von's face turns red.

Damn it, I should have taken an Italian class instead of that darn art class I took with Mick and Dex just to follow beautiful girls around campus, Von thinks. Sir Oliver looks surprised as he turns toward Von.

"Ya surprised me, lad. D'ya speak Italian as well?" he asks.

"No, not really. I know a few phrases, but that's about it," Von responds. The young girl comes back with a tray of orders for the three of them. Von shares his biscotti with Sir Oliver and his friend.

While sipping his coffee, Von looks around. The decorations remind him of *Lorenzo's* Ice Cream, where he worked during the summer. He is amazed that even the tin cans of biscuits look the same. He then wonders if they have gelato as well. He decides not to ask. He avoids speaking Italian to the young girl, who is eyeing him.

Von finishes his coffee and the rest of the biscotti. Then, he hears that Sir Oliver and his friend are discussing Marconi.

The man realizes Von has begun to listen, so he turns his attention to both Sir Oliver and Von. "In July 1897, the Wireless Telegraph and Signal Company was registered in the UK, having transferred Marconi's UK patent rights to the company for a cash payment of £15,000 and sixty percent of the shares. Marconi held the Italian rights, but he still had the shadow of military service hanging over him.

So, it was lifted by the King of Italy, who had him assigned as a naval cadet in training to the embassy in London."

"Von, ar' there ani events from the future that ye can share wiv me an me colleague? Oi 'ave explained ta 'im that y'ar' a time-travela' from the future." Sir Oliver wants Von to open up to him and his colleague, but Von is very hesitant and keeps his distance from the man. He doesn't mind sharing his knowledge about Marconi's success in the future to this man, but he is not confident enough to blurt it out. His instincts tell him that the man cannot be trusted.

"C'mon, lad, ya 'ave ta share somet'in' wiv mi' friend 'ere. 'E needs ta 'ear som' 'f Marconi's' success in the future. Yer not cross, ar' ya?" Sir Oliver insists.

"I don't get it. What do you mean?"

"Angry?"

"Me? No, are you?"

"Not aht ol, lad, not aht ol."

Von pauses for a moment and decides: Okay, I'll just say one thing from the future that has not been published about Marconi.

"When I was in school, my friends and I discovered a research paper in the library. It stated that there was an incident in 1909. The incident is that Marconi saves 1,700 lives through wireless distress calls when two liners collided and one of them sank off the coast of the U.S. He then shares the Nobel Prize for Physics with one of the founders of his company's rival, some German company," Von says hesitantly.

"Splendid, the Telefunken Company 'f Germany. Oi 'eard 'f that company a few months ago. Ani' otha' incidents ye' con share wiv us? Ani otha' interestin' events from the future?"

"Okay, another incident is in July 1910, or should I say two years from now. Marconi's wireless apparatus is applied for the first time to apprehend a dangerous criminal. On the SS Montrose, the captain asks Marconi's operator to send a brief message to England that they have strong suspicions that a killer they call Crippen, the London cellar murderer, and his female accomplice are among their passengers. The accomplice is dressed as boy. A detective from Scotland Yard boards a faster ship and arrests him and his accomplice before the SS Montrose docks in Montreal," Von says, while seeing that Sir Oliver's face as white as a ghost. Von doesn't bother to say anything else after that, since both men look surprised enough.

The man excuses himself from the table. Von and Sir Oliver continue their conversation. Von is excited that Sir Oliver promises to take him to the Olympics when they get back to England. It's been almost half an hour, and the man has not come back yet. They start to worry, so Sir Oliver asks the young Italian girl if she has seen their friend.

"Piazza! Piazza! Lui cammina al piazza," she replies to both of them.

"I think she said he walked to the public square," Von translates for Sir Oliver.

"Public square? W'y would 'e leave us 'ere?" Sir Oliver wonders.

Von and Sir Oliver decide to take a walk outside the plaza to see if they can find him. After a while, they run into him inside the telegraph company. Aldo is at the window sending a telegram.

"What the heck is he doing?" Von asks himself as Sir Oliver surprises Aldo by tapping his back. The man accidentally drops the piece of paper. Von picks it up to hand it back to him, but the man is so nervous that he yanks it out of Von's hand. The telegram rips in half. Von cannot resist reading the half he holds in his hand. The telegram reads:

"Professor Russo, Time-traveler found. Marconi involved. Leaving tomorrow. Inform Intention by wire. Ufficio Telegraphic: Signed: Aldo de Luca."

Von doesn't know what to think. He looks at Sir Oliver, who is also stunned. He gives Von a nudge, implying that Von should do what he needs to do. Aldo de Luca tries to grab Von's arm to stop him. He pulls out a pocket knife and swings it at Von just to scare him, but he slips and stabs him in his back twice. Von is knocked out on the ground. Sir Oliver is filled with the emotional impact of the incident, shocked that Aldo would do this. Sir Oliver screams for help.

Von comes to and clambers to get away from Aldo. He gets up and runs as fast as he can. He is on his feet, sprinting toward the market, while vaguely aware of footsteps behind him. His mind is focused on gaining distance from everyone. He is bleeding heavily and is in a lot of pain. He starts to get dizzy as he sees a policeman walking towards him. He hears someone yelling in Italian. He doesn't know what they are saying, so he proceeds to take a detour to the small alley towards the market. He loses whoever was following him, but he keeps walking until he can no longer walk.

"Shit! Shit! I got stabbed. Am I gonna die here? I will never be born in my time if I freakin' die here." He is entirely confused, and the pain is getting worse by the second. Von puzzles why Aldo would want to turn him in to the police and stab him after Sir Oliver assured him that Aldo was a decent and trustworthy man.

Von isn't thinking clearly. His body is starting to go into shock. Obviously, he cannot call Sir Oliver, because they don't have cell phones in this era. Von yearns to be in his own time. He is used to having the convenience of technology to reach people, anywhere and anytime.

Von tries to cross the street at an intersection. He sees an Italian man in uniform on the opposite corner and turns his head to avoid contact. He changes his pace to make it look natural. Everything seems okay for a moment, but then two more uniformed men walk his way. Von turns and crosses to the other street, leading to an alley. He tries to look away casually, but his pulse is starting to race as he tries to fight his paranoia of being spotted. Now he is walking briskly; surely they have seen him acting strangely. He emerges at the end of the alley onto a major *Vialle*.

"Where the hell is a cab when you need one? Shit, what am I thinking...cab, they don't have cabs. I guess they do, but it's a darn *carriage* and not a *metered* cab with a turbo engine, just like the real ones in the big cities." He turns quickly as he hears a carriage from behind him but decides not to take it because it's full of people. Besides, their carriage cab only seats three people at the most. "And how do you make a hasty retreat when the cab driver is busy swatting flies from the face of the get-away-horse!" Von whispers. He turns quickly as he hears a carriage from behind him but then realizes it already has a fare as the driver tips his hat and passes by Von. In full panic mode now, Von tries not to lose it when a young woman approaches him. She smiles as she watches him walk near her. Von is about to use his cell phone to call Mick to tell him about this ordeal – and to hopefully stay mentally alert after being stabbed twice. He feels the wetness of his own blood, and it's starting to make him feel woozy, along with the *piercing* pains that are shooting every second in the core of his flesh.

"What am I doing using my cell phone? Am I trying to get attention, or am I out of my mind?" He tucks the phone, still wrapped in a tiny plastic tube, inside the blazer that Sir Oliver bought him.

Von walks towards the Piazza Umberfina, the town's main square and the heart of the island's action. He tries to sit on a park bench and is ready to collapse. He is so dizzy but gets up and tries to keep walking towards the shore to stay away from the rest of the crowd. He shifts his position, clenching and unclenching his cold hand. He stretches his sleepy legs, careful not to skid. He moves a small rock behind him that has been chafing him, and he rubs his sore neck. As he stands on a high cliff overlooking the town, Von loses consciousness and falls.

CHAPTER TWELVE

INTO THE ITALIAN SEA

In the dead of night in the small, typical seaside town of *Piombino*, it is easy to become disoriented. The floating sensation of the boat rising and falling with each passing swell is like flying. There are only the soft sounds of water against the hull to remind a sailor of earthly connections.

The lookout holds a lantern off the bow as if to push back the curtain of inky blackness, attempting to guard the vessel and her crew against the unknown. The occasional log floats by, sometimes banging the side of the slow-moving fishing boat powered only by the gentle night breeze against the sails.

Back on shore an Italian sailor in his seventies is preparing to take his three older grandsons for an early boat ride. The serenity of the moment is broken by the sound of splashing just beyond the reach of the light of the dim lanterns over the rocks. He walks towards the water, shining his lantern over the tops of the jagged rocks. He climbs carefully over the edge of the first large rock, trying to get a look at an object that appears to be floating just beyond the rocks at the water's edge. Almost slipping on the slimy seaweed, he retreats landward to a drier rock to regain his footing.

"Nipote!" He yells to his grandson Filippo, who is already unfurling the sails, for help. The young man jumps out of the boat, running to the older man and sensing the danger in his voice.

"Nonno? Grandfather, what's wrong?" The young man asks.

The object seems to be moving with the water, flexing unlike the stiff bobbing of a tree trunk or stray shipping container. There is something in the water, it seems to be moving!

Watching his grandfather's reaction, the younger man in his twenties works his way out over the slippery rocks to the water's edge. Using the oar he brought to keep his balance he holds it with both hands by the flat end. Extending his reach as far as he can without falling in, he uses its tip to gently nudge the floating mass.

"Che cosa? What is it?" The older man asks and yells from the rocks.

"I need you to help me out here," the younger man yells back.

"Mi piacerebbe!" the old man yells back.

"Seconde me…," the other Italian man standing nearby starts to say something but decides not to say what's on his mind.

"Penso che sia morto! I think he is dead," the man announces. The body is bluish in color with dark blood all over.

"È un cadavere, per grazia divina!" an older tall skinny family friend yells.

"Un morto? Look at him, eh?"

"Look, *Penso che sia morto,*" one of the men says.

"*Per favore, un pó di rispetto, su!*" Then the "corpse" starts throwing up whatever is left in his stomach. Everyone goes ballistic as Von begins to breathe. Four of the men try to pick him up from the side of the rocks and carry him onto their small boat.

As Von's limp body is being lifted up onto the deck, a searing pain shoots through his back and shoulder, forcing a weak moan.

"*Come va?*" The grandfather asks his older grandson, while he shakes his head with suspicion, wondering who this young man is.

On contact, Von rolls over and extends his arm over the curved metal, enabling him to gasp for a breath. He is just moments from succumbing to the call of the darkness, when he feels life surge through his body as he finds the strength to reach for an outstretched hand.

The grandfather pushes aside the heavy sail bags from the clutter of the open boat, offering a makeshift bed among the ropes and fishing nets. The smells of the pungent remnants of day-old fish mixing with the balmy night air make Von throw up.

"*Scusate se la barca puzza. La puzza viene dal pesce di due giorni fa.* Sorry…the boat smells bad. The smell is from our two-day catch with my friends and family," the old man asserts. Von feels overwhelmed by the sickening smells, and as the Italian family helps him, he hurls the remaining contents of his stomach over the side. The younger men say something in Italian and share a laugh at Von's expense before he collapses.

"*Riportalo in cabina.*" An impatient younger brother, Francesco, watches from the helm and feels his way through the dirty compartment in search of his grandfather's needle and thread, which they use to repair their nets. Francesco is a full-blooded, strong Italian.

"I got the needle and thread. *Dai, Bruno, prendi una coperta coprilo,*" Francesco yells, struggling to pry open his grandfather's old wooden box, as Bruno, the grandfather, shakes his head, concerned that his headstrong offspring will rip off the top in his haste.

"*Va bène, dobriamo tirarlo su. Ma non facciamo altro, va be.*"

"We need to call the *polizia.*"

"Polizia?"

"*Davvero?*" Filippo asks.

"*Ma non midire!*" The other younger brother chimes in.

"No way! *Anche se muoro…Non m'interessa.* He's not going to die in my boat!" another young man insists.

"*Tai quello che puoi,* you understand me, Francesco?" Bruno insists.

"*Sì, Che vergogna!*"

"*Abbiamo di meglio da fare che aiutarlo.* Finish what you need to do, and I want him out of my boat!" Bruno shouts impatiently to the rest of his grandsons, then takes a quick pull on a bottle of *chianti* they stashed behind a wooden box. Francesco knows the wound on Von's back needs to be sewn closed, and as the most clearheaded, he is the only one to help Von.

Von lies on his stomach and groans indistinguishable words as Francesco gets to work with the needle and thread used to repair his grandfather's nets.

Bruno sees Von is beginning to move and turns the helm over to one of his grandsons.

"*Siete sveglio, Signóre? Mi sentite? Siete statu pugnalato, e sti amo cercando di aiutarla. Signóre?* Can you hear me? You've been hurt bad, we're trying to clean your wounds," Marcello explains.

"Wha…what?" Von barely opens his eyes.

"Di dove sei?"

"*Stavate galleggiando nella baia quando vi abbiamo tirato fuori.* You were floating near the rocks when we pulled you out," Giuseppe says

"Who are you?" Where's Sir Oliver? Von tries to speak in a very faint voice. Weak and in a lot of pain, his eyes blink uncontrollably as he tries to focus on the young Italian man's silhouette against the night sky.

"Cosa?"

"*Chi Sir Oliver?*" But Von didn't answer any of their questions

"*Siete sulla Pia, una barca da pesca. Ma le ho curato le ferite, sono brutte. Le ho cucite per bene,* You're on the *Pia,* my grandfather's fishing boat. Your wounds, it looks *buono.* I closed them good…with my grandfather's needle and thread we use for the nets," Francesco comments in some kind of pidgin English.

"Where did you find me?"

"My grandfather…hauling our nets. *Abbiamo sentito un grande tonfo dall'roccie sotto la scogliera.* We looked around, and there were no other boats around. We don't know where you came from – maybe from the sky. So, we pulled you out…near the rocks.

"How did you get here from the sky?" another man asks.

"*Chi siete?* Who are you?" Carlo asks, suspicious of Von's wound. Von doesn't answer, and another brother speaks.

"*Siete stato pugnalato nella schiena.* You were stabbed many times, *eh?* We are surprised you're alive at all. You *capis, Signore?*" Von tries to nod his acknowledgment. Uneasy with the cryptic answer, his nod is followed by a long pause.

"Are you from around here?" Francesco asks, acting a little concerned, knowing that he is responsible for bringing Von on board.

"I don't think so," Von responds. Under the pressure of his interrogation and the rolling sea, he is feeling queasy again. Francesco sees Von is in no condition to talk and works on Von's bandages.

"Sorry...!" Von whispers.

"Ho bisogno di riposare, per favore. You need to stay in your berth and stay calm. *Ti sentirai meglio. It will make you feel better,"* Francesco says.

"My wounds are hurting a lot, goddammit!" Von whispers, as he wipes his eyes with a dirty cloth. But physical pain is not what's troubling him right now. He gazes around the decrepit fishing boat, wondering how he got here, and he is thankful to be alive.

"Resto, eh? You need to rest, *por favore.* Do you like *vino?*

"No, thank you. Not now...I feel sick in my stomach..."

"Filippo, Dov'è..., never mind! I found it..."

Here, have some *chianti. Ti sentirai meglio?* It will make you feel *buono,"* Francesco reassures as he helps Von tip the bottle to his lips. Von swigs the bottle and falls back into his open berth beneath the stars, still dazed and wondering if this could all be real before falling off into sleep. When he wakes up, he sees Francesco beside the *galley.*

"What are you doing?" Startled, Von awakes to find Francesco searching through Von's pockets.

Francesco pulls back, holding a small case in his hand, and shows Von what he has.

"What do you have in your hand?" Von asks.

"Don't you know what this is?" Francesco asks surprisedly, bewildered as he opens it, revealing Von's cell phone.

"*È un telefono piccolo! It's a small telephone.*"Francesco stares at it, explaining to the others that the device is similar to a telephone handset. Francesco's amusement turns to doubt as he begins to question what he knows about this stranger that his grandfather found half-drowned and wounded.

"*È un piccolo telefono? Perchè è così piccolo?* Why does it look so strange? How did it get so small like this? Tell me, is this yours?" Francesco badgers Von.

"I don't know, I don't know," Von answers defensively.

"*Look,* veramente non vorrei essere coinvolto col suo problem e con la polizia," Francesco answers. "I have a family, okay? If you're in trouble with the polizia, please don't involve me." He walks towards Von and stares intently at him.

"How do you know that device is mine? I don't know if that thing is mine or how I got it," Von asks.

Francesco pulls out the bottle of *chianti* and takes a sip. Then he shakes his head, wondering who this young man is and if saving him was a mistake for all of them.

Von gets up and feels inexplicably lost and nauseous.

"*Cosa c'è che non va? Siete nei suai?* Are you in some kind of trouble? What's wrong?" Filippo asks, but Von doesn't answer. He just looks off into the darkness, aware of the pain that he is determined to ignore.

As the morning light begins Von is feeling better. A tawdry-looking Italian friend of Bruno with large, callused hands walks towards Von and gives him coffee.

Von rises slowly to his feet and realizes that he has also been ignoring the strong urge of nature's call.

"*Vuole usare il bagno? Non abbiamo il bagno su questa barca.* We don't have a bathroom in this boat."

"*What do you guys use to wash your face?*" Francesco does not understand him until Von makes a series of gestures to demonstrate the urgency of the matter. Francesco laughs and informs Von that they don't wash their faces. They do jump in the water to get clean up, and use the sea to urinate, and then he says, *"Por favore.* Tell Von to go ahead and use the rear of the boat to do his business."

The odor of dirty nets and feces wafting in the air starts to overwhelm him. Fighting off a case of dry heaves, Von returns to the foredeck, collapsing into the sail bags.

He awakens just as the boat touches the dock and the grandfather starts shouting commands.

"Make it fast, *Velocemente! il mio amico!*"

"May I get my clothes back?" Von asks Francesco.

Francesco points out to Von that most of his clothes are wet and ruined. Francesco reaches into an oilskin bag, removes some dry clothes, and hands them to Von. Then, he asks his grandfather for some lira and offers the money to Von.

"*Prenda questo.* Here...," Francesco says, offering the money to Von. "It's not much, eh? But it should get you where you need to go."

Von buttons up his borrowed clothes, takes the money, and puts it on his pocket. He feels dizzy again from the movement, so he sits down on a sail bag and reconsiders his situation.

"Dove state andando? Where are you going? Do you know of anyone in *Piombino?*"

"I don't know! But I would like to know how I can get to the Isle of *Elba,*" he says, accepting the money from Francesco. "I won't forget your kindness when I get back to England." Von shakes Francesco's hand and begins to climb out of the boat slowly.

"Davvero, eh?" Elba? Francesco looks into Von's sad, pale face. "This town stretches out into the sea; you can see the

nearby Island of *Elba*. Climb back, and we drop you there, take this...*ti sentira meglio*" Francesco says in his broken English.

The small boat powered by a dirty old sail takes Von to the Isle of Elba, one of the places that Sir Oliver mentioned as a safe haven, before they were separated.

After they drop him off. "A dopo, eh!"

"Lo stesso qui..." Von quickly smiles and leaves. He walks aimlessly through the town until he finds a bench. He sits and tries to get comfortable. He checks his funds and decides he has enough to splurge for a small loaf of bread. While having his bread, he notices that the town has a spectacular view of the island's cliffs. Once he feels safe, Von hunkers down for several long hours to heal and regain his strength. He uses the bathroom in a small restaurant and while there tries to call Mick. He enters a small restaurant that is getting ready to open. Before using the restroom, Von composes his language skills to ask a young man where he can find a train station on the mainland.

"Dove prendo il treno?" The man stares blankly at Von, so he asks again and this time speaks very slowly, thinking that he might have pronounced some words incorrectly. "Dove...prendo...il...treno? Do you know where I can take the train?"

The man explains to Von that he is new to the area but that his cousin will arrive in a few minutes, and his cousin will be able to answer any questions Von has about Piombino train schedules. Von is confused by the man's Italian, but he thinks that someone else is coming and can give him better directions. He decides to ask for the bathroom instead.

"C'e il bagno in questo ristorante? Do you have a bathroom in this restaurant?" Von asks politely.

"Toletta?" the man asks.

"Si, *signore*, ho bisogno di usare la toletta," Von replies. "I *need* to use the toilet," he whispers to himself impatiently. The man points left. Von goes inside the bathroom, which is completely dark because there is no electricity. There is a small window the size of a cat box split in half. Von takes out his cell phone. He presses Mick's speed dial number, but the reception has too much static. He tries to dial it manually, and this time he hears it ringing but it then it cuts off. He decides to get out of there and sit at the bench before hopping a fishing boat back to the mainland.

But why isn't he here yet? Where could he be? Did he know this might happen? Is that why he gave me some money just in case we get separated like this? Von thinks. *That would mean Sir Oliver knew that Aldo can't be trusted. He knew that there's a risk, a high risk, that he and I would get separated. He knew all along, but he took the risk for me, almost costing me my life.*

"Damn it, where could he be?" Von starts to get frustrated, looking around, hoping that Sir Oliver will show up any second. He waits for several hours and decides to start walking around the small town, until he finds a train station on the edge of town. While he is walking, his memory starts to fill in the gaps. He knows he needs to get to *Calais* on the coast of France, another place where Sir Oliver said he would find him if they were separated. The port of *Calais* is just across the channel from England, where steam-powered passenger boats make the easy crossing daily. He steps up to the counter at the station, and he asks the ticket agent, *"Potrei comprare un biglierro di sola andata, per favore, eh? Can I buy a one way ticket please?"*

"Yes. *Si.*" The ticket agent says.

"One way. Una *sola biglietto a la Calais, Francia*," Von responds softly.

"Dove vuole andare? Where do you want to travel? The ticket clerk asks.

"Vorrei un biglietto di sola andata per la Francia, per favore, Signore?" Von answers the ticket counter clerk and walks away.

Where do I go from here? he asks himself, half gazing at the scenery outside, half staring at his own reflection in the glass after boarding the train. He feels weak and lost. He knows he needs to reunite with Sir Oliver and get back to London, but he wonders if he even cares to go on. His face plunges into darkness as the train hits a bump and disappears into a tunnel. The loud *click-clack* noise as it passes underneath begins to fade in the distance echoing off the walls. Von gets some comfort, knowing that at least some sounds are familiar and the same in any time or place. As he drifts off into sleep, he remembers listening to his father's CD of train whistles as a child, and a smile comes to his sad face.

Hours turn into days. When the train comes to rest at its final stop on the northern coast of France, Von leaves the station, passing a small restaurant just as it is closing up for the night. He checks his funds and finds he has just enough after converting his *lira* into *francs* for a glass of wine but decides to save it for the crossing. He walks aimlessly through the streets until he finds a secluded bench. He sits and tries to get comfortable. The cold damp air coming off the English Channel is ushering in a thick fog, penetrating his light clothes and chilling him to the bone. Von knows this will have to do until the morning. Just as he is hunkering down for the long, cold night, a Frenchman in uniform approaches him.

"*Monsieur*, can't you read the signs? *Hors d'ici,*" the Frenchman says. "On your feet, and get out of here...*allez vous en!*

Vous n'allez pas dormer sur ce banc. Allez vous en d'ici. You are not going to sleep on that bench. Out of here!" the Frenchman yells.

"*N'avez vous pas un endroit ou aller? Allez chez vous aupres de votre famille?* Don't you have a place to go, Monsieur? Go home to your family," the Frenchman asks again.

Von stands and tries to regroup. He opens his side pocket on his worn Italian sailor's pants and unseals the wrapped wad that Francesco gave him days earlier. In the little pouch is his cell phone in a dry oilcloth with his PDA and a piece of paper with Sir Oliver's name and the name of the square where they are to meet.

"*Je vois que vous etes toujours la. Je vous aid it de ne pas rester ici? Allez dormer a l'hotel.* I can see that you are still here. Didn't I tell you not to hang around here? Get a hotel and sleep there," the Frenchman shouts at him.

He sits down on another bench and tries to recall the details of what happened the last time he was with Sir Oliver on the train. He recalls wrapping his electronic gadgets in some kind of a cloth tube that just fit inside his bulky pocket. This must be how Francesco spotted his gadgets when they fished him out of the sea. Von ponders how he got where he is now. As his tired mind tries to sort through the clues, he drifts off into sleep. In that moment of clarity before sleep, he remembers that he and Sir Oliver were separated...and that it was Aldo who stabbed him at the telegraph station.

When he awakens the next morning to first light, he begins to plan his next steps. He tries to clear his mind by studying the people walking by with their children. He tries to subtly connect with anyone who does not avert their eyes as they pass by him. One English gentleman who is on his way to breakfast before catching the early morning ferry to Dover sees his desperation and asks Von to join him.

"Voulez vous un café avec votre plat?" the waiter asks.

Von cannot believe how good the *café au lait* and *croissants* taste. He had forgotten the simple joys of French cuisine. After thanking the stranger, Von starts out to find the square where he hopes Sir Oliver will be waiting. He knows that this is the town where Sir Oliver told him they should meet if ever something went wrong, but he cannot recall if they discussed a date or time to meet. He only remembers Sir Oliver saying this is a place where nobody cares to know what you are doing. He remembered Sir Oliver making a wry joke about the French being very good at that sort of thing.

It's been several weeks since he saw him last, but Von still is determined to stay hopeful. By the third day, Von is feeling desperate and hungry, wondering if Sir Oliver will show up before his money and the locals' kindness runs out.

Tired, confused, and angry at the world, Von walks around the city, exploring the narrow, winding alleys near the square. He is careful not to draw unwanted attention from the locals, fearing that he might wind up arrested for vagrancy.

"I wonder if they do lock up people for vagrancy in this era," he whispers to himself while he looks around for Sir Oliver. He waits, but the waiting is in vain. After sitting for two hours on a park bench, Von starts to fall asleep, so he decides to ask for directions to see if he is in the right place.

With only the clothes he is wearing and his few chosen electronic gadgets, Von is plunged into an even more unbelievable journey; his courage is challenged, his integrity questioned, and his very existence hangs in the balance. He is put to the ultimate test by being here on his own.

With limited knowledge of French and only a little bit of money, Von has to find a new place to stay for the night. Having a hard time understanding the signs, he decides to sleep in the bushes for the night with just his suit jacket to keep him warm.

It is an uncomfortable yet peaceful night in the bushes. While lying on the ground, Von stares at the sky and admires the beautiful stars floating in it. The sounds of insects don't bother him anymore, and he falls asleep. Tired from the longest walk of his life, Von sleeps like a baby.

On the morning of the fourth day, an elderly man dressed in a suit carrying a long, wispy broom he uses to sweep the streets notices Von. He pokes Von to see if he is alive or dead, and Von awakens, startled to see this man with a broom on top of him, and jumps to his feet, startling the old man.

"Etes vous blesse, Monsieur? Be bougez pas, j'appele un medic in.

"S'il vous plait ne faite pas ca. Je veux dire ca va, je ne suis pas blesse.

"J'éi eu un etourdissement et suis tombé," Von says to the man sleepily. "Did I say it right? Did I say, 'I was dizzy and fell'?" Von asks, more to himself than to the man.

"N'appelez pas le docteur," the old French man say, looking very concerned for Von.

"No! Don't call the doctor. I am fine. Thank you," he says as he gets up, straightening his clothes, and runs away.

The elderly man shakes his head as he watches Von run back to ask him: "Puis je utiliser votre sale de bain pour me laver la figure et me nettoyer, je vous paierai pur ca."

The restaurant owner refuses to let Von use his bathroom. Von returns to the small bakery where he went several days before with the Englishman. They have seen him many times now and seem generally friendly once Von tells them he is waiting to meet someone. He has been able to clean up a little so as to not look out of place, but the real reason he returns to this bathroom is to use his cell phone. He has been in several others, but none has the good reception this one does. This will be his third attempt to call Mick, who for some reason is not answering. Von refuses to consider that Mick has fallen out of touch; he so desperately needs to hear a familiar voice.

Von finds the bathroom available and locks the door behind him. The small window is the only source of light. While inside, he realizes that he hasn't spoken to Mick for quite a while now and wonders what has happened to him. Mick always answers when the reception is good. Von takes out his cell phone and dials Mick's speed-dial number, but there is no sound at all – no ring or even a busy signal. Von wonders, "Could Mick have changed his number?" He tries to dial his number again and this time hears it ringing.

"Hello?" someone answers, but it isn't Mick's voice.

"Hello? Is Mick there? May I speak with Mick, please?" Von asks.

"Mick? Who is this? Hello? Hello? I can't hear you. Would you please speak louder?" the woman on the other end of the line says.

"Hello? Can you hear me? Hello, I said is Mick there?" Von begins to yell.

"Sorry, I can't seem to hear you, would you please call back?" The line goes dead, and Von hears static. He tries to dial Mick's number manually, but it doesn't work. He is about to put his phone back in his pocket when he decides to try one more time. This time, after he dials the number, he presses the icon for "Talk," and abruptly he feels that weird sensation again, like he is floating on air, and everything is dark. It is the same feeling that he had when he first disappeared at the dorm. A sudden, loud noise is heard outside the bathroom. There is a clap of thunder, and lightning spreads over the small French restaurant.

"*Monsieur, quel est ce bruit? J'ai entendu une explosion dans la salle de bain, est ce que ca va?* What was that sound? I heard an explosion inside the bathroom, are you all right?" the restaurant owner asks.

"*Monsieur, monsieur? S'il vous plait repondez moi, Monsieur ou j'appelle la police,*" a man insists from outside the bathroom door. He knocks to find out if everything is okay with Von. When no one answers, the man forces the door and finds the sink shattered, smoke filling the room, and Von nowhere to be seen.

"*Qu'est ce qu'il a fait dans cette salle de bain? Le lavabo est tout abime? Qu'est ce qui ne va pas chez ce type? Pourquoi est il venu faire ca dans mon restaurant?*" the man says in amazement. He shakes his head in disbelief, tugs his ear with his right hand, and goes back to the bakery counter, muttering something under his breath. "*Incroyable!*"

In the flash of an eye Von finds himself floating somewhere in total darkness.

"Where the heck am I?" Von asks himself. He can't even see his own hands. He remembers that whenever Mick forgot his dorm keys, he would flip open his cell phone use the light from it to light the door knob. Von does the same to figure out where he is, but it doesn't help. He tries to move around, but he realizes he can't go anywhere. He doesn't have enough space. He can't even get up or spread his arms.

"Whoa! Where am I?" he yells. He is trapped. "Help! Help! Is anyone out there?" It seems like no one is there to hear him. He tries to push whatever is in front of him. "Arrrghhhh! What the heck is this place? Am I in some kind of container or something? Shit! Shit. I hope I'm not stuck here for a long time. I can't stay in this position any longer. Damn it, I have a cramp in my leg. I can't move my freakin' leg!"

Since he can't go anywhere, he opens his cell phone again to try to see what's around him. Then, he feels like he is spinning. He sees what seems to be a clear object.

Von feels washed away in a dark ambience waiting for somebody to rescue him, waiting for the lifeline back to reality that will tell him he is not absolutely alone. He feels no sensation – no idea of weight or smell – nothing but the darkness surrounding him. He thinks he might be moving, but he can't tell if it's just his imagination. If time is passing in either direction, there is no way to tell. The quiet and darkness surround him. He decides to scream. It is important for him to let someone know he is there. He hopes desperately for someone to find him.

"Is anyone out there? Is anyone out there to hear me? Help!" *Okay, what was I doing before this happened?* he thinks, trying to trace his path before he was zapped to wherever he is. *Okay, Von, what where you doing? Yes, yes, I remember now...I was trying to call Mick, and then my phone malfunctioned. I think that's what happened before I got into this dark hole. Okay, let's see what'll happen if I dial his number manually again.* He feels a sudden spin and is knocked out cold.

CHAPTER THIRTEEN

DISPLACEMENT IN TIME

V on opens his eyes, looking up to the pure darkness of the night sky but is suddenly blinded by glaring lights. Disoriented, he tries to figure out where he is and what has awakened him so abruptly. Whatever it is startles him. His ears are blasted with the sound of deafeningly loud music. He finds that he is on stage. As he gets pulled to his feet he sees a banner: "Woodstock."

"Woodstock? In 1969? What the heck? Does this mean I'm heading back to 2008?" He realizes that the crowd is cheering for him or maybe at him. *Talk about being in the wrong place at the wrong time!* he thinks. Two security guards lift him up to his feet and with a hard shove send him staggering into the crowd below. As he struggles to regain his footing, he realizes that his cell phone is missing. Looking back at the stage, he sees all eyes are on Ravi Shankar, who is about to perform, and at his feet there is a cell phone. Von dashes back on stage, grabs the cell phone, and throws himself back into the frenzied crowd just as the security guards, looking all-business, are reacting to his unwelcome intrusion.

Damn! I'm at Woodstock. I just woke up next to Joan Baez who was waiting in the wings with John Sebastian and Tim

Hardin. Whoa! That beats dark limbo any day, Von says to himself.

Arlo Guthrie comes on and launches into a monologue having something to do with the Pharaoh. What was he talking about? He must be tripping, too. Cool!

Before he can grasp what is happening around him in this bizarre pastoral setting, hours have turned into days. Von is experiencing a shared sense of timelessness with tens of thousands of total strangers, a feeling that he has had to bear in his lonely journey but now seems to be part of everyone he sees. He never could have imagined that the feeling of belonging only to the moment could be so full of joy. If only it could last! Though he is of the moment, Von knows that eventually he will be alone again, and all of their communal celebration of life will be just a shared joyous moment with strangers. If he could just bring someone with him on his journey, perhaps the moment would last.

The music on Saturday doesn't begin until later in the day, and goes non-stop well into the next morning. Von doesn't sleep much through the event; nor does anybody else. He is mesmerized in front of the stage, watching the artists perform. He finds a spot so close to the stage that he can see details of the tie-dyed shirts on some of the musicians. During the lulls, he can make out comments and conversations shared by the roadies and the musicians. It is clear this is not just another concert to them, any more than it is to the thousands who listen, frolick, sleep and weep with joy in the hills and fields of this magical countryside for days on end without beginning.

Von has the time of his life. Janis Joplin is a symbol of the energy shared by all that day. High on life and something else, she sobs and yells, contorting her face with what looks like extreme pain mixed with joy as she belts out her songs from the heart. Her intensity and honesty incite the crowd to screams of approval.

During the Creedence Clearwater Revival performance, an anti-war activist wearing a wet tie-dyed shirt dripping in color staggers onto stage noticeably stoned and slurring his words. He tries to snatch the microphone to sing with them and say something about love and peace to the crowd. Security takes him away and pushes him back into the crowd, as they had done with Von and so many others. The message did not need to be said, as it is already in the hearts and minds of everyone who shares in the experience.

The Who performs the entire rock opera *Tommy*, bringing one million people to their feet. Von waits with excitement for Santana, charmed with the Latin rhythms and Carlos's serpentine guitar lines in "Soul Sacrifice." The crowd goes wild to their sultry Latin sound. Then, after Joan Baez's performance of "Joe Hill," they deliver a set of far more down-to-earth folk music. And it goes on until the wee hours.

Von, emotionally and physically wasted from dancing for hours with total strangers, as though they were long-lost friends, lies down next to a red cooler as if it might protect him from the chilling rain that seemed to go unnoticed until now.

Around one o'clock Sunday morning, the pouring rain wakes Von up behind someone's tent. The music had given him a headache and he needs some time out. Although he had seemed ready to go somewhere, he is feeling the need to recharge, and so he dozes off again. After a few hours he awakens to the pungent smell of pot wafting through the tent. Thanking his new friends for their offer to partake, he declines and sets out to reclaim his spot close to the stage.

Headache or not, he is compelled by the magnetism of the moment to watch the performances that would taper off mid-morning of the third day. He is hungry and thirsty beyond words, but tried to ignore it.

Jefferson Airplane plays "The Other Side of this Life." The music seems to provide sustenance in the absence of food and water. By this point, Von feels well past his limit; his head is pounding, and his ears are ringing. When Jefferson Airplane finishes playing, Von decides to finally call it a day and pushes his way through the crowds to someone's tent.

A couple of hippies offer Von something to drink. After drinking too much water, Von crashes beside a girl who, in what seems to Von to be in a stoned state, proclaims she could see his "aura" as dusty gold. Von ignores her drug-glazed stare, which seems to hold the unspoken offer of intimacy, and sleeps soundly and alone for four hours. When he wakes up, after ten in the morning, his muscles are sore and stiff from being in the same position for so long.

Von comes to realize that the euphoria of the day before is taking on a more desperate feel. The word is that Woodstock has been declared a national disaster area. Food shortages, water contamination, and sanitation problems ignored for the first two days are now taking a toll on those still living in the moment. Von listens to the helicopters whirring overhead, breaking the mood of the even the hard-core hippies. The real world is landing with food and medical supplies and taking off with the sick and injured. Nothing so good could last forever!

The weather Sunday afternoon is scorching, with only intermittent rain and electrical storms. But each time the thunder rumbles announcing an approaching storm cell, the music has to be shut down for safety concerns.

The worst storm of the day happens at around one in the afternoon when the wind picks up fast and furious, blowing about sixty miles per hour. The rain, thunder, and lightning follow seconds later. Von is caught in the crowd by the stage. Most are oblivious to the threat, under their ponchos and engrossed in a performance by Joe Cocker. Just as the show is hitting its stride, the storm shuts it all down. The turn in weather is at first met with disappointment, but as the cool rain begins to fall, it douses the intense heat which by then has claimed hundreds of victims. And then comes the mud. Easily ankle deep, it is glorious! Cool, soothing, soft, and wet, it is everywhere. Thousands of mostly middle-class, white hippies are transformed into primitive mud-people, worshiping this comforting gift from the heavens.

At about that time, Von thinks it might be a good idea to find his new friend's tent to avoid getting slathered in mud.

Four in the morning has come quickly when Von hears that Jimi Hendrix, the guru of acid rock who leads unchallenged with his combination of blues and heavy metal guitar, is supposed to come to stage, but Von feels dizzy from lack of food and is forced to pay attention to his body. He hasn't had anything to eat or drink for many hours. Getting just a few hours of sleep throughout the last three days only adds to his sudden sense of weakness.

But I've got to see this! His performance was supposed to be incredible, and I'll never get another chance like this! Von convinces himself to fight off the signals his body is sending him.

About half an hour later, just as the first rays of sunlight show up in the eastern sky, Hendrix finishes his last song. By now the crowd, which has dwindled to thirty or forty thousand, turns toward the cameramen filming the once-in-a-lifetime performance for what will be a documentary, and catches the eye of the camera lenses for just a moment. Then, he turns to the crowd and strums the crowning moment of his bizarre set – his rendition of the Star-Spangled Banner. Jimi plays solo while his band just sits and watches in awe. Hendrix's performance is stunning.

"This is it!" Von whispers to himself, feeling the hairs on the back of his neck stand on end. "This is the famous performance!"

He watches Jimi Hendrix, bigger than life, as he slowly concludes the Woodstock festival. His sound is all at once irreverent and patriotic, as he plays the familiar choruses connected by long, rambling, dizzying guitar riffs. The sound echoes across the silent countryside, where those who haven't yet left the festival watch the performance that now demands their attention even after their ears and their senses have long been numbed by too much stimulation. The feeling in the air is one of pure magic.

Von thinks of Mick again and the many times they had talked about what it would have been like to be a part of this historical moment. He wishes he could talk to him and tell him he is watching Woodstock in real time. He dials Mick's number, without thinking of the consequences that he faced every time he had reached across time before. A strange voice answers on the other end.

"Hello? Can I speak to Mick, please?" Von asks, thrilled that the call has gone through.

"Mick? I'm sorry, Mick isn't available," the voice says sadly.

"Where is he?" Von asks.

"I'm sorry to say that we're not sure…Mick was called into the war. I think he is a POW in North Korea." The man tells Von about the war and nuclear threat, but all Von can think about is his friend and how he must be suffering while Von is celebrating peace at an anti-war festival. Von drifts off into his own world as the voice on the other end vents about a place and time that has his friend in danger. *What? A war? I can't believe this!* Von thinks to himself, but doesn't say out loud.

The man adds, "*The military hasn't declared Mick dead… just missing in action. We haven't heard anything else.*"

Terrified and confused, Von hangs up the phone. A moment later, he decides he needs to know more, so he again dials Mick's number. But all at once, before Hendrix finishes his song, Von disappears into thin air, sending sparks of lightning onto the stage. Hendrix thinks it's part of his performance, and the crowd goes wild when what seems to be fireworks punctuates this riveting display of virtuosity. At that moment, Hendrix is immortalized, and Von sent into a dark familiar limbo. Jimi finishes and Woodstock is finally over.

Von wakes up in a daze, finding himself face-flat on the ground. He squints and rubs his eyes, and then he realizes he is in a garden near big flower bushes. He hears children's voices nearby.

"Hey, don't pull my hair. Stop it!" a young girl screams at the top of her lungs. Von peers through the bushes, and he hears someone's voice calling the little girl.

"It's time for your bath, Emma," a middle-aged woman tells the little girl.

"No! I don't want to take a bath. Am I being punished?" she asks.

"Of course not, silly, it's just time for you to get cleaned up," the woman answers with a smile.

"I said no! I don't want to get cleaned up!"

"Emma, you have to come and listen to your nanny," an older man calls to the little girl. Von slowly sneaks to the next set of bushes to see who these people are. Then, Von sees the little girl's nanny pick up the mess that is scattered all over the ground.

"Don't worry, Sir Oliver, she will have her bath very soon and be ready to go to her piano lesson," the nanny says.

"Is that Sir Oliver? Whoa! He aged! He doesn't have a British accent anymore; what happened?" Von says to himself. He looks at his own body and doesn't look any different. It feels strange to see how Sir Oliver has changed into an older man so quickly. For Von, it was just few hours ago that they were together. He feels the hair on his body stand up as he looks at the face of the little girl. Could this really be who he thinks it is?

"*Mom*?" Von says to himself in disbelief. He hides in the thick bushes as he sees this little girl, barely ten years old, who will one day be his mother.

While waiting for the right time to come out and introduce himself to Sir Oliver again, he stays in the bushes to observe. The nanny finally comes out with the little girl. The driver opens the car door, and the little girl and the nanny get inside. The car pulls away. Von wonders if he should go inside the house and introduce himself to Sir Oliver. He hopes Sir Oliver will recognize him. *He must be in his eighties now. Does this mean he got married late in life and has such a young daughter at this age? Mom didn't tell me this. Who is he, Hugh Hefner? I now remember that in those old pictures, Grandma did look much younger than Grandpa.*

The car returns with Emma and her nanny. They all go inside, and Von can't hear what they are saying. It's almost dark, and he still doesn't know how to approach Sir Oliver. He doesn't want to scare him or make him mad for putting him in this situation again. He goes for a walk around the neighborhood. He can't see anything to eat. Besides, he doesn't have any money, and if this is 1969, he definitely needs new currency. He goes back into the bushes and turns in for the night.

When he wakes up, the yard is full of tables with linens and chairs. *Are they getting ready for a party?* he wonders. He gets up and walks through the garden. He realizes that there is already a party. People are arriving in party dresses and nice clothes. Lights are lit around the garden. Young adults and some children come along with their parents. As dinner is served, Von sees the little girl running around with other children. She isn't paying attention to getting food to eat with the rest of the visitors. She starts talking with one of the guests' children.

"What is your name?" the little girl asks with a big smile in her face.

"Ehrina Kusmonov," a girl replies.

"My name is Emma," she says back in a different language, conversing for at least ten minutes.

What language was that? Von asks himself.

"Would you like to get some food? I'm really very hungry," the little girl tells the rest of the children.

Von almost falls from his hiding place in the little cabinet hole where he is sitting. He is stunned. *What were the two girls speaking?* Then, he realizes, *Did she say Ehrina Kusmonov? She must be Russian. Mom speaks Russian?*

Unbelievable! I never knew she could speak another language. I thought she learned some in college, not when she was young.

While listening and enjoying spying on his mother as a little girl, Von begins to feel hungry. He slowly gets out of his hiding place, walks toward the buffet table, and helps himself. He fills a big plate and stuffs his pockets with bread. He can't find a bottle of water, so he grabs a couple of sodas instead. *Dooble Coolah? What the heck is "Dooble Coolah"? Yuk! I wonder if it will give me a double stomach ache? Oh, hell, it'll satisfy my thirst, anyway.*

One of the servants sees Von with all the food in the bushes, so they go inside and call Sir Oliver. They bring Von to a private hallway. When he enters the room he sees Von sitting in a chair next to the kitchen.

Unwashed and unshaven from several days at Woodstock, Von is wrapped in a dirty kids' blanket he found in the bushes. By the looks on Sir Oliver's and the rest of the housekeepers' faces, Von could easily pose as a homeless man.

"What are you doing on my property?" Sir Oliver stoically greets Von. The first thing Von notices is that Sir Oliver has completely lost his British accent. Secondly, Sir Oliver clearly doesn't recognize him at all. Reality hits Von, and he realizes that if he went forward in his time-traveling from 1908 to 1969, it has been sixty-one years.

"Would you please tell me who you are and what are you doing on my property?" Sir Oliver asks again.

"Sir Oliver, don't you remember me? My name is Von, Von Muir Carmichael. We met many years ago in Oxford, England."

"Oxford?" Sir Oliver replies with surprise. "I haven't been to Oxford for many, many years. I don't recall meeting you."

"We met many years ago. It's been a while, so let me refresh your mind. You took me to the 1908 Olympics and invited me to Staffordshire. You also introduced me to Lady Stephanie, and we went to Italy to meet with Marconi...But something happened. Your friend Aldo de Luca was sending a telegram to someone about me, and I was scared. As I was trying to run away, he stabbed me, and I lost you after I escaped. Do you remember?"

"Was that you? You must be the time-traveler!" Sir Oliver looks at Von, admiring how young he still is. "Of course I remember you. I'd wondered what happened to you. When we got separated, I was questioned by the Italian police, and they took me back to Oxford. I was detained for several months regarding the murderer of those men in the dormitory. Nobody believed me when I told them the truth about you being a time-traveler. They thought I was losing my mind. It bothered me for several years, and until a few years ago, I was still thinking about you. What are you doing now? How did you survive your stab wound?"

"I fell off the cliff into the water and was fished out by some Italian fisherman who took care of me." Von conveys his misery to Sir Oliver.

"Look at you; you haven't changed a bit. Here I am in the winter of my life. You, you are still frozen in your youth."

"I know...I just want to go home. I still can't find the answer. In fact, my communication to my own time is getting worse. The technology has changed, and my gadgets have become obsolete. Every time I call my friend, his cell phone doesn't work. Every time I dial his number, I get zapped to another time or some kind of limbo," Von reveals.

"Well, I don't know what to tell you. I'm glad you have found me again. I don't know how you did it, but the important thing is you did," Sir Oliver replies. "Well, why don't you stay here with us until we can solve your dilemma? I'll tell the servants to have one of our guest rooms ready for you, so you can get cleaned up. Oh! I remember those clothes you're wearing. We purchased them in Oxford before we went to Italy." Sir Oliver laughs in surprise, and as he is about to leave the kitchen, the door opens.

"Yes, still the same clothes, except they were damaged when Aldo stabbed me. They shrank when I fell in the ocean. The fisherman who found me gave them back to me after I recovered from my stab wound."

A little girl interrupts their conversation. "Daddy, what are you doing in here?"

"I'm talking to a friend of mine," he replies. "Von, I want you to meet my younger daughter, Emma." The little girl looks at Von from head to toe, smiles, and starts fidgeting.

"Hello!" she says and runs out of the kitchen to play with the other kids. Von is shocked; it is very weird to meet this girl knowing she will be his mother. He sits down as a feeling of nausea and dizziness overtakes him.

"Are you all right?" Sir Oliver asks.

"Yes, it's just so crazy to meet my future mother as a young girl. It's making me sick," Von replies.

"Well, then, you should rest for the night, and we will talk in the morning," Sir Oliver instructs gently.

CHAPTER FOURTEEN

ROUNDABOUT PAST

The first thing Von becomes aware of when darkness abates is that his mouth is dry. Then, he feels the nauseating ache in his head and the terrible cramps in his stomach. Finally, for a few seconds, he resigns himself to open his eyes and winces. The pain in his head is like a million sharp daggers poking him in the eyes. He groans, pulls the blankets over his head, and rolls over. The move aggravates his stomach, which is informing him that he has only so long before it will rebel with a reprise of last night's dinner. He doesn't know if these reactions are real feelings or creations of his imagination. He slowly gets up and puts on the clothes that Sir Oliver gave him the previous night.

The breakfast table is set up, and Von is greeted by the little girl sitting at the table. She smiles at him and eats her food. A lady next to her tells her how to sit properly and how to hold her butter knife. The little girl pouts and gives the woman a hard time. She gets up from the table and demands to speak to her father. The nanny tells her that he has been out since early this morning and will be back before lunch. The nanny turns to Von and tells him to go ahead and have his breakfast. The servants serve him hot coffee and a full breakfast. After eating, he goes outside to the garden to get some fresh air. The little girl follows and sits next to him.

"Where are you from? How do you know my father?" she asks.

"Ahh…I met your father many years ago, and I am here to visit him for a short time," he replies. Von notices that the little girl is fidgety and cannot keep still in her chair. She gets up, runs around in circles, and finally sits down on the lawn.

"Do you know how to play the piano?" she asks curiously.

"Piano? No! Do you?"

"Of course! Watch me!" she responds as she runs inside the house and sits in front of the piano. She plays the piano and sings fluently in French. Von thought that his mother could not speak a language aside from English when she was young. How could this be possible? Is this really his mother as a little girl?

After playing few instrumental pieces, she says she is tired and wants to read her book in the living room. She gets up and takes a book from the family's bookshelf. Von asks her if she has a favorite book, and the little girl responds, "I love Marie-Catherine d'Aulnoy's series of short stories, like *La Chatte Blanche.*" She proudly hands her book to Von. He looks at each page and realizes that the book is written in French.

"What is it about?" Von asks and listens to the little girl, even though he knows what the book is about. He is familiar with *La Chatte Blanche*, or the *White She-cat.*

Von is more confused now than ever. He knows about his mother speaking and reading other languages as a linguist but not as a child. The little girl tells Von that her favorite song is in French. Then Von remembers one incident with his mother in their family room many years ago. He remembers seeing a very old copy of *Madame d'Aulnoy's books*. He remembers asking her about it, and her response was, "I got it in one of the antiquarian places in the city." Now Von wants to know what the connection to all of these events is. What is going on? What's the big deal? Why lie to him about the books and about being fluent in certain language since she was a child? What else will he find out about his mother?

Sir Oliver returns before lunch. He looks very tired and tells Von to meet him in his den in a few hours. Von goes outside again and sees that the nanny and the driver are preparing to take the little girl for a ride. The driver asks Von if he would like to go with them. Von nods and gets inside the car. He realizes that they are dropping the little girl off at school. Outside, a sign reads: "Language School for Girls." The driver tells Von that the little girl will be in school for several hours, so Von replies that he will walk around the area to keep himself busy and will meet them back at the car. The driver agrees, and Von leaves.

After several hours, the nanny picks up the little girl in front of the school. The girl is acting like a brat and is giving the nanny a hard time about how to carry her book bag. When they return to the house, the nanny takes her to her room to change clothes. When they come back downstairs for the little girl's snack, she is wearing overalls. She carries a sling-shot in her back pocket. Von now sees why Grandpa and the servants tell the little girl to wear her shoes. She wears them for a short time, and when no one is looking, she removes them and hides them somewhere where nobody can find them so that she can walk barefoot.

Von is surprised to see that his mother's upbringing was totally different from his. He was never allowed to be a brat. No wonder his mother knew how to discipline him all those years.

While waiting to meet with Sir Oliver, Von realizes that he has not used his BlackBerry for a while, so he decides to take it out of his jacket. The screen looks distorted for some reason, but it still shows some of the programs he needs. He searches the Internet news and is dumbfounded to find his name in the 1969 news: "BOY CASUALTY OF TUBER-CULOSIS EPIDEMIC, October 12, 1969." Von reads on: "The boy was given a BCG vaccine but did not survive." Von realizes that BCG is a tuberculin vaccine which was not yet widely used in the United States in the 1960s. He knows that a person given this vaccine will test positive when given a tuberculin skin test.

Oh damn, I've got to do something about this…October 12; that's four days from today. No wonder I started to not feel well this morning. I must've gotten a bug from time-traveling, Von thinks.

While Von debates whether he should tell Sir Oliver about the news, Sir Oliver comes down from his nap and shows Von to his den. Sir Oliver tells Von that while he was out earlier, he met with several old colleagues. He hands a note to Von, and it reads:

> There is a man by the name of Dr. Ali Javan, a scientist in New York, who invented a laser that can be used in telecommunication back when they first produced the gas laser beam. In fact, my colleague was there when they first tried it out.

He and his friend succeeded in creating the gas laser the next day, and he called a friend to the lab. One of the team members answered and asked them to hold the line for a moment. Then, they heard a voice somewhat quiver in the transmission and told them that the laser light was working. They heard the voice of Mr. Balik, who is now a professor in Canada. They were all ecstatic with the results. It was the first time in history that a telephone conversation had been transmitted by a laser beam. The date was December 13, 1960.

Sir Oliver, I thought this might help your time-traveling friend. We should see you both tomorrow. I have told one person about this highly secret situation.

The note is not signed. Von hands it back to Sir Oliver.

I am sorry I 'ad to divulge yer secret. 'E wouldn't tell me about t'e telecommunication machine if I didn't," Sir Oliver relates. Von notices that Sir Oliver's accent pops up in his speech once in a while.

"It's okay, Sir Oliver," Von replies. "I have another problem to tell you, though. I have found out through one of my gadgets that I will die in four days because of the BCG vaccine that will be given to me. I want you not to give me anything if I get sick. Promise me not to give me the vaccine."

"Oh, don't worry, lad. I promise ye not t' d' anythin' unless ye ask me t'."

Von tries to use his BlackBerry, but he is having trouble with it. He asks Sir Oliver where he can find the biggest technology corporation in the area so that he can connect to the twenty-first century. He knows that the first telephone conversation was transmitted by a laser beam on December 13, 1960, by Dr. Ali Javan, so Von thinks it's possible for him to trick some electrical wiring to connect his BlackBerry and scanner.

"Can you tell me more about Dr. Ali Javan? I have never heard anything about him," Von says.

"Well, we 'ave t' wait till t'morrow t' find out more 'bout t'is man," Sir Oliver replies.

"Wait a minute…Let me see if we can find something through my BlackBerry," Von says. He types "Dr. Ali Javan," and presses Enter. The PDA still does not work properly, but it gives some information. It says: "Dr. Javan tested a gas laser invention on December 12, 1960. The following day, he conducted an experiment of the first telephone conversation ever to be transmitted by laser beam. Then, nearly forty years later, laser telecommunication via fiber-optics is commonplace, comprising the key technology used in today's Internet. He anticipated that microchips will operate on light-wave frequencies, GHz, rather than the MHz radio frequencies."

"This is good news!" Von says with excitement. He indicates to Sir Oliver that he is receiving the information on his device.

"It's coming from outer space," Sir Oliver argues.

"I know I should avoid using my cell phone, but I think I should take a chance and dial my friend's number again to see if he answers." Von shakes his BlackBerry, but it again is not working. It turns off by itself, and when he tries to turn it on, he feels the static electricity all over his body.

"*NO!*" Von yells as he starts to dissipate, and Sir Oliver sees Von disappear right in front of him. He tries to grab him, but it is useless. The servants come to the den and ask Sir Oliver if everything is okay. They find Sir Oliver on the floor with his clothes torn and smoke coming from somewhere. The servants help Sir Oliver get up, and he reaches for his eyeglasses, which are still warm from the blast.

"Where is he now?" Sir Oliver whispers to himself, as he looks around the room with no Von in sight.

CHAPTER FIFTEEN

SHADOWS OF SUSPICION

Into the darkness, while the clock strikes into another dimension, Von is sweating a lot. He is breathing heavily and hanging on to his lifeline. Von had faith when he used to talk to Mick, and he is trying not to give up hope. He needs to talk to Mick or see Sir Oliver again. He needs more information about where Mick is. And where is Sir Oliver now?

Von must have fallen asleep while in limbo. He opens his eyes. His skin feels sticky, and he feels nauseous. A sharp pain stings at the back of his head. He moans softly as he shifts under the sheet that someone has apparently covered him with. He shifts to his right, and a cool, damp cloth brushes his forehead. To Von's dazed and aching head, it can mean only one thing.

"Mom," he whispers. "Is that you?"

"No, Von, it's Camilla."

"Where am I?" he asks, and he feels that his mouth is dry.

"You're in the servants' quarters," she says softly. "We were able to bring you here after the…incident."

"Servants' quarters? What incident? Who are you?"

"I'm Camilla. I'm the Roberts' housekeeper. Don't you remember me? Lie still, now."

Von follows her orders, letting his eyes fall shut again and relaxing as best as he can. He then opens his eyes and asks again, "What incident?" The back of his head throbs as he tries to bring everything into focus. "May I see Sir Oliver? I need to speak with Sir Oliver."

"No, you cannot speak with Sir Oliver."

"Ow! My head hurts really badly," Von says as he moves away from the housekeeper.

"I wouldn't doubt it, considering you were hit pretty hard. I'll see if I can get something to help that."

Von sees her shadow shift a bit, and a moment later, the table lamp near his bed comes to life. Camilla keeps the light dim, and Von turns his head away, shielding his eyes. Moving his head awakens new areas of pain, and he moans again.

"What happened?" he asks. "It feels like my brain is trying to escape out of the back of my head."

"Don't you remember what happened to you?"

"No! Tell me what happened," Von says, extremely curious.

"The Roberts' car exploded, and you barely made it. Nigel thinks you blew up the family car after you had an argument with him, but I know you didn't do it. We're quite certain we know who did, but unless we can find proof, the police will come back in a few days to question you at the station."

"Wait a minute, what do you mean? I don't understand what's going on." Von begins to panic.

"Poor boy! You must have really hurt your head," Camilla responds. "Don't you remember the car explosion?"

"What car?" Von asks.

"His classic Morgan," the housekeeper replies.

"I don't remember any car...That doesn't make sense. I was at the breakfast table, talking to Sir Oliver. That's as far as I can recall. After that, I guess everything is blurry," Von says, confused.

"The breakfast table? When did you have breakfast with Sir Oliver?" she asks curiously.

"Um, I think yesterday, with little Emma," Von replies.

"'Little Emma'? I don't remember you calling her 'Little Emma' since you moved in with them fifteen years ago, after you got hurt from some kind of a blasting mechanism in their kitchen. Boy! What happened to you? Don't you remember?"

"No! I don't remember anything like that," Von says, nearly breathless.

"Come on, you don't remember that you have been staying with the Roberts for fifteen years? Sir Oliver took care of you, and put you to work with him. Then, there was an accident a few weeks ago. You were working near the car when there was an explosion. You saw Sir Oliver, and you tried to save him, but he was badly hurt. We took him to the hospital, dear, but he didn't make it. This afternoon is his funeral."

"*Funeral?* He *died?* No!!! But...I was just talking to him...." Von can't grasp what Camilla is telling him.

"No, Von, you must be confused," the housekeeper tells him.

"But it's not possible. Little Emma and I had breakfast...We were all sitting at the breakfast table..." Von tries to explain.

"'Little Emma?'" she asks. "She's no longer a child. She's now a grown woman."

"Grown? What do you mean grown?" Von asks.

"I mean that she's an adult now, Von…She has been grown up, for quite a while now. The doctor at the hospital was right. You definitely have a concussion."

"This doesn't make sense at all. I was just talking to them…I was *just* talking to them," Von insists.

"That can't possibly be, Von," Camilla responds. "You were unconscious for several days. Sir Oliver passed away a week ago today. We have to wait for Emma to come home for the funeral because she has been out of the country."

"I'm sorry, but could you tell me what year this is?" Von asks.

"What do you mean what year it is? It's 1983, Von," the housekeeper answers, confused.

"1983? How old is Emma now?"

"Von, she just had her birthday. She's twenty-four years old, and she's engaged to be married."

"Oh, no…" Von whispers to himself as he tries not to scream. If that is the case, he will be born in three years, and if he doesn't make it back home soon, he will never be born.

"Well, listen, Von, you should get dressed. You can ride with me and Ethan to the funeral."

"Would you please tell me who Ethan is?" Von asks.

"Okay, don't tell me you have forgotten Ethan as well! He's your close friend. You two have been friends since you moved in with the Roberts. He is my oldest son!" Camilla says, shocked.

"I'm sorry. It must be the accident. I just don't remember anything at all. I'm sure I'll be fine soon," Von apologizes.

At the funeral, Von is able to slip in without attracting attention. He approaches the coffin to say a few words to Sir Oliver. As he looks around, he sees that there is a bigger crowd at the funeral than he has ever seen in his life in one room. The crowd is so big that children paying their respects are being carried on the shoulders of their fathers to make room for everyone.

Von is still weak and he trips. The people around him move but just enough to let him see the coffin, not enough to let him through. Von is having difficult digesting all that is happening, so he goes outside to get some fresh air. He waits for a few minutes to help carry the coffin to the funeral car, and everyone follows to the cemetery.

While at the funeral, Von sees that "Little Emma" is definitely no longer a child. She is with two middle-aged men. She comes to Von and asks if he is doing well. He responds by saying that he has felt better.

"How is your arm? Oh, and I can see that you're still limping a bit," she says.

"I'm okay, my leg doesn't really bother me," he says as he looks at her out of the corner of his eyes. And this time, he knows.

Oh, Mom…You don't even know it's me, he thinks. *I wish it could be as easy as getting into a machine and rewinding or fast-forwarding so that I can go home. Damn it, will I ever be home?*

In a public cemetery along a private lot next to Sir Oliver's, Von notices that there isn't much land left for new graves. Another funeral is taking place nearby. There are a lot of mourners in dark suits and dresses. The service is nearing its end.

Sir Oliver's newly dug grave is bordered with wildflowers of English origin. Von remembers seeing many in the formal garden of Sir Oliver's London estate. Emma stands with a solemn face, looking at the temporary marker and the flowers and big wreaths piled up against it. Then, they start to lower the casket into the ground. Nigel rests a floral arrangement against the pile of flowers. His hand drifts near a white gardenia wreath. There is a small envelope tucked beneath a blossom. He takes it and walks back to the car.

The funeral is over, and the mass of mourners, many wearing dark glasses, fan out toward a long line of cars. One of the mourners brushes past Emma. He looks up and tips his dark glasses down onto the edge of his nose, stares over them, and hugs her.

Von rides back to the Roberts' house with the housekeeper. He is sad to know that not only has he witnessed the loss of his grandfather, he has lost his only connection to the real world. Besides Mick, no one would believe he is who he is. He slowly walks back to the main house, and the housekeeper stops him.

"Where are you going?" she asks.

"I'll go back to my room," he responds sullenly.

"What room? You really don't remember that you've been staying with us at the servants' quarters?"

"Oh! I'm sorry. I must have forgotten. How long have I been staying with you and the rest of the housekeepers?"

"Since Sir Oliver's health began to fail. His oldest son, Nigel, handled their estate, and Nigel thought that you should stay at the housekeepers' quarters. Everyone knew that he was jealous of you while Sir Oliver took you under his wing as his young protégé. When Sir Oliver got sick, Nigel changed everything for you. Poor boy! You don't remember, huh?"

"It doesn't matter....," Von whispers. "What a nice guy Nigel is," he says sarcastically.

"I suppose I should remind you that this is the second time you have had a head injury. The first one was in 1969, when some kind of mechanism ignited in the main house, and the explosion caused your first head injury. They took you to the hospital, and the neurologist informed everyone that you had a bad concussion. Then, your second head injury was when you were trying to save Sir Oliver from the explosion few weeks ago. They said you had another concussion and a little swelling that was filled with blood resulting from a break in a blood vessel," the housekeeper clarifies to Von. "When you had your second head injury, Jenny and I alternated giving you your medicine three times per day. By the way, your medications are on top of your dresser."

After Camilla leaves Von alone to sort out his thoughts. He goes for a walk outside and sits at the bench in the garden. He remembers that it was the same bench that he sat on with little Emma many years ago. He hears footsteps behind him. He turns around and sees that Nigel is walking nearby. Von walks toward him and tells him how sorry he is about the death of Sir Oliver. He insists that he doesn't remember anything about the accident. He also tells Nigel that Camilla explained to him about the police who will be coming in a few days to question him regarding the explosion.

"You can stay with us for as long as you want. You will always have a space in the servants' quarters," Nigel tells him.

"Thank you, Nigel. I appreciate your kindness. I don't know where I would be without your father's generosity and hospitality all these years," Von responds.

"Don't worry. We just need to discuss what your plans are. Now that father is gone, things will change around here. Have you thought of what you're going to do now?" Nigel asks.

Von can't say anything. He cannot tell him that his plan is to go home to his own family in his own time. He can't tell him what he really wants to say. Only Sir Oliver could understand his situation. If he tells Nigel that he is a time-traveler, Nigel will think he is crazy and send him to an asylum.

He says, "Well, maybe I need to get myself organized and think about the future. I'll let you know what I decide to do."

"Okay, in the meantime, I want you to continue your job here with us. You will be helping the gardeners with the yard work since you are very good at that. Father once told me that he didn't agree with me when I gave you that job, but you seemed to adapt to it quite well."

"I'll be fine, Nigel."

"It's Mr. Robert. Call me Mr. Robert, okay, Von? By the way, I forget to tell you that your work around here will be long hours and not regular."

"I understand," Von responds.

"I can't pay you much the way Father pays you. Not for a temporary. When you don't have anything to do around the property, you'll have to turn your hand to whatever comes up – helping in the kitchen, running errands, seeing that my shoes are always polished...you got that?" Nigel asks.

Von shakes Nigel's hand and returns to the servants' quarters. He goes upstairs and realizes that he has been living in that space for a while. He notices that the clothes hanging in the closet are his. He walks toward the desk and sees a lot of pictures on it. The housekeeper knocks at his door, and when he opens it, he sees Camilla standing there with a large pile of laundry in her arms.

"Here. I washed and folded your clothes," she says with a smile as she hands him his laundry.

"Camille, I don't know what I've done to Nigel Robert. Why the attitude towards me?"

"Don't let it worry you, Von. You're doing just fine," Camille says encouragingly.

"By the way, whose photo albums are these? I found them here on the desk," Von asks.

"Oh! Don't worry. Those are all yours. You and Ethan put them together."

"And whose record player is this?" Von asks curiously.

"Come on, Von, Sir Oliver gave you that for Christmas a few years ago because you love music."

"Are you sure that these are all *my* records?" he asks.

"Yes, those are all yours."

"That can't possibly be. I never listen to GQ Disco Night Rock Freak, ABBA, and Olivia Newton-John," Von says as he tries to remember if he has ever owned a record-player or a vinyl album.

"Disco is one of your favorite genres. You play those records over and over again," Camilla reminds him.

"Really?" Von asks as he turns towards the window and notices a picture on top of the dresser. "Camilla, is this your daughter?" Camilla smiles at him and laughs.

"You are in big trouble, young man. Don't tell me you don't remember her, either. That's Jenny, your fiancée! You have been together for ten years now. She wasn't at the funeral today because she took her grandmother to surgery this morning. She will be over later to visit. Now stop this silliness, Von. I have to start cooking dinner," Camilla says, laughing as she leaves his room. On her way out, she says, "Okay, don't tell me you don't remember where the dinner table is. You eat with Ethan and me, not at the Roberts' dining table in the main house unless you're invited."

Camilla leaves the room with Von staring at the picture on top of his dresser. How can he not remember this beautiful girl if they've been together for ten years?

"My god, ten years? *Fiancée?* I have been dating this girl for ten years? Where was my mind all these years?" Von is confused as to how someone had fallen in love with him, and he is sad to know there is no future for them. *How do I react when I see her if I can't even remember any of this?* he wonders.

Why can't he remember what happened to Sir Oliver? Is his mind trapped in the dark limbo as well? Is this all because of his head injury, or did he black it all out in his head? Whatever the reason, it seems that his repeated attempts to get back home simply drop him into a variety of parallel universes. Is his mind playing with him? Is this real?

Through his time travels, Von realizes that he has experienced many perils. As he tries to recall what he has gone through, Von remembers a recent mysterious conversation he overheard while he was at the Roberts' main house.

He was putting away some old books that Nigel Robert wanted him to pack; Nigel was on the other side of the den speaking on the phone in a low tone of voice. Then, Von heard him scream to the person on the other end of the line: "Get rid of him, or I will personally get rid of you, do you understand? And make sure it looks like an accident."

Von remembers being shocked at what he had heard. He walked slowly away from the door to the other end of the room. Nigel heard noise from outside the den and swung open the door.

"How long have you been standing there?" he asked Von angrily.

"I just got here. Why? Have you been looking for me?" Von remembers saying. He pretended not to know anything.

He stares at Von, wondering if he really hadn't heard anything.

"Ahh! Yes, I forgot to tell you that those books need to be put in the attic after you box them up. Be sure that you seal the boxes properly, and let me know when you're finished,"

"Yes, of course. May I have your permission to go now to your library to finish my work?" Von asked.

"Most certainly, Von,"

Von did what Nigel Robert wanted him to do: box up all of Sir Oliver's old books and put them all up in the attic. Von was sad to see them confined in a brown box and not out where other people could see them or read the history in all of the books that Sir Oliver wrote himself. He couldn't understand why the new generation of the Robert family wanted to lock away its history.

As he finished locking up the attic, he heard a knock from somewhere in the main house. He came down the attic ladder slowly and tucked it away.

Von cannot believe what he is now remembering. What could this mean?

A young woman unexpectedly enters the room.

"Hey, I've been looking for you. How do you feel?" She approaches Von and kisses him on the lips.

Oh, boy, here we go… This must be Jenny, Von thinks.

"Hi! How did the surgery go?" he asks, remembering that Camilla said earlier that Jenny took her grandmother to the hospital for surgery.

"Well, she's feeling a bit tired, but it's to be expected. The doctor said it will be a few days before she can go back home," Jenny replies as she holds onto Von's hand. "Come on, give me a kiss. I'm glad to see you walking around and feeling better. You really had us worried there for a while.

Do you know that you've been calling someone's name in your sleep? Some name nobody knows."

"Name? What was the name?" Von asks, curious and surprised.

"Mick."

"Mick? Hmm, I don't know of anyone with that name," Von says, pretending not to know the name Jenny has mentioned. "It was probably a dream, one of those dreams when you call out a stranger's name, you know?" He smiles awkwardly.

"This must be quite a dream. You called him over and over again for several nights," Jenny says.

"Well, how was your day otherwise?" Von asks, trying to change the topic.

"Well, I'm here to remind you it's about time to take your medicine. You need to take them on time, okay?" she says sweetly.

"Yes, Camilla told me that earlier."

"I'm also here to pick you up to stay at my place tonight. I told Camilla, and she said that as long as I bring you back here early in the morning, Nigel won't be mad at you for not doing your morning chores."

"Umm…your place? What about your parents?" Von asks.

"My parents? Are you kidding me? I don't live with my parents. Have you forgotten that before the accident, you were ready to move in with me to get ready for our big day? We both agreed that it would be okay to move in together early to prepare ourselves for the wedding."

"The wedding? What wedding? I'm sorry, but since the accident, I guess I've become forgetful. When do we plan to get married?" he asks, trying not to act panic after hearing the word "wedding."

"Well, we *were* going to get married next month. That was our plan before you got your head injury, but I decided that we should really wait until you see the doctor at the end of this month. Is that okay with you, Von?" Jenny asks. Von is sweating just thinking all about it.

"While you where unconscious, I kept looking at my engagement ring. It was the only thing that kept me going when they told me about your injury. No one knew when you were going to wake up. I called Camilla earlier today, and she told me that you were up and feeling well enough to go to the funeral," she says. Jenny lifts up her hand and asks Von to kiss it as she flashes her ring. Von almost faints when he sees his grandmother's ring – the one that he was planning to give to Bessie.

"What's wrong, Von? You look like you've seen a ghost!"

"Oh, um, it must be from my head injury. I still feel a little lightheaded once in a while. Do you mind if I don't spend the night at your place tonight? I'll make it up to you, I promise, but not tonight," Von says.

"No problem, honey. I understand, and it's okay. You need your rest, and you'll be happier in your old bed, anyway. Just don't get used to it!" she replies, half joking. Jenny tells Von to relax and leaves. Von gets in his bed and thinks of all that is going on in his life.

The ring shocked me, damn it. That ring is supposed to be for Bessie. Bessie, I wonder where you are. Do you ever wonder where I am? Von thinks and then whispers, "I miss you so much."

The following morning, bright and early, Von gets up and eats his breakfast alone.

My mind really couldn't focus on Nigel's boxes today, so it's a good thing he's out of town. That means I won't be too busy working in the attic. I really need to make a phone call and satisfy my curiosity about what's out there, Von thinks. I don't even know if I should be doing this, but something tells me I should.

He looks around to see if anyone is there, and decides to use the Roberts' phone. He calls the operator, and they inform him that there is no Carmichael or Robert listed for the Florida address he provides, so he decides to ask the operator for Pascual Chevrier, Mick's dad. This is 1983, and he knows that the Chevriers moved to Florida in the early 80s. Von is happily surprised that the operator gives him a phone number. He hurriedly dials. Someone picks up, and Von quickly says, "Hello? May I please speak with Mick Chevrier?"

"Mick Chevrier? May I ask who this is? Mick can't come to the phone right now," the man responds.

"It's Von! Is Mick there, please?"

"Mick is taking a nap. Is this a joke?" the man asks seriously.

"No, sir, this is not a joke. Is this Mr. Pascual Chevrier?"

"Yes, this is he."

"Mr. Chevrier, this is Von, Von Carmichael. I'm Mick's best friend…since I was in third grade and also, his college roommate," Von says without thinking.

"Are you out of your mind, young man? Mick is three months old. He can't even talk, let alone go to school!" the man yells and hangs up the phone.

The sound of the dial tone brings Von back to reality. He recognizes that in 1983, he wasn't even born yet. He was born in 1986. Mick was born in 1983 and took a few more years to graduate college. All of these facts make Von realize that his mother isn't even married in 1983.

CHAPTER SIXTEEN

SNAPSHOT OF A PROTEUS LIFE

The wind howls. Von sits in a large chair, looking at the raindrops forming on the large picture window that nearly covers the backside of the Roberts' house. He begins to daydream and reflect on his freshman year at college. Camilla, Ethan, Emma, and Nigel are all out of the house. Von is left alone and as he relaxes with his thoughts and memories the familiar images begin to come into focus.

Soon, his memory takes him back to the first day of school, and he remembers vividly the details of that first year of independence and freedom. He remembers how he drove his metallic green, two-seater Porsche convertible down College Street and often stopped at the Maizen Beach Diner for a cup of *mocha latte*. His mind conjures the tastes and smells of the simple pleasure. He remembers how his mom and dad would visit every three months or so on a weekend and take him for dinner. These were such important moments for the three of them to bond, affirming his passage from adolescence to adulthood.

Such moments were part of the tapestry of Von's life, but with them also came the flaws. Life seemed to be orchestrated as though everything he did was part of a bigger plan. He was the legacy, simply a small part of a long tradition. Indeed, there would be no displays of emotion, just brief acknowledgment of goals obtained along the predetermined path.

He had been to Stephenson College many times with his family since he was a small boy, but before he started going to school there, it was different. In those days he was a spectator. Later, as graduation neared, he realized that he knew that would be handed his family's proverbial baton and would be expected to become one of the "white male leaders" that this bastion had molded for centuries into one of the future CEOs of a successful enterprise.

However, there would be no rite-of-passage ceremony. His parents were far too busy and too stoic for that. His mother did a lot of traveling back then for the UN; she had become one of their senior linguists, so there was never any time for hand-holding or nurturing. Accomplishments in life are expected in the Carmichael family, and Von's success at Stephenson was no exception to the rule. It was as though it was nothing, and at the same time, it was everything.

He remembers that when he was three, he received a miniature Alaskan husky for an Easter present instead of a bunny. As a three-year-old boy, he was very disappointed that the dog was not the bunny of his dreams. He was told that the Easter bunny did not give boys rabbits. Rabbits, it was said, are weak and unable to protect themselves. Their purpose was better served in stew!

Von soon learned that Alaskan husky has special attributes that make him the ideal gift for a young boy. He was told that the dog, unlike the rabbit, possesses tenacity, leadership, and other qualities shared by the men of Stephenson College. There was no doubt that this place was essential to a young man's rite of passage in the Carmichael family. As a child, Von only knew it as a place that was boring, hot, and humid. His first memories are of being dragged to the soccer games. After each game, his father would walk him through the Captain's Room, where he would gaze at his name carved into the back of the wooden bench among other team captains, always implying that it was expected that one day Von would join him there. Those were the days before recruiting forever changed college sports. Von wonders if his father had been disappointed that he only played intramural sports. He wonders if somehow he had failed the long legacy of leadership in his family's Stephenson tradition.

Von remembers being told about how one of his ancestors, a fellow Stephenson alumnus of course, was so brave that the British failed to break his silence when they caught him and tortured him as a spy during the Revolutionary War. The story goes on to say that he carried his Stephenson College diploma in his shoe and used it to steel his resolve through the course of his imprisonment.

Von wonders why anyone would carry his Stephenson College diploma in his shoe, and how in the world thinking about it could have helped him. No doubt the story had evolved through the ages as it was passed down.

Still, Von knows in his soul that within him lies the same fiber from which his family cloth has been cut for so many generations. He wonders if this is why his father seemed to cling to the outdated traditions. Von ponders that maybe by being part of something grander than themselves, his ancestors became bigger than life.

When his parents reprimanded him and he believed it to be unjust, Von would think about how much he hoped that he had a spirit as strong as that of his famed ancestor. He used to wonder if he would ever get the opportunity to prove himself, if family history would record him as a hero. He secretly prayed that he would get the chance to do something valiant. Taking measure of the moment at hand Von wonders if the opportunity to fulfill his legacy is within his grasp.

I guess this is the time to prove to myself that I am strong and brave, he thinks. And if he accomplished something valiant in his life, would history ever record it?

Von drinks his tea while he reminisces about his past and his missing friend Mick. While he sits outside the Roberts' house, he begins to daydream about how he and Mick imagined a wireless world discovery: a type of wireless remote.

He remembers that Mick always suggested a gadget that would remotely chill their beer or keg. Von's idea was to invent something that could stimulate the brain so that people could get drunk and high more easily, thus saving money.

He remembers they both decided that it would be stupid to try it. It would cost a lot of money, and they would need collateral. They agreed to halt this invention of theirs.

One semester, they decided that they should invest each of their small savings accounts on a girl-watching "breast-o-meter." When they took their idea to a bank, they were declined by their respective trust officers on the grounds that they could not possibly take a loan for this silly product. They were disappointed, so they withdrew what was left in their checking accounts, bought three kegs, and partied all weekend.

While they were both drunk, sitting on top of the keg, they came up with another idea: virtual pizza delivery. The concept was pizza that would stimulate nerve endings, but no weight would be gained. It would be beamed through a fax machine. They discussed the idea with only one of the trust officers this time. They hadn't even finished discussing the whole business proposal when the trust officer excused himself and left.

That same day, on their way to the elevator after being declined for the second time, they rushed back to the trust officer and demanded to see the bank's vice president to discuss their latest idea – a virtual tennis machine. They were both proud of their idea, but after that conversation, they were banned from both of their trust officers. The trust officers suggested to their parents that the boys needed some psychological counseling.

Stupid as it is, Von now begins to dream about something he has recently discovered on a trip to wi-fi wonderland. He wishes Mick were around to share in this with him.

A few years ago, the simplest way for Von to get online when he was away from home or school was to visit an Internet café and get a broadband signal. Now, as he has found from his PDA, that the old providers such as GoWired are no longer the booming trade in giving users web and e-mail access.

The latest technology is called Openzone, which is an access point at locations such as offices, hotels, and public spaces. You can wirelessly connect to the Internet on the new Widelink better than the old broadband speeds. It says that everywhere you go, there is Internet access – even in a public washroom.

Outcrash, the nation's first 25G Openzone multimedia technology, delivers over the new high-speed Evolution-

Data Optimized network with the highest-quality digital media format.

The new cell phones have become the dominant way to access data. There is now a new hybrid of the original smartphones. The information he finds on his now obsolete PDA says that devices such as his BlackBerry are now as archaic as a ten-pound walkie-talkie in a World War II movie.

The mobile or wireless Internet has also disappeared, as Internet Protocol is now the new technology that delivers data by either pushing or pulling it to a user.

Isn't that what everyone wants and even college students are willing to pay for – access to information they actually want and that isn't arbitrarily selected for them by their service provider or handset manufacturer? Von had thought when he read this.

Before he disappeared, Von heard of two companies in the San Francisco area with these ideas. Those two companies took content off of databases and allowed users to set up filters against the content before it is then pushed to them according to their preferences. He thought about doing business with them but never got the chance.

Von thinks, *People who have this system can choose to update their profiles to access more information. All the complexities of subscribing to a service can be accessed simply over their video cell phone.*

There is a knock at the door. Von snaps back from his memories to his new reality and hurriedly goes downstairs to answer the door.

"Damn, those where the good old days with Mick. Goddammit! I miss my buddy!" he whispers to himself while walking towards the door.

CHAPTER SEVENTEEN

PANDORA'S BOX

V on opens the front door, but no one is there. He assumes it was the wind that he heard earlier. A bolt of lightning strikes outside the large pane of glass, and Von stiffens as he worries about Camilla driving in the rain. He watches a raindrop slide all the way down the window as others combine to make a cascade. Von watches the droplets gather as he walks back to the Roberts' library to get more boxes to put away in the attic.

He begins to tape the boxes per Nigel's instructions and notices a journal lying on the floor with small notes partially exposed tucked inside. As he picks it up, the notes scribbled in had fall out.

Innocently he notices the references to his mother and begins to read. To his shock he discovers that his mother's career as a linguist is actually just a cover. Through reading the notes, he discovers his mother was groomed at an early age by his uncle to be an assassin and is in fact a sleeper agent. He also finds out that his uncle, known to be a gentle, retired vineyard owner, is a mercenary, trading in weapons, drugs and military secrets. He is an internationally wanted criminal.

An old newspaper clipping fell out of the stack of files he was arranging in one of the boxes. Von picks it up and sees the lead story. The faded newspaper is dated 1979 and it begins:

> Wearing a black label Armani outfit and dark sunglasses, Nigel Robert does not look the image of a notorious illegal drug and arms dealer. He was caught for illegal drug trafficking and money laundering, and was sentenced to five years in prison. Authorities said that he was seen months later in South America. His attorney, Christopher James, claims that he hasn't heard from Mr. Robert since last year.
>
> Three years later Nigel Robert is living in Spain, still brokering small arms and anti-aircraft missile launchers. In August 1978, one of his known associates, Topper Newton, was interrogated by a French judge for his role in the sale of arms and other contraband. Mr. Newton's attorney insists to the court that the two men don't know each other at all.
>
> Four days later, Topper Newton was found shot dead in his rented home in *Azerbaijan*. Investigator ruled the death a suicide. They found fifteen express delivery packages containing encrypted documents. One decrypted message urgently requested a shipment of 1,500 rifles to Gabon, Africa. It reportedly used his code name, and signed off with: "Funds are wired upon acceptance of the terms." The document is signed with scribbled initials.

Fascinated and nauseated by the revelation, Von searches through each article in the box of clippings. As he reads one after another, painting a new sickening picture of the man he has always revered, he looks for flaws in the story that might offer some plausible explanation. But each one seems worse than the last. He finds another clip and reads on, try-ing to piece together the truth about his beloved uncle.

The next clipping seems to be different newsprint – per-haps a different newspaper. The header has been torn off, concealing its origin, but he can still read the faded text:

CHILE FIREARM SALES: (1979–1981)

Nigel Robert is noted to be one of the most pow-erful arms dealers in the world. Well-educated, he exudes charm, and it is said that he can communicate in ten languages. In 1980, Interpol issued an inter-national "red notice" for Mr. Robert, a high-priority request for his immediate arrest and extradition. For nearly three years, the Justice Department has devi-ated from standard extradition procedure, refusing to arrest Robert, fueling speculation about his involve-ment with government agencies.

The investigation shows that since January of 1979, Nigel Robert secretly shipped Arms by boat from Bolivia to Santiago with a final destination set for Colombia, according to the indictment. The government's report goes on to say that during four years of trafficking under this charge, Nigel Robert delivered shipments totaling 8500 tons in small arms via six K-B line shipments to radicals in Lebanon at a street U.S. value of $80 million.

Under separate indictment, Nigel Robert is ac-cused of brokering the sale of more than 90 tons of rifles and ammunition to Ecuadorian rebels. Nigel Robert's case also involves a matrix of arms sales, corruption scandalss and terrorist bombings that have helped destabilize Chile in recent years. It was Chile's ongoing investigations into those events that led to Interpol's heightened red notice status for Mr. Robert.

Von can not believe that his uncle is an illegal arms dealer capable of heinous crimes against humanity. He learns that his uncle's business was conducted in the U.S through a number of corporate shells, some of which were owned and controlled by other family members. Now, Von has to wonder if his mother was involved as well. He is now incredulous. This is the uncle who taught him about the value of honesty, morals, and money. What's wrong with this picture? Could this be a wrong Nigel Robert?

He sits on the floor and reads through the stock of newspaper clippings, looking for a clue in desperate hopes of vindicating his family. Some of the clippings even have photographs of Nigel getting out of a car with his attorneys. Von feels like his world has collapsed. He pauses for a while and can't believe in his wildest dreams that this uncle who taught him so much about the world is truly a Jekyll-and-Hyde personality. He wishes he had never opened the box, and never learned that his life was a lie.

He doesn't know how to react to the family's underworld ties that expose a world of blackmail, murder, torture, and vendetta that challenges everything he knows to be true about his life. Then, he stumbles upon the clue he did not want to find in his mother's desk drawer. It reads: "Partnership: my brain, your expertise…" Von's search for the truth reveals a plot orchestrated by his uncle to kill an important European couple. He learns that his mother is somehow involved. While he searches through the desk, he sees the glasses Emma was wearing at the funeral. He goes to move them so that he can get at the rest of the notes, and suddenly the eyeglasses cast a light from the edge of the rim near the temple. It seems as though they transmit pictures into some kind of database with an inscription of none other than his uncle's initials.

"What the heck is this? What's with the glasses? Why does she need this? Is she some kind of spy?" Von whispers to himself. He rifles through all of the documents on the desk, in addition to the boxes that are to be stored in the attic, and he finds even more damning information about his mother and his uncle. He discovers what seems to be the business card of a dance instructor attached to a sticky note that reads: "Tango Instructor 'mole' of an underground secret operation. Emma's dance schedule will handle it."

"What? What's this?" Von asks himself; then a vinyl 45 rpm record "Por Una Cabeza" by Carlos Gardel caught Von's eye.

"Carlos Gardel? the King of Tango. Mom can't dance the tango. She has two left feet," Von says to himself. How can this be possible?

He tries to put everything back in its place, just as he found it. He needs time to process the information before approaching his family with his discovery. As he straightens the piles he finds another file implicating his mother in espionage that took place on June 7, 1981.

A Middle East jet aircraft accidentally bombed and destroyed a military barracks and weapons stockade in Kabul. Among the dozens declared missing was a former Mossad agent Rashid Majadin Azam. He was apparently working on a covert job with Von's mother, and abruptly vanished. No one knew where he went. Von wonders about his connection to the espionage and terrorism. There is a note attached to the file written in his mother's handwriting that reads: "The Cleaner was sent. Order was followed. The collision looks just like an accident. Collateral damage was unavoidable. An innocent little girl…" It is unsigned.

Von feels the hair all over his body stand straight up. He finds pictures of his mother and notes describing a failed murder attempt. An envelope shows that she was ordered to murder a man named Gus De La Serna, who was convicted in April 1981 of soliciting an undercover agent to kill Nigel. In the same file, Von uncovers papers suggesting that his mom attempted to assassinate a senator who had authorized an attempted execution of his grandfather. A newspaper clipping says that four bodies were found in a pool of blood in the Senate chamber very early on the morning of June 20, 1980, and a source said the victims were the senator's aides, secretaries, and other office staff. Apparently the Senator escaped and survived. Von is sick to his stomach thinking about his mother's secret life.

A handwritten note attached to the article Von recognizes as his mother's reads: "Please dispose of my things that were left behind in 'Tel Aviv'…" The note was unsigned.

"Holy crap…That's it. I don't want to know anything more than I already do," he whispers to himself in disbelief.

He is so upset that he pushes everything aside in a heap and leaves the attic. He cannot swallow the reality he has uncovered and decides that he must sit down with Nigel and tell him what he knows.

"I need to speak to either one of them. I don't care if they decide to put me away after I reveal that I am their future nephew and son. I need to hear the truth. I need to tell somebody, or I'll get myself to the loony bin."

As he moves one last box that is sealed with plastic wrap, a marked label catches his attention.

It reads: "Oliver Robert's confidential file." A note taped to it says: "To be incinerated." Again, Von's inquiring mind tugs at him to open the box. His mind is also out of control, imagining now that his friend who is actually his grandfather is also involved. Fearing the worst he is driven by his desire to find the truth to open the box. He hesitates for a moment to weigh the decision, then takes out that pocket knife that Camilla gave him and runs the blade cleanly down the seam.

Inside the box the old manila folders contain documents dating from the '50s and '60s. Von sits down on the floor and goes through each folder, absorbing every page. In one of the binders, notes handwritten by Sir Oliver detail its contents. They are files with several pages consisting of CIA files pertaining to a Soviet military intelligence officer and double-agent Colonel Boris Poriskova.

"What is this? Who is this dude? Who the heck is Boris Poriskova?" he asks himself.

The documents explain that Poriskova was the highest-level Soviet officer to ever spy for the United States and British Intelligence. The papers detail how Poriskova was observed by KGB agents after a meeting with British intelligence leading to his arrest, embarrassment to his community, and execution of his family.

Von reads through it learning how this Poriskova was involved with espionage, but when Von turns to the next page, he finds that the rest of it is gone.

"Where is the rest of this?" He slowly searches for it, piece by piece and realizes that maybe his grandfather took part of the files and was not able to put it back in the folder. It means that somehow, somewhere, there is a box with explanations about this cover-up operation…and his grandfather's real life.

"But where could it be?" Von asks himself, remembering the strange circumstances of his grandfather's death. Von's imagination runs with it: "Damn it to hell! Does this means that Grandpa was involved with a Russian spy? Why wasn't I informed about this? Was he killed by a double-agent?" Finishing the document, Von sets it aside and reaches for the next folder, excited to see what new revelations it might contain. A memorandum is on top of the next folder in the same box, and it reads:

CENTRAL INTELLIGENCE AGENCY
UNITED STATES OF AMERICA
WASHINGTON, D.C.

MEMORANDUM
TO: Director, Central Intelligence Agency
FROM: Joseph Kudrow
DATE: December 12, 1951
SUBJECT: Nuclear Preparedness;
By James D. Cooper

The enclosed article is for your review. It appears that the journal for Strategies *TOP SECRET* was acquired by our military assets within the KGB. However, its authenticity has been verified beyond doubt.

It is in our national interest that the source's identity remain confidential and further, that this material is to be handled as classified within your office. A request for duplicate copies of this report or any part of these documents is to be submitted only to me in writing.
Signed
Joseph Kudrow

Von is shaking with excitement as he finishes reading the memo. He can't believe what he has just read. He pauses for a while as he thinks, *Is my whole life a lie? Is my whole family legacy a cover-up? Is there truth to any to the reality I knew growing up? What were my mother's true intentions about pursuing the vendetta I has unraveled? Did she act on them?*

Von is certain that he needs to stop uncovering the past and move on. He has more than enough to process. Where to begin? How all this mess started from his time-travel... Right now, he just wants to go home and be with his friends and family in his own time and era. He knows he needs to hear it from the source. He needs to go back to his own time to confront his mother with the facts.

Before he can finish the task of moving the boxes into storage, the light begins to fade. He gets up from where he is sitting, looks at his watch, and realizes he has lost track of the time and has spent the entire day on a chore that was to have taken a couple hours. He tries to move a large box on top of the others as he stumbles and falls, rushing to put away the last file, and a piece of folded paper drops on the floor next to his foot.

"Oh, no, not again. Not another espionage memo." He picks it up and sees what seems to be another memo. Without thinking, he reads:

CENTRAL INTELLIGENCE AGENCY
UNITED STATES OF AMERICA
WASHINGTON, D.C.

MEMORANDUM
TO: Chief, Eastern European Division, C.I.A.
From: Oliver Robert
Date: May 10, 1953
SUBJECT: BORIS PORISKOVA

Regarding the discussion of May 7, I need your recommendations on the plan intended to accomplish the following goals:

Safeguarding the life of our most valuable asset, Boris Poriskova.

Reinforcing our organizational covert structures within the KGB & GRU; i.e., coordinating the effort within a spy network to protect our assets while demonstrating to our team that we are willing to make the necessary commitment to be successful.

Determining the workable plan for Poriskova's defection, this is to include compensation proportionate to his worth and to serve the dual purpose of sending the appropriate signal to his team members to up the morale.

Thank you for your urgent attention in this matter. As always, I am determined to see the mission to a very successful conclusion, and I await your decision.

Yours truly,

Oliver Robert

Von can't believe what he's seeing. "Goddammit! What is going on? Was Grandpa really involved with the CIA and some kind of a covert operation? Too bad I didn't have time to really get to know him. No wonder he helped me and understood my crazy situation," Von says to himself. "There goes one agent in the family I never thought I'd meet."

He begins to feel the slightest bit of sweat forming on his palms. "Von, get a grip," he says to himself.

He hears another knock at the door. He hurriedly goes to the door, and the lightning and rain grow stronger. Von closes all the shades and turns on the lights as it starts to get dark outside. Then, the power is gone.

"Damn! This is a bad storm. I hope Ethan and Camilla get home soon. This is not good driving weather," he says as he goes to the kitchen to look for a flashlight or candles. Finding neither he ends up sitting in the dark until a loud clap of thunder is followed by a blinding blue and white bolt of lightning. Von thinks to himself: "this one was much closer than the previous strikes." He can feel the electricity in the air, and hopes Ethan and Camilla are safe.

He sees through the window that Camilla accidentally left one of her cashmere sweaters outside earlier in the day, so he runs to get it. As he reaches for the sweater, a bolt of lightning strikes the chair a few feet away from him. He dives onto the ground, hitting his head on the corner of the door. As he crumples unconscious to the ground another bolt of lightning hits the neighboring house, killing the power to both houses.

Camilla and Ethan return and find the garage completely dark. The front door to the main house is wide open. Ethan runs to the main house to check things out, but he can't find Von. The power returns, so Camilla and Ethan go upstairs in the main house and find the attic door open. They climb up, but Von is nowhere to be found.

"Mom, where do you think he could be?" Ethan asks Camilla, looking at the boxes and the big mess that was left on the attic floor.

"He must have gone to Jenny's house for dinner," Camilla responds and shuts off some of the lights.

CHAPTER EIGHTEEN

CRUEL REALTY

V on is thrown about twenty feet away from the
Roberts' house when the lightning hits the ground.
However, as he lies there, he can't take his mind off
of the secrets he has discovered. He decides that he needs
to confront everyone, but he's not sure if he should confront
Nigel Robert, his future uncle, or call his real mother in the
future and give her a piece of his mind about her secrets.

He tries to think of how he can reach his parents. He
uses his cell phone to call his parents' house. While dialing,
he hopes that his parents still have their old phone number.

"Hello? Hello?" Von says as he hears someone pick up on
the other end of the line.

"Yes, hello?" the voice responds.

"Mom? Hello, Mom, can you hear me? It's Von. How
are you, Mom? Sorry I haven't called in a while, but I wanted you to know that I am stuck in some kind of time-travel.
I don't know how it happened, but it did. Mom, before you
say anything, I'm so angry because on top of this time-traveling, I had to find out that everything about our family is

a lie. I never had the slightest idea that you were a sleeper agent and grandpa was a spy!" Von blurts out in one breath.

"Hello? Who are you, and what do you want from me?" Von's mother replies. She hears the voice that sounds like Von, but she can't believe what she's hearing.

"Mom, it's me, Von. If you don't believe me, ask me something that only you and I know."

"Please, please, I beg you to stop calling here. I don't know who you are, but this doesn't make sense. My only son has been declared legally dead for almost forty years," his mother replies.

"Mom, really, it's me. How can I be dead when I'm right here talking to you? Mom, Mom, wait a minute. I haven't called you in a week…not forty years. Has it really been that long for you, Mom?" he asks.

She doesn't respond. She still believes that the U.S. government knows that she was a sleeper agent and took Von as punishment. She still thinks that the government continues to watch her and that the voice on the phone is simulated to seem like Von to entrap her. She is guarded in her remarks.

"Please, sir, I don't know who you are, but I beg of you… please stop harassing me…*please*," she pleads.

She cannot explain that she was recruited as a teen when her father survived being gunned down and that she believes the government had her father killed later on. She cannot explain to this person on the other end of the line how her heart still aches for her father's death and the accidental death of an innocent little girl in *Kabul* in 1981. An accident she will never forgive herself for and will never forget. She tried to save the girl playing near the explosives, and was too late to get her out of before the bomb exploded.

She pleads with the man on the other line not to torment her with her greatest pain and greatest loss...that of her only child, Von, who disappeared forty years ago.

Von realizes that he cannot change her perception regardless of what he says, even if he tells her the name of his childhood teddy bear or a nickname only the two of them know, as these would only convince her that the government has watched her every move.

She justifies the few hits that she did complete as a sleeper agent when she was young, including a Middle East murder that was never solved, by the fact that history proved that the people she murdered were not good people.

"Please don't ever call here again," her voice quivers as she begs for the last time and hangs up the phone. Von can hear her sobs before she puts down the receiver, and he can't bear to hear his mother's heart break. He decides that he will not put her through this again and that since he can't to talk to Mick or his mother, he needs to call Bessie. He knows that Bessie will understand him.

As soon as Von's mother hangs up the phone, she calls to her husband from the next room of the house and asks him to sit with her in the living room. She has decided to tell him the truth about her past. She knows that it will be hard for her to explain everything and that it's going to be a test of her husband's love.

It takes several hours for her to explain her previous life. Von's dad has a difficult time digesting what he has just heard. He cannot believe that the woman he's been with for more than forty years was a traitor to their country and lost his only son because of this.

After Von's mother is done with her explanation, his father hugs her, gets up, and tells her that he needs to go to bed and rest. She nods and quietly moves to their family room. She slumps into her favorite lounge chair and cries. She wonders if her husband will still feel the same about her now that she has confessed her past, and she wonders if she will one day find out what really happened to her only son who disappeared forty years ago.

Back at the Roberts' house, Von tries to call Bessie's old cell phone. His first attempt is not successful. He sits down in a small chair next to the Roberts' garden while he reminisces about his past with Bessie.

In the meantime, also in the future, Bessie locks the door to the place she works. She drives her small, slightly rusted car slowly back home, knowing everything that will occur for the rest of the evening since each day of her life for over forty years has been the same. And she never has gotten into the new flying cars.

She knows that her cats will be there to greet her: the only thin remnant of a love she barely can remember. She counts the time since Von disappeared not in months or years but rather by generations of their cats' propagation. It has been five generations of cats, but mysteriously, all have chosen to take their naps on top of the ancient telephone which she charges in vain, hoping for the call which she has sadly accepted will never come.

She knows that the phone can no longer be replaced, since she has tried more than six years ago to get a new one and conducted a national search for a reconditioned one...all to no avail. The phone does not have the proper replacements that are necessary to change to a new telephone number with an additional three digits to accommodate the new "multi-flexing phase in technology."

Bessie has tried not to think about the fact that one day the phone will be dead, and there will be nothing she can do. She nonetheless has tried over and over again to move the phone to locations where the cats would not be able to sleep on it, but they always seem to find a way to do so, as though it is part of their genetic legacy to wait for Von as she has.

She lands her vehicle in her driveway and walks up the stairs. She unlocks the door, greets her cat, and stares at it.

"Why do you need to take naps on top of the cell phone, huh?" she endearingly scolds. The cat just looks at Bessie and rolls over with his feet stretching out and up in the air waiting for his stomach to be rubbed. Bessie appeases him, and the cat returns to his nap.

Bessie puts on a pot of tea and again scolds the cat for sitting on the phone. She picks him up lovingly, talking sweetly. As she goes to nuzzle her nose against her cat's, the phone rings. The cat startles because it is *his* phone, scratches Bessie, hisses, and knocks over the phone. She hesitates, amazed that this old phone with its obsolete technology was ringing, then picks it up slowly placing it to her ears and for a second she hears Von's voice. The line disconnects immediately after the two get a glimmer of each other's voices. Her heart pounds, and she is frozen with disbelief.

"Hello? Hello?" she shouts, even though there is no longer a connection. She knows that voice in her heart. She sobs and wonders if she is losing her mind or if it really did happen. Did the phone really ring, or did it just break? She wonders if it was really Von's voice, but there is nothing she can do…The link is broken.

Frustrated and disappointed about the calls to Bessie and his mother, Von decides to call Mick's cell phone number one more time. He wants to find out more information on Mick's whereabouts. Without even finishing to dial Mick's old cell phone number, he is immediately thrown back into the unknown darkness. He closes his eyes and wonders what is next for him.

CHAPTER NINETEEN

UNRECRUITED

V on awakens in a daze outside the Roberts' house. His head aches and he wishes Sir Oliver or Mick were there to help him. He decides to search for his best friend. He has been completely cut off from all contact with him since his wireless device became obsolete. Mick is the only person with whom he can share what he has found out about his family. Somehow, Von continues to travel forward in time.

The last time he called Mick's cell phone was Woodstock. Whoever answered the phone said that even though the military draft for Vietnam ended in 1973, Congress reactivated it in the spring of 2010 when war broke out with North Korea, and Mick's number was called. The best *intel* was that evidently Mick was still alive as a POW in North Korea. Von also learned that China sided with North Korea under this nuclear weapon threat.

He remembers that the man said the military didn't declare Mick dead but "missing in action." Determined to change history and rescue his friend, Von searches for clues on how to reconnect with Mick. He knows that every time he has dialed Mick's old cell phone number, it triggers the mechanism that transports him to another time, so he decides to try it one more time.

Soon after he dials Mick's number, everything begins to spin around him. A familiar darkness surrounds him now. He closes his eyes and feels that sense of being out-of-body once again. Von knows he is being transported to another time – just when and where are beyond his grasp – as he drifts off into a sleep-like state.

Still surrounded by darkness as he regains consciousness, Von hears the thunderous pounding of what seems like artillery. As the darkness lifts from his eyes and Von returns to the conscious world, he senses that somehow he is on the right track and that Mick is near. Missiles roar overhead. The power of the Sm-3 missiles is astonishing; even at a distance, vibrations rattle through Von's body, the force of the fiery rocket blows against his face and leaves his ears ringing, as it fades into the distant sky.

Looking from a hill almost a mile inland, he sees the brilliant flash of light as the Airborne Laser (ABL) weapons shoot down enemy ballistic missiles. The airborne laser is attached to a huge Boeing 747-400F freighter with an ABL system. It is so powerful it seems to command the sky.

Von can see what looks like a Humvee sitting alone on the far side of the exposed hill. The three soldiers hunkered down by the vehicle are the only sign of life in this surreal, battle-torn countryside. He wonders if they are part of the Predator Unmanned Aerial System.

Then he hears a violent explosion. The loud blast must have woken the dead. The smell of burning flesh and jet fuel wafts over the airfield.

Von watches men who seem to be guarding a rough landing strip just to the south. Von thinks, *How could any plane land on that rutted surface?* Then he realizes it isn't for a plane. It's for Predator Unmanned Aerial Vehicles (UAV), which are equipped with reconnaissance equipment and Hellfire missiles. Von wonders if these drones are being controlled from the safety of a US base, far from the realty of war.

Amazed by his *futuristic* sorroundings, he recognizes what vaguely seems to be another Humvee.

Is that a Humvee? It looks like a Volkswagen Touareg but bigger and wider. Von thinks to himself, shaking his head, *Touareg, I don't think so! Whatever happened to the Humvee?* Von wonders if this version is any better at keeping its occupants safe or if they just don't make them anymore.

Then he realizes there are hundreds of legless, soft-bodied, wormlike larvae swarming through the pile of body parts around him. His head begins to swirl and before he can regain his equilibrium he starts to vomit convulsively, uncontrollably. Two unshaven soldiers in torn uniforms begin to move the body parts irreverently off to the side.

"Okay, let's go! Move, move, move!" a nasty-looking sergeant shouts. The new recruit's eyes are glued to the body parts being pushed aside. The blank expression of the men as they carry some kind of a large bag tells of the horror to come. Von approaches the men, hoping to find out more information about Mick's status.

Without warning, little canisters, submunition grenades, which are smaller explosive charges packed inside cluster bombs, drop from an unknown source. They are roughly the size and shape of a soft-drink can and explode on impact spraying the area around Von with deadly shrapnel. The next thing he can remember is the sky raining pieces of body parts down onto Von and everyone in the area who is still alive. The others do their best to stare straight ahead, but the carnage overwhelms them, and several soldiers break, falling to their knees, losing what little food they still had in their stomachs onto the bloody ground.

An officer smiles with reassuring confidence. "Well, sorry 'bout that, boys. This is North Korea, twenty-first-century nuke war," he says without showing any concern for the chaos around him. "That's the closest thing to a hot shower you're going to get for some time!"

"Do you think they'll nuke us?" a young recruit asks one of the grizzled unshaven men, as he wipes the vomit from the side of his mouth.

"Heck, no! I doubt it. Don't you see their own soldiers are all over? That would be like running the football into your own end zone! From what I've seen so far, that's the least of our problems."

Damn, I can't believe I'm in North Korea. How can the U.S. possibly be involved in this darn twenty-first-century North Korean Nuclear war? Thank God, I've made it. He peeks out of the bushes again, hoping to see Mick, but he then realizes Mick is one of the hundreds of POWs all over this province.

He senses that he needs to get to Mick fast, or he might be too late to save him. But how does he find him in this hell-hole? He sees a full duffel bag on the ground, slowly moves toward it, and searches inside. He finds some military clothes, and without even checking the size, he hurriedly puts them on. Von walks slowly toward the rest of the men in the company, hoping that in all the confusion, he can go unnoticed.

"Hey, where'd you come from? Where's your dog tag?" one recruit asks as he looks at Von's feet. "Have you lost your mind? You're not walking around without combat boots, are ya, man?"

"Ohh, um...I don't know what happened to my shoes. Too nervous, man. I must have lost them when we got off the plane," Von attempts an awkward lie.

"Don't let Sergeant see you like this, or you're in a hell of a lot of trouble...should be a Section 8. By the way, my name is Carl. I'm from Alabama. What about you, man?"

"Von, My name is Von, and I'm from Florida," he replies as they walk with the rest of the guys.

"Carl, what do you do around here?" Von asks.

"I'm a technical field specialist for the 101 Airborne Division."

"What's a technical field, dude?"

"My job is to guide intelligence gathering mobile drones over enemy territory. We can launch a drone from the back of a jeep sending fifty miles into enemy zones. We do detail aerial surveillance 24/7."

"Cool. How does it work?"

"Mobility is the key. Our unit can move out on a moment's notice. We can set up and launch a drone in less than ten minutes. By the time the enemy knows they're being watched, assuming they even do spot us, we can relocate and approach from a different flank. It's seamless and almost impossible to defend against."

Von looks back and is disturbed, feeling as if this young man is somehow not real, like he's a ghost. Von falls into rank and file with the stolen duffel bag slung on his shoulder and looks up at the sun burning rays in his face through the smoke-filled arena of body parts.

He marches with the recruits for more than an hour, heading for what he is told are enemy lines. He starts to feel sharp pains stabbing into his feet from a hard object. He glances down at his feet and is repulsed by the site of his own raw, bleeding sores. Struggling to maintain, he cannot let anyone see that he is losing it. Von slashes through the brush with total disregard for any enemy for traps. Suddenly, his nostrils spasm, repulsed by an unknown odor. He can feel himself start to gag. He knows instinctively that this is not right; he comes upon more body parts all over: the source of the foul smell. The lifeless bodies cover the ground. He can't stand the carnage strewn everywhere and the smell clings to his clothes like a damp bloody rag. Von gasps, horrified at the unholy sight. Someone appears from behind him.

"Move out, better you get this out of your system now than in the midst of a fire fight. These dead body parts shouldn't scare you boys half as much as the live ones," the officer screams with a sarcastic chuckle at Von's expense.

The soldier barking orders at Von has long since gone numb to death. Over the officer's radio, Von hears command: "Wild Tango, Wild Tango. What's the freakin' delay up there? Move it out on point. We're taking incoming missiles. We need to check out what's in front of us, over."

"Who was that?" Von asks.

"That's Lieutenant. He's nasty, and has this intense look like an animal on the prowl."

"Delta four, move it out. Zulu says to get that other new guy up here, *pronto*, over," Lieutenant Smith says over the radio.

"Which one, Lieutenant?" a man asks.

"The one who's slowing us down. I heard the kid's barefoot? Does he think his sunbathing in *Hawaii*? What the heck is he doing barefoot, waiting for his *pina colada*? Tell him to move it, on the double! He's supposed to be wearing his boots. Is he out of his freakin' mind? Working a Section

8, is he?" the Lieutenant yells. "I'll give him a real reason to go nuts!"

"Hey, *Barefoot*, keep moving, and get ready to meet the Lieutenant. He wants to see you now," the gruff officer shouts at Von.

"Yes, sir!" Von replies. As he surveys his surroundings, he sees that his squad is mostly full of tough, well-trained, twenty-year-olds; all are trying to block out the fear and hell around them…and just stay alive.

"Ain't war hell?" Von hears, as a skinny new recruit fires his IMI Tavor 2 machine gun.

As Von and his new friend Carl pick up their pace, Von becomes irritated at the officer's rebukes, but he can't let on that he is the only soldier who has no training, no business being there. He is soaked now from head to foot in sweat, and he is dizzy, feeling sick, about to vomit, just barely hanging on.

A medic comes over with Sergeant George, and in a calm manner, he asks, "Are you okay?"

"I think I'm okay," Von replies shakily.

"You look sick, man." The squad sergeant takes inventory of Von's duffel bag: grenade, gas mask, extra clothing, blankets, canned goods, sleeping bag, and books.

"Why are you carrying all this shit? You're carrying way too much. You brought the whole freaking *surplus store*, boy. You need to lighten up." The middle-aged sergeant shakes his head, amused; Von nods, out of breath. *He can't tell the sergeant that everything in the bag is not his*; he can't tell anybody that *he stole the bag* and *he isn't really a recruit*. Von realizes men pass, watching them. He feels terrible about this, as he was trying to keep up to the pace, and does not want to put the others in danger.

"You're really sick." Someone giving Von a hard time. Von tries to stand for a moment, fighting for his breath, and then he passes out, falling over with his 70-pound bag and hitting the ground unconscious with a loud thud.

"What in the hell…Hold it," Sergeant Raker screams, concerned. "He doesn't seem okay." "Goddammit! Move him to the side; he's probably dehydrated from carrying the whole freaking surplus store in his duffel bag!" They move quickly to help Von lie down on the ground next to the casualties. He moves his MK-47 advanced lightweight grenade launcher on the ground and yells.

"Damn it! His gaddam *surplus bag* is heavier than my 85-pound grenade launcher! Medic, Medic, keep us posted on his condition. Better off radioing the dispatch later," the Sergeant yells and instructs a young medic to move Von to the side of the field.

An hour later, Von wakes up on a cot still a bit dazed and dehydrated. He notices the military cot next to him. He rolls onto his side to get comfortable when a wounded soldier lying next to him asks Von to scratch his foot.

"Please, please, would you mind scratching my foot?" the guy asks.

"No problem…" Von raises the blanket that is covering the soldier only to discover that the soldier's leg has been amputated.

"Ahh!" Von is shocked, but since he doesn't want the soldier to see his reaction, he scratches the mattress instead.

"What the hell are you doing? I asked you a favor to scratch my foot. Why aren't you scratching it?" I can't feel it," the wounded soldier shouts. Obviously, the nerves are still sensitive, even though the limb itself has been amputated. The soldier has forgotten that he no longer has a leg.

"Sorry, I don't feel well myself. I need to lie down again. Would you mind?" Von lies. He would rather have somebody else tell the young wounded soldier that he no longer has a leg.

A medic approaches to check on Von, but Von tries to get up to show he is ready to move out with the men. He knows that to stay in one place behind the fight will put him at risk of being discovered.

"I'm okay, I'm okay now," he says, hurriedly following the medic to get the rest of his belongings, and nearly falling backwards again. Sergeant Raker helps him to get steady with his MK-47 on his shoulder before heading out. Fighting the urge to lie back down Von reminds himself of just why he is there, and how bad it must be for Mick.

I should ask anyone if they know Mick. "Sergeant, would you know of a soldier by the name of Mick? Mick Chevalier?" he asks Sergeant Elijah.

"Sorry, too many young men coming and going out here. Don't recall that one," the Sergeant replies. "Who is he?"

"An old friend, that's all," Von says.

As they walk, Sergeant George walks behind Von and shaking his head at Von's bare feet.

"I heard you asking for Mick Chevalier. You're a friend of his, I suppose?" he asks.

"Yes, do you know him, Sergeant George?"

"I know him, but it was a few years ago. I don't know where he is now. Last I heard, his company was captured on Hill 581." The Sergeant points to a hill nearby. "I haven't heard anything other than that. Some of them were taken to Panmun-gak, the headquarters of the North Korean Security Forces. Word is they torture their prisoners, but I'm not sure."

"Tortured?" Von asks.

"Yes, it usually happens when you get captured. The bastards don't give a shit about the Geneva Convention until they get captured. They do it to all POWs. I think they do the same all over Han'guk. Hey, you look pale," the Sergeant says.

"I'm okay, really I'm okay. What's Han'guk, Sergeant?" Von replies while thinking about Mick suffering in some rat-hole prison. Von feels helpless but is determined to help Mick. But he doesn't even have combat shoes much less the training to use a weapon big enough to do the job.

"It's slang for the North Korean country," the Sergeant smiles wryly.

"Sir, I've got command on line, they want you on the radio, sir," the man tells the Sergeant.

"Maybe this *nuke* shit is over," Von says, just as a mortar shell digs in to the hillside next to them without exploding, allowing them time to hit the dirt. After a few seconds, it explodes, sending debris and mud into the air. The Sergeant and Von rise, spitting out sludge but thankful for the near miss. The Sergeant looks dubiously at Von, wondering how the next batch of recruits could be any greener than the last.

"Keep your heads down, and cover me."

"Yes, sir," the man answers while the Sergeant talks over the radio.

"Okay, sir." I'll do my best and I'll bring this young man with me. His name, sir?

The Sergeant searches for Von's dog tag but can't see it. "What is your name young man, and where is your dog tag?"

"Von Muir Carmichael, sir."

"Colonel, his name is Von Muir Carmichael," the Sergeant repeats.

"Sergeant, I can't hear you. You don't have his name on your list of new recruits?"

"I don't understand. I'm looking at my list, and I don't have him either. It must be an error, Colonel," the Sergeant replies. "I'll include his name on my list, and you do the same. I'll investigate later on whoever released the list."

The Sergeant looks at Von and shakes his head. He walks to a dead soldier's body, removes his combat boots, and hands them to Von.

"Here, these look like they're your size. Goddammit, would you put them on, and that's an order," the Sergeant yells. "You're coming with me!"

Von puts on the boots that are still warm and bloody from the freshly slain soldier. He feels sick as he senses the wetness and thinks of the soldier's last moments fighting for life, but doesn't hesitate as he knows he needs them to survive.

"Sergeant, where are we going?" Von asks, as he looks around and sees a *non-line-of-sight-mortar*.

"I'll fill you in later. Right now, we are need-to-know only," the Sergeant replies.

"Sergeant, what is a *non-light-of-sight-mortar?* Von asks the Sergeant curiously.

"Soldier! Haven't you learned anything on your training? The mortar system and mortar platoon are designed to be flexible and agile in establishing sensor-shooter linkages. Its performance in all weather conditions at extended ranges is the critical advantage." The sergeant shakes his head, thinking that Von is not a good candidate for this mission.

"Sergeant, would you mind briefing me on the system. I am so nervous, that I must have forgotten exactly what it does." Von lies to the sergeant just to keep in engaged in conversation.

"Toughen up, Carmichael. May I remind you that this system supports the Modular Force Combined Arms Battalion maneuver units, you know...the CABs." The sergeant is annoyed that this soldier is unfamiliar with critical technology.

Von follows the Sergeant deeper into enemy territory. The Koreans are on the ridge above them in defensive positions. Von and the Sergeant struggle to hide in the woods below. The men behind them fire over their heads to give them cover. Grenades hurl above them and explode, raining shrapnel all over their position.

"Fall back!" the Sergeant yells. Von takes position behind the squad, as the boys return fire into the enemy's line. The explosions and a mortar round land in the distance.

"Get ready, Carmichael, you are coming with me. We need to climb later up to the *Bell 417* chopper. They are going to drop us at Panmunjeon village," the Sergeant yells over the noise.

"What's *Bell 417*, Sergeant?" Von asks.

"Damn it, soldier...Why the hell are you asking this now in the middle of battlefield? Don't you know, it's the new high tech chopper with modern *Chelton 'glass cockpit'* and new Honeywell HTS900 turbine engine delivering more than 970 SHP. Soldier...I swear, I'm sending you back to *boot camp* if you ever survive this mission...

"Sorry...Sarge...but...would you mind telling me, what's at the Panmunjeon village, Sergeant?" Von asks nervously.

"You'll find out," the Sergeant replies, a bit annoyed and with an ominous smile.

"A bro in intelligence says 'Korean' might try to pull off something big. They think it's a search-and-destroy mission." Von hears a soldier talking to the Sergeant.

Von and the Sergeant climb up to the chopper; the other boys blaze their MK-47 grenade launcher and Tavor 2 machine guns at the North Korean troops.

Once both men are settled into their harnesses on board the chopper, Von tries again to get an answer.

"Sergeant, what are we doing? Are we on a rescue mission?" Von asks. He hopes that he may be closer to finding his friend. Taking turns, the boys continued to fire up at the North Koreans to protect the chopper.

"No, but we *are* on a special mission," the Sergeant replies.

"May I ask what mission, sir?"

"We are going to the North Korean headquarters to get intel for the Colonel, and do a little search-and-destroy ourselves."

"Sir, why did you choose me for this mission? I don't belong to the special forces, sir," Von says.

"Let's just say you volunteered. Any man who is crazy enough to go into battle *barefoot* needs to be on this mission! You're a lucky one, boy!"

"Don't you think this is a suicide mission, Sergeant?" Von asks.

"Carmichael, when you're in a war, watching the sun come up is a suicide mission!" the Sergeant says, attempting a joke. Von sits in the corner of the chopper and wonders why he's in this situation.

When I imagined future military technology, I didn't conceive of some *giant* bipedal walking robots with individual human-like hand and fingers just like those machines out there. I expected more of stealth technology, intelligent drones, highly sophisticated intelligence gathering spider drones, clones, machines, Von thinks to himself.

The chopper makes a quick series of turns, and the pilot informs the Sergeant that they are ready to do the drop. Von and the Sergeant both jump with their parachutes. Von feels queasy with his parachute on, worried that he has not secured the straps. Finally, they both jump and land hard moments after the chutes open. They work quickly to hide their chutes and disguise themselves with underbrush. Quietly in the darkness, they take up positions to survey the perimeter security. The Sergeant decides that they are ready to make their play at the weakest point of the fence. *So far so good*, Von thinks to himself as they penetrate the barbed wire lines. Von is nervous and agitated. This not what he came to do. He'll be lucky to get out alive himself, if he stays with this Rambo-wanna-be.

They both realize that the Korean main gate of the base is high-tech security fencing. Their own *Precision Guided Mortar Munitions* are everywhere. While Von and the Sergeant hide, a Korean military helicopter lands.

Von looks around and sees his worst fear. The bodies of scores of men lay tangled, their shattered, stiff corpses covering one another. Could Mick be here? He pauses, thinking of the horrors his friend must have endured. The firing is almost constant. It seems to be coming from all sides.

They run as fast as they can across the open field with total abandon until Von falls. The Sergeant yanks Von's arms up and half-drags him to the edge of the field. They make it to the trees and keep running through the bushes and brambles for about thirty yards.

The sniper keeps firing. Von fires blindly, wildly, at every corner, doors and windows in the direction of the shot like a *wild banshee.*

Then, abruptly, the firing stops. Both the Sergeant and Von are struggling to catch their breath. They check their bodies, taking inventory and looking for signs of blood. They have their weapons and most of their gear, so they keep going deeper into the dark woods.

"Okay, here we are. We need to go inside and get the *micro chip*. It's in a metal vault with sensors around it," the Sergeant says.

"What are we here for, Sergeant?"

"These *bastards* took our prototype *Navstar GPS Block IIIF* satellite *micro chip*, known as *SV-2*.

"What? How the heck are we going to get it, Sergeant? I don't have a clue how to disassemble those sensors," Von blurts.

"Listen, boy, we are going to get this mission done no matter what happens, so stay on top of this, do you hear me?" the Sergeant says. Von is shaking with fear, and adrenaline pumps through his veins. All he wants to do is save Mick... not take on the North Korean Army. If ever he doubted it, now Von is sure that he will never be back in his own time – alive.

Damn! Why am I in this shit hole? I wonder if I can ever go back home? Maybe if my own world has not already been abandoned by the descendants of human beings and technology. It seems like the humanity has climbed out of the rubble of several global catastrophes and attempting to hopefully re-establish the previous life of my human culture. Is this what I should expect when I get back home? Von thinks sadly as he follows the sergeant around.

The Sergeant and Von circle back around to the camp for another attempt. "Listen, we are going to the building on the left. Can you remember that in case we get separated?" the Sergeant asks Von.

"Yes, sir," Von replies. "What's that other building, Sergeant? Is that the barracks?"

"I don't know. My guess is…that's where the prisoners are being held, but this is not a rescue mission. First, we need to get the key for the vault to complete our mission. An assault team is just behind us. Their mission is to evac the prisoners," the Sergeant relates.

Von is excited to hear that the other building is where the POWs are, but he notices that the building and all the windows are shattered. Its siding and roof are on the verge of collapse. After learning where his friend is being held, all he can think about is that there is a chance Mick is inside and how he can get there. The Sergeant tries to get Von's attention back on the mission, but Von's mind is focused somewhere else.

Von follows the Sergeant around the fenced perimeter, never taking his eyes off the hut. Their movements have caught the attention of two North Korean guards posted by a rear gate. Von sees them moving out in their direction. He hangs back under the cover of heavy undergrowth and fixes his rifle. The guards spot the Sergeant up ahead and start to take aim as they move within inches of Von. Von glances back at one of the Korean gate guards behind him, and the guy raising his IMI Tavor 2 hears him. Von thinks this is his chance and thrusts his serrated knife into the back of one enemy soldier, taking him to the ground. Yanking the steel from the writhing body in one fluid motion, he slashes with all of his might, catching the other soldier squarely in the face and sending him to the ground with blood gushing from his face. Out of nowhere, the Sergeant and two commandos spring on the fallen men, slitting their throats before either is able to make a sound.

In an instant, the bodies are pulled into the undergrowth and out of sight. The men pause in silence, waiting to see if any other Koreans have spotted them. Von looks at the unmanned gate and knows this is his chance to get to Mick. He leaps to his feet and runs through the gate, leaving a stunned team to watch what they see as the mission plan being rewritten before their eyes. The men know that Von has just saved them, and with a nod, the Sergeant gives the go signal to give support. They rush to take up positions at the gate; each covering the other they run through the open gate and into the door of the ramshackle hut.

"Let's move it! Down, boy; let's go!" the Sergeant commands. Von nods in total compliance. As he starts to drop out of sight, another North Korean soldier tries to grab him. Then, out of nowhere…*SNAP!* The soldier's arms shattered. The Sergeants is blown away by what Von has just done. "Amazing, boy, amazing."

A North Korean sergeant and two of his lieutenants react quickly by raising their weapons.

"Fire! Fire!" the sergeant yells in a heavy Korean accent, as Von lands hard on the ground, rolling away from the gate into the building and coming up with his assault rifle, swinging around as he searches for an escape route. Von drops to the ground again for cover and then sprints down a corridor. He tosses away his Tavor 2 after realizing he is out of ammunition, and he dashes into the building, frantic.

They take the front room of the target building without resistance. Everyone at the desk is half asleep. The Sergeant uses his metal pick to open the side of a bolted door. Their every move behind enemy territory is captured by the night-vision camera that the Sergeant carries on his pack. In case they don't make it, the next team will pick up where they left off. In this case, they know they will have some explaining to do.

"Cover me so I can get in, and then follow me."

"Yes, sir," Von says, snapping back into the moment.

A young Korean soldier walks nearby to get some hot water for his tea and hears sounds coming from inside the building. He surveys the area and finds nothing. He returns to his chair and drinks his tea when a siren blares. He jumps up and runs to check it out. Other Korean soldiers come running into the building, trapping Von and the Sergeant, who are hiding in the room with the vault. Just as the Sergeant sets the charge, a guard turns the light on and another Korean soldier's gun swings toward the Sergeant as Von jumps the man from behind, takes his gun, and fires it at a dozen soldiers running towards the sound of the gun. A grenade explodes in their midst. The Sergeant is able to get through the window just as they come into range.

"Check the second floor," the Sergeant motions Von. Von climbs the stairway, jumping three stairs at a time, racing up into the unknown. A deafening security alarm suddenly starts to scream – *bleep! bleep! bleep!* Von hears from the third floor's grand hallway. The alarm sounds everywhere. Caught by surprise, Von can feel the adrenaline coursing through his veins. The men shouting from the back of the building is the only sound he can hear over the alarm. There is no time to escape, so he braces for the fight. Three guards burst through the door at the end of the hallway and immediately begin firing their weapons at Von. One drops and rolls to the right, firing his stolen Tavor 2 assault rifle back at them, catching one in the leg and another in the arm. The Sergeant and the commandos stream into the room, putting down a hail of fire on the guards. When the shooting stops, the guards are lying dead, and the side of the building is riddled with quarter-sized bullet holes.

Three North Korean soldiers, armed and stoked, start up the stairs, leap-frogging in a point-to-point assault procedure, ready to target Von. The Sergeant loads his IMI Tavor

2 and fires every which way. All of the doors shatter, eaten up by the gunfire.

A dozen Korean soldiers lie dead. Their contorted bloody bodies are strewn about. Von hears another gun firing, and he dives to the floor. The bullets graze the back of his helmet. A Korean soldier comes running with his gun aiming at Von and the Sergeant. Bullets miss, spraying the walls all around them. The Sergeant fires back instinctively but misses. The Korean soldier is still laying down fire at both of them, now at close range.

CHAPTER TWENTY

UNKNOWN SOLDIER

(Man of Few Words)

V on follows the Sergeant, diving through the open window onto the ground outside the Korean campground with his *Tavor 2* machine gun. A deadly stream of bullets kicks up dirt, digging a path towards Von as he gets to his feet. Von falls again, just in time, as the spray penetrates the body of the dead Korean lying next to him by the crater. They both scramble to their feet, diving for cover in the thick underbrush.

Bullets are ripping through the brush all around them when Von hears the hollow sound of a bullet penetrating flesh. For a moment, he wonders if this is it. Then he hears the Sergeant groan and fall to the ground clutching his stomach, right in front of him. Von pulls the Sergeant toward him, trying to place his hands over the wound, but the blood is still flowing freely. The Sergeant's whole gut is wide open. The bullet has ripped it apart. His intestines are spilled out, collecting the dirt and leaves as he writhes in pain. Von is in shock and can hardly move upon seeing the carnage. Staying low, he crawls towards the Sergeant's backpack, which was thrown a few feet away from where he went down.

Von sees that the Sergeant is wide-eyed and fully aware that he is not going to make it; the Sergeant is breathing heavily and barely conscious, but blood is pumping out of him like a fire hose. The pain is searing his gut like a hot poker being thrust into him again and again. There is no way he can tourniquet the Sergeant's wound since it is the core of his body.

"Hello, hello, anyone there? Shit! I don't know how to use this damn thing…Betty Blue, Betty Blue, this is Rock Python, can anyone hear me? Shit! The Sergeant is down. I believe there is a possible strong enemy force occupying the whole building in front of us. Request immediate support. Over," Vons yells.

"Rock Phyton, take cover. We'll send support. Over," a man on the radio replies.

"I can't leave him out here. He's been hit a dozen fuckin' times in the gut! He can't wait that long; he's bleeding all over the fucking ground. His guts are ripped apart, man!" Von yells again over the radio.

"You aren't staying out there. We'll get him when the support tank comes up," a voice tells Von.

"Forget this! Forget it. I'll handle him myself. I am not leaving without him. Over," Von hang up and throws the radio on the ground.

"Damn it!" He shouts as he rummages through the Sergeant's backpack for morphine vial. The Sergeant begins to shake convulsively. Von pulls the Sergeant's hand from the wound. He gets a closer look at the wound and knows it's fatal.

"Don't worry, Sarge…I'll get you out of here safely. First, let's take care of your wounds. Then I need to put you on my shoulder and carry you out of here, Sarge" Von says as calmly as he can. He pulls his shirt over his head and presses it down over the Sergeant's wound.

"Ahhhhhhhh!" The sound of the Sergeant's pain fills the air. "Morphine...Give me the fuckin' morphine; it's in my freakin backpack," the Sergeant moans to Von.

"I got it, Sarge...I got it!"

"Shit, my guts are all over the place, Carmichael," the Sergeant looks around, and screams in pain. He is frozen in agony and watches Von preparing the morphine shot. They both know what it means.

"Shit!, how do I fuckin' do it? I don't know how to give a shot?" Von shaking uncontrollably.

"Make it fuckin' double, Carmichael," Von pumps the morphine straight into the Sergeant's artery. The Sergeant responds almost immediately as the medicine takes control, making the pain only slightly more bearable. The Sergeant groans as Von breaks open the sealed syringe to prepare the second shot. He's nervous, as he's never done this before. He plunges the second shot into the arm muscle, and he watches the Sergeant relax for a moment as the curtain of haze comes over the Sergeants' face. The Sergeant looks at Von and manages a pained smile. He whispers, "Go get 'em, soldier! You know what you have to do. I'm proud of you, Carmichael." The Sergeant's moans grow weaker as he begins to shiver with shock.

A moment later, the Sergeant lies dead; his eyes still focused on Von as if urging Von to go on, but Von sits frozen and begins to weep.

"Goddamn it...Goddamn it...Goddamn it," he whispers. He gently closes the Sergeant's eyes. His hand quivers slightly as he unclips one of Sergeant's dog tags. He fumbles and drops it, picks it up again, and puts it in his pocket.

"I don't want to fight the whole freakin' Korean army. I just want to save Mick. Where the hell is Mick, anyway?"

He looks back at the building and sees the bodies of the slain Koreans. The room where the vault is located is wide open from the blast. Von makes his move for the gate once more, enters the building unnoticed, and scales the stairs to the second floor.

"Damn, what's in here?" Von looks at stack of old Korean newspapers in the corner of the room and mildewed magazines piled all over the room. He moves towards a vault and opens it. Inside is a timer and what looks like a small bomb – a booby-trap. He notices an LED light flashing as he quickly but carefully moves closer. The laser is everywhere. Von sees an envelope on the inside of the vault, grabs it, and hides it inside his shirt.

"Okay, gotta move, gotta move fast," he urges himself. He hears a rapid ticking of the detonator…Von knows that if he doesn't get out there fast enough, he will get blown up, or gas poisoned.

He goes closer to the open window, which seems the size of a medium pizza box. He squeezes his body through the space and looks down, hanging tight; he has no choice but to go down.

"Damn, this is not one of my best plans," Von tries to convince himself that he has no choice. He thinks of jumping but hesitates. He freezes for a moment and then starts climbing down the back of the building. Holding onto a drain pipe, he swings to a better step, where he jumps to the ground.

"Okay, Von, just few more steps – a few more steps, and you'll be safe," he reassures himself. He drops to an old, rusted air-conditioner, grabbing another window frame just before the air-conditioner gives way to the weight he's just exerted upon it. Struggling to keep his balance, and as he reaches behind to shift himself, he drops the envelope. Now he has to go all the way.

Timing his next move he reaches another bracket and snags it. He tries to let go; before he falls backward, he catches a pipe, holding it just long enough to slow his fall. Then, he lets go for the last fifteen feet, and he hears noises coming from the porch along the outside of the building.

"Goddammit, if I jump this high I better not break my freakin' leg. How would I time-travel with a broken leg? Does anyone time-travel with a broken leg in a cast?" Von jumps, hitting the bottom of the muddy barracks.

Where is the sound of the bomb? Von thinks to himself. It didn't detonate. Could it be that it isn't a bomb? It must be a nerve gas, and that explains why the Koreans are not giving chase.

He holds his breath, picks up the envelope, and runs as fast as he can away from the building towards the gate. Finally, he lets out his breath and inhales deeply as he falls to the ground and crawls on his stomach into the underbrush.

He works his way back to the staging place where the Sergeant's body and radio are hidden. Hopefully, he remembers the radio code technique he's been hearing all day. He tries to use the radio again: "Betty Blue, Betty Blue, this is Rock Python again. Can you guys hear me at all? We got hit here really bad, man. The *Quack* doctor is dead. Operation *Ghost-town* is complete. Tell our boys to come in low from the east to pick me up."

"Okay, Fire fox, kick the tires, light the fires, select Zone 8, tag the bogey, but don't get in a dogfight. Don't boresight, check three, bingo to Mom – Got it?"

"Got it, dude!"

"Bravo Rock Python! Over," a man on the other end responds, seeming to know what Von hopes he said. "Snipers're all over this damn place. Operation Ghost town, over," Von says, and he puts the radio down and crawls back towards the prisoner building on the other side of compound outside the perimeter fence.

The rear gate is swarming with Korean guards. Von sees that the only chance to save Mick is through the main gate that is now under-guarded. A slow supply truck moving towards the main gate is just the break he needs. Von moves quickly into the darkness and in the chaos is able to ride the shadowed side of the truck hiding between two large spare tires through the gate. Once inside, he jumps off behind the deserted barracks and sees Korean inscription marks on the wall.

Looking almost cross-eyed through his *high-tech* radar telescope, Von immediately glances at the prisoner detention building. The doors and windows are boarded up tight. He double-checks one access point: a painted flat steel door. Then he tucks away his radar telescope device in his pants.

Though Von cannot see any of the North Korean soldiers, he knows the guards are positioned in the bluffs on either side of the barracks. If he makes a wrong move, the other team will suffer the consequences, and he won't stand a chance.

Feeling the humidity of the night, Von continues his plan to rescue Mick and whoever else is inside the building. He can no longer wait for the rescue team to back him up and provide cover. Invincible in the eyes of the enemy inside, Von waits silently until the change of guards is complete. As replacements are made, he is able to pinpoint the location of each guard. Von waits for the replacements to settle, hoping that they will let their guard down just long enough for him to slip by in the darkness. Von is careful to move slowly, staying unnoticed, when a big supply truck drives right past him, almost knocking him into the side of the guard tower.

To keep his mind alert, Von has to think about the good old days with Mick and the guys. He knows this is about duty and saving a friend's life. He experienced far worse things playing soccer in the hot Florida summer weather. For some reason, his joints hurt. He thinks that he is way too young for these arthritis pains. But the fact is that since he began time-traveling, he has been hurt several times. Time-travel has taken its toll. Perhaps this is why Von feels antsy as he waits for the right move to save Mick. He hopes he can rise once more to the occasion and get Mick out of this hell.

To Von's surprise, his perspective has been changing after the Sergeant died in front of him. He can't stop thinking about the Sergeant's last words to him. Von knows he has never been a team player, but somehow this experience left him with a new outlook. Working in a team with the military was not part of Von's job description. All he knows is that he must save his buddy Mick. A noise abruptly jerks Von back to reality.

He remembers what the Sergeant said: The prisoners are housed in two different buildings, and the rescue team needs to plan on the possibility that the guards will release poison nerve gas if they are overrun. The rescue team is still fighting the Korean forces in the jungle. The sound of assault rifle fire is still in the distance. Von knows they will never make it to the building before the enemy command gives the order to gas the prisoners. As far as Von can tell, the guards think that the battle is still being waged off in the jungle. He knows he has the element of surprise and that this is his best chance to sneak up on the building. He has no choice; it's his one last chance to find Mick alive.

He kicks off the barracks wall with his right foot and takes off running. He makes it to the metal door and gets inside the building, and for a moment, Von looks around. To his amazement, no one is guarding the access. Feeling his way in the dim light, he accidentally touches a switch on the walls. He slinks through each room using the Sergeant's night-vision goggles to see.

There are only two guards at the control desk trying to radio someone for help. Von sneaks past without the guards noticing him in the darkness. He hears someone moaning. He knows that the sound is familiar and follows the sound. Von sees the huddled prisoners lying on the floor inside a small room – all wounded. He walks towards them and finds one soldier's groans in the dark to be oddly familiar. The man's face is badly beaten; he is curled up into a ball and is hardly recognizable. He feels certain that he knows him. He leans forward toward the wounded man. The man looks older than his years as he lies groaning in pain.

"Mick, is that you?" Von whispers. There is no response. Sure enough, it's Mick and he looks at Von but can't speak. Von grabs his dog tag. On Mick's wrist is a small plastic envelope with his information. It says that he has a broken arm, a broken femur, a dislocated ankle, broken ribs, punctured lungs, and bullet wounds. It looks like a score card for some sick interrogator. Mick's color is bad, like old salami meat that has been left out for too long. Von senses that he does not have long to get Mick out of this torture room and take him to the medic.

He lifts him carefully, puts him over his shoulder, and slowly carries him out of the building. Moving in total darkness, he works his way back to the staging point and places Mick on the ground while he watches for Korean snipers. Von waits, hoping that a chopper will come and find them. Moving Mick has reopened his wounds, and Mick is bleeding out.

Then, a shot from the sniper ricochets off the wall a few inches behind Von's head. He ducks back around the corner, breathing hard. He carefully looks around the corner across the square at the back of the building, from where he thinks the shots were fired. Then he proceeds to take care of Mick.

All of a sudden, Bang! His leg is hit. The gunfire sprayed out metal everywhere and Von's leg fills the night air with blood and flesh. He throws himself forward and drops Mick to the ground to avoid having the sniper aim for a better second shot. Von's face goes white, and he falls to the ground with Mick. Von gets up and grabs his *Tavor 2* assault rifle. He glances at his bleeding leg, ignores it, picks Mick up, and throws him back on his shoulder again. Although he is weakened, he runs out staggering, loosing coordination in his movement.

"Don't worry buddy; we're good, we're fine. Mick, it's Von. Remember me, dude? I'm taking you out of here. I'll take good care of you. Hang on. Don't give up on me now." Mick opens his eyes, looks at Von, and can barely open his mouth.

"*Von?*" Mick whispers softly, but Von doesn't hear. Mick fades again and closes his eyes, gasping his last breath of life, and Von tells him the rescue helicopter is coming for them. Von clutches Mick's head and immediately vomits blood on him. He is so heartbroken about their situation.

"Mick…Mick, don't go…Dude, stay with me," Von says, wondering if he's losing Mick.

Von is in a lot of pain from his gunshot wound. He puts Mick down, cuts the side of his own pants, and examines the wound on his leg. He sees that he is bleeding heavily. He cuts the inside of his shirt and tightly wraps his leg to control the bleeding.

It is three o'clock in the morning, and Von is on his belly in deep mud inside the compound. Mick is motionless, showing no sign of life. Von has lost all contact with the rescue team but is confident they will be coming for him. He lifts his head and observes the dark barracks separated by a razor blade–sharp *concertina wire.* Through the dank air, the lights give off a faint yellow glow, like the end of cigarette. They also have a *laser emergency alarm,* so he needs to plan very carefully to save Mick. He knows that the guards will set off the poison gas killing the prisoners and everyone else if they suspect an enemy in the surrounding area. He feels dizzy from the gunshot wound.

Then he sees a signal from beyond: he knows his team is in position. He has to signal them before they move on the compound. He can see one commander is guarding the extraction point where the chopper will soon be touching down to get them out. Von crawls back to the bushes to get Mick.

Von sees Mick's condition is worsening; his body is beginning to shake as shock sets in. He can only think of the Sergeant and how quickly he died. Mick's eyelids drift together as Mick goes to a place deep within his own mind. A chopper suddenly drops into the landing zone to rescue them. As Mick slips off into unconsciousness from blood loss, Von watches helplessly as the medic begins his desperate work to save Mick. Von tries to tell Mick that he is there for him, but his words are drowned out by the roar of the rescue helicopter.

"I think we just lost this one," the medic says to Von as he tries to revive Mick.

"Nooooo! Nooooo! It can't be," Von yells.

"I'm sorry, we lost him." The medic shakes his head and starts to take care of Von's wounds and move on to the next wounded soldier.

"Please, please I beg of you – check him again. He was breathing a few seconds ago. Please…Von begs the medic.

"I'm sorry…" The medic says as he looks at Von.

As Von lurches next to Mick by the pen doorway inside the cabin, his cell phone, still hidden in his pocket, falls out. He tries to grab it when the helicopter makes a hard turn to avoid ground fire. Von accidentally presses Mick's speed dial number, opening the time-space continuum, and launches into a time warp once again.

"What the heck…? Where'd the kid go?" the medic asks the helicopter pilot, bewildered.

"What do you mean? He was there with you a second ago," the pilot responds, looking at the back of the helicopter.

"He couldn't have fallen out…he was at the very back and I'm pretty sure that door is locked," the medic says.

"Look, he left his duffel bag. We need to report to Colonel Bartley soon," the pilot notes.

"Green Panther, Green Panther. We need to speak with Colonel Bartley, over," the medic says.

"This is Black Jaguar Four," A very husky voice responds on the other end.

"Colonel, *Quack doctor* is dead, Sir.

"I heard that earlier!" a cold tone from the Colonel.

"I'm sorry to report Colonel, we have a missing soldier."

"Goddamn it, what do you mean you lost a soldier? Who?" the Colonel asks angrily.

"Carmichael, sir."

"How the hell'd you lose him? Was he captured?" the Colonel asks.

"No, sir, he disappeared right in front of us."

"Did you say he *disappeared*?" the Colonel asks.

"Yes, sir," the medic responds.

"Did he fall out of the chopper?" the Colonel wonders.

"No, sir. We can't explain it…He was wounded, but we can't explain how he just disappeared right in front of our eyes. His duffel bag is left here with us and inside it is the Operation Ghost-town package, sir," the medic tells the Colonel.

"Dammit! He was one of the good ones! Does anyone know what company he belongs to?"

"No idea, Colonel. He didn't even have a dog tag. His name isn't on any of the new recruit lists, either."

"What's the young man's name again?" the Colonel asks.

"Carmichael, sir," the medic shouts as the roar of the helicopter increases in strength.

CHAPTER TWENTY ONE

DETOUR

on's wireless device has again launched him into a time anomaly. After what seems like just a moment passing, Von finds himself waking on a hard floor. He was in a daze but he starts to get up, picks himself off, and abruptly falls back to the floor with a strange clattering sound and a searing pain in his leg. Von sees an open bed and makes his way back to it, collapsing into deep sleep. When he wakes up, he is back in his college dorm.

An old maintenance man heard the commotion and has been knocking on doors to see if anyone was hurt. He is in his seventies now, but as the doors opens he immediately recalls Von's face. The old man cannot believe his eyes. Scratching his head, wondering what Von is doing in the dorm, he asks Von if his father was a student at Stephenson College.

"Yap, but that was million years ago Mr. Sandler. I'm a student here...what do you mean? I'm still tired and I need to take a nap." Von responds and a look of shock comes over the old man's face. The old man shrugs his shoulders accepting this odd encounter as just another testament to what he calls his mad cow disease or in other words...senility.

"I know you! Yeah, I do remember you. Hey, what happened to you?" The old maintenance man asks.

"Amazing! I know you too Mr. Sandler. Darn, what happened to you? You look tired and got old on me, what a weekend you must have had, huh!?" Von makes a sarcastic remark intended to shorten the conversation while in bed. He wonders about the searing pain from his leg that makes it difficult to focus on chit-chat, and the blood stain soaking through the bed sheets has Mr. Sandler's full attention.

"Hey, you're blee..." The maintenance man gets interrupted by Von before Sandler can finish his sentence.

"Gotta go. Gotta get up, Sandler. I overslept. Okay? By the way, have you seen Mick?" Von added. Mr. Sandler closes the door as he walks away muttering something about "frat" boys under his breath. Von seems to have no clue that it is forty years into the future, and everything and everyone except for him has aged

Von finds himself angrily yelling out for Mick, but there is no answer. He can no longer stand the pain so he summons the courage to look under the sheet. Oh my God! He notices that his leg is heavily bleeding. He turns pale just before passing out at the sight of his own leg. He wakes again thinking it was all just a bad dream. To his horror he sees the blood stain is still moist and his worst fears may be true. Slowly he lifts the sheet, uncovering the source of the trickling blood. All he can see is a fleshy raw stump where his left leg should be. Even more bizarre is what appears to be a gun butt attached to it. He can see the metal screws attached to what looks like a mount penetrating into his thigh. A slow but steady flow of blood is coming from one of the screws. Where have I been? Von's mind races to find answers, but there are none other than the stark reality. Von's leg is gone and instead of a prosthesis, there is a gun attached to his body. A rounded wooden cap covering the business end of the gun works like a shoe. Von looks at it with detachment still searching his mind for an explanation. "God. It's not just a gun," he says to himself, "it's an old AK-52 machine gun! What the heck is this?" He checks to see if it is loaded and finds a full cartridge of ammunition. Trying to take some control over his situation, he reaches for the towel on the bedside chair and ties off the leg with a tourniquet, hoping to cut off the bleeding.

Von thinks to himself, If anybody sees me like this, they'll call the cops for sure.

A young man opens the door into the room and finds Von.

"Who are you? What are you doing in my room?" A freaked-out student in his twenties tries to calm Von, while he explains that he must have the wrong dorm room. Von insists that it is his room. The young man sees blood all over and runs outside as fast as he can in a panic

Von struggles to his feet, and tries to walk on his un-likely peg leg. The muzzle slips out from under him, and as he starts to fall, Von grabs for the chair. The motion fires off three rounds into the floor and sends Von into panic mode.

"Oh Jesus," he says aloud. Von can hear doors slamming and footsteps running down in the hallway. A knock on the door is followed by a commanding voice:

"We are Stephenson HumRob Security, you need to drop your weapon, and come out with your hands up, now".

"I don't have a weapon, it's my freakin' leg...I mean there's a machine gun attached to my leg!"

Seconds later, as Von is trying to get to his feet, the door swings open and two HumRobs burst into the room. Startled, Von falls back, setting off another short burst from his leg. The gun recoil sends searing pain up through his bloody stump into his hip. Both HumRobs fall to the floor twitching. A pool of red blood from their fleshy torsos begins to blend with a green fluid oozing from wounds on their robotic arms and legs. More HumRobs burst through the door with their *Tavor 2* assault rifles drawn aiming at Von's head.

"Don't shoot! Don't shoot!" Von shrieks. "This is all a mistake, please help me."

An ambulance arrives and paramedics try to stop the steady flow of blood from Von's leg wound, which opened in the fall.

"Be careful. That damn leg is loaded and has a hair trigger. No wonder it went off," shouts the head paramedic. He raises his head to ask, "Does anybody know where the safety is?" Von reaches to his leg, causing two HumRobs to pull their weapons.

"Easy guys," Von says, "I think I know how this works. Earlier I saw where the safety and lock are located." Without looking, Von finds the safety and locks it into place. Then he removes the ammo cartridge in one fluid movement. He presents it to the HumRobs before falling back onto the stretcher and staring at the ceiling in disbelief.

"I know that kid...I swear he used to be one of the college students who rented an apartment dorm many years ago. Something is terribly wrong here. I just don't understand why he hasn't aged? And his leg...what happened to his leg?" Mr. Sandler says. His words sound almost incoherent as he tries to give his statement to the HumRobs police officer.

"Mr. Sandler, Mr. Sandler, what the heck are you talking about? Damn, how the heck did I hurt my leg?" Von asks.

Von looks at his legs, saw blood gushing and dripping from his leg. "Excuse me, did I hear you correctly that a metal plate is holding this machine gun attached to my hip bone? Ahhhhhh!!! Would you please be gentle? It hurts really bad!" How did I get this?" He screams and is furious.

"I've seen attaching a hook as a hand, or maybe even using tool of some sort, but a machine-gun leg? There's something not right here. Did you see the detailed fit? Whoever did this procedure knew what they were doing. I don't see that kind of work coming from our HumRob Repair Services," says the HumRob security officer aiming a pen-like device at Von's irises to verify his real identity in the student database. A match blinks green on the device and Von is released into the custody of the paramedic, who gives him a shot of sedative and sends him on the stretcher to the ambulance.

Von didn't realize that he had been captured and tortured while trying to save Mick in the North Korean war. His Korean captors had amputated his leg to get intel. During his escape he attached an old AK-52 to his stump as his prosthesis, enabling him to escape to allied forces with Mick. Exactly how the AK-52 got bolted inside his thigh remains a mystery along with other gaps in his memory from the war.

Everyone notices that Von is wearing only knee-length underpants, a black sock with an elastic garter belt, and a military boot on his good leg. The undergarment has a button overlap in front and a drawstring at the waist in the back. It looks like a costume. They also notice that Von is holding an obsolete PDA and an ancient looking cell phone. One mystery is replaced by another.

Von's eyes grow heavy until the blur of the siren fades into silence. He awakes in a hospital bed to the sound of someone asking him questions. Von tries to focus on the man who seems to be talking at him standing with a clipboard wearing a lab coat. He is asking odd questions.

"Do you know where you are? And do you know who the president is..." and "Can you tell us what year it is?" Von tries to answer, but realizes he has made a mistake when he sees the man with the clipboard exchange an odd look over the top of his glasses with another man standing in the room wearing a police badge.

This can't be good, Von thinks to himself. Frustrated, he sits up and begins to rant.

The HumRob nurses react in unison injecting another sedative into Von's IV line. It is a fast-acting sedative and takes effect in a matter of nanoseconds. Von falls back into his bed almost immediately.

Von wakes up sometime later. The room is spinning and he feels more tired than before he went out.

Why do I feel off-center and lethargic? he wonders. *It must be whatever horse medication they gave me; I can hardly open my eyes.* A knock at the door interrupts Von's thoughts and someone enters the room.

"Hi," Von says, disappointed.

"Von? How are you feeling? I believe they are preparing you for the removal of your machine gun leg. How do you feel?" the robotic security cop asks.

"I'm fine. Have you found my friend yet? Tell me where he is. This is his entire fault."

The security guard tells Von that he needs to tell them more information about what happened. This usually involves finding that Von is in big trouble. Von is half-listening, mainly because his mind is focused on more pressing issues about his parents, Mick, and his leg. He sees a lone HumRob stationed at the end of the other door. He does not know how long he was out, but there is no sign of the men who were there earlier. Von gathers his wits and calls out, "Bring me my roommate. Bring me Mick."

"Who?" the HumRod officer asks.

"Mick Chevalier, my roommate. I will prove to you he can help me solve this mystery. I'll prove it to you. I swear," Von insists

"Sir, what are you talking about? Do you know how you ended up with a machine-gun leg? You're in trouble sir, and the sooner you give us answers, the better off you will be.."

"I don't know…I am puzzled. My mind is blank. I don't know what to tell you. Don't ask me how I lose my leg."

"We don't know, and we can't find anything on file in reference to a Mick Chevalier at Stephenson College." The HumRob Captain starts to tell Von what he knows.

"Excuse me, Captain…" a HumRob lieutenant walks through the door, holding a file folder in his hand and interrupts. "May I have a word with you? I found something here. I think you need to look at this, please." The Captain opens the file glances at the page for a moment. While the HumRob Captain inspects the file, the lieutenant steps through the door and starts right in on Von…

"Mr. Carmichael…We can't seem to locate a person named Mick Chevalier. However, your description of Mick Chevalier matches up to a nine-year-old boy, who was killed some time ago. Nothing in any of our database matches an adult description you gave us earlier…*sorry.*"

"What do you mean a nine-year-old boy? For heaven's sake, he is my college roommate. I've known him since I was seven. Find him, and I'll prove to you that I'm not psychotic

274 • E. I. Johnson

or some kind of lunatic," Von insists confidently. The Hum-Rob stares at Von, who is not making sense at all.

"Mr. Carmichael, are you saying that your friend is involved in doing a crime like this? Could it be that there is no Mick Chevalier? We believe he is a figment of your imagination! You just don't want to face the fact that you are responsible for shooting and killing two HumRobs. Who knows what other crimes there are? I'm sorry to tell you, but your phantom friend doesn't exist in any of our newest technology global databases. He doesn't exist period!!"

"What do you mean he doesn't exist? Mick Chevalier is my best friend and my college roommate. Forget this. I'll prove it to you that my friend got mixed up with the wrong crowd and he's involved with this," Von screams. The Hum-Rob officer shakes his head and leaves defiantly.

"Damn! What just happened here? What are these people trying to tell me, that I *time-traveled?*" Von whispers to himself. "How did I get this peg-leg and why is it a machine-gun prosthesis? I don't get it? And Von closes his eyes.

The HumRob police department tries to contact his parents, but they are nowhere to be found. Finally, after persistent searching, Von's parents are tracked, and they come to see him. When he sees his mother, who is obviously much much older, he faints.

When he regains consciousness, he is on a gurney on his way to surgery. It's been forty years since Von disappeared from his dorm...and was declared legally dead.

Von realizes when he wakes up that he is very tired and in a lot of pain. His Mom and Dad are sitting beside his bed. He is still groggy from the medication. He smiles at his parents and wants to discuss something. His father feels strange seeing Von for the first time after forty years. Von feels nauseous about seeing them. But that isn't the only reason why he doesn't want to speak to them…Von thinks that with his eyes closed he can ignore the information he received from the robotic cop so that he won't have to face them until he sees Mick.

Of course, these HumRob security people might love the idea Von really did go back in time. He must admit, for a moment it was great that if it really did happen, he gained some level of achievement. The consequences of it all excite and confuse everyone.

"It never happened, Mr. Carmichael. I'm sorry, but we don't know who did this to you. Look at your clothes. They seem to be forty years old or more."

Von responds, "For right now, I don't have the slightest idea what happened to me, and that is the honest-to-good-ness answer."

"Well, we both have no idea what really happened to you, Von. You do know that we found your parents, and now we are trying to locate your friend."

"Come on, please keep trying. Just try," Von begs and exasperated. "Please; you've got to believe me. This is getting too strange. Find all those people for me, and I'll prove to you that this is a mistake. Get my parents here, and find my friend Mick. Get out! Go!" Von yells, fed up with the same old routine and questions.

The robotic security guard leaves the room and goes to the nursing station.

"We need to put him temporarily in the psych ward. You need to call Dr. Bates. He specializes in psychiatry, and he'll process this situation right away. This young man is having severe hallucinations." he announces.

"Dr. Bates is temporarily out of service, Sir. He's being overhauled in the new medical tech services for new parts on his arms," the nurse responds.

"Fine! I don't care how you do it. I don't care who does it, but this young man needs to be moved. Do it as soon as possible, or there will be more problems with this matter. He should be kept under heavily guarded maximum security."

"I will do my best," the nurse replies and hurriedly walks away.

The HumRob officer leaves the ICU nurse station, Psychiatric ward floor in a bad mood.

CHAPTER TWENTY TWO

MIRROR OF HIS MIND

The HumRob police can't locate Mick. Von is left alone in the observation room. All of a sudden, he hears someone outside the door mention the name Bessie. He has not seen Bessie, his soon-to-be fiancée, for a long time. He wonders how she has aged and if she's in the hospital to find the answer to his mysterious disappearance. It seems that history remains unchanged, except for Von. What happened to Von in those forty years is what everyone wants to know...forty years ago, when everyone was twenty years old, just barely graduating from college.

"Mick, is that you, man?" Von sees a person enter the room. He is relieved and smiling.

"No, I'm not Mick. My name is Paschal Andre Chevrier. I'm his son. I was named after my grandfather. Dad is outside waiting for the doctors. He told me to come inside and tell you that he'll be coming in a few seconds."

"How old are you?" Von asks.

"I'm twenty-one. I just graduated from college," Paschal replies.

"Wow, you look just like your father....You're the spitting image of your father. A mirror of his youth," Von says, studying the young man carefully. He is sad to think that he doesn't remember what has happened to him. While he is trying to remember the past, the door opens.

Von sees a man in his sixties with a receding hairline come inside his hospital room. When the man comes closer, he realizes it's Mick. He is amazed to find that Mick has aged from a young, long-haired "dude" to what seems like a sixty-year-old man who is almost bald, with a beer belly and a wedding band.

"Von? It's me, Mick," he says somberly.

"Mick? Mick, is it really you?"

"Yes, it's me, man. I'm just a bit older with a bit of a beer gut," Mick replies.

"Dad, I'll wait outside," Von hears Mick's son Paschal says politely.

"Actually, why don't you come back and pick me up in an hour and a half?" Mick suggests.

Paschal approaches Von's hospital bed and says to him, "It is really nice to finally meet you; my father speaks very highly of you. He has a lot of pictures and wonderful memories of you." He shakes Von's hand and leaves the room.

The room is quiet for a few moments. Mick breaks the silence and starts talking. He asks, "What happened? Why did you stop calling me from wherever you were?"

"I called you? From where? Where was I?" Von asks.

"I think I called your cell phone back then, and every time you answered, you said you were in England with your grandfather. Well, first you disappeared. We thought you ran away with that girl from the party the night before our college graduation. Then, you didn't show up to graduation.

"Nobody knew where you were or what had happened to you. After forty-eight hours, your parents reported you missing. You were all over the news. The police came to our dorm room and tried to look for evidence. They didn't find anything, of course, except for one pair of ladies' shoes, badly torn, and an expensive silk ladies' garment, badly worn along the edges. You know, somewhat frazzled. I knew it didn't belong to either one of us, so I assumed it was Bessie's. She must've left it accidently, right? Here…I brought some of the old newspaper clippings I saved."

"Hey, buddy…that's a ton of newspaper you have there," Von says, startled.

"I know. You were in the national news for a while."

"So you said I called you? When was that? Was it before graduation? Where was I?" Von questions Mick.

"Well, the first time, I was the one who called you, the day after graduation. I remember I was still hungover from the previous night. I was looking for you and called your cell phone. You answered, and I remember it was such bad reception because you were yelling on the other end of the line.

"I didn't know where you were at first. I asked you to bring an extra keg to my party. Everyone thought you wouldn't come 'cause you'd chickened out on proposing to Bessie and decided to run away with the girl at the party – she didn't show up to graduation, either. But later on in the police investigation, we found out that she had alcohol poisoning and couldn't make it to graduation. Nobody knows what happened to that blonde girl after that incident."

"So what happened to me?" Von asks eagerly.

"I don't really know. When I spoke to you the day of my party to ask you about the keg, you told me that you were with your grandfather in England." Mick tells his side of the story.

"Grandfather from England? What grandfather?"

"You told me he was your mother's dad."

"My *grandfather*?" Von replies. "But that doesn't make any sense. He died before I was even born. I never met the man."

"I know, and that's what I told you on the phone, but you insisted that you were there. You sent me pictures from your cell phone of the British people and the surroundings. I thought it was some kind of school play," Mick says. "Here, these are the pictures you sent me. The police had copies made from my cell phone while they where investigating your disappearance."

"Where were those taken...really? Where was I? Who are those people?" Von asks.

"I don't know. At first, everyone thought I was on drugs when I told them what you told me."

"What did I tell you?" Von asks curiously.

"Well, you said that you traveled back in time. You said you were in Oxford, England. They put me on medication for a while, because they thought the stress from graduation was making me lose my mind."

"How long did they try to look for me?" Von wonders.

"For a long time, a very long time, maybe years...You called me several times, and then suddenly you stopped. I lost all communication with you. I didn't know how or where to reach you. I didn't know what had happened to you. I really do believe that you time-traveled, that you were out there somewhere.

"Look at you now...I don't really know where you've been all these years, but just look at yourself in the mirror. Then look at me. I've aged, but you haven't. What do you say to that?" Mick asks. "I was told that they have analyzed your clothes, and the investigator said they're museum quality, which means they're more than a hundred years old." The confusing part is…you're wearing bloody boots. The boots aren't museum quality. They seem to have been made during 2010, but the rest of your clothing is museum quality."

"Where did I get them?"

"I can't answer that. Only you can."

"Do you know how I got the gunshot wound?"

"Sorry, Von, I don't know. Nobody knows. They're still trying to figure it out, too."

"Damn, what just happened to me, Mick?

"I don't know…but here's another picture you sent me. Do you remember who this is?" Mick asks.

"No! Who is that?"

"It's your grandfather. Well, you said he's your grandfather. Here's another picture of the two of you together. When the investigator showed this to your mom, she passed out cold," Mick informs Von. "Your mother told mine in confidence that once in a while, she doesn't know what to believe. She wonders if maybe you really did time-travel.

"Some people told her that it was a hoax. They told her that someone must have kidnapped you and took your picture with someone who looks just like your grandfather. But now…when you appeared from somewhere and didn't age at all, everyone thinks that your body was frozen in time," "By the way, I was told that the HumRob Cops will reopen this case. Just to give you a heads-up. Everyone just wants to know what happened to you, and they need to start another investigation…some kind of a cold case investigation, but they're calling it 'frozen case.'

"Don't you remember anything at all? Don't you remember begging me on the phone to tell everyone that you time-traveled?"

"I don't know...I don't know...I don't remember anything. I don't know where I was, or where I've been. I don't have any recollection. Wait a second...I remember Dex knocked at my dorm apartment the night before graduation and asked me to help him load up his truck. He said he was moving to D.C., and that's the last thing I can remember to this day. That's it," Von recalls..

"Oh, yes, I remember Dex gave that information to the investigators back then. He flew back here to Florida for the investigation. He was so upset about your disappearance. He put off his training for a year to help find you. I told him about your time-travel, and he didn't believe me because every time you called, he wasn't around. He thought I was hallucinating," Mick goes on.

"How are Dex and Adam, do you still see them?" Von wonders.

"Oh, Dex's fine. He's still single; never did get married, definitely a confirmed bachelor, works with the Department of Defense in D.C. And he is the Special Assistant to the Secretary of Defense. I forget to tell you that he'll be flying down tonight to see you. Adam is in politics and is now in Europe. He came over to visit last year for a few weeks." Mick said.

"And you...What do you do now?" Von asks Mick.

"Well, I was an architect, but the architectural technology has changed so drastically. I'm kind of semi-retired right now. I designed several buildings all over the country, so I guess I've proven myself.

"Von, careers in this time are more like monkey bars or a jungle gym, with people moving up and down and jumping from one job to the other to develop a portfolio of skills.

"What do you mean monkey bars? I don't understand; what do you mean?" Von asks.

"There is no longer a corporate ladder to climb. Companies and employees have to be agile, innovative, and able to respond to unknown future events."

"How about the employers? What are they looking for?" Von asks.

"Employers provide access to the latest ideas, and technologies to attract the best staff. The future work force is all about choosing work that will let you update your skills. The convergence of information, biology, and business is the big technological wave after information technology. Do you remember information technology, Von?" Mick replies.

"Mick, I wish I'd become a security analyst specializing in software technologies. That's what I wanted to be before. Is that still part of today's business?" Von asks. "Are there any older people who still love to work? How do these companies know that the person that they are hiring is the best one?"

"Well, because of the aging population today, in 2048, older people have to keep working. If you're young, highly skilled, and adaptable, you'll have employers banging on your door or beeping your video screen," Mick says without blinking an eye.

"Are you saying that people out there need to have more skills than before?"

"What's really happening now is the major sociological problem that people who don't have access to skill development and communication technology find it increasingly difficult to find fulfilling employment," Mick says.

"So do people work more than forty hours a week?" Von asks.

"Yes, because the televisual society, mobile computing, and video communication technology mean that work infiltrates into your home even during weekends, creating less of a divide between work and leisure time. And because of this, there is a health cost associated with an increasingly stressed workforce."

"How can it be possible for a family of four to survive? Is there alternative work for older people?" Von wonders.

"With all the retired and dying baby boomers, more people have left the workforce than are joining it. To counter this, everyone is encouraged to work well into their seventies and maybe even in their eighties full time. Attitudes toward older workers have changed. Employers allow people to work part time and offer sabbaticals in order to keep as many older people as possible in the workforce."

"Do you know that I feel like I've only been gone for a week – not forty years, man…I've lost forty years of my life. I can't believe this…crap!" Von says sadly to Mick. "This sounds more depressing than our college life. Is this really what I missed for forty years? Let's change this depressing topic. How's your marriage?"

"Fine. Fine. I married Patrice. We have two wonderful kids. Chantal Genevieve is our daughter; she's in her junior year of college. She wants to be an architect as well. And you met Paschal Andre, our son. He just graduated; he majored in cyber technology," Mick shares proudly.

"How are your parents?" Von asks.

"Well, Dad's in his early eighties now. He hardly goes out unless he is being driven by his personal driver. He's been having eye problems recently. They gave him new robotic eyes, and he's still getting used to them. He has a new driver; we had to bring his old driver back to the shop because he was been malfunctioning. They almost got into an accident. So it's better for him to have a new one."

"What do you mean? You killed the old driver?" Von asks.

"No, No. Housekeepers, drivers, and yardmen...they're all personal electronic robots. They're almost like humans, but they don't last very long. If you get one that malfunctions all the time, you have a problem because some of the companies don't make the older parts anymore. It's often cheaper for them to make a new one."

"How long has this been going on?"

"Well, Dad bought his first personal robot in early 2015. It was one of the first household robots. He decided to invest in it. He said he knew it wouldn't last forever, but he figured it would be a good investment anyway."

"Wow. And how's your mom?" Von asks.

"Mom's doing better than Dad. She has a personal robotic physical trainer. I think it's added years to her life. She is healthy, eats a lot of good food, and keeps herself busy with the 'silver years crowd,'" Mick says.

"Tell me about my parents...How are they? How did they take my disappearance?"

"Well, your mom didn't take it too well. She was depressed for a long time. My mom still picks her up everyday and keeps her busy. Even though your mother's ten years younger than mine, she tags along with Mom and her robotic trainer. It took her a while to get to where she is now.

"And your dad was hospitalized several times when you disappeared. It was hard for both of them. It was hard for everyone," Mick says sadly.

"Tell me, Mick, what happened to Bessie?"

"Actually, Bessie never did get married. She has a little house where she keeps busy with her garden. She has several of *No-Neck's* great-great-grandchildren or 'grand-cats.' Remember your cat, Von? No-Neck died ten years after you disappeared. Bessie took care of her kittens.

"She has one that she calls No-Neck, Jr., and she's her only indoor cat. Believe it or not, No-Neck, Jr. is allergic to the rest of the cats. She has to get the new cat vaccine allergy shots. If she doesn't get a shot, she sneezes continuously until she passes out and needs to be put on an oxygen tank." Mick smiles while he tells Von the story.

Von looks toward the window, but the shades are pulled down. Mick sees this, so he walks to the window and opens the shades for Von to be able to see outside his room.

"Thank you," Von whispers softly." Wait, what are those things flying out there?"

"Oh! We now have flying bikes, cars, trains…you name it. Some of them run by solar power, and some electric."

"Unbelievable!" Von says.

"Von, *you* are unbelievable…I keep looking at you, and you haven't aged a bit. Dex will never believe this. You look the same as the last time we saw you."

"You are very lucky that you didn't get drafted in 2010 when the North Korean nuclear war started. I dreamed about you when I was in the war. In my dream you came to save me in a chopper," Mick says.

"Oh, yeah? Did you actually see me in your dreams?" Von asks.

"I don't remember anymore, but once in a while I still get flashbacks from it. It seems real. I really think that you were there for me," Mick explains. Von looks at Mick and they both stare at each other.

"After my rehabilitation, there was a military award ceremony honoring an unknown soldier. A soldier whose name was never on a list of recruits. The men who knew the unknown soldier's name all died in the war, so nobody knows the young man who saved me and a dozen other POW's." Mick says. "If not for him, I probably wouldn't have survived the ordeal."

"Sorry to hear about that. Hey, what about taking me for a drive after they release me?" Von changes the topic.

"Sure, old friend. I'll show you the latest video games kids are playing. You won't believe how amazing the new technology is. I'm not into it anymore, but I'm sure that you'll still enjoy them." A young woman enters the room. "Okay, your nurse is here. Just want to give you a heads-up, buddy. Nurses here are mostly HumRobs. It stands for Human Robotics. They have the intelligence of a human being – they can smell and feel like us – but they're robots. You really can't tell the difference unless you examine their mechanical parts." Mick smiles at Von and leaves the room.

CHAPTER TWENTY THREE

TIME OUT OF MIND

The year is 2048. President Arnold Schwarzenegger, Jr. and V.P. George Clooney III are now occupying the White House. *The OC* is long off the air, but it had become a box-office hit film with a successful sequel.

The *anime* cartoons have people going wilder than ever. A highway in the sky is now a reality. The major car and airplane manufacturers are scrambling to compete in the new market of personal aircraft. People can fly their vehicles over long and short distances with ease, like the Jetsons.

After what has only seemed like few minutes since the night before graduation, Von discovers that forty years have passed since he was declared missing and presumed dead. Even more mystifying to him is that he has no recollection of where he's been.

The hospital releases Von the following day. He is to come back the next day for follow-up with the specialist. After he is discharged, his mother wheels him out, while his now eighty-six-year-old dad, surprisingly spry for his age, brings the car around to the entrance to pick them up. While driving with his parents, Von sees a car passing – at least he thinks it is a car. This one sounds more like an aircraft than any road vehicle Von has ever seen. As he watches, it whines by and gracefully soars into the sky.

Inside his parent's car, Von notices the flow of traveler heading for the elevated Bzz-Tram terminal. It seems that everyone getting into the bus is elbow-to-elbow – an ample flow of everyday commuters. Bzz-Tram is the new transportation bus all over the metropolitan area.

While Von examines his outside surroundings, he sees a robot driving next to them. It is conspicuously a mechanical man, but it is designed partly like a human. This is clearly the HumRob that Mick was telling him about earlier at the hospital. Von can see the arm is made of some kind of an alloy metal and artificial resilient fiber.

"More like a thin aluminum foil that mom uses for cooking," he thinks to himself.

The HumRob senses his stare and rolls his window down. "Hi, there!" he yells and speeds up, whirling through the crowd and up into the sky before Von's father can say anything, leaving his mouth wide open.

Von gets a reality check, as he now realizes this must be "afterlife" – or is it really the *future?*

Von's father drives towards home, and Von comes across impressive skyscrapers. He wasn't aware of them the last time he drove home, which to him was just last week. The road and shortcuts he knows so well are no longer the same. The highway in the sky is packed with traffic. It seems that both young and old wear their personal computers like their clothes. He thinks that everyone is carrying a portable wireless on their body.

The streets are full of HumRob laborers with no human guidance whatsoever. He looks up the sky again with amazement, and he sees that it isn't empty. It is very crowded with more flying cars. Von stares at this impossible scene, and his jaw drops when another roaring whine immediately above him attracts his full attention.

"Are you okay, Von?" his eighty-eight-year-old mother asks. "How's your leg feel? You look tired. You need to rest as soon as we get home..."

"I'm fine, Mom. I still can't figure out how I lost my leg. And I'm just amazed at the new highway in the sky – just getting familiar with a lot of things I haven't seen," Von replies as he looks around. He sees another vehicle, but this time without a sleek aerodynamic modern design. He sees a '65 Mustang, heavily modified, cruising by about twenty feet overhead. He is amazed at what he just saw. For all he can tell, he doesn't even feel like he is on Earth.

"Oh, man," he sighs. His mind races with possibilities. He thinks, *Could it be some sort of amnesia, or maybe just a dream that would explain the gap in my memory...?*

A new disturbing possibility occurs to him: might this be the time to check into an asylum to be examined? After all, a reality check is in order! He hasn't thought of this before, but it could be a way to find out what really happened to him. They said he disappeared for forty years...But in Von's mind, it was just yesterday; and he can't remember any of it. Now, he sees himself an amputee and don't know how it happened. In his mind, it was just yesterday that he was in his dorm with his friends and now...he can't remember anything after that.

They arrive at his parents' house, and Von can't stop thinking, *Should I let fate take its course?* But time slowly wears on, and nothing happens. He begins to wish that fate would quit dragging its proverbial feet. As his friend Dex once said to him, "A wise man does not try to hurry history." Sound advice, but Dex had used it to try to be a "chick magnet," so Von isn't sure if the same theory applies to his current situation.

A low growl suddenly comes from his right. It is his mother's new RoDog. "Easy boy," Von instructs automatically. He notices the dog face is made of metal. The dog pauses enough to bark and bare its teeth and then returns to its discontented resting state in the corner, all the while making a loud rumbling sound. "Hey, Mom, this dog reminds me of *Swamp Dog*. Except Swamp despised going to the *Boww Wow Day Spa* and disapproved of sleeping in his organic cotton dog bed, which was perfect for a holistic dog lifestyle." Von says.

"Gee, son, I remember how *Swamp* loves to be pampered with organic *HOP-E Aromatherapy* coat spray and *chill* essential *Peppermint* dog breath drops, right?" his father proudly responds.

"Yah! By the way, when did *Swamp* die? And why did you guys get a RoDog instead of a real one?"

"*Swamp Dog* was run over by a drunk driver two days after you disappeared. If you remember, he couldn't see very well. The housekeeper left the front door open, and *Swamp Dog* crossed the road, probably looking for you. We cremated him and scattered his ashes on Casey Key beach, where you two always played together. We decided to get a RoDog a few years ago because they're good companions, they're easier to maintain, and they take care of themselves; we don't even need to walk him! RoDogs are pretty independent," his mother clarifies.

Distracted by an unfamiliar sound, Von glances out the window to see what caused it. What he sees is something that looks like a car passing his parents' house. It's another one of those cars of the future he saw on their way home.

Von swallows thickly, almost unsuccessfully. He doesn't know when or where he is, but one thing about this era has become very obvious: This isn't a time or place he knows.

Damn. What's happened to me? What have I missed? Where have I been all these years? he wonders sadly. None of this new world makes sense. This is getting very weird.

Von decides to see if he can get a look at himself. He bends down to look at a mirror in the kitchen only to be met by the hostile face of the dog, which he's forgotten about in the shock of his new surroundings. "Nice doggy," Von says with no hope for his statement turning into reality. "Everything's going to be all right. I'm just going to be using this spot for a short time. Just let me get a look at myself."

"Mom, I think your RoDog doesn't like me. Hey, where's Dad?" Von asks.

"I don't see why the dog wouldn't like you, Von. He might just need to get used to you. And I don't know where your father is. He might have gone to the store with his driver," his mother says, obviously concerned.

"Do me a favor, Von. Would you please turn on the green light on his collar? It is a radio, you know," his mother says.

"Radio station for a dog?" Von asks.

"Yes! We turn it on in the morning and they listen to it all day long."

"Crazy…Mom, would you show me how to use the new water system in your shower?"

"Of course. It's really easy. It's all based on your weight and height."

"What do you mean based on weight and height, Mom?"

"Well, it gives you more or less water depending on the scale that registers your information on shower floor. Go ahead – just stand there with your shorts on before the water turns on automatically. It'll talk to you and give you all the information that you need to activate the system."

"Can I still take long showers, Mom?" Von asks while he starts to play with the computerized water system.

"Of course. It will tell you if you're wasting water. It advises you that you have few seconds to finish before the automatic drying system will turn on. You don't need a towel. The system is good for older people, and it lessens your wash load," she tells.

"Do you need help getting ready?" his mother asks.

"No. I think I can manage. It seems like my body has adapted using my peg-leg. I must have had this peg-leg for quite a while and I don't even know it!"

"You mean your *machine gun* leg that they removed at the hospital? Well, we'll get to the bottom of this, Von. I promised you ..." his mother helps him with his shirt and leaves the room.

Von takes a shower and enjoys the new water system immensely. The modern faucet shows the time of the day and the temperature he is using. But then he remembers Mick was going to pick him up so that the two of them could go out to eat. He hurriedly finishes his shower and asks his mother if she has any clothes he could wear. His mother shows him his old clothes that they have kept. They still fit him, even though they are out of style. He chooses to wear jeans and the Hooters T-shirt that Mick gave him many years ago.

"Von, is Dex picking you up, or are you taking the new Bzz-Tram bus? Our driver can give you a ride wherever you want to go, too," his mother calls.

"I'm okay, Mom. Don't worry. I have a ride. I'll be right there, Mom," Von replies, feeling just like he's back to the good old days when he would come home from college.

Except the difference this time…Von has only one leg. Still confused and tired, he leaves his parents' house and meets his ride.

"Hey, Mick, how are you doin', buddy?"

"Von, I parked a couple of streets over, so we'll have to walk to the car. Do you think you can walk that far with your prosthesis?"

"No problem." Von is a bit afraid to cross the streets with cars flying overhead. There are only short landing areas and no landing roads. He's surprised that he has easily adjusted to his new leg.

"Damn, this is a little hard to move. I'll get used to it." Von frowns.

While they drive through a largely deserted area, Von sees an old convenient store that looks very much like any convenience store that he could ever imagine, just slicker.

He tells himself, *Either I accept that I'm in my own future or check myself in the nearest asylum and be sedated until I can make sense.*

"Hey, Von, what would you like to eat?" Mick asks.

"Anything is fine," he answers absentmindedly as he looks around him.

As they pass a sophisticated high-tech cyber store, Von sees a Mercedes Benz 570PA flying. It nestles adroitly between other personal flying crafts parked side by side just like the *Jetsons*. Mick and Von have pulled into a holographic gas station for a fill-up. It seems a dozen HumRobs swing into action like R2D2 in star wars, filling their tank. All Von can do is gawk and stay out of the way. He wonders if he will ever feel at home in this new reality. Every time he thinks he is getting used to it, something else amazes him.

"What does hydrogen gas mean?" Von asks.

"In 2048, vehicles are all using hydrogen – well, most of them – because it reduces greenhouse emissions and doesn't rely on the world's gas reserves. There are two ways of producing hydrogen: re-forming it from hydrocarbon sources such as natural gas or using electrolysis to release the hydrogen from water."

Is this the same as squeezing gas from a cow? I do remember back in college, they used to advertise that system to power our cars. They called it the *homegrown* gas, Von insisted

"Ahh, you mean the bio-gaz? That one is really from methane produced from slaughterhouse *poops*. They said whatever doesn't become burgers or strips of dried beef can be ground up and cooked in a special digester. That, my friend, later produces methane from the bacteria. Remember in our science class, they always told us it was highly combustible? Once the methane is produced, it is stored to a different station where it's needed. And it's just like propane or natural gas."

"What about public transportation? What do they use now?"

"Well, most buses and cars use a technology called Pro-Ton Energy Film (PTEF) to produce electricity. A fuel cell works like a battery that keeps recharging while people are using it. Instead of polluting with exhaust fumes of petrol and diesel gas, the hydrogen fuel only releases water," Mick replies.

"My parents told me that some cars make the electricity by splitting the electrons from hydrogen. My dad mentioned that the electric current arising from this electron flow drives the buses' electric motors. Is that really true?" Von asks.

"Well, hydrogen is quickly gaining acceptance as the eventual replacement for gasoline. Some older people are still adjusting to it, but believe me, it's really better for the environment and for our health."

"What does *this* car use?" Von questions.

"Some manufacturers' solution is to burn hydrogen in the car's rotary engine. Hydrogen combustion results in some emissions but far fewer than from a gasoline-only engine."

"Are hydrogen-fueling stations everywhere?" Von wonders.

"Believe it or not, some cars have a double-mobile power source with an electrical socket in the tailgate. Their concept is to run about 250 miles between fill-ups. Do you remember when we use to save gas in our utility shed because gas was so expensive? Well, people don't do that anymore," Mick chuckles.

"When I was at the hospital the other day I read in the *tel-a-paper* that there is now developmental research that putting a fuel cell in a small car saves space and energy on that car. It makes a car roomier than conventional cars because fuel cells don't need as much space for an engine and other mechanical parts. What's that all about?" Von asks, thinking he really missed a lot during those forty years.

"Some of the newer cars that came out a few months ago are all like that. Others have fuel-cell power from plant materials on their interior and exterior components. Power from potato skin fuels will start powering the whole world pretty soon. It's a new world out there, Von; it really is," Mick replies, half sadly.

"Mick, is that a police officer?" Von asks as he notices what looks to be a police officer turn on flashers as stunning as "full moon."

"Yes, it's a HumRob police officer."

They continue driving until they see a coffee shop, where they stop to talk just like the good old days. They go inside, walk to the counter, and look at the menu prices: "Coffee, $75.00."

"What the heck?" Von whispers to himself. Outside the restaurant is a dietary profile screen. Von sees Mick punch in some information, and he tries to look at what Mick is entering.

"What is that, Mick?"

"You see, dietary profiles are stored online. The list has the best food for people based on their medical history and genetic profile. All of the restaurants have these systems now. They use the information to suggest dishes that are good for your health and designed for you personally."

"Whoa, that's pretty awesome…but coffee for seventy-five dollars? What is it, rocket fuel?" Hauling out his wallet, he surveys the few hundred dollars he has in his old wallet that the police found at his dorm forty years ago when he disappeared. Then, a young waitress with "goth" makeup approaches Von and places a broken and barely used coffee cup in front of him.

Von just sits in place and stares. Something is most definitely wrong. What is this soda in front of him? It reads: 'Coeseven'.

It sounds like 'code seven'. Is this some kind of emergency drink? Yuk! Is that what I think it is? They combine 7-Up with something else? They wouldn't do that no matter what, would they? Von asks himself. It's really the menu combination that mystifies him, not the drinks.

"Will you be having lunch or early supper?" the waitress asks Von.

"My friend and I are both having coffee and maybe sandwiches," Von replies as the waitress shakes her head and stares at Von with her eyes wide open.

"Would you like to wait till he gets here, or would you rather order now while waiting for him?"

"We can order now, he's right here next to me."

"*Oooookay*! Whatever you say," the waitress answers sarcastically, looking around. "Our coffee of the day is copper green with a dash of new-and-improved metallic powder. Any takers?" She looks at Von and then turns her head with a grin, snapping her gum.

Von scoots over so fast to the side, scared that he might get spit at and is lost by the coffee choices. "Um…Do you have any regular coffee, please?" he asks. Then he whispers, "Hey Mick, I don't think the waiter likes you. She's pretending like you're not even here. I think you're not her type, man," Von says to Mick with a big smile in his face.

"Yeah, I get that a lot with women!" Mick responds.

"Hey buddy, what the hell is copper green coffee, and what's a metallic powder?"

"Those are the coffees for the HumRobs: metallic powder is their half and half creamer," Von hears Mick whisper back.

"They eat and drink, too?" Von asks, surprised.

"Yep. Don't ask me how it works. All I know is they are same as humans, except their organs are mechanical. To be honest with you, I've never seen their body parts…" Mick laughs.

"Are you serious? They have the same body parts and organs like we do?" Von whispers.

"Yep, and be careful talking about it in public. You never know who's sitting next to you. Anyway, where would you like to go from here?"

"Do you mind if you just leave me here? I really want to explore on my own if that's okay, and I don't want my parents to worry about me being in a new environment," Von says.

"Are you sure?" Mick asks.

"I'm positive."

"Okay, let me pick you up around six o'clock – before sundown," Mick says as he looks down at his wristwatch, which contains GPS and video-conferencing.

"What kind of watch is that?" Von asks.

"It's one of the new high-tech watches. It gives you accurate readings on your health; it beeps at you when you are feeling nauseous, when you are close to fainting, and when you have other health issues. Since I'm in my early sixties now, I decided I could use one of these," Mick details. "As we get older, we want medical solutions to keep us alive longer. More and more older people want to live longer and healthier lives and will require large investments in medical research."

"Oh...really?" Von responds, confused and intrigued.

"Yes. As a matter of fact, this innovative technological treatment will cost a lot of money, which everyone will be able to afford."

"What do you do?" Von asks.

"Well, in order for me to keep my family alive and healthy, I need extra insurance for higher technology so that they can keep me posted on the best medicine out there. Otherwise, I'll be like the rest of the population who's having a hard time keeping up with the latest medical research. Artificial organs are now the future of health," Mick relates.

"What do you mean?"

"To keep people healthier and alive longer, there will need to be a focus on improving the general well-being of the population."

"Is that possible?"

"It may be impossible to fund high-technology inventions for the increasing number of older people, so some other individuals have to pay an extra fee to keep them aware of the new medical technology. Like the newest medications and all of that stuff, you know?"

"Is that good or bad?" Von asks.

"Well, it's good *and* bad, I guess, but by putting money into helping the population live a happier and healthier life, there is less demand on hospitals and nursing homes."

"We can now do simple skin grafting by using *skinpotatoe.*"

"Potato skin? Why potato skin?"

"I don't know!"

"Why are there a lot of robotic nurses in the hospital?"

"They're HumRobs. There's a difference," Mick explains. "HumRobs are partly human, while robots are purely mechanical. Their skin is partly made of clay and terracotta. Heck, I don't know the technicalities. You have to ask my son. He's really knowledgeable about all of this. We should get together with my kids after your surgery, okay?" Mick suggests.

"Is everything okay here? Would you like some more coffee?"

"Nope! My friend and I are just finishing our coffee, and we are on our way out," Von replies to the waitress.

"Whatever you say!" the waitress answers sarcastically again.

"Okay, let me take care of this bill, and I'll see you later in front of the library," Von says to Mick.

"Which library?" Mick asks.

"That small one downtown," Von answers.

"That library is huge now. Believe me, you won't even recognize it. Okay, I'll see you later," Mick says as Von sees him leaves the coffee shop. Von finishes his cup of coffee, and pulls out two of his fifty-dollar bills.

"Well, excuse me, I can't tell you the exchange of old currency, we don't accept that here," she says as though Von is trying to cheat her.

"Old currency? What do you mean old?"

"Old, as in ancient, no longer in use? What's wrong with you? Where have you been? Nobody uses that anymore. You should have asked your *friend* to pay the bill instead. Is he still here?" She looks around, shakes her head again, and gives Von a weird look while she cleans the counter and snap her bubble gum.

"No! He left, and I promised him I would pay for his coffee. Sorry, I had a brain injury. I don't remember the changes in the new currency," Von lies, hating it.

"Okayyy! Just pay the bill, please? Or...I'll call the cops."

A middle-aged woman with a metal arm is waiting for her take-out order at the counter and overhears the conversation. She walks over to Von and say, "My son owns an old currency store next door. I know something about the market. Do you want to sell those?" the woman asks a confused Von.

Von hands her the bills, and the woman holds them to the light. Von notices her arm is partly *metal* and assumes that she must be a HumRob. The woman makes a more-than-generous offer to Von for his old bills, noting that one of them is worth twice the face value of the bill.

"Here, ma'am," Von says with a smile. He settles the bill and leaves the coffee shop without leaving a tip, and sets out on foot to see the town.

He crosses the street and stops, dazzled by the new surroundings, only to be dazzled again by the sudden, stunning outlook of the city.

First, he notices the quality of the architecture; everything seems surreal. Then, there is the reduced ozone that is formed naturally in the atmosphere. The towers everywhere in downtown have escalated the office buildings, which outshine the horizon. Older building construction squeezes into limited spaces among the new, shielded by colossal steel.

As he gets closer to where he is going, Von sees that the old roads he knows are jam-packed. The freeways begin to disappear from a series of underground tunnels. Ancient-looking streets have become monstrous. The young and old have strange fashions and hairstyles. For Von, everything is an astonishing sight. Everything is opulence, as if the small town where he used to live has turned into the new world of the HumRobs.

"I never thought I'd see this time," he says to himself. He notices the new Circuit City, so he decides to take a look inside. He is greeted by a young man.

"Good afternoon, Mr. Carmichael," the young man says.

"Oh, hi! Do I know you from somewhere?" Von asks, wondering how the young man knows his name.

"No! We don't know each other. I just know who you are from reading your iris-recognition identity through mine," the young man tells Von.

"Oh, I forgot about that," Von says as the man wonders if Von has a short circuit in his memory.

"Sir, it can recognize and match every person's identity in seconds. You do know that, don't you, Mr. Carmichael? Everyone knows the process makes it impossible to falsify a person's data or identity. The details of each person's iris are typically unique. No two are exactly alike - even among twins or in your own two eyes. There's no way to fool the system," the young man preaches.

"Thanks for reminding me, and I apologize for the inconvenience I caused you. I had a head injury and have become very forgetful recently," Von lies and realizes that this young man must be one of the HumRobs Mick told him about earlier. The man walks away, and Von browses on his own.

He pauses while looking at the information desk, and he now remembers that Mick warned him about the iris-recognition system. Mick mentioned that they now use it everywhere. Von forgot that that is how they were able to discover his identity and track his parents when they found him in his old dorm room.

He walks around the store and is fascinated by 2048's new technology. Their televisions are no longer plasma. They now have holographic televisions with screen as wide as a regular bedroom. Von goes ahead and speaks with one of the sales people.

"Excuse me, what does this sign mean?" He points to the sign near the holographic tubes.

"It means you can literally smell anything inside the television while watching; flowers, fragrances being use by any entertainers, just about anything. It's the new-and-improved *Smell-O-Vision* system," the salesman explains.

"Wow! Does that mean I can smell a cooking show as well? Damn, that's great, and the holographic television is so big it's like God coming to pay a visit," he whispers to himself with a smile.

Watching one is a true theater-like experience, plus it also serves as a security system and connects to a holographic doctor.

He leaves the store and walks a few blocks. The sights of the city now seem hostile. A homeless person with a scruffy dog begs Von for money. Remembering that he has not eaten since lunch yesterday, the homeless man wills his weak body to move and goes to the nearest garbage can. He scavenges through it, sniffing the pile of trash. He soon finds what he is looking for – a big, empty can of Coke and an old, dried hamburger on a wet bun. He sniffs it – the smell of the onions in it is lost in the mix of other trash, gum, empty chocolate shake containers, bugs, and used baby diapers. He reaches for the old hamburger and starts eating it.

He smirks toothlessly, pets his cranky pooch, and watches Von walk near him with curiosity. "We haven't eaten in four days, have we, pup?" The limp and dirty dog, like the beggar himself, is busy licking the sores at his foot and looks at the man, then scampers away whining back into his kennel made of a paper box covered with duct tape.

The beggar stretches out his hand one more time, making a pitiful face, and begs Von for money. Von takes a bill from his wallet and gives it to the homeless man. The beggar's dirty and calloused fingers tightly grip the bill. He watches Von leave, eventually losing sight of him in a crowd. Then he opens his fist and sees the folded fifty-dollar bill. He smiles. With the money in his hands, he thinks of the three days' worth of alcohol he can finally buy.

Von crosses to the next lane and sees a *Holoservice* newsstand. The rack looks more like a sophisticated futuristic television set. Von thinks, *You would have thought by now they would have made these things obsolete!* He remembers earlier that a man at the café stood in front of the eye scanner and looked into some sort of identification slot on the vending machine to buy cigarettes.

Von puts his eyes in front of the icon and looks into the machine's sensor plate. A flickering light flashes and Identiskans his iris. A beautiful female with a lovely voice speaks: "Hello, Mr. Carmichael. What is your choice for today's news?"

"Um, what are the selections?" he stammers, shocked by the personalized response and blushes a little bit, feeling like he is talking to a real person.

"What are your choices? What are your choices?" the machine repeats like a broken record. "One moment, please, one moment, please" the box spins.

A man next to Von demonstrates, wafts his hand across the *Holoservice News*. It cuts through it with a holographic ripple effect. "First time I used one of these, I asked her out on a date…I didn't know how to use it either. I didn't even know it's a hologram," the man says, grinning graciously, examining Von's face.

"Thanks!" Von says appreciatively. He hears a whirring sound coming from the *Holoservice News* and sees a flashing light. A bell rings, and a fresh newspaper pops out from a slot in the side of the machine. The paper is still extremely hot, like newly baked bread. The ink on some parts of the paper is still a bit smeary.

Then the voice comes on again: "Thank you, Mr. Carmichael, for choosing *Holoservice News*."

Von looks at the *machine* with his eyes partly closed. He wafts his hand across the box, and the *Holoservice* flinches at the impact. Von composes himself and smiles bashfully.

"I'm so sorry," he says. "I didn't mean to do that." Von apologizes as if he is talking to a human being.

"It's okay. Really. I get that a lot," the *Holoservice* responds back and winks at him.

Von wonders why they even have newspapers anymore. He remembers how everyone was getting the news from online services, and that was years ago. Curiously, he looks at the front page and notices something is different. All the bylines are time-stamped, and some are as recent as minutes and hours ago. Somehow, the paper was updated just before he pulled it from the receptacle!

He sits down on a nearby bench and reads the paper. A man next to him stares at him while he reads.

"Would you like to read the paper?" Von asks.

"No, thank you. I already read it through my eye-vision system channels," the man replies.

"Would you mind telling me what those are?" Von curiously asks.

"You don't know?" the man looks at Von with bewilderment.

"Sorry, I don't remember. I've had a head injury, and I've been forgetting a lot of things lately," he says, deciding this is the best explanation.

"Oh, one of those things, huh?" the man replies. "Well, eye-vision channels are a system you can get through your optician. They put little microchips in your eyeglasses, and your brain automatically reacts with the power coming from your retina. When you have the system, you can access any news or weather report from wherever you are," the man says. "I have to get going. Have a good day." He then walks away.

CHAPTER TWENTY FOUR

CARPE DIEM

Von stands outside for a moment looking up at the new 21st-century public library entrance. The thought of no archived books seems somehow as odd as the futuristic newspaper stand. He takes a deep breath as he enters the building, not knowing what to expect next and wondering whether he will be able to find what he is looking for – information about his disappearance forty years ago.

Inside, Von sees that it looks pretty much as he remembers except for the holographic computers on a nearby console instead of desktop computers. They don't even have a check-out desk, so he walks to the woman standing behind it who seems to be in charge. His eyes wander around the large room with the familiar stacks of books. At the end of each stack, there is a holographic computer station on which a classic *Bibliothec*, a professional trained in library science and engaged in library service, smiles at Von.

The woman looks amazingly similar to the young lady behind the holographic computers, and she beckons users to stop for assistance. Von sees the telltale red flicker in the corner of the woman's eye, identifying her as a Humrob.

"Of course," Von thinks to himself. "Why would they use people for jobs like this when they can program robots to know so much more?"

Undaunted, Von asks the HumRob administrator for directions to the historical records section. She smiles at Von and points to the rows of holographic computer terminals behind the stacks, explaining that the books are the reserve section but mostly are only for effect. She says that the data accessible only from libraries is all stored in a central database on a supercomputer. Von smiles, accepting that he has been duped into believing a quaint colloquialism to be real.

He sits down at one of the stations, hoping no humans have seen his gaffe. Minutes turn into hours as he negotiates the system. Each path takes him with lightning speed close to finding his own disappearance only to cut off with an error message that reads:

Inconclusive Data Search; please try another query.

Von senses something is not right and that for some unknown reason, he is being blocked.

"Good afternoon, Mr. Carmichael. Are you having difficulty with our system?" a voice in the holographic monitor says.

"Damn, doesn't anyone have privacy around here?" Von whispers to himself while looking at the blinking holographic monitor talking to him.

Somewhat embarrassed by his outburst, he shuts down the computer without signing out causing the alarm to sound. A couple of HumRob administrative assistants come over to where Von is sitting. They each check the holographic system with a tiny *micro chips* and swipe it out. The alarm stops and the two HumRob assistants walk away. Von feels his neck hair bristle as he senses someone standing next to him again. When he turns around, he finds a young lady passing him; she is being followed by a small robotic mechanical cart full of books. The girl is pretty. He thinks she is human and that she is made more so by her infectious smile. She is pretty in a wholesome way and wears very simple clothes.

She put him at ease and he fumbles with an apology, "I was wondering if you can help me. Are you..." Von wants to ask if she is human but embarrassed to ask so he changed his mind and instead asks a different question. "Sorry, I just can't find what I need. I was hoping for more facts. I need more information."

"I know what you mean. I'm one of the many human library clerks that are left, and I work regularly around here. Just so you know, the library has indexed everything to a big central database to the point of losing the essence of the old-fashioned research. Remember how we used index files in the old days? We don't do that anymore. All we do now is ask *CLEO*."

"Did you say...Ask *Cleo?* What is Cleo, or who is Cleo?"

"C.L.E.O. stands for Computerized Library Educational Organization," the young girl responds.

"What does it do?"

"Well, it gives all the information you need as long as it is available in our master computer and database."

"Really? All I have to do is mention something, and CLEO will get it for me?"

"Yeah, that's right. Then, you can touch any of the information in front of you. It doesn't even need to be a holographic computer. As long as CLEO can reach the signal, it will feed you the information right there and then. Why don't you know the system? Where have you been?"

"Ahhh! I had a brain surgery, and I easily forget some-times," Von lies again, uncomfortably.

"Sorry to hear that." There is sadness in her voice. Shy-ly, she extends her hand. "By the way, my name is Lexielle. Hey! Do I know you from somewhere? Have I met you somewhere before?"

"I doubt it. I don't think so. Was I just talking really loudly there for a minute? Sorry if I am. By the way, I'm Von. My name is Von," he says, shaking her hand and reveling in its smooth warmth.

"Nah! You're fine. You're not loud at all." Broadening her smile, she says, "And let me get rid of this cart, I'll be right back to assist you." She enters a couple of codes into the side of the mechanical cart, and it goes away on its own.

He watches her hurry away, pleased for more reasons than he can admit. She helps relieve some of his loneliness and frustration. He hopes she really will come back.

She does and says, "Let me take you to the tower where all of the old files are located at."

"Tower?" Von whispers to himself. They find piles of time-worn newspapers covering every available space, leaving just enough room for the tables and holographic computer screen.

Von grins and scratches his head. "Isn't there anything left of the old system?"

She sits at the holographic computer. "There used to be a catalogue until a few years ago, but they locked it up in the *black tower* when they changed over to HOLFXNEWS2 deliveries.

"Did you say *black tower*? What is '*black tower*'?"

"Only the head of the HumRob police department can access those old files. I was informed that the library has everything recorded, but I don't believe it."

Looking up at him standing beside her, she needs to distract him from his gaze, which is roaming over her. "What do you need to see?" she says, blushing a little.

"Oh, uh, can you keep a secret?"

"Sure!" Try me…the girl was curious to hear what Von is about to say.

"Well, I think I have a clone somewhere."

"You're joking, right?" Von immediately laughs hoping he can convince the girl that he was just teasing.

"Do you think we can find out if anyone has a clone somewhere?" he insists again.

"Okay. That doesn't sound too hard." She begins typing, thinking that either Von is serious or he is a joker.

"This acts just like the central data bank. Tell me the dates, and I'll dig up the information for you."

"Do you remember when they cloned you? Do you know which scientist did it?"

"Nah! I don't have a clue.

She looks further and is able to eliminate unnecessary write-ups or feature columns about suspected cloning. Her search is narrowed down to only eleven instances in which "Von" is never mentioned, of course. Then Von comes upon the desired issue that he wants. The girl begins to look for the appropriate newspaper publication, but finds it's not about cloning but about a disappearance of a college student.

When she has found the papers, she stops, removes her eyeglasses, and looks at him more closely. "Gosh, are you really a clone? How can this be?"

Von back off, and swerves. He didn't expect to see his close-up head shot.

She exclaims, "Did they really clone you forty years ago?"

"That's what I wanted to know because I always see someone who looks just like me and has the same mannerisms as I have." He feels a bit awkward about the lie he's been telling the girl as her eyes scan over him.

"Why would you want to know if you're a clone? If you ask me...I wouldn't want to know," the girl asks, continuing to look at Von's face.

"I'm sorry to say this, but he really looks like your twin brother. I'm going to say this to you again: I really think you're a clone...Do you know this man?" She looks at Von more closely, inspecting every angle of his face. Von doesn't responds to her questions.

She looks at Von again and read some of the articles. Most are about Von's vanishing act in his dorm in 2008. The next article mentions a college kid who disappeared without a trace.

Von is so disappointed that he can't find more of the older files about his disappearance at the dorm and he really hates to continue lying to Lexielle. She tells Von it will take several weeks for her to go through the database in order for her to find out the real story behind all those old newspapers. She mentions that there was an accident at the main electrical power plant, and some of the *nano* micro chips were destroyed.

He turns to her and says, "Is there any other Carmichael family who've cloned themselves? Is there any news similar to cloning?" He feels awkward again about the lie he's been telling this girl, but he needs to look further on their old archives.

"If you really are interested in those old archive files, I need to go through the database. Sorry to tell you that it can't possibly happen today or tomorrow. It can be done but not right now. You really need to wait till everything is done in the power plant." Her smile is reassuring. "I promise. I'll help you." The green lamp sheds light on her shiny hair as she puts the older file away. The smell of shampoo fills Von's head with a scent that makes him realize how long it's been since he has thought of any woman other than Bessie. She smiles at him, and he returns the smile.

They share a look which, without an explanation, expresses their connection. They continue to work. Von asks another question, and as she reaches across him to grab another microfiche, by accident her chest grazes the length of his arm that is holding the computer mouse. Chills run into Von's stomach, and he is shocked by his body's undeniable response to the young woman. The feeling reminds him of the first time he discovered his father's *Playboy* magazine hidden under the fishing tackle box.

He looks at her, noticing how kind and soft her brown eyes are. He notices how flawless her skin is and how beautiful the angles of her high, rosy cheekbones are. Von becomes warm and feels his face flush uncontrollably.

She notices his blushing face, and she blushes, too. She moves a strand of hair that has fallen over her angelic face. Their eyes lock. They are drawn together and are about to kiss when the head HumRob librarian interrupts.

"Miss Kostan, I need you immediately at the front desk. There is a line of nearly thirty students waiting to check out." Von sees the telltale red flicker in the corner of the woman's eye, identifying her as a Humrob.

The moment is gone. Von recuperates and slowly gets up, leaves, and meets Mick outside the library.

He realizes that he doesn't have the time to wait for the library file in the next few weeks. He is supposed to undergo a medical procedure that his parents and the doctors want him to do. His parents will take him the following day for his medical observation in the hospital. He is told that after the procedure, he can go home the same day and will be treated by the holographic doctor in case there are complications.

A car is waiting for Von outside the library. As soon as Von crosses the street, he sees Mick on the driver's side.

"What's wrong, buddy?" Von asks.

"My asthma is bothering me lately. I need to see my holographic doctors when I get home. It must be from the smoke at the restaurant earlier."

"Hey, tell me more about the holographic doctors. What're they all about?"

"Well, they're pretty good. It's a good system, especially for older people who have trouble leaving their houses. What it is, is a personal monitoring system that records your vital signs, heart rate, and breathing and tracks your movements through the house. It quickly alerts medical services or your family in the event of a fall, accident, or drastic change in your heart rate.".

"How do the doctors know all these things?"

"They check your conditions and provide support via a voice and video communications system. Your holographic doctors are at your door within seconds."

"What do you mean? It sounds like they're on call just for you," Von wonders.

"In some ways, they are, but it's amazing how the technology has changed since you disappeared."

"Do the holographic doctors check you just like the old-fashioned doctors?" Von asks.

"Actually, the chemicals in your breath can be monitored to provide more information about other potential health problems. There is a system called My-Health-Check that is hidden in every household bathroom mirror. You don't have to worry about your procedure. You're in good hands." Mick smiles sympathetically and encouragingly at Von.

When Von reaches his house, he invites Mick in, but Mick declines, saying his wife Patrice has prepared dinner for him. He invites Von to join them, but Von decides to stay home to spend some time with his parents.

Dinner is ready when Von walks in the door. He helps his mother in the kitchen just like he used to. His mom cooks his favorite meal while the RoDog keeps them company.

"How was your day?" his mother asks.

"It was great, Mom. Everything is so different around here, and I had a great time."

"Who gave you a ride?"

"Mick…Mick gave me a ride, Mom," he whispers.

"Mick?" she asks.

"Yes, mother, Mick."

"Oh, okay…" she responds and looks at Von with a loving smile.

Arrffff, Arrffff.

"Keep still, Fluffy. You know you can't eat this kind of food. It'll make you sick," Von's father says.

"Mom, this meal is delicious. It tastes just as I remember it. And your new kitchen is cool. Is that the style these days?"

"Yes, and you don't have to worry about helping me in the kitchen after dinner, dear," his mother says.

"What do you mean? Of course I'll help," Von says, confused.

"No, really! We now have nanometer technology in our kitchen and bathrooms. It repels any dirt that touches any of the surfaces. The architect who built this house told me and your dad that the molecules in the surface layers of the kitchen and bathroom will break apart and repel all organic materials, which eliminates the use of cleaning chemicals, dear. Every surface in our kitchen and in all of our bathrooms is dirt-free and water-repellent."

"That is so cool, Mom. Hey, Dad, I noticed that the water system is totally different – very high-tech. What's with the new system?"

"The architect talked me into it. It was just a simple addition to our plumbing to capture the water from the sinks, showers, and our washing machines. The grey water is now filtered and stored in tanks to be used for watering gardens and flushing the toilet. By law, we need to recycle grey water in all new houses," his father explains.

"Have you seen the newly installed *tov-si-gerator* in our guest house?

"What's a *tov-si-gerator*, dad?"

"It's a stove, sink and refrigerator in one. It's good for efficiency apartment style.

"Wow. There's so much for me to catch up on," Von says and then takes the dishes to the kitchen. The HumRob housekeeper cleans them.

"Von, would you come to the den, please?" his dad asks gently.

"Sure, Dad."

"Hey, I want you to watch our housekeeper. Her mechanical parts haven't been functioning well recently. If you see something smoking around her, it means she's short-circuiting. You have to gently reach behind her neck to the small button. Press that button, which should eliminate more damage, but remember not to let her know what you're doing, or she may hurt you. She might think that you're trying to shoot down her system, so be careful, okay?" his dad says.

"Dad, how can I do all that without her knowing it? She'll see me," Von worries.

"Just do the best you can. I don't want to come home to see that the housekeeper has knocked you out cold," his father says with a smile.

"Okay, I'll try my best, but aren't you going to have her system fixed?"

"Yes, we have ordered the parts, but it's taking a while for them to get here."

"Well, it's time for me to retire for the night. Do you know how to use the new holographic TV?" his dad asks sleepily.

"I'll figure it out, Dad. Thanks," Von says.

"Hey Von, your favorite gal from that show *The OC* has five kids of her own and weighs two-hundred-fifty pounds! The times have changed, my boy, time really has changed!"

"Are you serious? What happened to her? She must have eaten too many pizzas and hamburgers, huh?" Von says, half-joking.

"I don't think so. We all have to watch our diets now. It's now the law that everyone needs to watch what we eat."

"Damn, that's weird," Von says and starts to look at the family pictures on a table. "Hey, Mom, what happened to Uncle Nigel?"

"Von, he passed away a few years ago," his mother replies sadly.

"What did he die off? Was he really a retired vineyard owner, Mom?" Von asks.

"He died of old age. He was in his nineties when he passed away. And to answer your questions...yes, of course your uncle Nigel was a retired vineyard owner, dear. What made you ask?"

"Nothing, really. I'm just curious," Von replies. "Oh, and Mom, when did you retire from your job at the UN, and did you like it?"

"What a silly question, son. Of course I enjoyed it then. I've been retired since a few years after you disappeared. I thought it was about time for me to just stay home," his mother replies, somewhat anxiously. "Why all these questions, Von? You have never been interested in my work, so why now?"

Von doesn't answer the question and continues looking at the rest of the family pictures on the top of the shelves in their living room. He notices an old metal picture frame. He picks it up and stares at it for a long time.

"Mom, who's this man in the picture next to Grandpa?"

"Oh, that's Michael, Grandpa's best friend when he was young. He came from England and became Grandpa's business confidant," his mother says.

"He looks familiar to me," Von says.

"Oh, yeah? I don't think you met him. I did, when I was very young. He was a very successful businessman in England, and everyone thinks he looks just like you."

"It's so weird…he looks really familiar," Von insists and puts the picture frame back on the shelf as he stares at it.

"Well, good night, son!" his dad says.

When his parents go to their room, Von tries to figure out the new television system in the living room. He can't find anything to watch, so he goes to his room and goes to sleep.

The following morning, they all wake up early. Von isn't allowed to eat anything because of the procedure, so he sits down with his parents and just has a glass of water. After his parents finish their breakfast, they drive him to the hospital.

On the way to the hospital the sirens blare on and off. The ambulance zooms to the hospital, weaving in and out of air traffic. The girl from the library races in her car to keep up. Four minutes…Four minutes is something that no technology has changed. In four minutes, her little brother will be brain-dead due to a lack of oxygen.

He had taken her new technology gum out of her purse, not knowing that only one piece could be eaten at a time and that there are strict directions not to swallow it. The warning label is not attached in the container. He did not know that it was saliva-activated to expand and that it grows if swallowed. He was choking before she knew it. He was gasping for life, and the Heimlich maneuver didn't work. As she dialed in fury for help, his body went blue until it was lifeless. Her heart broke as she watched her brother's life be stolen by her high-tech gum.

She suddenly looks up as she is about to crash into another vehicle that is turning slowly into the hospital parking lot. As the other car comes painfully close, she sees Von inside the car with his parents, and Von sees her, but she cannot waste a moment. She tears into the hospital after the stretcher, and Von knows that there is something terribly wrong.

When they enter the hospital, Von looks around and sees Mick, Patrice, and Dex. Next to them is a petite, well-dressed woman in her fifties. Dex walks towards Von and shakes his hand.

"It's been a while, man…It's been a while, and you look the same. Wow, you haven't changed a bit. I'm shocked, I don't know what to say," Dex says.

"I'm glad you came. I missed you, man!" Von whispers as the petite woman walks towards Von and gives him a long hug.

"Von, it's been a while," the woman whispers softly as tears fill her eyes.

"Hello, Bessie. You look as pretty as the last time I saw you. You really haven't changed," Von says.

"Older…I look older," she says.

"Ah! I love older women," Von whispers into her ear teasingly, squeezing her hand. Bessie blushes and squeezes back.

"I am so sorry that I didn't come to see you the other day. I was in shock and didn't know how to react. It's been so many years. I waited and waited until I decided it was time to let go." Tears are now running down her cheeks as she speaks. His parents, Mick, and Patrice walk down the hall to give Von and Bessie privacy.

The two of them sit down and talk for at least half an hour, holding hands the entire time. Then, Bessie decides that Von should spend some time with his parents before the procedure. They continue to hold hands and walk toward the others.

"Oh, Bessie…" Von whispers softly as he looks at everyone. He is uncomfortable seeing everyone is old except for him. His dad walks toward him and gives him a big hug. Mick shakes his hand and tells him how much he's missed him. His mother is crying and tells him everything will be okay. They know that the procedure will help him find the answers he needs.

"I'll see you guys later. I love you," he says to his parents.

Two doctors come forward and speak to Von about the procedure, explaining that it is very safe and has been done many times before. A younger nurse is with them and takes notes. One of the doctors tells his parents that they will now take him to the procedure room. Von gives everyone another hug.

"We'll be right here waiting for you..." Bessie whispers in his ear. She sits back while Dex comforts her.

"Please do...Would you please excuse me, I need to speak with Mick privately," Von whispers to Bessie as she looks towards the sliding door, trying to see where Von is heading.

"Where are you going, Von?" Dex asks.

"I need to discuss some things with Mick. I need to ask him if he can be my medical surrogate. I'll be right back, man."

"Who do you need to speak to? And what's with the medical surrogate?

"I'll explain later," Von whispers, and Bessie sees Von talking on the other side of the corridor. Von whispers back and walks away with the doctors. He knows that this is the best thing to do for everyone to find out what happened to him. He knows that relying on the medical field search for answers is the best thing to do to end this mystery.

Von is hooked up to all kinds of equipment during the examination. They have decided that in order to find out what is wrong with him, he needs to have a transgression hypnosis and holographic surgery, in which doctors can look at a three-dimensional CAT scan and take measurements within the holographic image of his organs and other parts of his body. Von is very nervous, but everyone has assured him that it is a safe and simple procedure. They put him on an examining table and start the process.

Von undergoes transgression hypnosis by the chief of psychiatry to determine if he is having delusions or if he is indeed a time-traveler. He is taken back to another time, and he sees he is married to an Edwardian lady and has children. He is the owner of a big corporation. Then, he sees a fleeting stranger with beautiful blonde hair. Von talks through his hypnosis to the psychiatrist, who sees Von's internal struggle to be true to Bessie while he is very drawn to the beautiful blonde. He wants her and gasps that she is like an angel. He feels a stronger connection with her than he has ever felt toward anyone else without even knowing her.

The doctor tries to determine what role this woman plays in Von's life: a wife, a relative, or something else. Von does not know the answer. He only knows that she has won his heart.

The psychiatrist announces that Von is not psychotic and is, quite to the contrary, very psychologically healthy, considering what it appears he has been through. The doctor says he believes Von is a time-traveler and refers him to the only expert surgeon who can deal with these delicate matters.

The surgeon is introduced to Von and his family, and he outlines their choices: If it turns out that his brain is older, and only his body is young, Von can undergo surgery to make his body catch up. However, this will make him die sooner even though he will fit in with Mick, his parents, and Bessie.

If he has both a young body and young brain, he can try to fix it so that he will age like other young people, but there is no guarantee of the unknown. Another option is for the surgeon to try an unproven concept of exploding Von so that he would probably go back to the Edwardian time and his wife and children, for whom he currently has no feelings.

Von struggles with the pros and cons and weighs the options in his head. An earlier death, no guarantee of the unknown, or a life back in time with no connection?

"The enzyme that we will use on you will turn your facial muscles soft and spongy. You won't look like the same man. You will look older, perhaps much older, depending on how your body reacts to the enzyme. It's vicious but very effective," the specialist explains.

Von looks at his family, hugs his mother and father, says goodbye to Dex, and wishes them all well. He holds Bessie's hand and tells her how much he loves her and has loved her all this time. He looks at the surgeon and enters the operating room. He knows that there is no such thing as a free ride and that he has to be man enough to face a tough decision.

Von enters the operating room and surveys everyone uneasily. He's not nervous about the procedure but rather about the whole setup, the robotic needles and scalpels, and the modern medical technology, which Von truly does not care for.

An operating room aide says to Von, "Don't worry. These doctors could open your abdomen, sew a dead mouse or squirrel in there, and you'd never get an infection. Not with the kind of nano-reconstruction enzyme they'll be giving you."

"What enzyme would that be?" Von asks.

"It's the new Tuf-fu-Organ-neck-macro-bi-tek enzyme." the hospital aide reiterates as he leaves the room in a hurry.

"I am ready now, Doctor," Von says.

"All right. Lie down on this table, and Nurse Evans will prepare you for the procedure," the doctor responds.

Von removes his clothes and shoes. He lies down on the operating table stares at the ceiling. He knows that he has chosen the best decision and closes his eyes as they give him the oxygen mask and make him count backwards. Within seconds, he is out cold.

A biotechnician doctor peers through his microscope and is starting to work at the stainless steel table. He is dissecting and examining protoplasmic tissue masses that they will use for Von. Then he uses robotic arms to manipulate organic tissue behind a glass barrier that protects it from other microbes.

The head scientist tests neurotissue that will be used for Von's muscles. Four HumRob surgeons and two human surgeons perform the procedure. They look at each other through their surgical masks and shake their heads. They know what Von wants, and there is nothing they can do about changing his mind. They asked him repeatedly, and he insisted that it is his own decision and that no one else is liable. He said that he is not changing his mind. He knows the risk he is taking. He knows that there is a big possibility of danger, but it is what he wants to do.

While the doctors are busy with Von's procedure, the electrical devices interact with the other medical machinery. The power in the operating room is shut off, and a loud noise echoes throughout the hospital. The operating room is a disaster. The hospital security arrives to inspect the commotion.

The electrical backup in the hospital is turned on, and the doctors remove their surgical masks and leave the operating room.

Von walks out of the room, looks down, and sees his aged body. Von feels the skin on both of his cheeks begin to pucker. The muscle goes soft, and his chin begins to sag like an old man's. His forehead starts to wrinkle, the healthy pink inside his eyes is bloodless gray, and the skin under his eyes droops. This is the effect: he has aged fifty years.

When the door opens toward the lobby where everyone waits for him, an unhealthy-looking older man walks slowly out of the procedure room. He nods and walks past the nurse, who watches his uncertainty as he wanders off to his family.

"Hello Von," a voice whisper .

He lovingly looks at Bessie's wrinkles like they are badges of honor earned by a never-ending love for him.

As he walks through the lobby of the hospital, he sees gorgeous Lexielle. She looks at him, sees that he looks older with wrinkles and frail body, and is limping with a cane.

Von slowly excuses himself from his parents, Mick, and Bessie. He struggles to walk towards Lexielle. She slowly walks toward him, meeting him halfway the lobby. Their eyes meet again. This time, she is teary-eyed.

"It was you in the archives forty years ago?" she asks, looking at him with her tear-filled eyes.

"They didn't *clone* you...you disappeared mysteriously." Lexielle whispers.

"Yes!" he answers, trying not to look at her.

"Was that you earlier chasing the ambulance?" Von asks as he tries to grip his cane.

"Yes. My younger brother swallowed a piece of my new technology gum. I was hoping he'd be okay. I thought he'd make it through the night. I'm so scared. I lost him a few hours ago...he's gone!" Lexielle starts to sob.

"I'm so sorry to hear that. Are your parents here with you?" Von asks while he looks around the hospital lobby.

"No...Both of my parents passed away in an automobile accident a few years ago in the new sky highway. They were on their way to a hospital gala when the accident happened." She blows her nose into a tissue and sobs. "They are not my real parents. I was adopted. They found me in one of the bad sections of town, badly beaten, unconscious, and suffering from amnesia. They took care of me until I got better."

"How nice of them to care for you," Von responds.

"Yeah. Nobody knows who my birth parents are. Nobody claimed me after they posted my face all over the media. So they legally adopted me. Several years later, my younger brother was born. It was the happiest time for all of us. Now it's just me. Our parents were both only children, and no grandparents."

"Wow, how sad. I'm so sorry." Von looks at Lexielle, who seems determined to cope with whatever life deals her.

"So...you chose this procedure," she says sadly.

"Yes." Von answers without looking at Lexielle's sad face.

"My father was in one of the first groups of expert surgeons who did delicate procedures like yours in this hospital several years ago," Lexielle says.

"Your father was a surgeon in this hospital? They have great surgeons here."

"Are you happy with the procedure?" she asks.

"Well, it was the right decision. It may not be the best one, but I can live with it," Von responds.

"How long do you have?" she asks, and *Von reveals his choice — one that will affect the rest of his life and could leave him with many regrets. The pair reveal their dreams and disappointments, and without many words a connection is made.*

"Six months, but really nobody knows for sure. At least I'll be with my family, friends, and people I knew all my life." Von's frail body shakes. The pain is sincere and grave, as both grieve the short encounter they had.

She weeps because they did not get the chance to enjoy their experience together for more time. But in the end, Lexielle is happy to know that they had lived their whole life in a few seconds – a few seconds at the library after this courteous stranger approached her for information.

"I'll be at the library three times a week. If you decide to read some of the old books, I'll be there to assist you," she says as she looks at him sadly.

"Thank you, and I'll forever be grateful for the short moment we shared. You were actually a part of my decision. You helped make it possible for me to make the right choice," Von whispers and shakes her hands while tightly gripping his cane.

Lexielle smiles sweetly. She realizes her life is forever altered by their hidden affection during that short encounter at the library

"Why should I long for something that was never ours?" she says to him, as she looks at Von's face for the last time. They both know in their hearts that this is it, this is the last time they will ever see each other.

"I have to go…I need to claim my brother's body at the morgue and make necessary arrangements for the funeral. Take care of yourself, and be well," she whispers into his ears. She understands the choices one must make in both life and love.

In her mind, it's a slate with one message; she admires Von for the man of commitment he is and is happy that she shared a few moments when time, space, and their separate lives did not interfere, and she slowly walks away.

Von sees Mick walking towards him. "I overheard the nurses say that you have twelve hours – twelve hours to reverse the procedure. Otherwise, you are forever stuck in this old body. I'm proud of you, but I don't think I am as strong of a man as you are."

Von grips his cane and manages to pull something in his pocket. It takes him several minutes to fish it out, and his legs wobble. He grabs the object and hands it over to Mick.

Mick looks at it, and his jaw drops. He stares at Von, and tears begin to fall down his cheeks. "Where did you get this? This is my missing dog tag." Mick looks at Von. "You're the unknown soldier, aren't you? You were there for me, you were really there for me." Mick's weeping turns into sobs.

"I'm sorry, I don't remember, Mick, I just don't remember. I found this inside the clothes that I was wearing when I came back," Von says.

"Von, why did you decide on this procedure? Why would you waste your stolen youth? You should have a life, just like the rest of us had forty years ago; you should have kept the healthy life," Mick says as he looks at Von's frail body.

"Look at you, how could you agree to this? How could you let this happen?"

"Mick, what are you saying?" Von asks, and sees Mick shakes his head and doesn't respond.

"Von, if I had a choice, I would be young and healthy again, like the good old days, you know?" Mick shakes his head and stares at Von, studying his face for signs of doubt.

Von turns away and looks at Bessie sitting in the hallway and then focuses on the empty sliding door where Lexielle has just exited. He looks outside for a few moments, contemplates, gazes for the longest time into a sad, familiar face, and closes his eyes.

"Von," a soft voice whispers. "Hold my hand. I'm right here for you."

"Who are you? I can't see, and I can't hear very well. Let me have a seat, please. It seems like I have cotton balls stuffed inside my ears," Von says.

Opening his eyes, he sees nothing at all. It is dark, and his eyes are watering; the strain to see is painful. Then, he hears voices coming from somewhere, but he can't see who they are.

"Von, it's me, don't be afraid," a voice reaches out to him.

"Where am I? What is this place? I can't see a darn thing; it is so dark. I can't see or hear anything!" Von responds, and then a deafening noise echoes in his ears. The sound reverberates in his head. Instinctively, he covers his ears with both hands and wipes his watering eyes with his forearms. He tries to open his eyes again and squints at the light. This time he can make something out but not clearly. He looks around and realizes he is in a different place, not altogether sure if it's a familiar place or not.

In his mind, he guesses that losing his eyesight and hearing is part of the medical procedure they just did to him. He shudders at the thought that his next move will be to an adult living facility where he can join other old people who have been abandoned to spend the end of life with strangers. For a moment, he sees the irony in his ending life this way.

"Where are we?" Von gets up and repeats the question.

"What do you mean?" a female voice asks.

Von wipes his eyes and looks around. He sees someone holding a newspaper standing nearby and can just make out the banner, it reads:

Maizen Beach Florida News / Herald Tribune /
June 12, 2008

As he is about to turn around, someone *taps* his shoulder.

"Are you *lovebirds* going to stand there and smooch all day? You know, ever since you guys met at the *frat party*, you haven't come up for air. C'mon dude, take a break for few minutes. Let's go! I've been waiting for hours to get some *latte*. From looking at my watch here, you guys have been sacked out on that park *bench* all day. Your lips are turning into dry prunes man. Get up, get up!"

Mick yells, "Heads up!" and throws a soccer ball to Von, who catches it by reflex.

"C'mon, Von, you need to help Bessie and Dex move out of their apartment before moving to D.C." Mick says, regaining his composure. Von looks at Lexielle's eyes.

"Was it a dream?" he asks.

"Dream? What are you talking about?" Lexielle whispers in disbelief, grabbing his hand and leading him away from the *bench*. When he stands up he notices that he isn't limping. His right leg is no longer shorter.

"What just happened? Look. Look at my leg. My leg is okay. I'm not limping."

"Limping? Since when did you start limping? You're such a dork." Lexielle grabs the newspaper and smacks him on his head thinking it was a tribute to their passionate display.

Was it a dream? Was I dreaming? Von looks at his legs again as he gets up from the bench, tries to feel them, and shakes them out. He doesn't know how or why, but he is haunted by faint images of time-traveling or a dream.

Then he hears Mick yell, "Hey, would you guys like to check out my new car?"

"Awesome! When did you get this, dude?" Von admires the ultra-sleek, modern car with big smile.

"Who are you talking to, Von?" Lexielle asks as she looks around. "By the way, I know you're still not used to it, but just to remind you, this is your car. Your parents gave this to you for your graduation, don't you remember?" Lexielle shakes her head. "Seriously, who are you talking to?"

"Mick! It's Mick!" Von yells.

"Von…Von, don't you think it's about time…?"

"What?" Von asks hesitantly.

"…It's about time to let go of Mick. Stop blaming your-self, after all these years. You were both young, and you did your best to save him. There's nothing you did wrong. You tried your very best to save Mick, but he just didn't have a lot of time on earth," Lexielle clarifies.

"Would you stop it! I don't want to hear it, Lexielle. You're right. It's about time for me to let go of my dear friend. I hate to let go, but I'll try."

Lexielle holds his hand and reminds Von that Mick was the nine-year-old boy who used to live next door to his par-ents' house. There had been an accident one summer…The boys were having a great time swimming in a pond when Mick hit his head on a rock and lost consciousness. Seven-year-old Von helplessly tried to save his friend and get help, but Mick died on the way to the hospital. Von never re-covered from Mick's death. In his heart and mind, he has really never believed that Mick died. Every now and then, he thinks he sees Mick and speaks to him.

"Lexielle, this week, Mick's been dead for fifteen years. He and I could have been roommates in college, he could have been in the new military draft, or maybe even have a girl of his own," Von walks away sullenly to the other side of the car. When he opens the door for Lexielle, a familiar song is playing on the holographic MP3 player.

As he listens to the song, Von remembers the tragic accident with Mick in the summer of 1997. A confused Von walks into the driver side, and as he searches for his keys in his pants, a folded piece of paper falls out of his pocket unnoticed, and the light breeze whisks it under the car into the drainage ditch. As the paper drifts slowly towards an underground pipe, it begins to unravel, revealing for a moment the answer to Von's questions, before disappearing into the dark abyss:

Highway In The Sky Medical Center
216 Orbit Circle, Maizen Beach, Florida 34567

Patient Discharge Slip (Home Care)
Instructions for Exploratory Surgery
Procedure: Total Body Reconstruction   Parts Use: Robotics
Patient Name: Carmichael, Von Muir   Sex: Male
<u>Age of Present Body</u>: 62 yrs old
<u>Age of Present Mind</u>: 22 yrs old
Admission Date: June 19, 2048
Discharge Date: June 21, 2048
Medical Surrogate: Mick Chevalier
Contact Info: Unknown

~

Please contact your physician if you do not get relief from the pain medication prescribed, if the intensity of your pain increases, or if pain is interfering with any of your activity or rest. For additional healthcare information and resources, visit our website at www.highwayintheskymedicalcenter.com or call our Health Life Line 24/7 at 941.123.4567 and a HumRob health care representative will assist you for transport to our outpatient recondition skyway facility site.

Then, all of a sudden the sound of a door closing sends Von's mind off into another place and time. He thinks that time-travel and the surgery have taken a toll. Von's body is inexplicably aging at an accelerated rate, while his mind is slipping into dementia, unable to distinguish reality from fantasy, past from present and future.

Von feels trapped in his mind, now a soup of mixed memories – one moment remembering chatting up a beautiful young lady at a banquet in Edwardian England, the next waking up in the bleak fog of war in North Korea under the nuclear weapon threat, feeling the sudden rush that comes from being hunted by an enemy. Then, he recalls a mixed memory of having an exploratory surgery in 2048.

He slowly begins to doubt his sanity as increasingly bizarre things start to arise which no one seems to think exist. He knows that his greatest strength has always been his ability to distinguish and adapt to changing realities. Though he time-traveled seemingly without control, somehow his youthful resiliency enabled him to cope with each new remarkable twist in his life. Weakened and confused, Von faces a kaleidoscope of images whizzing by without context or meaning, spiraling inward to a place deep within his mind. This kaleidoscope of images is getting inside his head and doing more damage as he thinks. If only he could unlock it. He feels a ball-peen hammer inside his brain; it wants to leave psychic flash burns on his soul and leaves him feeling he was smashed across his face with a 2x4.

For the last time unable to distinguish reality, he sees his life flash before his eyes, and he wonders if these are the last few seconds before he dies…

In the dark underground of his subconscious, the sound of a woman's voice asking him a question jolts his mind, and he opens his eyes to the warmth of a fire in what seems a familiar setting. A nurse approaches from behind his chair acting as if she knows him. Von strains to see her name badge, which says Lexielle, RN, Health Life Services, Inc. She smiles at him saying, "Mr. Carmichael, you gave us quite a scare when you pressed the panic button. It's good to see you are with us now. When I got the call, I came as fast as I could. Sometimes when you go off like that, I worry and wonder when you will be back." Von smiles knowingly, as the nurse continues her consoling banter.

His eyes are drawn towards the flickering flame, away from the words and sounds of Nurse Lexielle, setting his mind adrift. He abruptly hears another voice, with a British accent:

"Von Muir Carmichael, you 'ave been charged and found guilty on the following counts. That you did on the 12th day of June in the year of our lord, nineteen hundred and eight ya' murder Andrew Ainsworth, Austin Breton, and Clive Schellden by means of strangulation and mutilation of their bodies. Do you 'ave anything to say before yar sentence is prescribed?"

Von's eyes open to the horror of a courtroom surrounded by men with white powdered wigs dressed in drab Edwardian morning suits. Throngs of angry men and women fill the gallery. Von looks at the man in the seat next to his offering only a vacant stare. The man stands to say:

"Your Honor, my client has no words to add." Grasping the finality of the moment, Von leaps to his feet, shouting.

"Your Honor, there has been a terrible mistake, I'm innocent!"

The Judge bangs his gavel, then asks that the defendant rise to receive sentencing. Von's attorney takes him by the arm and stands with him as the surreal play is acted out in front of him. Von's mind flashes to that awful first day of time travel. He can still see the blood and the dead bodies and the faces of his accusers as they approached to extract their street justice. "My God!" Von thinks to himself, "How can this be real?"

Then the Judge looks unflinchingly at Von and begins speaking the stern, cold words that could only be intended for someone else:

"The sentence of the court upon you is that you be taken from this place to a lawful prison in which you shall be confined until your execution and thence to a place of execution you will be hanged by the neck until you are dead; afterwards you will be buried in the shallow graves of the prison yard if no individual will collect your remains. And may the Lord have mercy upon your soul."

Von is immediately led off through the cheering mob that convulses with hatred, spitting into Von's face as he is forced to go near. Others hurl rotten fruit and vegetables they have kept hidden for just this moment. Von closes his eyes, hoping that somehow he will time-travel one more time, leaving this horror behind like the bad dream it is. Minutes go by before he hears the sound of a heavy door close and lock behind him. He opens his eyes to the dark, dirty walls of his cell. With almost no light, he can feel how small it is by the rank and fetid smells they give off after years of confining the wretches of society. Rats scurry around his feet, sniffing at his clothes for clues of new flesh to gnaw. Von's mind races from images to images trying to make sense of this strange new reality.

The next three days are a daze, punctuated only by the sound of the door opening for the first time. Von squints into the light hoping to see a familiar face, perhaps Sir

Robert with news of the court's apology for this travesty of justice.

The light silhouettes the Priest's face, making his eyes indiscernible. Only his bald head and collar are showing. Behind him is another man who looks ungodly in his demeanor. He steps in front of the Priest grabbing Von's arm saying, "Y'ar coming with us lad."

Von hears his footsteps echoing on the cavernous walls of the prison as they walk through the tunnel leading to a courtyard. All the while, the Priest is reciting psalms about redemption and forgiveness to the back of his head. The large wooden doors open to the courtyard, revealing the gallows standing high in the middle. Von hears the excited sounds of a crowd just outside the prison wall. Von feels weakness overcome his body but now is almost floating as he walks with guards holding him up by his arms tied behind his back.

They climb the stairs towards the hooded man in black. Unable to distinguish reality from fantasy, past from present and future…Von's mind flashes back to the park bench where he thinks Lexielle so tenderly touched his face with her hands. Von closes his eyes and can see only her face. He can taste her lips and feel the promise in her kiss. In his mind he hears Matt Goss's song *It's the End of the Road*, like it was a mantra:

Yesterday a clear horizon / Now the clouds are rollin' in it's disappeared / The one thing that I've always believed in / It's strange how right now it all seems so unclear / I consult my soul / And it tells me that it knows / There's no doubt one day I'm gonna fly / Gotta stand up / Dust myself off / Just for now / It's the end of the road / When something ends / something begins / But now it's the end of the road / When someone loses, someone wins / I know it's the end of the road…

Then without warning, Von hears the sound of a grating hinged trapdoor in need of oil in the gallows and feels the floating sensation of weightlessness that signals change is coming...

• END •

Printed in the United States
66624LVS00004B/45

9 781592 992393